Through the Deep Forest

THE DARK FILAMENT EPHEMERIS

VOLUME I

RUSSELL C. CONNOR

DARKFILAMENT.COM

Contact the author at
facebook.com/russellcconnor
Or follow on Twitter @russellcconnor

Cover Art by SaberCore23 Artwork Studio
For commissions, visit sabercore23art.com

ISBN:
978-0-7331133-7-3

First Edition: 2019

TABLE OF CONTENTS

The Last Fathers

BEYOND THE BARRIER

1

On the morning of his sixteenth birthday, Korden Bright broke the law.

But, in his defense, 'law' didn't really seem a fitting word for it. Laws, to him, were foreign concepts, remnants of the long dead world that Tash and the rest of the Last Fathers once inhabited. He'd always imagined them written down in thick, dusty tomes by hooded figures, and enforced by those gallant guardians of the land called 'policemen.' Such as those hadn't existed since long before he was born, if they ever truly had at all.

No, Korden told himself his transgression wasn't so much the breaking of a *law*, but rather, a *rule*. One simple little rule. A suggestion, really.

Considering that suggestion had been hammered into his head from the moment he was old enough to understand it, these excuses did nothing to alleviate his guilt.

Especially when his entire life came crashing down around him.

2

He rose early, dressed in the dark in a pair of worn deer-skin dungarees, slipped the strap of his carry-pouch over his head, and padded barefoot and silent out of the thatched roof *hucté* he shared with his father.

Outside, the sliver of an archer's moon cast a pale glow on the empty hilltop where their dwelling sat. Stars blazed in scrimshaw patterns overhead. The early morning air hung heavy with cool dew, turning the bare flesh of his lean shoulders and back into a carpet of prickles. *Gooseflesh*, he'd once heard the Olders call it, a term that baffled him.

Much like everything that crossed their ancient, wrinkled lips.

A dirt path began just beyond the door and twisted along the curve of the hillside. He started along it, taking stealthy steps to be sure his father didn't come tearing out after him. Then, beneath the sickly pallor of the waning moon and that sky full of blue-tinged stars, Korden cut away from the dirt path his feet knew by heart, into a meadow thick with skilne grass that led away from the tiny village nestled in the shallow floor of the valley. The plant stalks—what his father called 'thinking grass'—came alive at his passage, turning and bending to follow the heat of his body, snatching weakly at his limbs.

He relaxed his tense efforts at silence amid the waist-high blades and allowed his legs to stretch into a run. A stiff wind sprang up, shushing through the grass like the murmur of distant voices. Korden stretched his arms into it, closed his eyes, and pushed himself harder, ignoring the fire in his muscles and the rattling wheeze in his chest. The feel of his bare feet on the soggy earth and the skilne blades grasping at his torso fell away. He concentrated only on the imagined sensation of flight, a flight that would, in his mind, take him far from here, to distant lands so strange he couldn't imagine them.

When at last he opened his eyes again, the boughs of the mammoth sequoias towered over him like an army of giants.

He came to a halt at the edge of the meadow, then doubled over to catch his huffing breath. The Olders called his sickness 'as-mah,' a lingering symptom from a fever that almost killed him at the age of nine. At its best, like now, it was little more than an annoyance. At its worst, he felt as though the air had turned to honey and clogged every inch of his throat and lungs.

When his breathing finally evened, Korden looked up, squinting into the forbidding wall of the tree line along the ridge ahead. The mighty redwoods formed a natural border east of the village. The sound of chirping crickets and the insistent click of the golas taking shelter in the forest seemed deafening, amplified in that way noises always seemed to be in the stillness of the night.

He couldn't catch so much as a glimpse of what he sought, but this must be the place. The geography of the land rolling away to his left and the angle of the trees told him this was exactly where he'd stood mere hours before, after Skewtz let him out of his reading class early.

His destination couldn't be more than a quarter span away, somewhere beyond the first imposing trees, in the undergrowth of the forest. A few hundred pargs. A ten minute walk, perhaps.

But he would have to defy every person he'd ever known to reach it.

No more carefree running now. Instead, he inched forward cautiously, taking each step one at a time, shoulders hunched defensively, like a man expecting a sharp blow at any second. Even though this stretch of meadow looked no different from the rest, his jaw clenched in anticipation.

Korden had no idea what would happen next. He always expected there would be *something*, some precursor...and then, here it was: a curious tingling ran the length of his body before culminating in a shiver. Every hair on his body stood up.

He had reached the Barrier.

3

It had encircled him his entire life, or at least as far back as he could recall, and he'd never crossed its invisible boundary. Not once, in sixteen long years. This was the closest he'd ever come to its edge.

He could remember once, when he must've been close to five, slipping away from his father's side while Redfen argued with several of the Olders. Korden had chased a butterfly down the broad dirt lane through the middle of the village and out toward the empty plains to the south. His innocent flight had been short, nowhere near close enough to the Barrier to feel the physical effects, as he did now. But the way his father screamed in abject panic, chased him down, and gave him a whaling his backside still regretted was more than enough reminder that his existence had severe limitations.

In one of Skewtz' old, musty books, Korden had read about a place called 'prison.' A place where, before the Purges, people were locked away when they committed misdeeds. When they *broke the law*.

Around the time of his eleventh birthday, Korden began to think of himself as a prisoner. He could see the sky and roam about the village and surrounding lands, but all the time the Barrier sat over him, a great, upside-down cup plopped down over the entire village like one might catch a bug.

Over the entire village…but not for the *sake* of the entire village. Woven from the fabric of the Olders' strongest artcrafts, the Barrier had been created to protect and hide only one person. Everyone else within it could come and go freely. Not that they ever did, but at least it was their *choice*.

Korden Bright, today a sixteen-year-old prisoner, had been afforded no such choice.

And he'd grown so sick of it, he could scream.

4

Korden moved forward another step in the night, and then another. The trilling sensation within him continued to rise, causing one hand to shake as he lifted it in front of him and held it there, palm out. The raw power within the Barrier's invisible construction was as strong as any artcraft he'd ever seen, far beyond anything he could hope to conjure. Given enough time, he thought he might be able to cobble together a wordspell to make it visible, perhaps as a shimmery wall, but that would serve no purpose. He stepped forward again, waiting for a jolt of pain. Or maybe just to come up against an obstruction as hard and unyielding as stone.

But there was nothing. If he went any further, he would just push right through. Korden hung there a moment, breath hitching, and tried to decide if he wanted this.

Do it, an insistent, constantly impatient voice told him.

Just do it Kord, or we're going to be stuck in this village until we make the Olders look like young men.

That wasn't true; his prison sentence would last only another two years, at most.

But right now, that two years seemed an *eternity*.

Korden stepped forward one more pace.

There was the delicate sensation of something gossamer giving way in a great rush, like the bursting of a soap bubble, and the tingling sensation vanished.

He'd done it. He'd crossed the Barrier. It'd been so easy, it was almost disappointing.

He reexamined the night around him, ready to bolt back into its safety at the first sign of the horrors his father had promised awaited him on the other side.

Nothing was different. The air still tasted muggy and wet, the sounds of crickets and golas still floated on the breeze.

Part of him felt embarrassed. Ashamed to have listened to their stories for so long. It was all too easy to believe, in that moment of anticlimactic release, that it had all been an elaborate lie, a measure to control him: the Barrier, the Purges, the Incarnates...everything.

Then again, did he actually *want* those inhuman creatures to be waiting for him in the dark?

Actually...yes, he found that he did. The excitement of such an encounter—of something new and foreign and...*different*— would have been well worth the danger.

Yeh want excitement, ghammer, *then go find it. Yeh dint cross tha Barrier just ta say yeh crossed it, now did yeh? That would truly be a fool's errand.*

The voice of Tash filled his head this time. It spoke true; breaching this boundary was nothing more than an obstacle in the path to his true destination.

There was still adventure to be had this night.

Korden grinned and ran forward, out of his prison for the first time.

5

The forest had always been just out of reach on the other side of the Barrier, a strange land to be gazed upon but never entered. This restriction suited him just fine; something about this place seemed unnatural when compared to the oak grove on the far northwest side of the village, and not just because of its gargantuan timber. These trees exuded a glowering essence, an alert, watchful, sullen vibe that had frightened Korden for as long as he could remember. Tash said they were even older than the Last Fathers, that history itself had been writ upon their massive trunks.

As he approached, the golas fell silent. Black wells of shadow gaped obscenely between the branches where they nested. The canopy far above his head was too thick for the wan moonlight to reach even the limbs of the smaller pines and alders nestled amid the redwoods, much less the underbrush on the forest floor. A chill prickled Korden's skin at the thought of entering such darkness, but he'd come too far to turn back.

The air smelled pleasant, rich, dark earth and sweet resin. His bare feet trod a rough carpet of fern leaves and pine needles. He slowed his pace before he encountered a root to trip over and rummaged through the carry-pouch slung around his neck.

Korden withdrew the homemade charcoal pencil and leather-bound journal he kept on him at all times. He flipped the book open and leafed through pages. It was too dark to read his haphazard writing, but he found a blank spot and paused with the tip of the pencil hanging above the paper.

A hundred fragmentary thoughts and ideas whirled through his head. His imagination was a vast, untamed place, where he could play for hours. He forced himself to focus and scrawled down a two-line couplet, the first thing that came to mind:

> *The trees are looking down on me,*
> *Don't they wish they could be free?*

Not his best work, but it didn't matter. The use of imagination would bolster his will, and, as he'd been told countless times, only the will mattered in the practice of artcraft.

That, and faith, of course.

He bent, found a good-sized acorn on the ground, and held it in his open palm.

"*Demno,*" he muttered in the Craften tongue, concentrating.

Light—a pure, soft, bluish-white glow—sprang forth from the seed's shell in all directions like his father's lantern, illuminating a wide stretch of the forest, chasing shadows into holes and crevices. A simple wordspell, and one of the few he could perform consistently.

With the light to aid him, Korden reevaluated the trees. He'd been on a far hillside yesterday afternoon on his way home when the setting sun glinted off something in the distance, sharp enough to sting his eyes. Korden had cut across the meadow toward it, keeping that glitter within sight at all times, and found himself as close to the Barrier as he'd ever come before this morning.

Whatever it was, it sat deep within the tree line, hidden behind a screen of forest. That chip of light looked too sharp to be a water reflection. Metal, perhaps? It faded a few minutes later as the sun moved away, which meant he would've missed it entirely if Skewtz hadn't let him go early.

His first instinct had been to tell someone, but suddenly that glint seemed like a sign meant only for him; the chance of him happening by at a time and place where it would catch his attention was a message directly from the Upper. If he told the Olders, they might attempt to find the source, but you could be sure he wouldn't go with them.

And something in his very soul insisted that he *had* to.

That it might be the most important thing he ever did.

Korden looked back at the meadow, trying to compare the glint's position relative to where he thought he stood now. It'd seemed to come from farther south. He turned and continued into the forest, driving away the darkness before him with the glowing acorn.

He went only a handful of steps before emerging between two redwoods and found himself in front of a surface the likes of which he'd never seen.

6

Flat.

That was the first attribute his mind fixed upon. This new terrain lay perfectly flat and even under his feet. He'd never walked on anything so level, not even the most hard-packed dirt.

The odd surface stretched in front of him for only ten paces or so, clearing a short strip in the forest floor, but to his left—north—the ribbon curved out of sight behind the bulk of a tree. To the right, it ran endless, spreading out far beyond the limits of his conjured light. He knelt over it, bringing the illumination closer.

The material was rough and hard as stone, grayish black in color. In places, deep cracks cleaved across it, from which grass sprouted. Then he saw the faded yellow dashes up the middle, and understood.

He was looking at a real, honest-to-Upper *road*.

A relic from the time before the Purges, made from the substance his father called 'crete'. The Olders talked often about the autos that once used these paths to carry people far across the land. He had no idea that one lay so close to the village.

For a moment, Korden stared up that road to the north and wondered where it led after it curved out of sight, what waited at the other end.

He turned the opposite direction and moved along the hard surface, feet making sharp slapping sounds now. The light in his hand continued to jump and play among the trees until at last he came around a scarred old redwood trunk whose base could've squashed his entire home. There, he found the source of the glittering flash he'd spotted from the hill.

7

With the reality of the road settled in his head, he found it much easier to identify the large, boxy shape in front of him, sitting against the far side of the gnarled and pitted tree trunk, even covered with a crusted shell of dirt, leaves, and skilne.

An auto.

A car.

So far as he knew, his father had never even seen one. The few instances when Korden heard him mention the self-moving carts, his voice filled with a reverence and awe that was contagious.

It stood three-quarters as tall as Korden and twice as long, and rested on tattered wheels made of some material that had long since rotted away from their metallic hubs. Foliage sprouted through the shredded remains, giving the appearance that the whole thing had grown right out of the ground. From what he could tell, its body had once been sheets of polished black metal, but beneath the layer of debris, rust had eaten jagged holes in the machine.

On its side, in small, upraised letters just visible under a gob of mud, was the curious word 'TOYOTA.'

The front of the vehicle was wrapped around the tree trunk, crushed from collision. Random bits of strange metal jutted from an interior chamber where the engine that powered it must have been kept. This entire end bore signs of scorching, but that long ago fire petered out before consuming the rest of the auto.

Korden brought the glowing acorn closer to the point of impact. The scarring of this behemoth tree had been deep enough that it still had yet to recover. Patches of bark were stripped and gouged away, leaving the core open to the elements.

He walked along the car's body, to the long sheet of sloped glass at the front end. Thick mud caked the surface, obscuring the interior. He raised a hand and wiped at it, cleaning away layers of encrusted muck, and leaned in.

The gaunt face of a human skull leered back at him from the opposite side.

Korden yelped and jumped away. His outburst startled something in the bushes on the other side of the auto into flight. He looked around, peering into the shadows that crouched beyond the *demno*'s light, his breathing sudden-ly husky. From somewhere in the woods, an owl hooted cautiously, but other than that, not even the wind made a sound.

He waited for his breathing to calm, then leaned against the window once more, cupping his hand over the glass to cut down the glare. When his eyes adjusted to the even deeper darkness of the vehicle's cockpit, he could make out the occupants.

There were two, both in the front seat, no more than skeletons in shreds of clothing. The one closest to him seemed to be the captain, for he was draped across a large wheel that seemed to have crushed his midsection during the crash. His head gazed emptily at Korden from a shelf above the steering wheel, white, skinless hands thrown up against the glass as if to stop the tree from smashing into them. And the other one...

The other one had been a *woman*.

Korden wasn't sure how he knew this. Something in the general shape of the bones perhaps, the delicate form they suggested. As he stared, an amazement stole over him that put everything else he'd experienced this morning to shame.

Because, like the road and the auto, he'd never seen one of these before either.

He stood mesmerized. Not by the bones, but by the idea they were once been a living, breathing female. He'd been having dreams about them lately. Dreams about soft, spectral beings that his imagination conjured with the help of what little input it had on the subject, dreams where he awoke lightheaded and with his groin aching and his penis stiff enough to be used as a walking stick.

The form slumped against the door on the far side of the car, turned away so that the curve of her spine showed, clothed in the rotting remains of a blouse. He could see part of her head was shattered, but her arms were crossed tightly in front of her, clutching something to her ribcage.

An object so important that she clung to it during the violent crash, even as her life bled away.

8

Korden went behind the auto, then shuffled through the dense foliage on the far side. A fat purple snake hissed at him before crawling away, but he gave it no notice. He'd become aware of how fast time was slipping away, of how his conjured light became less necessary with each passing minute.

He studied the door of the carriage, searching for a way to open it. At last he found a handle buried under a sheen of dried mud and pulled upward.

A crack sounded as the ancient seal broke, and the door separated from the frame with a rusted creak. Korden muscled it open a few more pargs and hunkered in the gap.

The skeleton watched him, its blank face somehow pleading even without eyes and features. He wondered what the fractured skull had once looked like. If he'd been a powerful enough craftsman—far more than even Tash—he might've been able to find out.

He could see now that she held a bound book to her chest, much thicker and wider than his journal. Korden reached out and touched it gingerly, ready for the body to come to life and fly at him for this intrusion. When the apprehension passed, he grasped the tome on both sides and gave it a gentle tug.

The skeleton disintegrated at every joint simultaneously. Bones clattered into the floor and spilled onto the ground at his feet. A disembodied hand clung to the book by several ivory fingers.

Korden waited for his heart to drop out of his throat and then shifted from knees to bottom, sitting cross-legged on the forest floor. He drew the tome into his lap, tilting it so the hand fell off. It landed on the ground with a soft clatter, palm up and slim fingers reaching toward the stars, where it would stay until the world came to the limping end it seemed headed toward.

He brushed dust from the book's cover, revealing writing. Gold letters in a fancy script that read, 'Our Family.' He pulled open the thick cover to the first page, holding his glowing acorn close.

A delighted gasp escaped him.

Pictures—not drawings, but square images capturing real life—were mounted side-by-side on the page. It was like looking through a series of tiny windows into worlds frozen in time. His jaw dropped at the sheer strangeness of the scenes they contained.

His wish had been granted, for now he knew what the woman in front of him looked like in life. She hadn't always been a grinning skull; she once possessed muted red hair the color of Harvest leaves spilling down her shoulders, and freckle-covered skin over her skeleton, and a pretty face with a nose that turned up just the tiniest bit at the tip. She had been tall and slender, with those mounds on her chest (*breasts, they were called breasts*) that pushed out the front of every strange article of clothing she wore, and hips that curved ever so slightly at the sides in a way that stirred something in the pit of his stomach.

In most of these pictures was another man, presumably her riding companion, and behind them a variety of fantastical settings. In one, they stood in front of a large window overlooking a road where more autos zoomed back and forth, blurred by their speed, some of them hovering a few pargs off the ground on orbs of pale yellow light, and beyond that, rows upon rows of the tallest and straightest structures he'd ever seen marched to the horizon. The man had his arm around the woman, and they both smiled in a spirited, carefree way that was just as alien as everything else about them.

Korden flipped through pages, all thoughts of the coming morning gone, lost in this magic portal through time. Here was one of the woman at a large, square pit in the ground, filled with the clearest water he'd ever seen. She sat on the edge and dangled her feet in. Here was one of the man holding a small, brown animal that looked like a wolf cub while it licked his face. Here was one of both in front of a bright green tree growing in the middle of a room, an evergreen festooned with brightly colored lights and baubles.

He kept turning, unable to tear himself away from this story of their lives.

At last he came to a picture of the woman in a strange bed with metal fencing along its sides and surrounded by a plethora of electronic gadgets, looking exhausted and haggard, but in her arms sat a small, chubby creature, face screwed up in a violent shade of red, plump little hands balled into fists.

A baby.

It was revolting…and yet precious at the same time. Had he ever looked like this, been this small and defenseless in the arms of his own mother, whose face he couldn't even remember? Had the *Olders?*

Korden went further, and now the couple was joined in their pictures by a little girl, and, soon after, a boy. These two grew up before his eyes, jumping seasons and years between pages. Where were these children when their parents perished? He stopped turning at one picture of the girl from the shoulders up in front of a brilliant, blue background, long black hair spilling down her neck and chest, staring into his eyes with a pleasant grin.

Looking at her, his heart beat against the inside of his chest.

'Beautiful' wasn't a word he'd been able to use often in his life, but it was the only one he could think of to describe this exotic specimen from another time.

And suddenly, Korden suspected he knew why the woman in the car gripped this book so tightly as she died. The children were absent because they had been taken in the Purges. Stolen away by Incarnates. Perhaps these two (*mother and father*, his mind whispered, uniting the new texture of the former with the familiarity of the latter) thought they were on their way to find them, or just trying to escape the pain of their loss.

In that second of revelation, Korden Bright understood the full magnitude of the situation the Olders prattled on about. They were dying, all of them, every last one, the human species dwindling without a new crop to replace them. Someday the Olders would be gone—their arts kept them long-lived, but not immortal—then his father would die in the natural order, and then…

Then he would be all alone.

Korden hugged the book to his chest in the same way the woman in the auto had, and tried not to let fear and loneliness overtake him.

REDFEN

1

As he made his way out of the forest, Korden's heart still felt heavy. All the excitement of the secret expedition had been leeched away. If it'd been part of the Upper's *divine plan* (another of Tash's favorite terms) for him to find the auto and its occupants, he didn't understand the purpose, other than to start his birthday on a depressing note.

He found himself far south of where he'd entered the trees, on the opposite side of the village proper. He was inside the Barrier once more, although he had no idea exactly when he crossed its border; there had been no buzzing sensation upon reentry. This might've bothered him if he'd stopped to consider it, but the need to get home superseded all else. The quickest route would be to cut as close as possible around the east side of the tiny settlement and hope he didn't get caught.

Speed would have to trump discretion. Color bled into the morning sky at an alarming rate, even though the sun itself would remain hidden behind the black Shroud for another hour. The village would be about the day's business soon.

He ran again, pumping his legs as fast as he dared without bringing on a fit of gasping from his weak lungs. He spotted the high roof of the *hangala* first, from its position on the far southwest edge of the village. The building was by far the largest, constructed in the same fashion as the *huctés*: a sturdy wooden frame and floor, walls and ceiling filled in by artcraft-hardened mud, and the roof further protected by a tightly-woven layer of dried skilne grass. Painted Craften symbols adorned the exterior, incantations of good fortune, tranquility, and abundance. He faithed in this building every Seventh Day Morn with the Olders, leaving his father behind to grumble and fume.

Korden crested a last low hill. The rest of the village lay spread out before him.

A wide, dirt avenue snaked up the middle, the result of feet and cartwheels passing over the valley floor for countless years. On either side were the humble homes of the Olders, each of the forty men living in solitude with only space to eat, sleep, and faith within. Korden and his father would've been welcome here if they were willing to live with the same simplicity. Which was exactly why Redfen moved them as far away as possible.

All of the Olders' domiciles were dark, their elderly residents still asleep.

Save one.

As Korden cut behind the eastern row of dwellings to continue toward home, he looked over and saw the pure glow of a *demno* coming through the window of one home on the opposite side.

"Tash," he whispered. He pictured his *den-so*'s face, so deeply-lined it might've been carved from tree bark, the long jowls and grey eyes glazed with milky whiteness. "Why are you up so early?"

Korden reached out with his mind, attempting to read the man's *mohol*. He must be delicate about it; if he pushed too hard, Tash would sense him prying.

From this distance, he received only the briefest flashes of emotion, expressed in his head through color. Tash's usual stoic slate on top, the same color as his eyes, but beneath that, an undercoat of sickly yellow nervousness punctuated by dark bursts of...

Fear?

Korden reeled back his mental probe in a hurry. The idea that Tash—with his dry, unflappable demeanor—could ever be afraid seemed unthinkable. He wanted to reach out again, make sure of what he sensed, but the risk of exposure was too great. Besides, whatever ailed the old man wasn't his business.

He angled farther right, taking him around the hovels, passing through several fruit and vegetable gardens that complemented the village's diet of fish and whatever meat the 30-day hunts brought. He heard a soft whinny to his right and turned to see Mulder, the decrepit village plow horse, standing motionless in the shadow of an orange tree, regarding him with narrowed eyes. The horse chuffed and wrinkled back its lips in a toothy sneer.

"*Shhh!*" he hissed. The beast raised its head in defiance and brayed. Korden shot him a nasty look as he moved on.

Then it was past Skewtz' library, the tiny classroom that had been built for the village's sole student, and the social hall, where most of the Last Fathers—as they preferred to call themselves—whiled away the hours playing chess or hands of totala. Then a series of small foothills interrupted the valley floor, and he found the dirt path that would take him home.

His bare feet were filthy. He stopped to clean them in a puddle just beyond the dooryard and studied the mud face of the only home he'd ever known. Korden loved his father fiercely, but the man remained oblivious of the way those brown walls seemed to shrink each passing year. Then, with supreme smugness, Korden slipped inside the doorway and crept through the common room, heading toward bed, where he could replay the morning's events. He was so good at this, he might have to sneak out every—

"I hope for your sake that sleepwalking is a consequence of all that garbage Tash fills your head with," a voice said behind him.

2

Redfen Bright regarded his son from his seat at the supping table, already dressed in a light tunic and denim pants so patched with animal hide hardly any of the original material remained. Even in the dark, he could see the guilty flush that bloomed on the boy's cheeks and spread down his neck. He reached over and turned up the lantern flame beside him, filling the room with shifting light.

"R-Redfen," Korden sputtered.

"Where were you?" Redfen asked, working hard to keep his voice neutral.

"Down the hill. Practicing. Tash, he…gave me some new wordspells to try." Then the boy hurried to add, "It's my birthday!"

"I know. So imagine my surprise when I got up early to make you breakfast with the last of that possum jerky you love, only to find your bed empty."

"I'm really sorry, I—"

"So the least you could do," he continued, "is be honest, and tell me where you *really* were."

"Just...out walking. I wanted to find a quiet place to write. To have some time to myself."

"When you want time to yourself, you tell me and I'll go with you."

Korden squinted at him, as though trying to tell if he'd meant it as a joke.

"Do you have any idea what I thought when I couldn't find you? I was one very short minute away from waking every last one of those toothless old bodlas and mounting a search party when I heard you splashing around outside." This was exaggeration. In truth, the frantic inspection of the *hucté* left him so paralyzed with fear he'd been forced to sit down until the strength came back to his legs. Now that he could see the boy was safe (and had gone out without shirt nor shoes) all that icy fear melted into anger. "What were you thinking?"

"But I didn't—!"

"No, you didn't. I've told you time and again, just because you're inside the Barrier is no reason to trust that you're safe. It doesn't keep the Incarnates out, it only hides your presence from them. One could still wander in here at any moment. We have to stay cautious, especially at night." He snorted and balled his hands into helpless fists on the table. "You just...*you can't be so framming reckless!*"

Korden dropped his head in defeat and said nothing.

Redfen glared at him a moment longer and then sighed. What good did it do to be angry? He remembered what went on in the minds and hearts of fifteen—no, *sixteen*-year-old boys. He hated to constantly reprimand his son when the boy only wanted a little space.

But a little space will get him killed, his mind countered. *He wasn't raised like you, to be wary. This place may've provided a sanctuary, but it's also coddled him. He has no idea what the rest of the world is like.*

Redfen stood up and came around the table. He bore almost no resemblance to the boy across the room. Korden was lanky, too thin for his height—as evidenced by the ribs that visibly banded his bare waist—with skin so pale and fair it glowed in the darkness. Redfen possessed a lean, muscular build in contrast to his son's slightly wasted torso, his skin a more coppery hue. Whereas Korden's face looked narrow and angular, framed by a sheet of thick brown hair and punctuated by brilliant green eyes flecked with amber, Redfen's was broad and rough, with a scar twisting along the left temple, blond hair pulled back in a tail and murky blue eyes.

But then, the lack of familial likeness had never surprised Redfen.

"Two more years, Kord." He put his hands on the boy's bare shoulders. "Just two more years, and then you're safe. We're so close. Once you turn eighteen, we can leave here, go wherever you want. Curse, don't you think I'd love to get away from these mouthy old warlocks? But until then...we both just have to be patient."

"But Redfen." Korden looked up, and Redfen was surprised to see a depth and maturity in his face that had never been there before, as if he'd woken up this morning much more than just another year older. "What if...the Incarnates are all gone? What if the Purges are over and we've been stuck here under the Barrier all this time for nothing? No one from the village has had any contact with the outside world since before I was born."

"And with good reason," Redfen countered, before the boy could finish. He knew this argument would come one day, had prepared himself for it, yet it still seemed to be happening too soon. "You were too young to remember life before the Olders took us in. The Incarnates hunted us every night, and most days, too. Things were bad when I was a boy, but at least back then, we stood a chance at fighting them off. But when you entered the world, an entire *army* showed up outside the walls of the fortress we lived in hours before you were even born."

"I remember the story," Korden told him.

"I'm not surprised. Upper knows I've told it to you enough times. So please trust me when I tell you that if you were to leave the Barrier, they would sense you from the farthest reaches of the land, and they would come."

Something flickered in the boy's vivid eyes. Fear, perhaps. Good; he should be afraid.

Redfen went to the door and beckoned Korden to him. When they both stood outside the shack, he pointed to the east. The sun stood high enough to be seen, but on the horizon just below it, barely visible over the high sequoia treetops along the slope of the valley, an inky black blob stretched across the heavens, as if the night there refused to submit to the coming morning. Even from such a great distance, this viscous darkness could never be mistaken for a storm cloud.

"You see that? That's all the proof you need that the armies of the Dark Filament are still out there. They say the Shroud used to move, blotting out the sky and bringing the Incarnates, until something held them up out there for a long, long time. But one day, the Shroud will start getting bigger again, spreading farther. Tash and I don't agree on much, but I think he's absolutely right about that darkness. When the Incarnates finish the work they began with the Purges, that shadow will cover the face of the entire world."

In other words, when they finish trimming each family tree of all its branches, he thought, a visual put in his head by someone long, long ago.

Korden still didn't speak, just stared off to the east at that roiling shade, which was already disappearing behind a lazy band of white clouds blowing in from the south. Another pang of longing speared through Redfen's heart. As eager as he was for the boy to reach free age, seeing him grow up was a pain all its own.

"I only want to protect you. Someday, when you have a son of your own, you'll understand." A cruel thing to say perhaps, considering the likelihood of Korden ever siring a child. He ruffled the boy's hair. "All right, enough of this gloom. It's your birthday, and you must have a present on your birthday."

Korden plucked at the hem of his dungarees, which Redfen had sewn himself the year before. "But these still fit me just fine."

"No, no clothes this year. I have something different for you."

Back inside, Redfen went into his room and removed a rag-wrapped bundle from under his straw mattress. He placed this on the table in front of Korden, who stared at it with a cocked eyebrow. "Go ahead, open it."

An excited smile crept onto the boy's face as he unwrapped the gift. There were so few surprises for him here. When he had it open, he lifted out the burnished piece of black metal with the scuffed brown inlays and looked at it in amazement. On one side, the words SPRINGFIELD AR-MORY were still visible.

"Do you know what that is?" Redfen asked.

His son nodded slowly. "A shooter. This type was called a *pistol*."

Of course he knew. The boy had read every one of Skewtz' books a hundred times, both the true and made-up ones. He seemed obsessed with learning all he could about that lost world and its inhabitants, much to Tash's dismay. That old coot never stopped harping about the 'fallen ways' that broke humanity's self-sufficiency and replaced his precious Upper. He looked at Redfen as a fool just for using a lantern. Well, he may've apprenticed Korden into his mystical arts—with Redfen's reluctant agreement—but at least he hadn't managed to prejudice the boy against the past and its many marvels.

"Is this…?" Korden began.

"Yes. The weapon that saved my life on the day you were born. It hasn't been fired since, mostly because there's no more ammunition for it. But I've kept it clean and oiled with deer fat, so I could give it to you one day."

Korden examined the shooter from all directions, then grasped the handle experimentally in both hands with his fingers on the trigger, and swung it around the room like one of the stick swords he loved to play with.

Redfen laughed. "Like this." He took the weapon, made a show of ejecting the empty clip and then shoving it back in, then held it in one hand, aimed at the wall, sighted down the barrel, and pulled the trigger. Only a dry click sounded, but he made the pistol buck in his hand and mimicked the explosive sound of a gunshot. "The real noise is much louder. But you must be careful, even though it isn't loaded. It isn't a toy. My father used to say, never point it at anything or anyone that you don't intend to kill."

Korden accepted the pistol again reverently and held it like he'd been shown. "But…what will I do with it?"

"I dunno. Keep it as a trophy. Or, if you run into someone else that knows what it is, a threat can be just as good as a shot. Just don't let Tash know. I grow as tired of his lectures as you do of mine."

"All right," the boy agreed.

Redfen planted a kiss on top of his head, which smelled of sweet pine mingled with the earthy aroma of the outdoors. "Why don't you get some sleep before your lessons? I'll make you breakfast and then I have to go."

"Where are you going?"

"On a hunt with some of the others."

"But why? The 30-day hunt isn't for another two weeks!"

"Fortholm believes the ramlar migration is coming early this year. Upper knows we need the meat."

"Oh." The boy's face fell. "I just thought…that we would celebrate. Like last year."

"Don't worry, I'll be back well before you get home. I happen to know that a huge birthday dinner is being planned for tonight, and I don't want to miss it. All right?"

Korden nodded happily, then went into his bedroom clutching his birthday present and his carry-pouch. Redfen watched him go and thought, as usual, how he would do anything to keep the boy safe. Indeed, he already had.

Except there may come a day when you're not around to do so anymore. And what then?

Redfen hoped that day would never come, not suspecting for a moment that it already had.

3

In his room, Korden spent a few minutes practicing the actions his father had shown him with the gun. It was a fantastic gift, but his mind remained too preoccupied to truly appreciate it.

He opened the small trunk beside his bed, which held the few items he treasured in this world: various shells and rocks found around the village, a few of his favorite books, and the ragged blue blanket his mother wrapped him in, before the Incarnates killed her on the night of his birth.

His father talked about the woman little. Just a single story about how they'd met. The image of her Korden held in his head was nothing more than an amalgam of Redfen's scant descriptions coupled with storybook princesses.

Korden placed the pistol inside the trunk, atop the blanket, then climbed into bed with his carry-pouch and pulled the thick quilt over his head. Once he felt secure, he created a *demno* on the tip of his pencil, producing a thread of illumination, just enough to see beneath the blanket. One hand wormed into his carry-pouch, feeling for the picture he'd taken.

The idea of leaving the auto without some memento of his trip had been unbearable. The volume itself he'd closed back up with its owners, the only burial honor he could afford those skeletal lovers, but he allowed himself to choose just one of their paper windows to keep.

He examined the picture. It was the one of the girl (*the daughter*, he amended) from the shoulders up, posing primly in front of that unnaturally blue background, as though she knew this second would be captured for all time. He noticed now that her nose turned up at the end in imitation of her mother. He wished he could see her *mohol*, to know how she felt at this frozen moment, but the picture offered none of her aura.

A girl, he thought, still awed. He understood the biological basics of what men and women did together, but reading mechanical descriptions from dense textbooks hadn't prepared him for the sensations that would accompany them.

What was this power she seemed to have over him? That grin made him feel dizzy. His stomach fluttered. He would've been frightened, if it didn't all feel so wonderful.

Praise the Upper, if a mere picture of a female could do this to him, what would it be like if he ever actually *met* one?

Without thinking, he brought the paper up to his face and brushed his lips against those of the girl. It felt no different than kissing a page from a book, but a small, secret thrill rocketed through him anyway. A fantasy formed in the halls of his incredible imagination, one that he would explore fully when he wasn't so tired.

Korden slipped the picture back in the pouch, clutched the bag to his chest, and closed his eyes.

Just before tumbling into sleep, his father's warning rang through his thoughts one last time, that leaving the Barrier would bring the Incarnates after him, like wolves tracking the scent of a wounded animal.

MODERATION

1

Redfen decided to let Korden sleep rather than wake him to say goodbye. As much as he fretted over his son's safety, he felt much better about the boy being out of his sight during the day, especially when his lessons would keep him busy. Still, if he had his way, Korden would be by his side even for this, learning to hunt. The invitation would be certain to thrill him, but their expedition would take them far beyond the limits of the Barrier, where his son could not go.

So Redfen collected his bow and quiver, and slipped out of the *hucté*.

Outside, the coolness of the morning had already been lost to the coming day's heat. It was the tail end of the Bloom, and, judging by the higher temperatures escorting it in, Burning Season looked to be scathing this year. Redfen didn't relish the idea of working in it, neither today nor in the coming weeks. Sweat beaded on his brow by the time he traversed the path down to the village, where he'd agreed to meet the others for an early start.

The hunting parties always consisted of eight men. When he and Korden settled here, Redfen was quick to volunteer for the duty, eager to prove his value to the tiny community. He lived in terror that they would be deemed too much trouble and sent out again on their own. Back then, the spots were assigned on a rotating basis, as were most jobs in the village, so that he only had to go once or twice a year. But the pool of able-bodied men shrank rapidly since then, leaving this task and many others to the few hands in good enough health to perform them. With Korden busy at his lessons—not to mention the new rigmarole Tash was teaching him—Redfen would spend the next season chopping firewood and lugging water from the spring by himself.

Not that he minded. He considered it more than fair trade for the peace and security the Olders gave them in return.

However, his skill with a bow left much to be desired. He often felt like a burden on these trips. But for the ramlar migration, their prey was so densely packed (and slowed by the Olders' mental magics) that he only needed to draw string to do his part. His mouth watered at the anticipation of that strange meat they were treated to but once a year.

A few minutes after leaving his home, he found himself behind the *hangala*, where seven other figures gathered.

2

Redfen had lived with these elderly men for fifteen years, since the rainy night he'd stumbled onto Bibb's doorstep with an infant in his arms and two Incarnates on his trail, after an entire season of working his way north through the flatlands and avoiding other people. He spoke with them every day and, in most cases, knew the more intimate details of their lives. And yet, the extreme age difference between himself and them never ceased to surprise him.

Like Korden, Redfen played with no other children as a boy. He'd been around people much older than himself his entire life, but all the men waiting on him now—including Fortholm, the youngest of the entire village and the one he most considered a friend—had stooped or outright hunched backs, thinning hair, and spotted, papery skin. Few looked spry enough for a venture into the wilderness to hunt wild game.

And even their elderly appearance didn't reveal the complete truth, that their magics had kept them alive much longer than anyone he'd ever met, far longer than humanly possible. Hard to tell just exactly how long, since he could never get a straight answer out of any of them.

But every last one said they'd ridden in hovering autos and sky carriers. Shopped at stores and watched 'teevee.'

They all claimed to have been active members of the great society that existed before the Purges.

The Last Fathers, they called themselves. *Olders*, Korden named them, since he was old enough to talk. Redfen had always heard the term *Crafters* for those whose faith in the Upper allowed them to perform strange and impossible feats. He'd never met one before coming here, didn't entirely believe that such people could exist. A man named Payt was the only person Redfen ever knew that preached faith in the Upper, and he certainly had no special abilities.

Redfen had lived among them long enough to see that their power was real, but knew he would always be the lone outsider unless he embraced their strange religion, as his son did. Not a week went by where they didn't invite him to attend the high-peaked building on the edge of the village.

What the Olders didn't seem to grasp is that Redfen had come to believe in the Upper just as much as His polar opposite; he'd seen enough cruelty and death to justify that one's existence, and if the Stranger existed, it only stood to reason that the Upper did too.

No, the real reason he chose not to worship with the Last Fathers was because he just couldn't hold the Great Interceder in as high regard as they did. With the way things were going in these, humanity's last days, it just seemed like the forces of evil had more interest in the dealings of mankind than the Upper did.

They certainly had more time and energy invested.

3

Ahead of him, the hunting party worked to lash a wooden cart to Mulder's sagging back. The plow horse snorted angrily and shifted his weight between hooves. This group of Last Fathers had shed their pious brown robes today, in favor of less constrictive tunics and breeches.

"Hail, Brother Redfen!" Fortholm greeted him warmly in his creaking, raspy voice. Redfen grasped the man's gaunt left shoulder and had the gesture returned, although the grip was so weak he could scarcely feel it. Fortholm might be younger than the others, but his health deteriorated much faster. He had no business undertaking such a strenuous task, but each time he insisted he be allowed on the hunting party. The nest of wrinkles at the corner of each of his eyes bunched into a mighty fold as he grinned.

"Good tidings to all." Redfen glanced around at the others as he spoke, then asked, "Eddas, would you like a hand?"

The Older—big as a bear, with a sloping bulge of stomach and one bad eye amidst the crags of his weathered face—strained as he lifted the front end of the cart high enough for Tiller and Santo to finish attaching it to Mulder's yoke. He was too out of breath to answer, purple veins pulsing at his white-haired temples, but he managed to shake his head.

Redfen turned back to Fortholm and Allin. "Isn't there a bit of wizardry you could use for that?"

"Artcraft is a well that must be refreshed, my friend! If we used it for every trivial matter in life, it would go dry quickly."

"What he means," Allin added, his syrupy drawl giving the word several extra vowels, "is that this ol' ox gotta take ev'ry opportunity to show off what's lefta his muscles!"

Eddas gave a grunting sigh of relief as the weight came off his back and the cart balanced on its own two wheels. He wobbled as he straightened to his full seven-feet, a height attained even with the drastic curve to his upper spine that made the top of his head just about level with his shoulders. "Once upon a time, I crushed men like you with my bare hands in the ring, Allin," he growled. "You remember that."

"Yeah, well, I think the only crushin you could do these days is if ya sat on me." After hoisting his little finger in response to the other man's scowl, Allin asked Redfen, "So what's the kiddo doin for his birthday this mornin?"

"He was still in bed when I left."

"I'll bet. Sleepin's about tha only thing for a kid his age ta do 'round here." He gave a low whistle, an easy feat with his many missing teeth. "Curse, can ya imagine? Sixteen years old and stuck out here with us dusty fossils?"

"He does get a little bored," Redfen admitted.

"*Bored?* Shoot, that don't tell the half of it. All those teenage hormones, never seen a woman, not so much as a single picture for jerk off material? That ain't natural. Poor li'l guy probably wouldn't know what ta do with an erection if it bit 'im."

Eddas groaned.

"Brother Allin," Fortholm chided, and *tssk*ed between his teeth.

"Oh come on Fortholm, ya know as well as I do the kid's miserable."

Fortholm shook his head. "Be that as it may, let us hope he makes it to his lessons promptly today. Tash is...in a strange mood."

Beyond him, the last two members of the party, Del and Port, stood with their heads bowed in the intimate conversation of lovers, Port's hand gently rubbing the back of Del's neck. Redfen saw many such pairings even before coming to the village; same sex relationships presented fewer dangers and complications. In many of the towns he'd come across while on the run, men and women were forbidden from even touching. As Redfen waved to the couple, Tiller came around the cart.

"Let's get moving," he told the group. He was a quick, lithe man with veiny ropes of muscle on his forearms and silver hair cut so close the scalp could be seen through the bristles. He was also one of the few Olders in as good a shape as Redfen himself, so he often led the hunting expeditions. "I want to be at the canyons before midday."

"Are we certain about this?" Redfen asked. "This is a full thirty days early for the ramlar migration. Not that I'm complaining, I'd much rather do it now than when the heat is at its worst, but..." He let the sentence hang, knowing it was stupid to question their insight.

"You heard Tiller." This came from Santo, a Hispanic

man with a fist-sized goiter stretching the right side of his neck and a voice like a bullfrog. "Stop jabbering and help Fortholm into the cart. If the stubborn bastard insists on coming with us, at least he won't slow us down."

Redfen, Eddas, and Allin all moved to aid Fortholm, gently lifting his brittle body by waist and legs so he could step up on the cart's bench. After he settled, he leaned down, back popping audibly, and whispered to Redfen, "They're coming, all right. I'm not good for much these days, but I can still feel them when they're on their way. Their migration pattern has shortened. I think...they're being pushed westward."

Before Redfen could ask what that might mean, Mulder neighed as Tiller slapped him on the rump. The cart started forward on squalling wheels. Redfen fell into line beside it with the other six men as the sun beat down on them from above.

4

Korden awakened from a nightmare in which a dark, savage force hunted him through the forest.

He'd been with the girl from the picture, sitting with her at first in the most wonderfully awkward silence in the same clearing where he'd found her parents. She wore an outfit from one of her other images; a breezy yellow blouse with no sleeves and a wide V neck, and a strange black garment around her waist that only covered her hips and thighs; he thought it was called a 'skirt'. They stared at their feet, glancing up at one another furtively, until he gathered his courage and reached over to hold her hand, a gesture he only knew about from his books.

She turned to him and grinned—that same dazzling smile as in her picture—then leaned into him, encircling his chest with her arms. A tingle ran across his scalp as they reclined on the forest floor, their bodies pressing against one another. His groin felt hot and tight. As her hands moved down to it, caressing and tickling, the aching pleasure of it all made him press his eyes closed. And then the contact vanished. When he opened his eyes again, she had disappeared, and a cold wind gusted through the trees, carrying a stench of decay.

An overwhelming sense of impending disaster filled him.

He leapt to his feet just in time to hear something snarl. A pair of red eyes like smoldering coals appeared in the underbrush beside him. Korden backed away from it, gaping in horror, then turned and ran. The beast gave chase, staying just on his heels. The clack of its teeth echoed in his ears.

Rather than catapulting from sleep, he came to consciousness so gradually that the line between dream and reality blurred. For just a moment, he lay in bed, feet still pedaling, and thought he could hear the creature's jaws. The sense of foreboding followed him all the way back into the land of waking, and throbbed in the back of his head as he opened his eyes.

Usually, with a dream this vivid, he would scribble a description in his journal. He liked to remember them, not just for creative fodder, but for the secrets they might hold. Tash said that sometimes the Upper communicated in sleep what the heart knew but the mind could not interpret. Like when Micka told them of a nightmare in which he'd been drowning in a frothing flood and, the next day, it rained so hard that an entire wall of his *hucté* collapsed.

The problem was, you could never tell if a dream mattered until it was too late.

Today though, there was no time for reflection. The light trickling into his room around the window braces looked bright. Too bright. He was exhausted from staying awake all night, and now he would probably be late to his lesson. Tash would not be happy.

It's my birthday. I can be late if I want.

Such excuses would mean nothing to his *den-so*.

And, aside from his father, there was no one he liked disappointing less.

He got out of bed, still clad in his dungarees, and pulled on a green, half-sleeved shirt woven from tight mesh, and the leather boots Eddas crafted for him when his feet outgrew the last pair. These already felt a little cramped, with a worn spot in one sole, but he could easily make them last another few seasons.

His carry-pouch lay beside the bed. He paused just before picking it up.

The picture was still inside. He considered taking it out to hide in his room, but then realized it would make no difference. If he remained this preoccupied with it during his lessons, Tash would sense his distraction. The only way to avoid getting caught would be to put it out of his thoughts entirely. He tried to do just that as he picked up the bag and pulled the strap over his head.

Breakfast waited for him on the table. He wolfed it down in three bites without stopping on his way to the door.

Outside, he reveled in the sunshine and warm air. It had been a long, wet Stilling, and the damp cold always worsened his health. This year alone had seen two fevers and a handful of colds. His good mood allowed his worries about the Barrier and the last vestiges of his nightmare to fade from his thoughts. Excitement overtook him instead, at what he knew waited just ahead.

The village was alive this time as he approached, the residents going about the few menial tasks that made up the majority of their days. Palo balanced on a ladder, using complicated crafting gestures to repair a hole in the thatching of his roof, his bird legs wobbling beneath the hem of his robe. Feegran, the town healer, stood just outside his own *hucté*, examining a rash on Matar's arm while a line of other Olders waited with their own ailments, which seemed to grow more numerous each day. Coomb, Dillish, and Bant sat on the steps of the social hall in their wheeled chairs, clutching totala hands, where they would remain all day until they fell asleep drooling over their suppers.

Birthday wishes rang out from all corners when he entered the village proper. As always, the Olders perked up when they saw him, rousing from their half-asleep existences with a twinkle in their eyes. He'd been told many times that his presence here kept them young more so than the artcraft. Korden waved to each of them and called out greetings.

He loved these men as much as he did his father. They had been nothing but kind to him, and many of them imparted their knowledge to him both in and out of the classroom; reading, writing, mathematics, and— most important of all—his various artistic tutelages.

Besides Redfen, the Last Fathers were his only family.

But, no matter how strong his affection, he didn't want to end up like them. The thought of living in this village for as long as they had made him feel the same way his as-mah attacks did: as though an iron vice was clamped tight around his chest.

To his left, Skewtz emerged from his library, raised a hand and called out in his high, quivery voice, "Hail Brother Korden!"

"Hail Brother Skewtz," he shouted back, without stopping his hurried pace.

"Tell me, how goes the reading assignment?"

"Good. It's just that…" Korden paused. "How did all those warriors fit inside that one horse?"

"Well, it was huge! It towered as big as the city walls!"

"Oh." He swept a few locks of hair thoughtfully out of his eyes. "But…did they take all the guts out first? And why did the people in the city want a big, dead horse?"

Skewtz stared at him for a long moment, tongue bobbing, then burst into a fit of laughter that sounded like hiccups. "I think you missed something in the translation on that one, my boy. We'll talk more about it in our next session. You better run along to Tash."

Korden did run along, but he didn't go straight to his session. He had one other stop to make first, one he had anticipated for days. It wouldn't matter anyway; to Tash, late was late, whether a minute or an hour.

Instead, he took an abrupt turn just before reaching his classroom and ducked through Bibb's door without knocking.

5

The interior of the *hucté* was sparse, barely two rooms, the only furniture a rocking chair, a feather-stuffed mattress on the floor indented from its owner's weight, and a large wooden trunk in the corner. Bibb himself sat in the chair, with a hand-carved clay pipe in one hand that smelled of the spiced tobacco he grew, and a thick book in the other. He glanced up as Korden entered and peered at him from behind smudged glasses. A mischievous smirk split his sagging face.

"So the birthday boy has come to pay me a visit," he teased.

"Show me," Korden commanded.

Bibb's eyes twinkled as he said, with exaggerated innocence, "Whatever do you mean, lad?"

"You know what I mean! Hurry up, I'm already late for my lesson with Tash!"

"That is *your* fault, not mine," he scolded, but the tone remained mocking. He paused, perhaps considering if he wanted to pursue the jest, then relented and said, "Oh, all right. Have a look outside then, make sure no one is coming."

Korden did, but already knew the other Olders—the ones not on the hunt with his father—were not liable to come busting in unannounced. By the time he turned back, Bibb had set aside his pipe and book, lugged his pear-shaped body from the chair, and waddled to the trunk in the corner. He opened the lid while still several steps away with a flick of two fingers. One hand went to the small of his back as he squatted awkwardly to rummage inside. Korden denied the urge to leap to his side and gaze in at the contents.

Finally Bibb straightened and turned, holding up a small object light gray in color and badly scarred, with a broad, rectangular face and width no more than a single cupit. On the side facing Korden was a square window with a black circle beneath.

"I've been saving this one until you were old enough to appreciate it," the Older said.

Each year, on Korden's birthday, Bibb pulled some new wonder from the past out of his trunk to show off, then it went back in, never to be seen again. Last year, it had been a mechanical challi bird that flew around the room after Bibb turned a tiny wheel under its fourth wing, its flight directed by movements of his hand that seemed like artcraft, but were entirely technologic. Before that there had been many toys that once belonged to his children, and a game where one pulled tiny pieces out of a drawing of a man, which, through the magic of electricity, buzzed loudly if one touched the sides of the opening. Once there had even been a device that Bibb called a 'holo-cast,' a silvery disc that produced images in mid-air—so intangible you could put your hand right through them—of a cat and mouse that chased one another in endless circles. *An-eh-mae-shun*, Bibb explained. None of the other Olders knew about his stash, which was the way he preferred it.

He handed the slim box to Korden, who turned it over and over in his hands. He might've recognized his father's gift, but he had no idea about this. It was made of a material slicker than wood and lighter than metal; probably plastic, a substance that he once heard Tash refer to as 'a prime example of the fallen ways.' There was no writing of any kind, just a glass window spiderwebbed with cracks and several arrows on the black circle beneath.

And on the back, above a series of small holes laid out in neat rows, was a slightly upraised insignia in the shape of an apple, with a missing chunk on the side.

Korden looked up at Bibb questioningly.

The Older reached out with one pudgy, yellow-nailed finger and touched a spot on the black circle.

A sound blasted out of the thing, a noise so high-pitched and startling that Korden almost fumbled the device out of his grip. A screeching wail vacillated between notes faster than he could keep up with them, joined a few seconds later by a voice whose tenor matched the piercing squeals, the words threatening something about making him sweat, making him 'groove.' It seemed to be coming from the small holes in the back. Bibb hurriedly slid his finger around the circle. The volume lowered, but the pitch did not.

"What is that?" Korden asked, somewhat frantic. On the cracked window, an image tried to resolve, but it flickered with a thousand scattered black and white speckles.

"That, lad, is rock and roll. I listened to that song when I was your age. Of course, it was nearly a hundred years old even then, but I always had a fondness for the classics."

"You mean music?" The sounds behind the singing were nothing like the lilting melodies Santo would sometimes play on his guitar, or even the quick-tempoed songs Coomb produced on his harmonica, which made them all clap and dance. "It just sounds like a bunch of noise."

"Well, it's not everyone's cup of tea, but that certainly takes me back." Bibb sighed wistfully. "Anyway, this gizmo is called…an iFod. Or Bod. I-something or other, they put that letter in front of everything for a while. It's taken a beating—with the screen broken, there's no way to control what song you'll get next—but the battery in that will be around long after you and I are dust. For all I know, it may very well be the last collection of musical culture left from before the Purges."

Korden put his thumb on the circle and pressed. The song cut off and a new one began, this one a twangy jangle over a voice pleading for mercy for his 'achy-breaky' heart.

Bibb blushed all the way across his jowls. "Yes, well, ahem, when it looked like the M-Net was going to collapse, I packed a little of everything onto that gadget. Try another."

Korden did, thinking again how, when the Olders spoke of the world before the Purges, he understood only one word in five. He continued pressing the button, skipping through song after song, each one completely different from the last, styles as distinct and nuanced as each person's emotional aura tended to be. Then a song came forth that was deeper, slower, more melodic...and soulfully beautiful in ways he could not describe.

"Opera," Bibb mused. "From *Rigoletto*, I believe. I haven't heard it in so long. Please, leave it on this one."

A voice began singing against the rich strains, a high-pitched, lilting falsetto that made him blurt, "Is that...a *woman?*"

"Indeed."

Korden listened, fascinated for so many reasons. The woman sang in a language he didn't understand, but it didn't matter; the emotion conveyed the basic sentiment, perhaps more so than if the words had been familiar. They listened in silence all the way through, Bibb easing back into his chair to sit with his eyes closed while his *mohol* ran cool with peaceful blues and greens. The song sounded so delicate and harmonious, Korden wished it would never end, but when it did, he reluctantly surrendered the device.

"Bibb...why do you keep these things?" He'd never thought to ask this question before, when the excitement of these treasures and the promise of keeping them secret overshadowed all other concerns. But lately, he had more and more trouble accepting at face value the world he'd taken for granted. "If the Last Fathers believe technology and science are so bad, then why not get rid of them?"

"It's not that we think they're inherently bad. You won't find a single one of us that will tell you that, Korden. Not even Tash, as much as he blusters. Did that song seem evil to you?"

"No. Not at all. It was wonderful."

"Of course it was. And technology was responsible for much good in the world. But too much, just as with anything in life, can be destructive. Do you know the word 'moderation'?"

Korden shook his head, frowning.

"It means stopping yourself from doing something before it becomes a habit, or even an addiction." Bibb held up the iFod. "Toward the end, moderation fell by the wayside. Society invested so much of its time in gadgets just like this, in wires and chips and circuits and guns and bombs. We forgot about art and creativity and faith, even those that purported to worship in one of the countless religious sects. That's why the Filament gained a foothold in the first place, or so I believe. But science is not meant to be abandoned completely. The only reason we don't allow it here is the same reason we allow no women: because of the distraction it would bring. But, to put things in perspective, a deep enough trust in artcraft can corrupt just as easily as technology." He poked Korden in the forehead. "You remember that word 'moderation,' lad. Balance is the key. Never shut yourself off from any possibility, but don't let that possibility control you, either."

"I'll remember," Korden agreed.

"Good. Now get to your lesson. If Tash seeks to punish you, I'll not have the blame on me."

Korden nodded, and reluctantly left the *hucté*.

6

The classroom where Korden spent the majority of his days was bigger than any of the Olders' homes, a square room ten pargs to a side whose sole piece of furniture was a desk built specifically for him. Long windows spanned each wall, their braces open to allow in breeze and the day's light. The rest of the walls were decorated with his best attempts at drawing and painting throughout the years. A scratched and pitted chalkboard—scavenged somewhere beyond the village—stood in one corner, but they'd run out of chalk years ago. Today, for some reason, a wooden crate of freshly-pulled carrots waited beside his desk.

His various instructors alternated the room's usage, bringing in their own teaching implements when needed, but only Tash, it had been determined long ago, would instruct him in the usage of artcraft, if he wanted to learn. His answer on that subject had been a resolute 'yes' since the age of five, after witnessing everything the Olders accomplished through their faith. Unfortunately, Redfen did not share his son's enthusiasm. Only after much pleading and persuasion did he finally agree to let Korden apprentice. The lessons began exactly one year ago today.

At the classroom's eastward facing window, Korden's *den-so* stood gazing out toward the blackness of the Shroud, now hidden behind the overcast sky. Except the man wasn't really gazing at anything, since he could hardly see the end of his own crooked nose thanks to the opaque sheen across his eyes. A long, brown robe hung off his bowed back, the hem puddled around his feet.

Korden waited half a minute for the man to speak first. He suspected the silence was a precursor to some rebuke about his tardiness. When he could stand the quiet no longer, he tentatively said, "Tash?"

To his surprise, the leader of the Last Fathers—and by far the oldest man in the village—flinched at the sound of his voice, like a person startled out of sleep. Tash had never been prone to dozing or wandering in his thoughts (*cotton-picking*, as Allin called it) like so many others. His mind remained as sharp as a blade while his body aged. And indeed, when the man turned around to face him, Korden thought he looked as alert as ever. His expression, however, was drawn and pained.

"*Ghammer*," Tash uttered, sounding relieved. The term for an artcraft apprentice was far more derogatory than the formal *den-ret*, but from Tash, it was always said with fondness. A mane of silken, white hair framed his wizened face, flowing like a waterfall from crown to shoulders. Once his eyes had been a grey the color of angry thunderheads, until the disease slowly robbing him of his vision muted their color to a pearlescent ash. As his sightless eyes roamed across Korden, one gaunt, fisted hand rubbed at the center of his chest in slow circles. Something about the gesture caused a spring of anxiety to bubble up in Korden.

"Are...are you all right?" he asked. He couldn't help recalling that light this morning, the one shining out from the man's *hucté* long before the village awoke. Korden gauged the man's emotional spectrum, and received that same queasy, nervous yellow as before.

Tash blinked a few times, opened his mouth as his brow drew together, then shook his head. The yellow in his *mohol* faded. "Fine, *ghammer*. Jes ruminatin." His odd accent turned every 'R' into a trill. "That's all yeh'll do when yeh get ta be my age."

That was it. Not a word about his lateness. Korden didn't know whether to be relieved or concerned.

The old man started across the room. Despite his near-blindness, his steps were sure-footed and quick. He came to a stop just in front of Korden, his height barely bringing his chin level with the top of the boy's head.

He jabbed a finger at the vegetable box on the floor. "That is a fresh box straight from tha harvest. Among them is a single carrot on which I carved yehr own name. Find it, and place it in my hand within a thirty count. And if yeh so much as *touch* any o' them, I'll keep yeh faithing here 'til this time tomorrow." He held out his hand, palm up.

Korden's gut clenched. Curse Tash's constant surprise tests! At least he was acting more like himself again. Korden let none of his consternation show as he closed his eyes and concentrated on the Upper, opening his heart and mind to that presence, feeling it flow through him like warm cider on a chilly night. As he shed the inattentiveness of youth, this state became increasingly easier to reach. And whenever that conduit opened, he got a glimpse of something power-ful, something that made him feel tiny and insignificant, yet infinitely strong at the same time.

"Nine...ten..." Tash counted.

His will, honed by faith, was a tool ready to do his bid-ding, but where to direct it? What wordspell from his limited arsenal should he use? He could try to levitate the carrots out of the box so he could inspect each one, but that would take far too long, even if he managed to keep more than a few in the air at a time. He might be able to make his target glow with a focused *demno*, but that wouldn't get it into Tash's hand. Or was there a trick to the instructions, and he only needed to find some physical object with which to sift through the box's contents without touching them? The old man was certainly sly enough to devise such a test, just to further test his problem solving.

"Yeh're overthinkin it, *ghammer*. Remember, only tha will matters. Imagine yehr goal an' then *force* it inta being."

The carrot, Korden willed. A single bead of sweat rolled down the side of his face. *No, not just any carrot, the one with my name on it. Be in Tash's hand. Be there.*

He opened his eyes, full of hope.

Nothing had changed. Tash's bony hand remained empty.

Korden's shoulders slumped. "I can't do it."

"Not with that attitude, yeh can't," Tash snapped. He slapped the back of one hand into the palm of the other. "Don't rely so much on what yeh know. Craften is not but a nonsense language made up by artcraftsmen without enough faith in themselves. It helps ta build concentration, which is why I taught a little ta yeh, but such wordspells also keep yehr mind chained. Yeh must work at sheddin yehrself o' them. Too many here have yet ta do that."

"Yes sir."

Tash's sightless eyes flicked back and forth. His voice softened the slightest bit as he added, "Yeh have a bigger imagination than anyone I've ever met, *ghammer*; if yeh can just learn ta call upon it when yeh most need it—instead o' only usin it ta daydream—there is almost nothin yeh won't be able ta accomplish. Yeh might even be able ta cure yehrself o' those constant sicknesses which have plagued yeh fer so long."

"I'll keep practicing."

"Yes. Yeh will. Startin right now."

Today's Problem

1

They headed west, toward the ocean.

Redfen had seen that vast blue expanse three times in his life, on hunting expeditions that yielded little game and forced them to range far from the village. After they pitched camp, he would stay up late and watch the waves come rolling in on the shores of a place Fortholm told him had once been called Californya. The sheer might of those waters stretching to a clear, unmarred horizon was unparalleled in Redfen's limited travels. It was the first place he wanted to bring Korden, when the boy was free of the Barrier once and for all.

Today's hunt would not take them so far. The ramlars were always steadfast in the route of their migration toward the sea and then up the coast to the north. The expedition would be a simple matter of intercepting the herd on their closest approach northwest of the village, twenty or so spans away, then taking down enough of the creatures to provide meat through the end of the season.

They trekked across hilly, open fields at first, before entering a light wood of oak and birch. The shade provided a nice respite from the heat, but the trees grew so dense at times they were forced to seek out paths wide enough for Mulder to pull their cart through. Redfen had no trouble keeping up with the pace Tiller set, but as the terrain took its toll on his elderly companions, he found himself having to slow his steps so he didn't outdistance them. Several of the Olders began to grumble about various aches and pains, to which Santo barked that they could keep their complaints to themselves.

Only Fortholm seemed in good cheer. After they emerged from the trees and started down a grassy slope that would lead into the canyons below, he climbed down from the cart and insisted Del and Allin ride the rest of the way. Then he hobbled to catch up with Redfen.

"So tell me," he rasped, "how *is* the boy? Speak true, now."

A question Redfen heard often. The Olders' concern for Korden was never-ending, but it felt different from Redfen's own worries. At times they seemed in awe of him, as though they expected him to suddenly sprout wings and fly away.

For all he knew, that might be exactly what they believed.

"As restless as ever. Even after all my cautions, he went out in the middle of the night to do Upper knows what. I caught him creeping back inside early this morning. Said he wanted *time alone*."

Fortholm nodded knowingly. "The Barrier grows smaller around him each day. When I was his age, I ran away from my parents' house. If memory serves, it was because they wouldn't let me smoke cigarettes with my hoodlum friends." He smiled at the memory, revealing a very few teeth clinging to his shriveled gums. "I made it two blocks—that's how we lived, in groups of homes called 'blocks'—before I turned around and came back. But still, I felt I accomplished my goal. That's what young men do, Redfen; it's what they were made for, even in times as dark as these. To rebel. To push at boundaries, so they can do the things old men like us no longer can."

"Speak for yourself," Redfen objected. From the cart behind them, Allin snorted laughter as he eavesdropped on their conversation. "The problem is that Korden *can't* rebel, and it's…it's stealing the fire of his youth. The only things he truly seems to enjoy anymore are his writing and Tash's lessons."

"Then aren't you glad you relented and let him learn?"

Redfen readjusted the bow and quiver on his shoulder and decided not to answer such a complicated question. While he hated Tash's constant meddling in the boy's upbringing, he was thankful for the apprenticeship. Artcraft was a tool, a weapon that would help ensure Korden's safety, just as training in archery or swordsmanship would, or even a few bullets for that old, useless shooter. Even if it made him a pariah, it would give him power, and power was essential for survival. But all the time, in the back of Redfen's mind, he would always be resentful because…well, because…

Because it's his birthright, a voice answered for him. *Because every spell Tash teaches him just brings the boy one step closer to being what they say he is.*

He swallowed a heavy lump that formed in his throat. "Even if we get him to eighteen safely, he'll still be eager to leave. And he won't be satisfied with staying isolated; he'll want to see what's become of the cities he fantasizes about. But there's more than just Incarnates out there that could harm him. The world is a strange and desperate place now, and becoming more so by the day. I know, I've seen it. I was out in it long after the lot of you hid yourselves away to practice weaving your magic."

The land began to level out as they talked. Somewhere ahead would be a small ridge overlooking a shallow valley full of interwoven ravines, canals carved deep into the earth from the seasonal floods of the Bloom and separated from one another by narrow dirt walls. From there, they would have a perfect vantage point to see the ramlars sweep in from the east and pass just below. But Redfen's thoughts turned to Korden, feeding him visions of the boy in trouble, of him alone in the thick, haunted umbrage of the redwood forest and surrounded on all sides by unseen enemies.

"Brother Redfen, do you know the story of the shnikyun beast and the chipmunk?" Fortholm asked abruptly.

"Oh Upper, here we go," Allin groaned behind them. "We'll all be asleep in no time."

Redfen hid a grin by rubbing his chin pensively. "Can't say that one's familiar."

"Well, the shnikyun beast, when its kind appeared some years ago, found it easiest to prey on rodents, but it had a particular taste for chipmunk. Its front tentacles reach into the holes where they take shelter and snatch them out, turning what was an instinctive defense into a trap.

"One day, a particularly clever shnikyun beast came upon a chipmunk standing outside the entrance to his home in the base of a tree. Now, this shnikyun beast wanted to make a meal out of the chipmunk, but before he could chase him inside and pull him back out, the rodent began to laugh.

"'Why do you laugh at me, little chipmunk?' the shnikyun beast asked.

"'Because,' said the chipmunk, 'you will never be able to catch me with your long tentacles. The hole in this tree goes much deeper than you can reach, and before you get here, I will be safe at the farthest end!'

"The shnikyun beast thought quickly, and said, 'But my little friend, I haven't come to eat you, but to spread a warning to all the inhabitants of the forest. A terrible winter is coming, and food will be scarce. You must gather everything you can find to store up so that you might survive the famine.' And, with that, the shnikyun wisely slithered away before the chipmunk could ask why the beast cared to save his life.

"The chipmunk soon became worried and worked day and night, gathering nuts to get himself through the harsh winter the shnikyun predicted. He worked until his entire cubby was filled with nuts and he had more food than he could eat in a lifetime.

"After giving the chipmunk ample time, the shnikyun came back and found him once again outside his hole. He didn't waste time on words, but charged forward and chased the chipmunk back into his hole, where the little rodent discovered he'd left himself no room to hide from the shnikyun's questing tentacle, and was dragged out and eaten.

"Now, I ask you, Redfen." Fortholm paused to give a harsh, ragged cough from using his voice so much, then wiped sweat from around the neck of his tunic. "What is the moral of this story?"

Before Redfen could answer, Allin shouted from the cart, "If ya can trick someone inta puttin nuts down their hole, you'll be able ta eat 'em out!"

"*Shut UP, Allin!*" Eddas roared from somewhere at the rear of the caravan.

"Was that right?" Redfen teased.

Fortholm gave a wheezy sigh that sounded like Korden

during one of his attacks. "Try again, considering it from the chipmunk's point of view."

"I don't know, Fort." Redfen threw up his hands. "Why don't you tell me what I was supposed to get out of that?"

"The lesson is about the future, my friend. You see, the chipmunk was so concerned with the danger in the distance, he never stopped to prepare for the one that was staring him in the face."

The caravan slowed as the ridgeline came into view. Redfen stopped walking and studied Fortholm. The old man's eyes met his, and, though the skin around them drooped and sagged with age, the orbs within them were still young and full of life. He reached out and put a dry, shaking hand on Redfen's forearm.

"It does no good to worry about what *might* be," he explained. "Focus on today's problems. There's more than enough of those."

Then he turned and limped toward the canyons with Eddas and Del on either side.

2

The approaching ramlars were heralded by a grumble in the air like thunder and a slight vibration underfoot, followed by a cloud of dust rising to the east. The sound soon swelled to a headache-inducing drum beat of thousands of stamping feet. Any second now, the first tufted, rotund bodies would be visible in the canal just twenty or thirty pargs below. Then the main body of the light brown herd would thunder through the short valley's chokepoint, divided temporarily into jostling lines as they hurtled through the maze of narrow ravines and then regrouped on the other side.

Redfen had never heard of the bipedal creatures until he came to live with the Olders, but he looked forward to their succulent meat each year. He knelt, unslung his bow and quiver, and nocked his first arrow. Beside him, Allin did the same, giving Redfen a toothy grin before pointing his own weapon down into the valley. The others spread out along the ridgeline.

Redfen glanced up once as the stampede drew closer. The sky remained cloudless, the noon sun directly overhead. They would be home tonight well before dinner just as he promised, and he could spend the evening celebrating his son's sixteenth birthday, a feat he never dreamed possible on the child's first. With a smile of his own, he pulled his arrow tight, right hand all the way against his shoulder, left arm taut and straight, and waited to see the teeming mass of fuzzy bodies appear below him.

And waited.

And waited still longer.

He could feel tension overtake the others. The sound of the ramlars came from their right…grew to a roar…and then swept by them in the farthest ravines, where their arrows couldn't reach.

Redfen blinked in confusion. It was as though the beasts consciously avoided the pathways closest to them.

"*They're on to us!*" Santo shouted over the noise of the herd.

"*Can't be!*" Allin answered. "*They ain't smart enough!*"

"*Something has them spooked!*" Fortholm yelled from Redfen's right, his hoarse cry barely audible. He pointed out over the short valley, toward the thick screen of dirt rising into the air. "*Look, there, you can see them on the other side of those trees, through the opening in the canyon wall!*

They're frenzied! Open your hearts and you can feel the fear coming off them in waves!"

Redfen could feel no such thing, but from the moment his friend made this declaration, something dark bloomed in him. His thoughts immediately went to Korden. Behind them, Mulder bucked so hard the cart almost overturned. Eddas ran to calm the horse.

"Can you soothe them?" Tiller shouted to Fortholm. *"Lure them to us?"*

"Their terror is too great! I would never be able to manipulate their emotions enough to overcome it!"

"Then if they won't come to us, we go to them! Climb down, and for Upper's sake, don't get crushed in the stampede!"

Redfen slung his bow and quiver back over his shoulder. They moved single-file, leaving Mulder tied to a tree, and Tiller led the way down a less steep section of the slope and into the floor of the canyon. The going was rough, uneven and full of ground fissures, so Redfen didn't see how the more decrepit members of their party could possibly make it down. He stayed close behind Fortholm, ready to catch the man if he fell, but it was Redfen whose foot flew out from under him on a patch of loose rocks. He tumbled backward to smash against the ground.

Or would have, if Eddas hadn't snagged his arm in one of his huge bear paws. The Older set him back on his feet and sent him on his way with a pat between the shoulders.

They helped Fortholm down off the last shallow ledge and then the eight of them spread out across the ravine floor, heading into a thicket of gnarled trees growing from the coarse soil. Just on the other side, through the break in the ravine wall, the roving migration was visible in the next narrow canal. If they could fire on the animals without crossing over, they wouldn't have to risk getting trampled.

This close, their pounding feet were almost deafening. The musty odor of the beasts' bodies mingled with the smell of churned earth. It attempted to steal the hunters' breath and cloud their eyes. Tiller and Port released the first arrows, taking down two fat ramlars near the edge of the crowd. They gave deep, bass honks as they fell, but the flood of their kin just parted around them and kept going. The hunters would only have another minute or so before the migration passed them by.

Redfen fiddled with his bow, trying to get his hands to stop shaking so he could ready an arrow. The dreadful assurance that this turn of events had something to do with Korden—*Korden in danger, a great wrong with Korden*—settled over his head like a noose.

His persistent unease must have been apparent, because Fortholm turned to him before firing his own bow. "*Remember the chipmunk, Redfen!*" he shouted. "*Hunt now, worry later!*"

Redfen furrowed his brow, made a silent vow to heed this advice, and nodded.

Then a figure emerged from the shadows of a tree and buried an axe in the back of Fortholm's head.

3

There was no time to act, no time to even shout a warning. The dark shape lurched out and brought the heavy blade whistling down all in one smooth motion. Fortholm's head wasn't so much split as it was crushed from the force of the blow, the entire top caving in so much that the old man's bleary eyeballs bulged from their sockets. Wet droplets spattered across Redfen's face. Fortholm collapsed into a heap in front of him, the weapon jutting from the top of his head like some strange hat.

The figure stepped into full view, bent, and gave the handle of the axe a solid jerk to separate it from Fortholm's shattered skull. It lingered in the shadow of the overhanging tree, blocked from the direct rays of the sun, but there was more than enough light for Redfen to recognize what he looked at.

Not *who*; the face was always different with these beings, and never an indicator of what lurked beneath. All the same, this was a familiar monster.

An Incarnate.

4

It'd been years since he'd faced one, and none of them were in this poor of condition. He'd assured himself that he was finished with these abominations.

The creature stumbled forward, careful to stay in the scant flutters of shadow provided by the treetops. Redfen could see that its body was on the verge of giving out, rotted by light exposure and beaten apart by the forces that had commandeered it. It wore only the merest tatters of clothing, exposing skin that was either covered in blackish green discoloration or missing in chunks and patches. The flesh of its stomach had worn through at some point, spilling half-hardened viscera down to its groin, where the last shredded remains of a penis dangled free. Its limbs were little more than bones with skin pulled taut across them.

Distantly, Redfen was aware that the ramlar herd had thinned, enough that he could hear the alarmed shouts of the rest of the hunting party. But he remained rooted to the ground, unable to look away from the thing shambling toward him, caught in a cycle of terror and disgust.

The face it wore was cracked and pitted with sores, the hair long fallen out, the nose no more than a scabrous crater. Its eyes were little red embers buried deep in their sockets, and they fixed on Redfen with murderous rage as the demon came on.

"*Lrgggggggsssssshhh*," it growled, before its jaw gave way at both joints, hung for a second by the scraps of decayed flesh covering them, and then tumbled through the air to land at its feet. There were a few crooked teeth left in those gums. They looked very white against the reddish soil of the ravine floor.

It all happened with the unrelenting slowness of an awful dream. Redfen remained frozen even as the Incarnate hefted its weapon again, and made to swing it down upon him with the same deadly force that ended Fortholm's life.

"*Move!*" Santo bellowed, shoving him aside with a strength that had to've been artcraft granted. The axe blade whistled through the space where Redfen's neck had been and bit into the meat of Santo's upper arm instead. He screamed and jumped away, clutching the wound as blood gushed through his fingers.

Redfen fell across the ravine floor beside Fortholm's remains, his bow snapping beneath him, and the world resumed its normal pace in a great, whirling rush. Beyond the ravine wall, the last of the ramlars passed them by, leaving a void of silence in their wake. The Incarnate loomed over him. Port helped Santo to a safe distance as the rest of the hunting party cautiously moved in. Redfen realized it was probably the first time most—if not all—of them had ever seen one of these creatures. They lived sheltered lives here also, hidden away in the wilderness since the Purges began.

Allin acted first, hobbling forward to tackle the creature to the ground just a few pargs from where Redfen lay.

"*I got 'im, I got the sonuvabitch!*" he bawled. The Incarnate struggled feebly beneath him, unable to lift its axe for another swing. Allin tried to sit up while planting a hand on the creature's chest to hold it down. The torso caved beneath his weight, brittle ribs snapping with the dryness of dead wood. His arm plunged into the body cavity up to the forearm. He made a snorting sound of disgust and wrenched his hand free. It came out covered with blackish, clotted blood and chunks of rotted organs.

Beneath him, the Incarnate made weak gasping noises. That dark blood gurgled up from the hole of its exposed throat. Its eyes rolled in their sockets, the glow in them guttering like a weak candle flame. Some vital piece of its stolen body had been mortally damaged, and it was surely dying.

Dying.

But that meant…

"*Allin, get away from it!*" Redfen shouted as he scrambled to his feet. The implications of a dead Incarnate came to him much faster than anyone else, but still not soon enough.

Allin glanced at him in confusion and then back down at the body beneath him.

Just in time for a little black funnel of smoke to drift from the eyes of the demon and into his own.

5

The transformation happened fast. One second it was Allin staring out of those wide, brown eyes, and in the next, they glowed red as the Incarnate possessed him.

Allin—no longer the easy-going man that always tried to

make Korden laugh, the Older whom the others teased about being a 'red-neck'—pushed off the ground and reclaimed the axe from the hand of its former host. It looked around at the six remaining members of the hunting party, face cloaked in shadow, mouth contorted into a feral snarl. Its eyes pulsed with that fiery red heat.

"A new body," it said, in a gruff, growling approximation of Allin's voice. It looked down at itself, raising the tan, wrinkled arms with their stringy muscles for inspection. "An old body…but beggars can't be choosers. Anything is better than returning to oblivion."

Eddas threw up a hand and shouted one of their spells, a collection of strange syllables that sounded to Redfen like, "*Mish'aka!*"

Whatever he intended for the spell to do, it failed. An emerald green shimmer appeared in the air just in front of his palm and then faded away. Eddas stared in blank amazement as the Incarnate chortled. "Crafters, is it? I might've known. Your spells are as useless as you are. Your faith has grown too weak to give you power over the Filament."

"What do you want here, demon?" Tiller demanded.

The Incarnate's lips parted in a sneer that could chill beating blood, and then it said something that shattered the comfortable life Redfen had enjoyed for the past sixteen years.

"You know exactly what I want. Give me the Light, and you and your ilk can go back to worshipping your dormant god for the last remaining hours this doomed world has left."

6

Silence fell. The hunters shifted uncomfortably. Santo— breathing raggedly as Port attempted to tie cloth around his injury—shot a glance at Eddas. Redfen's mouth went completely dry at the implication of what this monster just said.

"You're mistaken, as you can surely see," Tiller told the creature in a much calmer tone. Too calm, Redfen thought; such a response reeked of bald-faced deceit, like a totala player with a horrible bluff. "There are no children here. We are all far past the days where we would be of any interest to the Filament."

"Not *you*, you worthless sin cows," the Incarnate hissed through clenched teeth. "The one I sensed this morning, before the accursed sun rose and trapped me here. I felt it, so clear and so close for but an hour, and then its scent... dampened. I can still taste its foulness though, even now..." The Incarnate drifted off, raising its face to the stiff breeze blowing through the thicket, and then snapped abruptly back to attention. "If you harbor the one I seek, you will be destroyed along with it."

"You will never touch him!" Redfen shouted, unable to control his anger at the monster's presumption. They were all like this, all the servants of the Dark Filament he'd ever encountered, so sure of themselves and their mission. He wanted to hit this being, to pummel at him until nothing remained.

"Shut your mouth, Redfen!" Tiller commanded.

But the damage was done. The Incarnate's glowing eyes turned to him. "So there is one among you who knows where I can find this Light. Tell me, and you will be allowed to continue your pathetic existence." It sneered again, its use of a human mouth obscene.

Something hard snapped inside Redfen. He flew forward, crossing the five paces separating him from the creature in a heartbeat, and raised his hands to do just what he'd envisioned.

The Incarnate was ready. Had probably baited him for just such a reaction. It batted away Redfen's questing hands with the axe handle and used its free arm to grip Redfen's throat. He felt a curious lifting sensation, and then the Incarnate had him suspended above the ground by his neck in an iron grip that must have been forged in the Stranger's own furnace, held so high his head brushed against the branches of the overhanging tree. He scrabbled at the fingers, trying to prise them open far enough to catch a breath.

Tiller and Eddas started forward on one side, Del on the other.

The Incarnate raised the axe above his shoulder and flung it. The blade spun expertly through the air and caught Del just above the collarbone, sinking to the hilt. A torrent of blood cascaded down his chest as the old man fell to his knees, choking and gasping through the ruins of his windpipe. Port screamed, an anguished, small sound in the stillness of the ravine, and left Santo's side to run to his lover.

"Not another step," the Incarnate growled at Tiller, "or I break this one's neck."

"It'll be the last thing you ever do," Tiller promised. No bluff in his hard eyes this time.

"Perhaps. But there will be more. There will *always* be more." It turned its fiery eyes up to Redfen, still hanging at arm's length above him. "Nothing stands in the way of the Filament."

Black spots danced in Redfen's vision. His eyes rolled up, to the leafy canopy just above his head where light dappled through the leaves in tiny chinks. With the last of his strength, he raised a hand and pulled one of those branches aside.

A flood of sunlight fell directly onto Allin's upturned face.

The Incarnate roared in pain, then dropped Redfen and flung up its arm to protect its eyes. It doubled over and drove the heels of both hands into the sockets.

Redfen crashed down in a heap and coughed as air filled his lungs. He watched Eddas approach the Incarnate from behind and wrap his massive arms around it, subduing the creature by crushing it to his chest. As the Incarnate struggled, the Older slid one arm up against its windpipe and applied enough pressure to seal off the passage.

"Stop, you fool!" Santo cried.

"This isn't Allin anymore," Eddas said gravely. "You know that."

"Yes, but if you kill it like that and it gets into your body, it'll tear through us all!"

Reluctantly, Eddas eased up enough to allow the Incarnate to breathe, but not speak. It snarled and gnashed its teeth instead. "Fine. Ready your arrows and I'll set it free. We'll give him a makeover a porcupine would envy."

"We're not killing it," Tiller told him. "We'll bind it with rope and lash it to the cart."

Eddas looked at him with shock drawing his good eye wide. "You want to bring this demon to the village?"

Tiller nodded. "Tash might want to question it, to find out how it knew about…" He broke off and looked at Redfen. Eddas and Santo did the same, while Port continued to weep over Del's body. Fortholm still lay where he'd fallen, and beside him, the remains of the Incarnate's original body were quickly putrefying into an oily sludge in the sun's heat.

Redfen felt a knot of panic rise into his throat.

"We have to get back," he whispered. "Right now."

Monster in the Flesh

1

Practice lasted for two hours, until Korden's muscles felt weak, his head ached from concentrating, and he barely had enough artcraft flowing through him to levitate a dandelion pod. Tash ran him through a rapid-fire succession of drills to test his mastery of the various disciplines they'd been working on, and his wisdom in deciding which one to use in any given situation. These were punctuated by short faithing breaks where they sat on the floor, closed their eyes, and cleared their minds of everything but their connection to the Upper, an exercise meant to widen his personal conduit so his artcraft could flow more freely. This was followed by creativity strengthening, which, for Korden, meant writing in his journal.

"Tha imagination is a muscle all its own, *ghammer*. An' jes like any other muscle, it becomes stronger with exercise," Tash had told him countless times. Most of the Olders painted or sang or played an instrument. Korden tried all of these, but, in the end, it had been writing that drew him. He loved creating his own characters, getting lost in stories whose outcomes he could control, or just scribbling lines of rhyming verse that came to him. Some of these he shared with the rest of the village, holding the Last Fathers in thrall with public readings in the social hall; others he kept private. There were no limitations in these made-up worlds, no Barriers to hold him back. Sometimes he felt his mind slipping into them even when he should be paying attention in his lessons.

His longest running work, begun when he was twelve, was the saga of Sheriff Protector, a grizzled policeman errant that travelled the land in a roaring red auto, rescuing children and fighting Incarnates with nothing but a bow, a sword, and his scarred knuckles. The character had been with Korden so long, he felt real at times, as though he would come driving into the village at any moment.

Today though, a different inspiration struck, and he started writing a much more mundane tale, the story of an ordinary young girl who lived long ago, before the Purges. In his head, she bore a striking resemblance to the girl from the picture.

This one would probably be for his eyes only.

Tash worked alongside him at an easel, using homemade paint and canvas to create one of his blurry compositions, which he called 'impressionist'. Even though he could never tell what they were supposed to be, Korden still thought they were remarkable for a blind man working entirely from memory and instinct. The brush swooped through the air, held aloft in a glimmering grey haze and guided by Tash's mind, adding a line here or flourish there.

They spoke little during this time. Korden was afraid the other man would notice his preoccupation, but it turned out to be the Older who seemed distracted. Korden could feel that same trepidation coming off him in waves, like heat from a fire, but couldn't discern the reason.

Finally, after looking up from his writing to discover his den-so's brush hovering forgotten over the canvas, while his clouded eyes roamed the ceiling, Korden asked, "Tash… what's wrong?"

The old man shook his head slowly, coming out of the trance. His snow white hair floated about his face. At first, Korden thought he would again deny the question, but instead, he muttered, "Somethin…somethin is not right."

A thread of guilty fear wove through Korden, but he squashed it down before it could show in his *mohol*. "What do you mean?"

Tash stood, joints creaking as he rose from his hunkered position on the floor, and moved back toward the window once more. "The world, *ghammer*. The world feels like its spinnin in tha wrong direction. Has since I woke this mornin." He turned to face Korden. "Yeh're tha best *den-ret* I could ever've hoped fer, boy. I hope yeh know that."

Korden tried to answer, but the words felt stale. Tash had never, not once, spoken to him so earnestly. His dream came back to him—that awful feeling of doom slavering at his heels—and made his stomach plummet even further.

This time, Tash did notice. He turned his blind face to Korden with drawn brow before nodding suddenly, as if the boy's silence confirmed something he already suspected. "There're times when yeh remind me so much o' my own son."

"You had a son?" Korden realized, for the first time, how little he knew about the man in front of him. The other Last Fathers spoke often of their lives before they withdrew from the world, always with the loss of their friends and families hanging heavy about them, even after so much time. But on this topic, as with so many others, Tash kept his own counsel.

"Aye," he said sadly, after several heartbeats. "Long ago."

"Did he...die in the Purges?"

"No, no, he was much too old fer that. He served in tha military, went off ta fight in tha first o' tha Dark Wars against tha Filament, once mankind began ta understand what a threat they were. Died defendin his country—nay, his planet—from their evil."

"A *war?*" Korden leaned forward eagerly, his fascination eclipsing his earlier dread. He knew the term, but no one had ever mentioned one in reference to the Filament.

Tash tried to lower himself gently onto the windowsill, but plopped down hard as his bony legs gave beneath his robe. "Tha war ta end all wars, they called it. The zealots and Jesus freaks—that's one o' tha old religions, mind yeh—all claimed it ta be Armageddon, but, even then, I believed that to be fancy. Whatever it was though, it was too late. Not even tha combined forces o' every nation on earth were enough ta overcome tha might o' tha Dark Filament. And then, when our defenses were gone...tha Purges *really* began, and civilization came apart at tha seams."

"I don't understand." Korden saw an opportunity to have the questions he'd been pondering for so long answered, and he didn't intend to waste it. "Where did they come from in the first place?"

"No one truly knows, *ghammer*, an' those that say they do are lyin. At first they were jes ghost stories, random horror on tha news about some maniac slaughterin a school full o' children. But their numbers grew greater and their sightings increased, until we began ta understand we were facin an enemy unlike anythin we could imagine." He grunted. "'Course, by tha time they showed up, we'd already done most o' their work fer 'em. Abandonin art fer science, dividin ourselves with technology, poisonin nature, abusin our children. Perhaps we could've saved ourselves without tha Upper's intervention if we'd just kept tha scales balanced. In the end though…our apathy was our undoin."

There was that word again: *balance*. "But if we did that, if we…*balanced these scales*…would that put things right again?"

Tash shrugged…but Korden thought a strange look crossed his face as he did. "Even if it would, I have no more idea how one would go about doin that than yeh do, *ghammer*. Nor do I know what tha Filament will do after they've accomplished their terrible goal. I only suspect there must still be some other children left somewhere to tha east, or that ugly black cloud would be hangin over our heads right now instead o' keepin to tha horizon."

"Then maybe we just need to make more children. We could go out and find women, let them into the village…"

At this, Tash let out a sharp bark of laughter. "And jes what do yeh know about makin bebies, *ghammer?*"

Korden felt his cheeks redden. He was glad the Older couldn't see it. "I know enough."

"Yes, I imagine Skewtz gave yeh quite tha bumblin explanation. And considerin we'd be hard pressed ta find some Viagra, who would volunteer ta impregnate these women if we found them and brought them here? Yeh?"

The heat in Korden's face became a raging inferno.

"Ah," Tash said. "So yeh're already preoccupied with tha fairer sex. I feared this day fer long. But it's a notion yeh must not dwell on. Tha Barrier is a delicate thing. It couldn't hide anyone else. Frankly, I'm surprised it lasted this long." Korden's disappointment must've been palpable, because he added, in that same uncharacteristically soft tone, "I know it doesn't seem like it, but things *will* change fer yeh one day, *ghammer*. Perhaps faster than yeh would like. If anything good has come from tha Filament, it's tha yeh came inta tha world. I've watched yeh grow from a tiny pup into tha young man before me, and I've seen all tha progress yeh've made in yehr trainin over tha last year. Soon, I'm sure I'll see yeh leave this place. What yeh do after that…could be important to us all."

And then Korden's teacher tumbled off the windowsill and into the floor.

2

"Tash!" Korden jumped up from his desk and crossed the room. The old man lay curled in an unmoving ball on the floor. Korden had a vision similar to the one this morning, when he sat beside the crashed auto: the Olders finally dying to leave him here all alone in this empty village.

But his *den-so* looked up. One hand fisted against his chest again and rubbed in those small circles. "Not me," he wheezed, and took a long, shuddering breath. "Tha others. It jes…jes hit me all at once. Somethin…" Korden could see the stark fear swimming in his eyes even through the milky glaze. "Oh dear Upper, somethin terrible has happened."

Korden extended his senses and realized he could feel it too: a massive wall of terror and grief emanating from just outside the classroom. The sensation was so heavy and un-expected it almost bowled him over too.

And beneath this overpowering mental explosion, he glimpsed something else.

A black mass amid the sorrow, a color of the emotional spectrum so dark it took him a moment to recognize it as such.

Shouts drifted in through the open window, along with running footsteps. Feegran limped by, heading toward the northern end of the village. As Korden strained to hear what was happening, his worries went from Tash to his father.

"Help me up, *ghammer*," Tash ordered, his voice strong and resolute once more. Korden slipped an arm around his shoulder and pulled the man to his feet, the weight little more than a stack of kindling. He made sure Tash was steady before racing ahead to the door.

"Korden, no! Wait!"

He'd never ignored one of Tash's commands, but he did this one, bursting out into the afternoon sunlight, then blinking around at the chaos.

Olders shuffled in all directions, yelling to one another. He tried to read their auras once more, to see if he could discern the source of the distress, but the jumble of their emotions assaulted him; it was like trying to read a book in a pelting thunderstorm. To his left, Santo stood covered in blood from a gaping wound to his shoulder. Feegran hurriedly applied a poultice and dressing while muttering a string of healing wordspells. Further along, two forms lay on the ground covered in a roughspun blanket. Port sat beside them, holding a limp hand that protruded from the fabric and weeping uncontrollably as Coomb tried to console him. The sight made Korden weak with fear.

His father.

Where was Redfen Bright?

Most of the crowd was centered just outside the social hall, around Mulder and the old wooden cart. After some effort, Korden spotted his father on the far side of the gathering, standing with the mountainous form of Eddas. Relief made him momentarily weak, but then he started to run again.

Korden squirmed into the crowd, weaving between the Olders to get to his father. Everyone seemed to be talking at once, paying him no mind. He heard the word 'Incarnate' mentioned more than once.

At last he broke through to the center, easing around Bibb's wide girth, and found the object of everyone's attention.

3

The open back end of the cart faced him. Another blanket had been stretched tight over the top, providing a low ceiling. Beneath was a well of shadows that—in conjunction with the layer of loose straw that littered the floor of the cart—reminded Korden of a musty animal's den.

And inside lay the animal.

It was Allin's face staring out from the darkness, yet clearly not Allin at the same time; Korden needed no one to tell him that much. He lay on his stomach, arms pulled back and bound at the wrists to his ankles, so that his gangly, withered body was contorted into a painful pyramid. A tight gag sat across his mouth, but his eyes were free and open.

The centers of them burned with blood red light.

As soon as Korden broke through the knot of Olders, Allin's gaze latched on to him with a hatred that was palpable. A low growl built in the man's throat. He thrashed at his bindings, hard enough to rock the cart back and forth on its wheels. Mulder gave a nervous whinny and pawed at the ground restlessly.

Korden took one more half-step forward, trying to see further into that tight wedge of darkness, and then had his view cut off as his father leapt in front of him.

"Get back! *Get back!*" Redfen shouted, shielding Korden with his body as he forced him back through the throng. He was shocked to see a ring of dark bruises around his father's neck, the shape of purple fingers clearly visible against his skin.

"What happened to you? What's wrong with Allin?"

"Never mind! Just stay away! I don't want you anywhere near that thing!"

Tash brushed past them, heading in the opposite direction. Redfen froze in the act of herding Korden and they both turned to watch as Tash hobbled determinedly toward the crowd. The Olders parted for him, giving their leader a clear path to the cart and its contents.

The old man examined Allin—not with his eyes surely, but with his mind—then turned and demanded, "Why in Upper's name would yeh bring that foul thing *here?*"

Tiller stepped forward from the crowd. "We thought... you would want to question it."

"I've no interest in anythin it has ta say! And by bringin it here yeh've endangered us all!"

"But it *knew*, Tash," Tiller murmured. He tried to keep his voice low, but Korden still heard him easily in the silence that fell over the village proper, broken only by Port's soft weeping. "It already knew, and it sensed..." He cast a hesitant glance at Korden after trailing off.

The anger melted from Tash's face. He tilted his head back for a moment, his unseeing eyes flicking back and forth across the few clouds in the sky, then pointed at Allin. "Get that creature into tha social hall and make sure it's tied well. Leave no guard; I'll not give it another body ta steal if finds a way ta kill itself. Everyone else, into tha *hangala*. Including yeh, *ghammer*. We must sort out exactly what has happened."

4

Their worship building—the first structure the Olders built upon founding the village—looked even bigger on the inside. Its interior was painted a faded gold the color of Bloom sunlight and hung with tapestries created by several of the men that depicted, in broad, abstract strokes, such events as the Purges, the fall of the old world, and the discovery (or rather, *re*discovery) of artcraft. Korden had studied them all countless times. The high peaked ceiling had a rectangular skylight cut through the middle of the wood and thatching that ran the length of the *hangala*. On Sunday mornings, with the rain curtain pulled away, a flood of sunlight poured through the opening to brighten the entire room and turn the walls into a beautiful, blazing array, but now the afternoon rays slanted too steeply to provide much illumination. Instead, a host of *demnos* in every color of the rainbow blazed in each corner of the room, intricate structures made from twigs that cast the light upward rather than out so as not to dazzle the eyes.

Three rows of long, wooden pews stretched across the front of the room, filled with thirty-four of the remaining Last Fathers, who mumbled quietly to each other. All of them seemed to be watching Korden. He could feel their eyes on him where he sat with his father, right in the middle of the first row, but whenever he looked back at any of them, they stopped their whispering and averted their gaze.

Because they know. They all know what you did.

Surely not. They had no way to read his thoughts, but they could probably sense the terrible churning in the pit of his stomach, a gurgling mixture of cold fear and warm guilt.

And he wasn't the only one unsettled. Redfen Bright

squirmed uncomfortably beside him, radiating jagged orange waves of his own anxiety. In the light of the demnos, the bruises on his throat looked even more stark.

Korden realized his father had never been inside this building. He often made jokes about the goats they must sacrifice in here, a reference Korden understood only enough to recognize it as one of his jabs at Tash and the Olders.

He saw Korden watching him and whispered, "It's all right. Don't worry. They'll know what to do."

About what? Korden wanted to ask. He still wasn't entirely sure he understood the implications of whatever had happened, and no one seemed eager to explain it. They undoubtedly thought they were protecting him by keeping him in the dark. Acting in his 'best interest.' He was surprised they even let him attend this gathering.

Would it always be like this? Even when he turned eighteen, would they still view him as a child to be shielded from the world? If that happened, he felt sure he would suffocate, that his deficient lungs would collapse altogether from the pressure of their smothering.

Tash stood at the front of the room, where he'd been conferring quietly with Feegran and Bibb. The three of them were unquestionably the strongest artcraftsmen in the village. Finally, their palaver broke, and Tash turned to face the congregation of Olders. He held up his gnarled hands for attention.

"Today, we have suffered a grave tragedy," he said, his voice a low rumble throughout the *hangala*. "Three members o' our family have been taken from us. Two have gone inta tha merciful arms o' tha Upper, an' tha other…well, let us hope he finds his way home as well."

Death. Korden never knew anyone who died. How was it possible that he would never hear Fortholm or Del speak or laugh ever again? He understood fundamentally what it meant to be dead, but the whole concept suddenly seemed supremely stupid and wasteful, a pitiful way to finish out one's existence, by closing your eyes and lying still and never getting up again.

"However, tha time ta mourn must come later, fer there're more dire problems facin us." Tash paused, frowned and swallowed, the prominent lump in his throat bobbing. "After some deliberation, we have determined…that tha Barrier is falling."

This proclamation was met with instant uproar from the audience. The churning in Korden's stomach became even more violent. Beside him, Redfen sat bolt upright on the bench, every muscle rigid.

"This can't be right!" someone shouted over the clamor from the back of the room.

"How did it happen?" Dillish asked from his wheeled chair at the far end of the first row.

"We don't know," Tash answered, but Korden had an awful suspicion that he might have an idea even if his *denso* didn't. After quiet fell once more, Tash continued. "It doesn't seem ta be a degradation o' tha artcraft itself, but rather somethin that triggered its demise. Fer tha moment, it seems ta be stable, but we don't believe that will last. We must determine what caused tha problem if we're ta have any hope o'—"

"I did it," Korden said. The words rattled in his throat like a mouthful of dust, escaping before he even realized he planned to say them. His breathing hitched as he added, "It's my fault. I…I crossed the Barrier this morning."

Once again, gasps filled the room as every eye turned to him. Tash regarded him sternly from the pulpit, but his father looked at him with horror etched across his drawn face. "Korden…please say you didn't…"

"I'm sorry." Scalding tears spilled down both cheeks. He recalled Tash's words from earlier this very day, about the delicate nature of the Barrier. What had he been thinking? That the Upper's hand itself guided him to that rotted husk in the woods? How childish that sounded now. "I-I didn't mean for this to happen, for anyone to get hurt, I just wanted t-to see what it was like. I can show you where if that will help."

"No, that's quite all right, *ghammer*." Tash sounded more tired than angry. He came forward, robe sweeping the ground behind him, and stood in front of Korden with his blind eyes fixed on the space above the boy's head. "Fer now, what I need yeh ta do is leave us. We have matters we need ta discuss with yehr father, matters that're long overdue. Go home and wait for us to call on yeh."

Redfen jumped to his feet and declared, "Absolutely not! I'm not letting him out of my sight! There could be more of those things coming!"

"He is safe fer tha time bein. Tha Barrier is holdin, an' if any more o' them were ta approach the village, we would sense them." Tash's brow rose. "Unless yeh want ta have this conversation in front o' him."

Redfen glared at the Older for another few heartbeats before turning to Korden. "Go straight home and wait there. Do you understand me?"

"But Dad—!"

"*No*, Korden." Redfen's words were so sharp, his son flinched and shrank away. "*Go home.*"

Korden moved past him and hurried down the main aisle of the *hangala* with his head down, unable to meet anyone's eye. He'd never felt so ashamed in his life. But mixed with that shame was also a kernel of indignant resentment. He was *sixteen*, Upper damn it, too young, perhaps, to be safe from the Filament's clutches, but too old to be treated like this anymore. Maybe if they ever bothered to truly explain anything to him, treated him as a man, he wouldn't have done this in the first place.

That's right, Korden; blame them *for* your *foolishness.*

He wasn't blaming them, he felt guiltier than he could've ever thought possible, but the Olders and his father had been hiding something from him all his life. It felt like an itching bug bite on the back of his head, and stubborn determination blazed in him now to find out what it was, the same obstinacy that led him to cross the Barrier in the first place this morning.

Tash would've recognized the ironclad resolve that served the boy so well in his study of artcraft.

Instead of going home, Korden hurried to retrieve the ladder Palo had been using to repair his roof.

5

"So what are you saying?" Redfen demanded, still standing at the front of the congregation. Eddas put one large hand on his shoulder from the second row, trying to get him to sit again, but he shook it off. His anger at the old man using Korden to manipulate him still blazed in his chest like one of their damned magic glow sticks.

Tash's answer this time was just as maddeningly calm as the ones before. "Tha Barrier will fall. It's only a matter o' time. Hours, if we're lucky. Prob'ly less."

"Just because he *crossed* it?" Redfen put a shaking hand to his forehead. This couldn't be real. It was too much like every nightmare he'd had since coming to live here. For just a heartbeat or two, everything that happened this day—the shock of losing Fortholm, the fight with the Incarnate, the fear that gripped him during the rush to make it back to the village—weighed on him so heavily he thought his back would break. "I don't understand how that can be. We go across it all the time!"

"But it wasn't meant fer *us*, Redfen. Tha artcraft was always focused on Korden, and relied upon his cooperation. When he breached it, tha covenant was broken."

"All right, then just…conjure another one! You did it before, so do it again!"

Tash crossed his arms, hands slipping inside the sleeves of his robe. Behind him, a pained expression dampened Feegran's face, and Bibb looked like he might be ready to blubber. "Of course we will try, but I don't expect it ta work. It took all o' us ta create tha Barrier before, usin every bit o' artcraft we could muster. But now, with our numbers lessened an' powers faded…I think it will be a lost cause."

Redfen's jaw clenched in frustration. He wanted to grab the man and shake him, slap him, anything to get a suitable reaction. "Damn it, do you understand what this means? The Incarnates will come for him, just as the other one did this morning!"

The old man's brow lowered, his cataract-laden eyes drilling into Redfen. "Then perhaps it is time we talk about tha boy's past…and his future."

Redfen took a step back as though the words physically pushed him. And maybe they had; he had no idea how their powers worked. He stumbled as the pew struck his legs and then sliced his arms through the air after regaining his balance in a desperate gesture of denial. "No, I won't listen to more of your lunacy!"

"We have held our tongues fer far too long already, Redfen."

"And you can keep on holding them for the rest of your cursedly long lives, for all I care!"

"The boy is special," Tash persisted. "You told us that yehrself. Or was that only so yeh could dupe a village full of old men inta protectin the two o' yeh?"

"But...b-but...it's just a *story!*" Redfen sputtered. The old man's accusation sent him reeling...but only because there was a healthy dose of truth to it. "It was told to me the same way I told it to you! I don't even know if it's true! And even if it was, what does it matter? It has no bearing on Korden!"

"I have seen fer myself how powerful he is. He has more artcraft flowing through him than the rest o' us combined, even at our height. He just must learn ta harness it."

"Fine, teach him! I'm not stopping you! Turn him into another wise old sage! But I won't let you fill him with crazy prophecies and send him off to wage a war against the Filament!"

"Redfen." Tash's words were tinged with the first hints of impatience. "Tha last thing I want is ta put tha boy in danger. But if he has any purpose in tha Upper, a role he must play in our final hours, then I fear his chance ta do so will expire in another two years, when he reaches the age of safety. For Upper's sake, we must prepare him ta—"

"*Curse the Upper!*" Redfen shouted, the effort tearing at his bruised throat. An outraged cry rose up from the gallery of Olders at his back. "The Upper takes what He wants from this world, but He can't have my boy! I won't let you do this, you're *not* his father!"

"*An' neither are YEH!*" Tash roared, temper flaring at last.

An uncomfortable hush fell in the worship hall, during which Redfen fervently wished, for just a moment, that he'd never told these ancient men the truth. Or, better yet, that he'd bypassed this village entirely, kept running with the child that had been entrusted to him, taken his chances on his own.

You never would've made it. Korden would be dead by now, and you most likely with him.

"*I* raised him," he said. "*I* kept him safe before we ever got here. Not behind some magic wall, but with my own two hands. I'm the only father he's ever known, and you won't take that away from him." *Or me.*

Tash nodded, and this time his voice was neither angry nor infuriatingly calm, but gentler than Redfen had ever heard it. "I would never do such a thing, but don't yeh see, Redfen, yehr love fer him has blinded yeh. Mine has done tha same. I think I would've been content ta keep him safe, ta continue his trainin here in the village right up until his eighteenth. So perhaps everythin that happened today was fer tha best." He frowned. "Because now...tha choice has been taken away from all o' us."

The tension and anger evaporated from Redfen, leaving him as weak and limp as a dead fish. The old man was right; he and Korden had a nice respite from the horrors of the world for the past fifteen years, but now, regardless of what Tash or Redfen or anyone else believed, that world was about to catch up to them in a big hurry.

The only way to go was forward, but the idea of running again made him feel as old as the men around him.

"What do we do?" he asked softly.

"First, we must deal with our visitor. Then we will faith, and do what we can ta shore up tha Barrier, ta buy as much time as possible. Yeh go and…tell the boy tha truth."

"Please…I can't…" Redfen pleaded. The soreness in his throat moved down to his chest. It sat there, squeezing his heart. "You don't know what you're asking."

But Tash's face held no mercy. "Tell the boy tha truth. Or Upper so help me, *I* will."

6

Korden lay stretched out on the roof of the *hangala* on his stomach, listening to the argument drift up through the skylight. Any of them could have sensed him at any moment, but they were far too preoccupied. When Tash raised his voice for the first and only time, what he yelled caused Korden to push away from the window and roll onto his back in shock. He slid a few feet down the inclined surface before he could catch himself, then lay there panting as the shouted accusation echoed through his head.

Redfen Bright not his father? No; that idea wasn't just frightening, it was unthinkable. He had precious few attributes that made up what he thought of as his identity, and this was the bedrock that all the rest were built upon.

He realized, with the brutality of a striking hammer, that they'd lied to him. *All* of them, every last person he'd ever known in his life. Even Tash had been in on the betrayal. The world seemed to be melting around him, colors running together, reality blurring.

He felt tears welling and wiped them away. How could he believe anything they said? He just wanted someone who had no reason to lie, who would tell him the truth about the world and his place in it.

There is one such person.

Korden stayed where he was another few seconds, considering this new idea that popped into his head, then scrambled to the edge of the roof and hurried down the ladder. He left it in place and ran across the dirt lane to the door of the social hall. The wide, covered porch offered shade, and he stood in it for a few seconds, waiting for his jangled nerves to even out. Above the door, a cloth banner had already been hung in anticipation of his birthday celebration later this night. The sight of it made him ill. Korden forced himself to pass beneath the bright letters and push his way through the swinging entrance.

Inside, he found a silent, cold darkness coiled beyond the threshold. Usually the long hall—where the Olders gathered for meals and spent their days gabbing, playing totala, and drinking the mead that Bant distilled—was full of light and laughter, but shadows filled every corner today. The drapes were drawn shut across the open windows, sealing out every last ray of sunlight. Korden denied the urge to conjure a *demno* as he entered the building and crept between the gaming tables, which had also been decorated for tonight's feast.

Fear danced just beneath his skin, prickling the hairs. His breaths shortened until they were little more than ragged pants. He inched forward, fighting panic, trying to peer into every corner simultaneously.

At the far end of the room was a tiny stage where some of the Olders played instruments to entertain the village, and where Korden would sit to hold public readings of his poetry and Sheriff Protector exploits. A lumpy shape sat huddled on one end, next to one of the building's thick support posts. The dark form didn't move.

He stopped several pargs away and quested out tentatively with his mind.

"I wouldn't do that if I were you." The voice—a sneering, harsh baritone—startled Korden so much his bowels clenched. "You might not like what you find."

Korden backed away as the figure's head lifted. Two blazing red pinpricks turned on him, casting a pale glow around the figure. This close, he could recognize Allin's features in the hellish light. His hands and ankles were fastened around the support post with iron manacles that Korden had never seen before, but he appeared to have chewed through the gag around his head. Allin's lips drew back in a gruesome sneer as the Older regarded him, the expression utterly alien on his kindly face.

"Such a brave young Lightbringer," he purred. Allin slouched forward against the post as though to peer at him. A smell of something moist and rotten drifted into Korden's nostrils. "Come closer, where I can see you."

Korden ignored the invitation, thinking of an old tale Skewtz had told him about a wolf who dressed up as a grandmother. "You're not Allin. Where is he? What did you do to him?"

"Your friend is roasting in the fires of Magdenom as we speak. If we listen hard, we might hear the scream as his soul is ripped asunder." The claim—which made Korden's stomach give another watery heave—was spoken plainly, with no more concern than the announcement of the evening meal. "His body, however...that belongs to me now."

Korden swallowed and stiffened his spine. He refused to give this creature the satisfaction of his fear. Ignoring the previous warning, he sent his mind out once more, needing to see for himself if any part of his friend remained.

The cheerful purples that made up the base of Allin's emotional rainbow were gone. This thing's *mohol* was nothing but an oily blackness so putrid, it made Korden feel filthy to touch upon it. It held no emotion, but rather, a *negativity*, an absolute absence of feeling that chilled him as effectively as the deepest Stilling wind. He pulled back just as fast as before, shivering in disgust.

The creature in Allin's body chuckled languidly. "Can't say I didn't warn you."

"Who are you?" Korden asked.

That awful sneer grew wider, wider, impossibly wide, until every tooth in Allin's mouth—what few were left—showed through his thin lips. The light in those eyes pulsed slowly. Korden remembered the monster that chased him through the dark forest in his dream. "I have no identity. I am one of many, an emissary of the Stranger, the Dowser Beast, Lord of the Dark Filament and all it surveys, dedicated to the extinction of the last flickers of Light remaining on this pathetic plane."

Korden didn't understand most of its words, but enough to be sure of the truth.

"You're...an Incarnate."

"Yes. That's what generations of your people have called us."

Korden's next breath wouldn't come. This was one of the monsters he'd been warned about his entire life. No longer a story, but flesh and blood. After a few seconds, his chest ached for air. He doubled over, concentrated on the wooden planks of the floor, and waited for the episode to pass.

The Incarnate gave that slow, dry laugh again. "Poor little Lightbringer. I can cure you of everything that ails you, if you but come a few steps closer."

"Why do you...keep calling...me that?" The question came out a high, choppy whisper as air found its way back into Korden's chest.

"Because children are the flame that keeps the darkness away. Once you are all gone, and we have removed the slightest spark of hope for your return, this world will wither and die, and the Filament will move on."

"Move on to where?"

"The next plane to be ravaged."

The answer brought to mind the swarms of locust that would sometimes decimate the Olders' meager crops. "But... but *why?* Why do you hate us so much?"

"I have no need to explain. Your death is the only thing that matters to me."

Korden watched the Incarnate without speaking for a long moment, this hateful, hunched ghoul wearing the face of one of his friends, and then asked the question he came here to ask. "Were you looking...for me? I mean, *me*, in particular? Is there...is there something special about me?"

This time it was the Incarnate's turn at silence. It tilted its head back and drew in a long, sharp breath, the nostrils of Allin's nose flaring. "Perhaps I could tell, if I could catch your scent."

"My *scent?*"

"Your warlocks have their powers, Lightbringer; we have ours. How do you think I found you in the first place? Now come nearer, or leave me be."

Korden was instantly skeptical...but there would be no danger in moving just a little closer. He took a few more steps while the Incarnate continued to sniff the air. He was still well out of range of its hands. He took another and another, easing toward it, and thought of the girl from his picture, who had probably been murdered by a creature very much like—

He saw his mistake at the last moment as the Incarnate lunged. By leaning forward with one shoulder, the crafty creature had hidden the actual amount of freedom it had against the post, and now it slid forward and stretched its arms to their fullest. Hooked fingers grazed Korden's nose as he jumped away, the same fingers that had left those bruises on his father's throat. He landed on his side and scrambled backward.

"*Curse you!*" it snarled, gnashing its teeth as it thrashed against the pole. "Don't think your Crafter friends can hide you forever! Their magic is stale and dying!"

"No." Korden pulled himself up by one of the room's chairs. He'd been arrogant, he saw now, to ever wish to see one of these creatures. "That's not true."

"Oh, but it is! And even if they work up the courage to dispatch me, there are *thousands* more that will come for you! Tens of thousands! They will sweep through this valley and slaughter anyone that harbors you!"

Korden stumbled away, heading not toward the door, where voices could be heard from the direction of the *hangala*, but to the closest draped window.

"*You can't escape!*" the Incarnate screamed after him. "*Our work here is almost finished! When the human race is broken, darkness will spread over the face of this world like fresh earth over a grave!*"

Korden pulled the drape open, allowing a shaft of sunlight to stream into the room. It fell across the Incarnate, who shrieked and covered what had once been Allin's face, then shrank into a pitiful ball on the floor. Korden swung a leg over the sill and ran toward home with tears running down both cheeks.

Bedrock Crumbling

1

Dread filled Redfen as he reached the *hucté* far up on the hillside. He'd hoped this day would never come, the day when he finally revealed the truth to Korden, but all along, in the back of his head, he knew he was only putting off the inevitable. Tash's claims—bitter though they might be to hear—were accurate: the boy was special, Redfen felt it in his heart the moment he laid eyes on him, and yet he'd tried his hardest to bury that knowledge as the years passed and his affinity for Korden grew into the genuine love of a father for his son.

But the time for pretend was over. The make believe world he'd worked so hard to build was about to come tumbling down.

It hurt to think the last sixteen years had just been one long stage-and-curtain show for the benefit of…who? Himself? Korden? Redfen couldn't even remember why he'd told the boy that he was his father in the first place. It just seemed such a natural lie, one told to keep him from asking questions whose answers would only confuse him.

And that also let you feel like a father, if only for a short time.

There it was, the true heart of the matter. His own selfishness. He wanted the boy to be his son so much that the lie became a truth in his own head.

And today, he would lose that son.

He stood in the doorway of their dwelling, listening to the silence within.

"Korden?" he called.

There was no answer.

Then he caught sight of the boy just before panic could hook its claws into him once more. Korden sat beneath a single elm that grew in the field beside the *hucté*, a place where Redfen often found him stretched out with his nose in a book. He leaned against the base of the tree with his back to their home, head down and staring at his lap.

Redfen approached slowly, shuffling his feet through the dirt to announce his presence. Korden gave him no notice. When he got close enough, Redfen peered over the boy's shoulder to see which of Skewtz's dusty titles held his attention, but it was no book he studied this time.

"Where did you get that?" he asked in amazement.

Korden held out the square of slick paper, letting him see the young girl smiling on it. "I found it when I crossed the Barrier. It was in a crashed auto."

Redfen hunkered down beside him and accepted the picture. The girl was pretty, exactly the sort to steal the hearts of boys Korden's age. Even Redfen, who hadn't seen a female himself in half a lifetime, found his own eyes eager to study her. He handed the paper back. "When I was your age, a man in the town I lived in had a machine that made those. He called them 'fotos'."

Korden gave the picture another glance, as if considering the name, and then opened the flap of his carry-pouch beside him and tucked the picture inside. He sat for another moment, thinking so hard the wheels in his head were practically visible, then turned to Redfen.

For Upper's sake, he was still so *young*. So full of innocence. What did Tash think he was going to do? He looked at Redfen, gaze roaming up and down, as if seeking something. Then, without warning, his entire face screwed up in anguish.

"I didn't mean to," he said softly, choking on tears. "I just…wanted to see what it was like. And now Fortholm and Del are dead, and Allin…" He buried his head in the crook of his elbow.

Redfen put a hand on his neck and squeezed gently. "It's not your fault."

The boy's voice was muffled by his arm. "But it is. *I* left the Barrier. It was a choice *I* made."

"They wouldn't be dead, and you wouldn't be stuck beneath the Barrier, and the whole world wouldn't be slipping into darkness in the first place if it weren't for the Filament."

Korden stiffened and lifted his head. "What will happen to Allin?"

"That's not Allin. That's just a creature that stole his body."

"I'm not talking about the Incarnate, I'm talking about *Allin*. Can he…can he be saved?"

Redfen hesitated, choosing his words carefully. "You must understand, Allin's thoughts and beliefs and opinions—everything that makes him Allin—has either been destroyed or shoved so far down that it amounts to the same. Incarnates are not but parasites, and no one has ever found a way of removing them that doesn't kill the host."

"But they'll at least try. Won't they?"

"Korden, I think…I think Tash intends to have the demon…disposed of."

He expected more tears, but the boy only nodded glumly. "How?"

"Well, not with artcraft, that's for sure. Their magic didn't seem to have much effect on it. Frankly, I don't want to know what they do with it, so long as it can never hurt us again."

They lapsed into a tense silence. Redfen leaned back against the tree and looked up at the sky. The sun was beginning its downward crawl as afternoon dwindled; otherwise, azure blue stretched from horizon to horizon. It was so calm and peaceful here in this field, it was impossible to believe how close death had come to them this day.

Then the dark smudge of the Filament caught his eye to the east, barely visible behind a scrim of clouds, and he remembered it had been there all along.

"Korden," he said, "I have something to tell you."

"I know." The boy flapped a dismissive hand without looking at him. "You're not my father."

2

He threw it out as a test, hoping that Redfen Bright's *mohol* would show genuine surprise at the accusation. He would ask where Korden got such a ridiculous idea, and then they would talk, and Korden would realize he misheard.

But Redfen said nothing. Korden glanced up after a few seconds and saw that the shadows thrown by the afternoon sun on the bough of the elm tree had turned the man's scar into a dark rift across his temple, his bruised throat into a patchwork quilt of colors.

As it turned out, Korden didn't need artcraft to sense the man's mood. There was no surprise on his face. Just quiet pain.

"Who am I?" Korden asked. That bedrock was crumbling beneath him, and he felt as though he were falling down into a yawning black abyss of uncertainty. "Is Korden even my real name?"

"It's the only name you were ever given. By me."

"But where did I come from? Where are my real parents?"

"I don't know. I was asked to take charge of you on the night you were born, to protect you from the Incarnates, and I've done so ever since."

"By who?"

"Your mother." The man sounded resigned and mechanical, as though he had started this story and now wanted to see it through to the end. "Sixteen years ago, I lived in a town called Bright. That's where I took our last name from. I thought it might be safer to start fresh, in case someone took up my—*our*—trail. Bright was…a sort of fortified village. A castle, built after the Purges, mostly to keep out marauders. We never had trouble with Incarnates because we didn't have anything they wanted. No one made babies; the town council made sure of that. I was the youngest person there, and even I was in my early twenties.

"Then one day a woman, one a few years older than myself, wondered into town, and the council voted to take her in. Her name was Celia. I remember thinking it was all very hurried, like they were trying to keep something secret. When pressed by the rest of the town, they gave a reason, and then I understood. Or thought I did. She…she was a Crafter."

"A Crafter?" Korden sat bolt upright.

Redfen nodded, the pads of his thumbs rubbing nervously across his knees. "She'd come from one of the colonies up north, one that shunned all women, like Tash and the others have done here. Everyone figured they wanted her to stay so she could cast a few spells to help out, but a lot of people wanted her expelled. Some of them left in anger when they let her stay."

"Why?"

Redfen ducked his head and shrugged uncomfortably. "People who can do what you do…they're not always welcomed by others."

Korden sat silent for a long time with his face turned into the breeze and his eyes closed, trying to digest this mountain of information. "So my mother…she was an Older?" Somehow, it never even occurred to him that there were more Crafters out there in the world, beyond their hidden village.

"No, not like they are. She wasn't one of the originals. She didn't discover it, she was taught artcraft the same way you were."

"So she didn't live on a farm? She didn't fall in love with you because you brought her a wild rose?"

A flush of scarlet more vivid than any flower worked its way across Redfen's face from ear to ear; his aura turned a matching hue. His thumbs moved faster, scratching across the fabric of his pants. "That was…just a story I made up. In truth, I barely said two whole sentences to her the whole time she was there."

"Is there anything you *didn't* lie about?" Korden demanded suddenly. Another horrible thought occurred to him as he watched the man's *mohol* recoil in shades of yellow guilt, and he blurted, "That's why you kept me from learning artcraft for so long, isn't it? So I wouldn't be able to see right through you!"

"Son, it's not like that—!"

"Don't call me that!" He brought up his hands, meaning to cover his ears, and then left them hanging in the air in front of him. The fingertips crackled with arcs of cerulean light until he clenched his fists again. "Finish the story!"

"There's not much to tell," Redfen said miserably. "Less than a week after she arrived, the town council announced she was pregnant and then—three seasons later—you were born. That same night, an army of Incarnates descended on Bright; that part is true. They were waiting for you; I think they enjoy making us give up our children rather than taking them. Helps to break our spirits, I suppose; ensure the lesson is learned. Anyway, we convinced the men of the town to fight for you, and when daybreak came and the Incarnates retreated, the town asked me to take you away. Not because they trusted me, or because I was the most capable, but simply because I was the youngest. I agreed, and that was the last time I saw them or your mother."

Redfen appeared to age as he told this tale, dark circles appearing under his eyes, a few wrinkles to either side deepening. He seemed to realize what his hands were doing and, with some effort, lifted them from his legs, put them in the grass to either side, and waited.

"So my mother...is alive?"

"The last time I saw her. But that was a long time ago."

"Then who was my father?"

Redfen sighed, and something in its soft sound made Korden realize this was the thing he'd most wanted to hold back, the reason why Tash felt he needed to hear this now. "They told us it was a man named Jenner, a man from town, but...that wasn't true. They didn't think we would believe the truth, or maybe they just didn't want to make you a bigger target than you already were. They only let me in on the secret when they tried to convince—"

"*Just tell me!*" Korden shouted, all semblance of patience dried up like mud in the Burning season sun. "*Who…was… my father?*"

Redfen's sunken eyes widened in shock at the outburst. "You…you didn't have one. That's what she claimed, at least."

"I don't understand." Korden shook his head.

"She said that…that she was a virgin. That means—"

"I know what it means."

"Oh. All right." Redfen gnawed at his lower lip. "I don't know if she was crazy or not, but Korden, I never meant to lie to you. I just knew you would be confused if I told you. And somewhere along the way, it became easier to tell people you were my son. And then, when you were old enough, it was simple enough to tell you the same." He held out a hand, but cautiously, as one might to a wild animal. "Please forgive me. You *are* my son, and I only tried to do what was best for you."

Korden looked at the offered hand. He wanted to take it. Or to slap it away.

But before he could do either, a scream drifted up from the village below.

3

"What is that?" Korden put a hand over his eyes to block the sun and peered down into the village, where a cloud of gray smoke was forming. Another distant, plaintive cry echoed up before being abruptly cut off.

In his head, he saw Allin's remade face. Those glowing eyes. That awful grin.

"Inside. *Go*," Redfen commanded. He grabbed Korden's shoulder and gave him a shove toward the *hucté*, then ran ahead to the door. "Help me, Kord. Grab whatever you can carry. We have to leave."

"What?" The helplessness in his own voice made Korden feel even more panicked. He couldn't think suddenly, his mind had turned to molasses. "Where are we going?"

"Upper help me, I don't know. Away from the village, for a start."

Korden hesitated, standing in the shade of the tree where he whiled away so many hours of his youth, and wondered if he would ever do so again.

Redfen reached the door, realized he wasn't being followed, then turned back and beckoned urgently. "Come on, hurry!"

"But…what about the others?"

"They can take care of themselves! Keeping you safe is the only thing that matters! We have to go, right now!"

Korden shook his head. He caused this whole nightmare, with his boyish impatience and selfish whims, and if he ever wanted to become a man, he couldn't run from his mistakes now.

Before Redfen could say anything else, he turned and flew down the path toward the village.

4

Gray tendrils of smoke stole along the hillside. With no breeze to carry it away, the cloud squatted low to the ground, smelling of wood and the sweet piquant of burning skilne. Korden plunged into it, running even faster than this morning, pushing his wheezing lungs to work.

Somewhere behind him, he could hear Redfen giving chase, shouting his name, but he was no match for the speed of Korden's youth, even with the as-mah forcing him to fight for breath.

He could hear the crackle of fire as he closed in on the village. Red and orange flames peeked through the smoke like razor-sharp teeth biting into a hank of meat. He thought several of the Olders' *huctés* must be burning. Just before Korden reached the first of them, a huge, dark shape loomed out of the haze, barreling straight at him. He recognized Mulder and leapt aside just before the horse would've tromped over him. The animal gave a terrified squall and galloped away without stopping.

Korden moved on. He could see the first homes now, their roofs indeed aflame.

And just beyond them, he stumbled over the first body.

5

It was Coomb, his frail form stretched on its side upon the ground, bony legs tangled in the spokes of his overturned wheeled chair. Korden couldn't see what was wrong with him, but his *mohol* was gone, his aura extinguished. A few feet away was Tiller, a large wound in his stomach from which blood still bubbled, and further up the dirt avenue was another form so bruised and battered he couldn't even identify it.

Even through the still-thickening smoke, he could see bodies everywhere, all of them wearing brown robes. He spied Bant and Feegran among them, the healer's head sitting backward on his neck.

Something moist and acidic crept up the back of Korden's throat.

So many of the Last Fathers slain at his feet. The idea seemed more like a dream than reality. He wanted to feel sorrow or anger, but instead there was just a dizzy numbness that crept along his limbs as he wandered through the massacre.

Ahead, he could hear grunts of effort and the bangs and clatter of combat. He could make out several forms scuffling in the middle of the dirt lane. Korden moved closer, trying not to cough from the smoke.

In the broad shadow thrown by the *hangala* in the late afternoon sun, Eddas and Santo stood facing one another, and between them was a gaunt wraith whose red eyes swirled in the haze, like a fat baker's moon through a wispy cloud bank. It towered nearly seven feet tall, and wore plates of tarnished silver armor across its narrow chest and arms, reminding him of the descriptions of the Roman soldiers in his current reading assignment. Its head was bald, its skin a mottled green the color of a putrid banana. In one hand, it hefted a four-parg long sword of rusted metal, with a hilt made from gleaming bone that twisted around its forearm to the elbow.

As Korden watched, it slashed at Eddas, who managed to suck his sloping stomach in far enough to narrowly avoid having his guts spilled. He roared and reached for the Incarnate's arm, but it pulled away and caught him with a vicious back swing that opened his cheek to the bone.

While it was distracted, Santo levitated a log from the woodpile beside the social hall. With a flick of his wrist, he sent it hurtling through the air. The projectile smashed into the back of the demon's head, knocking it off balance. It sprawled in the dirt and rose back up on one arm, ready to rejoin the fray, but then caught sight of Korden.

"*Lightbrinnngerrrr,*" it gurgled.

"*Korden, get back!*" Eddas bounded forward and brought one gigantic foot smashing down on the creature's head. It burst apart like a rotted melon, spraying a viscous, black fluid. Eddas slung an arm around Korden's waist and carried him away from the body before he could see anything else.

"What's happening?" he asked, when the Older set him down again. His eyes watered from the smoke. Flames leapt from building to building. The whole village seemed to be burning down around them.

"More Incarnates," Eddas said vacantly. A sheet of blood cascaded down his face from his sliced cheek. "They set the *huctés* ablaze, then cut the weaker men down as they fled." He shook his head. "It happened so fast. We sensed them, but we just didn't have time to... "

"Where—?" Korden began, and coughed so hard a burst of stars flashed behind his eyelids. "Where is Tash? Is there anyone left?"

"I don't know. I don't know where anyone is, nor how many of those demons remain." Eddas gripped the sides of Korden's head with a gentleness that his size denied. "But it's you they want. We have to get you away."

A pain-filled scream issued from within Skewtz' library, which was just beginning to smolder. Another Incarnate emerged from the door, this one as big as Eddas, holding the skinny librarian by the throat so that his feet dangled above the ground. A strange pair of black-tinted glasses were strapped tight around its head, the lenses dark enough to contain the glow from its eyes. Unlike its brothers, the sun seemed to cause this one no problems as it strode into the street and tossed Skewtz aside like garbage. Korden's literature teacher hit the side of the building with an audible crunch and lay unmoving.

"That is the one we seek!" the Incarnate barked, pointing a crooked dagger at Korden. "Give him to me or we will slaughter *every one of you!*"

Eddas let go of Korden and straightened to his full height, a formidable tower of muscle even wrapped in the wrinkled, spotted skin of an old man. He brought his fists up in front of his face and clenched them so hard the knuckles cracked. "Do. Your. Worst. Demon." He issued a mad bellow as he charged at the creature, who rushed to meet him.

"Run, Korden!" Santo urged. "Get as far from here as possible!" The Older went to join Eddas where he scrabbled with the Incarnate.

Before, the idea of fleeing seemed cowardly and repulsive to Korden, but that had been an eternity ago, when he'd been safe far up the hillside, viewing all this from a distance. But here, knee-deep in death and chaos, he could think of nothing he wanted more than to escape it all. Korden backed away from the fight, then did as he was told, running toward the closest gap between *huctés*. He looked back only once, and saw Santo impaled through the eye by the Incarnate's dagger just before they were all swallowed up in the haze.

He ran on, choking on tears and smoke, unable to see more than a few feet ahead in the narrow, dark alley between buildings. A sob tore out of his throat just before it closed up for good, sealing off the last of his air. He sank to all fours on the ground, where the fumes were thinnest, and tried to calm himself enough to catch a breath.

A shape appeared at the far end of the alley. One whose eyes burned away the darkness. Allin's face swam out of the haze as the figure strode toward him. The Incarnate had picked up a wicked sword since Korden last saw it.

"Well, well, little Lightbringer," it said, swiping the weapon through the air. "Looks like it will be me that cures you after all."

Korden scrambled backward away from it as black spots crowded in at the edges of his vision. The alley spun. His arms felt limp and distant, as though they belonged to someone else. The Incarnate advanced, jabbing at him on the ground playfully with the sword tip.

Then it stopped abruptly and looked over Korden's head.

"Get away from my son."

Redfen stepped in front of Korden, swinging a piece of flaming timber at the demon. The Incarnate backed away, snarling.

"Get up, Kord!" Redfen shouted. "Stay behind me!"

He continued to swing the burning wood, driving the Incarnate back one step at a time toward the end of the alley, where a few strangled rays of sunlight filtered down through the smoke. Korden tried to obey him, but could only suck in the thinnest dribbles of air. He still felt too lightheaded to stand.

"Korden—?" Redfen turned his head to look over his shoulder.

The Incarnate grabbed the fire with its bare hand, the flesh charring instantly. It pushed the wood aside and drove its sword into the other man's chest.

"*Redfen!*" Korden wailed, finding his breath at last.

The weapon penetrated straight through Redfen Bright's torso. The timber slipped from his hand, and, when the Incarnate yanked the blade from him, he crashed to the ground.

"No one can protect you," the demon said, coming at him once more.

A red, undeniable rage rippled throughout Korden's body, turning every nerve ending into a twitching inferno.

He wanted to kill this creature, to destroy it, to make it feel this pain that tore at him. He opened himself to the Upper completely, calling upon the artcraft, but instead of attempting to manipulate it, as he usually did, he allowed it to channel through him like a raging river.

The force of his will was all-consuming. A command to be given to the universe itself. His skull ached from the pressure. It had to be released.

Korden focused on the Incarnate, envisioned his goal, and pushed with his mind.

He felt something massive leave him, a surge of energy visible only as cerulean waves that leapt across the short space separating him from the creature. The Incarnate stopped as suddenly as if it had run into a wall. Allin's scraggly hair and wrinkled skin blew backward in a sudden wind strong enough to stagger him back a step but that did nothing to disturb the smoke around them.

And then that skin began to peel away.

As Korden watched, the Incarnate dissipated into fragments that quickly swirled away in the haze. Its flesh unraveled, like threads from a cloth, revealing layers of muscle and veins. Allin's face dissolved. The demon howled—more in anger than pain, Korden thought—but the sound was cut short when its throat stripped away and blew into a million tiny pieces. Within seconds, the creature was nothing but clean ivory bones standing inside a tunic and breeches. They clattered to the dirt.

A funnel of oily blackness drifted up from the pile, but it too broke apart and vanished into the smoke from the burning houses.

Korden got to his knees and scrambled past the bones to Redfen's side, then turned the man over on his back.

The hole in his chest barely leaked any blood. His eyes were open, and they fixed upon Korden glassily. One shaking hand rose and touched the hair at the boy's forehead, as it had so many times before.

"I didn't mean it," Korden told him desperately, as though the words could create a tether to keep him here. "You're my father. You always have been."

A dreamy smile crossed Redfen Bright's face. "You are… special," he whispered, before his mouth went slack. Korden touched his mind in time to see the last of the color fade from his aura.

Then he put his head against his father's chest and sobbed.

The Heavy Cloak

1

When Tash found him, he still sat next to Redfen's body, eyes dry and fixed on nothing as he cradled the man's head. The smoke had cleared, and the hungry sounds of the fire were fading, but these changes barely registered in Korden's dulled thoughts. He had no idea how long he'd sat like this; the passage of time was marked only by the creeping shadows of late afternoon and the distant, frantic voices calling his name. If another Incarnate had come upon him like this, he would've been easy prey.

"Thank tha Upper," Tash panted. "I couldn't sense yeh, *ghammer*. All our powers're drained dry. We were about ta start searchin tha forest. I feared…" His voice broke on the last word. It was this momentary slip that finally interrupted Korden's trance. He dragged his attention away from the corpse to study his *den-so*. The old man was filthy, robe torn to tatters. A runner of blood trickled down the left side of his head, a brilliant line of vermillion against his snow white hair. Moisture glistened in the web of wrinkles along his cheeks, either tears or sweat.

"They killed him, Tash," Korden murmured, smoothing hair from his father's forehead. Again, as he said this, there was no emotion to accompany it. It was just a fact, like something read in one of his books, no different than bees pollinating flowers or water flowing downhill. When he tried to force himself to feel something, *anything*, there was only that emptiness in his chest, a hole that felt big enough to swallow him.

"I know," Tash told him. "I'm so sorry. We tried ta stop them, ta protect yeh as we always vowed, but…" He trailed once more, and his cloudy eyes flicked to the pile of bones further up the alley. His mouth firmed into a tight line, the way it did on the few occasions when Korden passed one of his surprise tests.

"We have to bury him," Korden said. "Him, and all the others. That's what you do when someone dies, right? Put them in the ground?"

"Aye, *ghammer*, that's right. And we'll do jes that, I promise. But for now…I need yeh to come with me."

He held out a shaking hand. Something brown was crusted under his ragged nails. Korden stared at it and blinked several times before accepting dazedly. He lowered his father's head gently, but had trouble standing. He understood what Tash meant; he felt as limp as a rag doll, so devoid of artcraft after his encounter that he barely had enough willpower left to move his limbs. Yet he found the strength to hold back when the Older tried to guide him away.

"I can't leave him. Not like this."

Without a word, Tash slipped off his tattered robe. Beneath was a tan, long-sleeve tunic and a pair of worn breeches, the most informal garb Korden had ever seen him in. He took the robe and draped it gently across Redfen Bright. Korden took a last look at his father as the brown cloth settled over him.

"Yeh mustn't think on it; not now. We need action, or all is lost."

This time, Korden allowed himself to be led back out to the dirt lane up the center of the village. Or what was left of it. With the smoke gone, the extent of the destruction could be seen. A good portion of the *huctés* and the library were nothing but burnt cinders, and the high roof of the *hangala* had collapsed into the building's ornate interior. A handful of Olders were busy extinguishing the few remaining fires, treating wounds, or carrying limp bodies inside the social hall. Bibb was among those still on his feet, as well as Port and Eddas, the latter two attempting to free a badly burned Dillish from the wreckage of his home. Korden and Tash stood aside, unnoticed, and observed the devastation.

"How many...?" Korden asked, too afraid to finish the question, much less hear the answer.

"Sixteen o' us remain," Tash answered solemnly. "And I expect three more ta expire from their injuries by nightfall."

Korden drew in a quick, harsh breath. More than half the village slaughtered.

Outside the ashes of the library lay the large Incarnate that wore the dark lenses to protect its eyes. The patches of its skin exposed to the sun were quickly melting into greenish-brown slag. Korden knew that light damaged the bodies once these demons took them over, especially their eyes, but the process seemed to quicken after they expired, as if the world wanted to rid itself of them as fast as possible.

"Are they all dead?"

"Aye. We cut down tha four in tha group that attacked us, and as for tha prisoner they released...I believe yeh took care o' that one yehrself."

"*Five?* Just five of them were able to do all of this?"

"They are vicious, brutal creatures, created for nothing but combat and murder. We fought as best we could, but, in the end..." He sounded ashamed as he finished with, "We are not but used-up bodlas, *ghammer*."

"But you said you would know if more were coming!" Korden shouted. His voice rolled up and down through the desolate village, causing the Olders to stop their work. Their gloomy faces lit up when they spotted Korden, and all who were able came running.

Tash winced at his accusation. Before the others arrived, he said softly, "And I truly thought we would. Our powers are even more diminished than I realized. I was wrong, and many people paid fer it with their lives, yehr father among them. So if yeh feel tha need ta hate someone...let it be me."

The sorrow hit Korden then, a delayed wave of black grief that struck him like a hard fist in the stomach. He wrapped his arms around his torso and clenched his jaw until the muscles on either side hardened into stone, and waited for the pain to pass, much like he did with his as-mah attacks.

But he couldn't hate Tash.

Because right now...he hated himself far too much.

And then the remaining Olders—the last of the Last Fathers—swept him up in a tide of relief and cries of joy.

Eddas wept as he threw his massive arms around Korden and lifted him skyward. A cloth bandage stretched across the side of his face that the Incarnate sliced open. "I thought we'd lost ya, boy!"

"Enough," Tash ordered, when they'd all taken a turn. "I must have words with him."

"Not now, Tash," Bibb scolded. A crack ran up the middle of one of his spectacle lenses. "The boy needs to rest. Can't you see he's in shock?"

"There is no time fer rest. We must put an end ta this, and quickest done is least painful."

The gathered group of men fell into uncomfortable, chastised silence.

"What is it?" Korden demanded. "For once, stop protecting me and just tell me what you have to say!"

"There will be more," Tash said plainly. "We chose to settle here because o' its isolation, so, chances are, these Incarnates jes happened ta be close by ta arrive here so quickly. A stroke o' bad luck that is, but yeh can bet they won't be tha last ta seek yeh. They could come tomorrow or tha next day or five minutes from now, drawn here like iron ta a magnet."

"Isn't there...some way to hide me again?"

Bibb removed his broken glasses and daubed at his eyes. "There's no place you could hide from them except behind the Barrier, lad. And with so few of us left, we would never be able to rebuild it strong enough to shield you."

"Then what do we do?"

There was no answer for what felt like ages, and Korden was on the verge of asking again when Tash said, "Yeh must make a choice, *ghammer*, one that we will all abide by: stay...or go."

"Go? Go *where?*"

Tash met this question with one of his own. "Yehr father. What did he tell yeh?"

Korden paused, hesitant to repeat the strange story, to give it any more power than it already had. "He said that... that he wasn't really my father. That I had no father."

"That's right. He told us tha same story tha night he brought yeh here, but even if he hadn't, I would've known. I think we all would've."

"But how can that be true? It doesn't make sense!"

"No. It doesn't." Tash drew in a breath that seemed to have no end. "But I believe…yeh were meant fer something grand, Korden. Destiny hangs about yeh like a heavy cloak, and yehr potential fer artcraft is seemingly limitless. But if there *is* a task before yeh, I fear tha time left ta accomplish it may grow short."

"Accomplish *what?*" Korden cried. Part of him realized that his *den-so* had just used his name for the first time that he could remember, but he was too caught up in what the man was telling him to marvel at it. "Just tell me where I'm supposed to go!"

Still facing Korden, Tash raised one arm and extended a finger toward the eastern horizon, where the black shroud of the Filament was still visible against the coming of the bruised twilight.

2

Korden couldn't speak. He was too afraid if he tried, his throat would clamp shut again.

Yes, he'd long dreamed of leaving the village…but not to go in *that* direction.

"I don't know how yeh'll get there or what yeh'll find when yeh do," Tash said, "but I believe, deep in my heart, that yehr fate lies within that darkness."

"So…I'm to be banished from the village?"

Tash surprised him by bursting into laughter. The rest of the group joined him. "Never in life! I said yeh had a choice, and I meant it. If yeh decide ta stay, we will face whatever comes with yeh."

"That's right, Korden!" Eddas agreed. "We'll fight at your side to the last man!"

Korden gave him a grateful smile. Considering that five Incarnates had been enough to raze the village to the ground, he wondered how much time this offer would buy them.

"But if yeh go," Tash continued, "yeh will leave today, this very hour, and yeh will go alone. Yeh'll travel fast and light, be wary in tha day and even more so by night. And, most important o' all, yeh'll keep yehr faith at all times. Tha choice is yours, but it must be made now, so that we can prepare either way."

The Olders watched him in silence, but he could sense them probing him gently with their minds for his reaction. For some reason, Tash's phrase about destiny hanging on him like a cloak echoed in his head. Korden thought he could feel that cloak wrapped around him now, just as he had this morning, before setting all these events in motion with his damned *adventure*. And this cloak wasn't just heavy, as Tash claimed.

It was suffocating.

"I'll go," he said, too softly to hear the words himself, and then repeated louder, "I'll go."

Their reaction confused him. Instead of being cheerful, the group of old men gave each other crestfallen looks. Their *mohols* all blended into the same dejected shade of midnight blue shot through with tense crimson. Port bowed his head and sniffled, while a small, strangled squawk escaped Bibb.

Had they actually *wanted* him to refuse?

Bibb confirmed his suspicion a moment later when he asked, "Are you *sure* this is what you want, lad?"

Korden nodded. "Yes. I won't let anyone else risk their life for me."

"Oh, but it's not about that! Not at all! If you stay, I'm sure we can figure out a plan, we can—!"

"Do not undermine his decision." Tash's voice cut through Bibb's plea with unquestioning authority. He addressed the others. "We will not make this harder on him than it has ta be. For now…let us prepare him fer life beyond tha village as best we can."

3

They were reluctant to even let him return home without an escort—insisting he be kept in a ring of Olders, or, at the very least, that Eddas be sent at his side—until he pointed out that soon he would be away from the village, entirely on his own. If he couldn't take care of himself here, how would he ever do it out there?

His strength had begun to return, but Korden stood outside his *hucté* for several long minutes. The idea of going inside sent a pang through his heart. This place looked different to him, lonely and somehow darker in a way that had nothing to do with the dimness of the afternoon, as if its mud walls had once been imbued with a sheen that was now faded.

Things will *change fer yeh one day,* ghammer. *Perhaps faster than yeh would like.*

Tash's words. As usual, he'd been right.

His carry pouch sat beneath the tree where he left it. He went to retrieve the bag to delay going inside. The picture of the girl was still tucked beneath the bag's flap, and he pulled it out to look at it.

Whatever magic it once held for him had vanished also. Something felt broken inside him, disconnected, like the wires that made all of Bibb's fantastic gadgets run, and he wondered if he would ever be able to find joy in anything so trivial again. He opened his hand and let the breeze carry the square of paper away. It danced along the grass, heading back toward the forest where he found it.

The very same enormous, brooding forest he would soon be entering.

Korden might not be able to feel happiness, but he found fear was still in ready supply.

You don't have to go! a panicked voice in his head insisted. *You could stay here!*

Only until the next envoy of Incarnates arrived, and then they would finish what the others started.

Bibb said you could figure out a plan! You can fight, make weapons, fortify the village, maybe—!

They're old men, not soldiers. They can't fight a war to save me, even if they're willing to. And if I thought this place was a prison before, it'll be worse when I'm trapped here with them hanging over me more than Redfen ever did, waiting to see if each day is my last. He swallowed against a lump that felt as large as a fist in his throat. *I won't let them die for me. I won't. I would rather be dead myself than see any more of them hurt.*

But that's just it. The anxiety was gone from this intrusive voice, replaced by a blunt callousness. *They're not asking you to die. Closing your eyes and lying down and never getting back up again? Anyone can do that. But what can they possibly expect you to do against the Dark Filament? Might as well ask you to push down one of those redwoods with your bare hands.*

Korden bowed his head until his chin pressed into his chest, as if dragged down by the weight of Tash's invisible cloak. He'd delayed long enough. If he wanted to get away from the village before dark, he would have to hurry.

With the carry pouch's strap now resting on his shoulder, he made himself go through the door of his home.

That empty darkness had gotten inside the *hucté* as well. His father was in every corner of this place, and the memories were like a raw, open wound. Korden felt tears pressing at the backs of his eyes again and ignored them.

In his room, he took the only other pair of dungarees that still fit him, several light tunics, the thick woolen coat that Bant sewed for him just this past year, and the thin feather pad from atop his bed. These items were tightly folded and rolled and then went into the pouch alongside his journal, and were joined by several books and odds and ends from his collection.

The pistol waited in the bottom of his chest, still wrapped in the tiny blanket. Korden held it in both hands for what seemed like an hour before tucking it too into his bag.

At the door, he paused to take one last look around the *hucté*, at the table where he'd eaten countless meals with his father and the chair where the man sat by the fire while Korden sprawled in the floor with a book.

Instinct told him he would never see this place again, but he wasn't sure he wanted to anyway.

4

Korden met those that were well enough to say goodbye at the easternmost edge of the village, a group of stoop-shouldered old men that he loved with all his heart. The sun was a red ball riding the distant spine of the low mountain peaks northwest of the village, thrusting the Last Fathers' shadows into long, jagged ghosts behind them and turning the tears on their creased cheeks into lines of golden fire.

They stood side-by-side, each of them waiting for their turn to say goodbye and offer him trinkets to remember them by or to help him on his journey, until his carry pouch bulged with their gifts. He received a bladder of water, enough for a week if he rationed, and several weeks worth of dried deer and possum jerky. The idea of how he would get nourishment had never entered his mind, but now it was a whole new problem to worry. Port must have seen it in his eyes, for he gripped Korden's bicep and said, "Trust in the Upper, and He will provide."

From Eddas, he received a bone-hilt knife whetted to razor sharpness, in a leather sheath that tied around his waist. The bear-of-a-man wiped snot from his nose with the back of one hand and said, "We would give you Mulder to speed you on the journey, but that old nag would be riding you before too long. Just keep on the move, it'll prevent the Incarnates from getting an exact bead on you. If you happen to take one of them down, it's very important that you stay away from the body, all right? Remember all those wrestling holds I showed you, too. And for Upper's sweet sake, don't trust *anyone!* There'll be far worse out there than those demons, believe you me!"

"All right," Korden agreed, before the Older could ramble on. "I will, I promise."

"Happy birthday, Brother Korden. I'm so sorry it ended this way."

His birthday. He'd forgotten all about it. The boy that woke up so full of excitement this morning had died today also, along with Redfen Bright and many more.

Bibb waited last in line, now with soot smeared across his face beneath his cracked glasses. He glanced nervously at the others and then leaned close to Korden.

"It all burned," he whispered sadly. "All my treasures, gone." His frown curled slowly upward, tugging at his jowls. "Except for one I'd been keeping separate from the others, in case Tash ever made me get rid of them. I always planned to give you this when you left the village one day. Consider it a last birthday present." He extended his fist palm down, using one flap of his robe to hide it from the others.

Korden held out his own hand, surprised to find a kernel of excitement taking root in him. Bibb dropped something smooth and round into his palm. Korden reeled it in, eager to find out what magnificent object from the old world had been bequeathed to him...

"It's a rock," he said, staring at the smooth-edged, reddish white pebble.

"Nope, it's a *stone*," Bibb corrected, with a mirthful wink. "Take care of yourself, lad. And remember what I told you about moderation."

He gave the man a hug and dropped the odd gift into the bottom of his carry pouch, where he promptly forgot about it.

Tash—dressed in a fresh robe and with the blood and dirt cleaned from his skin—waited patiently while Korden finished his goodbyes, then stepped forward and took his arm. "I will escort my *den-ret* as far as tha road. Tha rest o' you...get about tha task at hand."

The two of them started across the field toward the waiting forest, where the shadows grew hungry once more in the fading light. This time, when they crossed the space where the Barrier had once been, there was no tingle, and certainly no exhilaration. Korden turned around to look back only one time as they entered the tree line, all that he could bear.

The Last Fathers still watched him, some of them weeping. He opened his heart, wanting to experience their auras one last time, and found a blaze of conflicting emotion surrounding them, happiness and sorrow and regret and fear in one smeared palette, but, standing above them all, the pure white brilliance of hope. Korden saw Eddas touch two fingers to his forehead in a brief salute just before the dense network of trees hid him from sight.

5

He and Tash walked through the dim forest in a comfortable silence. Now, in the fading daylight, Korden could marvel at just how tall these trees were, looming over him until they seemed to touch the sky. The air was moist and heavy with the smell of sap and the sweet fragrance of catkin blossoms from the pines and alders growing amid the sequoias. His *den-so* kept one hand locked around his elbow, but he needed guidance here no more than he did in the village. Every step found its way around roots and underbrush to a sure footing as they worked their way around the giant redwoods.

"I'll have to light a *demno* soon," Korden remarked. "It's getting too dark to see."

"Why don't yeh just cut out tha middle man like I do, and command yehr eyes ta work?"

Korden gaped at him. "You mean, all this time, you were able to…?"

"I know my art looks like it was created by a blind man, but how else do yeh think I stay so spry?" A smug grin tugged at the corners of Tash's mouth. "What have I told yeh? If tha Crafter is strong enough, there is nothing he can't accomplish. One's own body…even tha very laws o' nature!…will all bend ta his will." Then the smile fell away, and he added, "But I suspect yeh already know that…don't yeh?"

"The Incarnate," Korden said quietly.

Tash kept silent, but his thin lips pursed once more, as when he'd come across the pile of bones back in the village which, Korden now realized, he had probably been able to see.

"I don't know what happened! I didn't mean to—!"

"Yes, yeh did. Yeh focused on a goal—one yeh hadn't been taught and practiced a hundred times—then made it come true."

"One second, I was mad, and the next…it was just… *there*. Inside my head." He saw it all once more—the Incarnate coming at him, encountering that ghostly blue wind, and then disintegrating in a fine mist—but he could no longer remember how it felt to have that energy building inside him. He couldn't even recall how he released it.

It just came to him when he needed it.

Tash was nodding. "Anger—or any strong emotion—can be a powerful boost to yehr will, if used correctly. But yeh must not rely on it, *ghammer*, or yehr artcraft will be erratic and unreliable, at best. At worse, it'll corrupt every part o' yeh. Everything in its time and place."

"Moderation?" Korden asked.

"I see yeh've been talkin ta Bibb." The old man's brow furrowed into a great pile in the middle of his forehead. "Killin an Incarnate by any means, much less with artcraft, is a difficult task. It takes faith, yeh see? And as we found out today, it apparently takes more than we have left in our used-up bodies ta even conjure against those abominations." Tash sighed softly. "Faith is fer tha young, before tha world has a chance ta wear yeh down. That's why they want yeh so bad in tha first place, ta snuff out that hope which burns inside all o' yeh. So keep up with yehr lessons, stretch yehr creative muscle, and never, *ever* let go of yehr beliefs."

Through the trees, Korden caught a quick glimpse of lighter gray against the ground. They had reached the road already. Another burst of panic burned in his chest as they came to a stop at its edge. A thousand questions sprang to the tip of his tongue, but one burned brighter than any of the others.

"Tash...what Redfen told me...about my real mother and...and father..."

"Is somethin best put out o' yehr head fer tha time bein. Fer all intents and purposes, Redfen Bright was—*is*—yehr father, and that's all that matters. That other is not but a story."

"But if it's true, what does it mean?"

"Maybe nothin. Maybe everythin. If it was true, would it change who yeh are, or what yeh think?"

"No," Korden said. "I guess not."

"No one, not even tha Upper, can tell us who we are, Korden. If He wants yeh ta know more about where yeh came from, He'll reveal it ta yeh, and then you'll have ta choose what ta do with it. All right?"

Korden shrugged reluctantly. "All right."

"And now, yeh face yet another choice, in what I'm sure will be a long line ahead o' yeh." Tash swept an arm to the right. "If memory serves, in this direction, tha road winds back ta tha west, far around tha village and toward tha ocean beyond. Yeh might be safe if yeh went that way and then headed into the frigid Rim territories, kept ahead o' tha Incarnates. But *that* way—" Tash pointed past him, to the left, "—will eventually take yeh east, out o' tha forest. I haven't been that way since the Purges first began, but there used ta be a few towns and settlements that direction. Upper knows what yeh'll find now."

"I'll go east," Korden said without hesitation.

Tash acknowledged this with a nod, as though it made not the slightest difference to him. "No matter where yeh go, stick ta the road, at least until yeh're out o' tha forest. It'll keep yeh from gettin lost. These woods are old, fearsome, and liable ta be full o' creatures yeh don't want ta meet. Sometimes the trees themselves almost seem to be…" He trailed for a moment, looked around at the towering trunks, then dismissed the thought with a shake of his head. "And yeh must be just as wary o' other people as Eddas said. Yeh're still a child, and that's not somethin anyone has likely ta have seen in a long, long time. Some o' them might be dangerous ta yeh fer reasons all their own. But somewhere out there, *someone* must be throwin a wrench into tha Filament's plans. I recommend yeh start with tryin ta find them and see what yeh can do ta help."

Korden nodded. "I'll come back," he vowed. "After I've done whatever it is I'm supposed to do, I'll come back here. If…if I can."

"Aye," Tash agreed, then looked away quickly.

But his *mohol* deepened into the bright, blushing red of discomfort.

The Older's last order to the others came back to Korden, about 'getting to the task at hand.' He thought the man meant rebuilding the village, but now a sudden suspicion popped into his head.

"What are you going to do?" he demanded.

Tash set his narrow jaw as he stared into the forest, then

shook his head. "That's our business."

"Keep no more secrets from me, Tash," Korden warned, sounding like anything other than a child. The gruff timbre jerked the old man's face back toward him. "Not now."

His mentor hesitated, but only for a moment. "Just because we don't have tha power ta shield yeh, doesn't mean we can't conjure up somethin ta draw tha Incarnates ta us. If we make them think we have a village fulla children, keep their focus on us, it might give yeh tha head start yeh need."

"You can't do that!" Korden cried. He couldn't imagine what those creatures would do when they descended upon the few remaining inhabitants and realized they'd been tricked. "I won't let you!"

He tried to pull free of Tash so he could run back and put a stop to this suicidal notion, but his *den-so* clamped down on his arm and dragged him back. Korden spun, meaning to shove him away, and instead fell against his thin chest. He wept as the man's arms encircled him.

"Please, *please* don't do this!" he pleaded. "You were supposed to be safe if I left!"

"Oh Korden. Oh my dear, sweet boy, don't yeh see? It *has* ta be this way." Even without looking up, Korden could hear the tears in his words. "We have a role ta play, every bit as much as yeh do. We pledged our lives fer yehrs many years ago."

"*But I don't want to do this by myself!*" Korden wailed.

"And I would go with yeh on this journey, if I could. But, besides tha fact that these old bones would only slow yeh down, destiny is a delicate thing, and we can't take tha risk that our presence could influence or interfere with yehrs. Yeh may very well be tha last chance we have ta set things right, ta balance tha scales."

Korden pulled away from his embrace, and wiped the dampness from his eyes angrily. "I didn't ask to be the last chance."

"I know. Tha Upper doesn't always ask us before He sets about makin plans." Tash took a step backward. "I'm proud o' yeh, Korden. So was yehr father. And when we get to the fount beyond this world, I know we'll see yeh there."

Something was happening. Tash continued to move away from him, but with each step he seemed to be fading, using artcraft to melt into the shadows.

"Wait, Tash, don't go! I'm not ready!"

"Goodbye, *ghammer*. May all yehr choices be true."

Then he was gone, and, for the first time in his life, Korden Bright found himself completely and utterly alone as the sun set on his sixteenth birthday.

On the Road

KEEP WALKING

1

It took him several long minutes to move from the spot where Tash abandoned him, like the siblings in the tale of the witch that lived in a house made of sugar. Another of Skewtz' 'fairy tales', told in the social hall one night, and Korden remembered thinking that the real villain was not the witch, even if she'd used her artcraft for cannibalism; it was the terrible father who left his children to fend for themselves in the woods, and now Tash had done the same thing to him. He knew in his heart this wasn't true, but it felt that way, all the same. Korden stood beside the road, pleading for the man to come back, then clenched his fists and shook them at the trees around him, which remained as tall and silent as they had for countless years, giving no indication that they cared about his tantrum. And when he finally did move, it was back in the direction of the village.

He just could not do this. It was too much to ask of anyone. He would go back and tell them they could find some other child to send into the forest.

Don't let the first choice you make on your own be the wrong one.

After a few steps, he halted, turned around, and set off before his body could mutiny.

2

The surface of the road felt strange under his boots. Hard and unyielding. He kept to the middle of the path, straddling the faded yellow line up the middle, and concentrated only on putting down one foot after the other. The repetitiveness helped to occupy his mind, kept his despair at bay. Five or ten minutes after he started—judged solely by the amount of ground the shadows devoured as they stretched longer and longer—he reached the wrecked auto with its mummified passengers. This time, he moved past without stopping. That relic had gotten him in too much trouble already.

He wanted to feel brave. Like Sheriff Protector, riding into battle in his fiery metal steed. Or, if he could only recapture that sense of destiny that had driven him through this long day—the destiny that Tash claimed he could sense from the moment Korden arrived at the village, as though it were a strong body odor oozing from his very pores—then at least it might seem like all this had some purpose, had happened for a reason.

But Korden didn't feel like someone of importance any more, heading toward some predestined location where he would alter the course of history.

He just felt like a scared kid, trudging through the deep forest and trying not to think about his murdered father or the demons that could be stalking him at this very moment.

That first night came swiftly among the dense trees, skipping over dusk entirely and plunging him into full darkness. Korden kept his head down and continued walking until he could no longer see the yellow line, until only the sound of his feet slapping on the road told him he was even still on course. He might have kept going even then, plodding doggedly along, but his boot heel came down in a crack across the pavement, and his ankle twisted painfully. He stopped and looked up for the first time.

Which proved to be a mistake. He'd barely even been allowed outside after nightfall his entire life, much less in the sparse woods that sat within the Barrier. And the forest—with its thick roof of interwoven branches—was pitch black, much more so than when he crept out in the watery yellow dimness of early morning, with a heart full of optimism to buoy his spirits. His eyes could scarcely pick out the shape of the enormous tree trunks lining the sides of the road. The whole world had become nothing but a black void filled with unknown cracks and creaks and rustlings, and the realization sent him into a fit of panicked half-breaths.

He thought he could feel countless eyes watching him, but that had to be his out-of-control imagination. Still, his hand went to the knife at his hip and hovered there.

Korden wanted to lie down, curl into a ball, and close his eyes until morning came, but he couldn't stop for the night yet. How far could he possibly have gone? A mere span? Two, at the most? Upper only knew how many still lay ahead. At the moment though, he needed only to concern himself with getting as far away from the village as possible, or the Olders' sacrifice would be in vain. Even so, he couldn't continue without some sort of illumination to guide him.

He knelt and felt around the ground at his feet until his hands encountered a chunk of pavement that would make for a good *demno*, but he stopped just short of igniting the artificial fire. A bright light would completely expose him among the dark trees, making him a target.

And Incarnates weren't the only danger here. Tash just said these woods could be full of creatures he didn't want to meet. Now he wished he'd asked his *den-so* to elaborate. A squirming ball of fear travelled from his stomach up to the back of his throat as his mind conjured an array of horrors.

Several years ago, a wounded mountain cat limped into the village on a broken hind leg. Fortholm—who'd always been the most skilled in animal communing—managed to entrance it so Feegran could mend the appendage, and while he kept it hypnotized, he let Korden come in to see the animal. It'd been as long as his own body from head to tail and twice as heavy, its torso and shoulders banded with rippling muscle. Feegran raised the cat's tawny paw, which was big enough to cover Korden's face, and pressed the pad on the underside to unsheathe curved claws at least six cupits long. The healer assured him that such talons could tear him apart in the blink of an eye.

Of course, if such a beast were around now, it would probably only need to follow its keen nose to find Korden, but there was no sense giving it any assistance if he didn't have to.

So just make your eyes see in the dark.

Could he do that? He'd used artcraft to ease pain and even increase his strength, but this sort of augmentation was far beyond that. Yet Tash made it sound so easy. Korden closed his eyes. Swept his mind of extraneous thoughts. Opened his heart to the Upper and felt the flow of artcraft. He envisioned his intention, saw it as clearly as possible in his mind, then tried to give that same mental push as back in the village. He strained to the point that a dull ache developed in the center of his forehead.

When he opened his eyes, the forest remained just as imperceptible as before.

"So much for that," he muttered. A new idea came to him. Instead of trying to see in the dark, he stretched his senses out in all directions, and suddenly the *mohols* of the surrounding wildlife blazed into existence, pinpricks of light in his head. He could discern the auras of snakes and rodents and squirrels amid the underbrush, an owl on a high roost in the sequoia beside him, a nest of golas dangling from a branch ahead. They glowed in calm tones of aquamarine or, in the case of several of the snakes, the tense, ruddy hues of a coiled predator, ready to strike. The brief glimpse made him feel secure enough to light up the hunk of pavement in his hand. The white glow drove away the darkness.

He continued on for another hour, this time trying to divide his concentration between the road and his awareness of his surroundings, but even that proved a challenge. The pavement became more deteriorated the further he went. The earth beneath had worked relentlessly to break apart the crete over the long years. Jagged cracks stretched in all directions, making the remaining sections of road look like ice floes on a frozen pond as the Bloom thaw begins. Exposed tree roots surfaced here and there, humping the road into uneven hills. And the shoulders were overgrown by encroaching undergrowth much too thick for him to push through. Korden picked his way through the rubble until his growling stomach became yet another distraction. He realized he hadn't eaten a full meal since the breakfast that Redfen prepared him.

A few pargs off the road to his right, the trees and brush cleared out for a short stretch. Korden stepped into this glen, performed another quick scan of the area, and sat down. His legs and feet tingled unpleasantly; before now; the only walking he did was back and forth from his house to the village. The Olders spent so much time exercising his mind, but perhaps not enough on his body.

While he rested, he pulled his carry-pouch into his lap and dug through the contents by the light of his *demno* until he found his jerky and water bladder. He allowed himself only two strips of the dried deer though his belly demanded more, and only one swallow of water though the cured meat made his mouth feel full of sand. The stores looked like a lot when he took them—especially with their weight added to his already heavy pouch—but now a few weeks worth didn't seem much at all. He would have to try hunting down game in a few days if he found no other alternative.

Even if you'd ever hunted a day in your life, what would you use? You didn't even bring a bow. The Olders prepared you really well, didn't they?

I don't need a bow. The Upper will provide, remember?

Unless the Upper is just another one of their stories.

The thought—popping into his head completely unbidden—caused Korden to jump so hard the bladder slipped from his hand and sent a splash of water into the grass between his legs. He snatched it back up and replaced the cap with shaking hands.

Of course the Upper was real. Couldn't he feel that presence when he concentrated? To think otherwise was a blight upon one's faith. Doubt would choke off his conduit to the artcraft just as his sickly lungs did to his air supply.

And how do you even know that much is true? Because they told you it was?

Korden's cheeks burned. Less than five hours on his own, and already he questioned everything he'd been taught. If this had all been another of Tash's tests, he would be failing spectacularly.

Of course, he'd also doubted their claims about the Barrier, and look how that turned out.

3

He considered going on, but was just too exhausted. This would have to be his camp for the night, even though the idea of closing his eyes and leaving himself defenseless put him instantly on the raw edge of panic.

But thinking about the Barrier gave him an idea. He got back up and formed a rough perimeter around the tiny meadow with broken tree branches, and lashed them together with strips of sapling bark he peeled with his knife. Then he enchanted each joint, instructing them to buzz like a hive of hornets if their bindings were broken, a variation on a wordspell that Del once showed him for keeping pests out of the garden. Then he covered his entire invention with enough grass and brush to camouflage it.

All in all, a simple alarm system, one that would give him only a few seconds of warning if something approached in the night, but far better than nothing. He thought Tash would've been proud of the ingenuity.

Korden lay out his bedroll in the grass and bundled his coat under his head for a pillow. He slid his boots and socks off to let his sore feet rest, but kept his clothes on, even though they still smelled of smoke.

The ground was hard and slightly damp. He missed his bed. Only after laying his knife at his side, within easy reach, did he extinguish the *demno*.

Darkness leapt back in at him once more. But overhead, the clearing gave way to a blazing sliver of sky through the redwood canopy. Hundreds of stars were packed into the small space, more than he could count. Their muted glow twinkled in a display that was somehow comforting.

He realized he'd never slept outside before. His father promised they would someday, when they were able to leave the village at last. Deep down, Redfen Bright understood—and perhaps even shared—Korden's need for adventure. He'd told the boy that no one could ever truly experience life until they'd slept beneath the stars.

If only the man had known he would never live to see the night his son finally got to do so.

Except Redfen never had a son...

A single tear slipped along the side of Korden's temple. He wiped it away, too tired to cry again, then turned on his side and squeezed his eyes shut against the tide of memories and doubts and regrets that tried to invade his head.

He figured he would lie awake all night, but exertion and stress had taken its toll. Sleep swept over him surprisingly fast. Just as he surrendered to its warm embrace, sinking past the point where reality began to blur, a tiny, faraway voice whispered a string of nonsense into his ear that his weary brain immediately dismissed as a dream.

It sounded like, KINETIC BATTERY CHARGE TO 20 PERCENT...

4

Korden awakened to shrill bird song high above. He opened his eyes and then clamped them shut again immediately. The same gap in the treetops that provided him starlight now allowed a stream of morning sunshine to hit him square in the face. He blinked in the glare until his pupils adjusted and then sat up.

The forest had transformed into a pleasant, otherworldly

place now that day had broken. The canopy was a smattering of vivid greens, like one of Tash's blurry paintings. Weak streams of light seeped between the massive tree trunks on a steep diagonal, worming their way through the woods and softening the rough texture of the bark with a haze of shadows. The redwoods—not quite so ominous now—marched away from him in rows, forming endless corridors populated by smaller trees and rife with undergrowth. If not for having the road as an anchor, he could easily see himself getting lost in them. They actually made him feel a little claustrophobic, as though he would never be able to escape their embrace. No matter how far he walked, there would always just be more forest, ready to swallow him up, so that he never saw the open sky again.

He pulled himself away from these thoughts before they could bring him down. His sleep had been full of terrible dreams, but still deep enough to relieve him of his anxiety, rejuvenating his mood.

Too bad the same couldn't be said for the rest of him. His body ached. The backs of his calves were tight as drumskin, and the bottoms of his feet still maintained a grumbling soreness, the left one bearing the beginnings of a blister on the side. Korden slid his boots back on and then made himself a meager breakfast from several fistfuls of wild whortleberry he spotted just a few steps from his camp. He set off his own alarm in the process of harvesting them, the sudden buzzing in his ears tearing through his nerves until he was able to release the enchantment.

The plants tasted bitter without being boiled, but he was far too hungry to care. He took another few swallows of water to wash them down and then sat contemplating all that empty space at the top of the bladder.

With the trees blocking any view of the sun, he couldn't judge the time or figure how long he slept. As eager as he was to get on the move again, Korden forced himself to take out his journal and scribble a page on the story he started yesterday. It felt good to create again; the action not only added a comforting touch of normalcy and familiarity, but provided a mental escape from the sadness that constantly waited at the edge of his thoughts. He wrote about the girl from the photo, and described the outfit she'd worn in his dream. Afterward, he crossed his legs and took a short faithing break, just long enough to prepare himself for the day, but had trouble maintaining that state of perfect communing with the Upper.

Then it was up and walking. He soon found that movement helped too; the changing scenery prevented him from slipping back into grief. The road continued on in a broken jumble, forcing him to tread carefully, but after the first hour, he reached another smooth section and picked up his pace considerably, reaching a light run. The trees flew by on either side for several minutes, until he realized how pointless it was to hurry when he didn't even know where he was going. And, though it was cool along the forest floor with the canopy providing shade, the temperature was still more than hot enough for running to tire him. He found a tread he could manage without too much exertion and made himself to keep to it.

Watching the road unspool quickly became dull. Korden tried to read the books he'd brought, but the path became treacherous too often for him not to have his eyes on it. Instead he took out his knife and threw it at trees along the way as he walked, aiming for a particular knot and trying to sink the blade in it, a feat he accomplished only once out of dozens of throws. He talked aloud to himself, spinning Sheriff Protector stories and acting out the parts. Then he got in his artcraft practice for the day, coming up with his own tests in lieu of Tash's guidance: conjuring fire from thin air (the best he could usually manage was a small burst of blue flame from his fingertip), stretching his senses into knotholes or dark crevices to explore the interior, levitating logs and rocks, and manipulating objects to make them obey his wishes with only the force of his will.

Simple motions were always the easiest. Tash compared learning artcraft to being an infant once more, mastering the clunky motions of crawling before graduating to fine, precise control. Korden considered it a major victory when he maneuvered a stick through the air dexterously enough to have it spell his name—albeit illegibly—in the soil beside the road.

But, try as he might, he couldn't seem to find that place in his head again, the one that had blown the conduit wide open and unleashed the furious waves on the Incarnate in the village.

Midway through the day, the landscape began to climb. Korden found himself working up a steep slope, the road once more in overgrown shambles where large slices of pavement had broken free and tumbled downhill. The sequoias receded, leaving behind a collection of stunted pine trees that clung to the hillside at acute angles to the ground and giving him clear access to the sky for the first time since entering the forest. Sweat poured down Korden's brow as he ascended, each step an exhausted drudgery, each breath a wheeze. His carry-pouch dragged at his neck and back until every muscle groaned.

And then, just as his stomach began to demand lunch, he crested the top of the hill and found himself looking down upon a rolling valley unlike anything he'd ever imagined.

5

The land descended on the other side of the ridge just as steeply as it had risen, but plummeted farther, so much that Korden could see above the redwoods where they resumed at the foot of the hillside below. The lush, green tops were laid out in front of him like a rug, hiding the long valley beneath, except for a body of turquoise water off to his left that sparkled in the sun. He followed the road with his eye as far as possible, but after winding down the slope, he lost it among the trees. Some unknowable distance away though, at the very edge of vision, he could make out where the behemoths petered for good, replaced by a rich emerald timberland of firs and smaller evergreens all the way to the horizon.

The beauty of it all made him want to sit down and write in his journal, to describe it so he would never forget.

Except for one thing.

At some point in his travels, the road had indeed curved to the east as Tash promised. From this high vantage, Korden had a better view of the skyline in this direction than he ever did back home. The inky black smudge of the Dark Filament hung over this gorgeous vista, an ugly lid on the end of the world. It didn't appear to be any closer, but up here, in the thinner air, he could see how crisp its edges were, as though a titanic blade had carved away the azure sky like a slice of meat from a roasted goose.

That's where I'm going, he thought. Now that he'd been on his own for nearly an entire day—had seen that it wasn't quite so horrible to be alone—this idea didn't inspire fear anymore so much as it did amazement. *It's so far. It'll take me a hundred years to get there.*

Just keep walking. That's all you can do. This morning

you thought the forest would have no end, but you can see it for yourself right there. Eventually you'll get where you're going.

Kinetic battery charge to 50 percent...

Korden jumped and spun around to face the person who'd snuck up on him to whisper in his ear.

There was no one there. He was alone on the road.

"Who said that?" he shouted. Except he wasn't completely sure that anyone actually *said* anything; the words had sounded too contained to have been spoken aloud, the way they would indoors. His own voice came out flat and small on the open hilltop.

In fact...it seemed like this disembodied voice had been in his *head*.

"Hello?" he asked cautiously. "Is anyone there?"

A bird chirped, but otherwise, he received no answer. After standing still for another few minutes—straining his ears and scanning the surrounding area for signs of unfamiliar life—he readjusted his carry-pouch and started down the hill.

S.T.O.N.E.

1

The last half of the day proved to be much more enjoyable than the first, despite numerous complaints from his body. He ate a midday meal as he walked, allowing himself a larger helping of jerky and water to assuage his growing hunger, which had become a constantly niggling presence behind his thoughts. All this exercise must be burning through his energy reserves as fast as he could fill them back up. And the downhill direction gave his lungs a rest, but didn't do much for his sore feet. His good mood carried him onward though, even when the thick redwood canopy closed over him once more. He even found himself singing while he walked, belting out some of the bawdy chants that Allin had been so fond of, and trying to recreate that enchanting song Bibb played for him on his musical gadget. With the device burned to a cinder, the lovely voice singing in its exotic foreign language might exist only in his memory now.

As dusk descended, he came upon another vehicle rotting in the undergrowth by the side of the road. This one, however, was *huge*, and seemed to be comprised of two parts: a towering, rusted cockpit in front with only a few flakes of dark blue paint left to hint at its original color, and a boxy white wagon sixty or seventy pargs long that rolled behind it on a double row of wheels, many of which had been bent out of shape by the vehicle's weight. A phrase had once been written down the side in letters as tall as his leg, but they'd weathered away until he could only make out 'CNWA TRUKG.' He could only guess what must have powered a massive chariot like this, or what it had been used for. Maybe it had been some sort of armored troop transport for the Dark Wars that Tash told him about.

He climbed up inside the cockpit first, which stank of mildew. No bodies here, skeletal or otherwise, just two cracked leather seats and a dust-covered instrument panel. In the floor, he found a collection of waxy, crumpled paper bearing such exotic names as 'McDonalds', 'Taco Bell', and 'White Fortress', but a compartment set into the front panel contained a paper packet coated in some slick covering that unfolded into a huge rectangle. A collection of irregular, interlocked shapes of various colors splashed across the page, crisscrossed with squiggly lines and full of tiny labels. As usual, only his vast reading about the old world allowed him a frame of reference.

A map. He'd never seen one before, never needed one. The paper was yellowed and faded with age, but its glossy outer shell seemed to have prevented it from disintegrating entirely. Korden refolded it carefully and stuffed it into his bag for later inspection.

Before leaving, he sat in the pilot's chair and pretended to drive the huge vehicle. He turned the steering wheel, poked at buttons, turned dials, all while imagining himself driving through an actual city full of autos. A wire ran across the ceiling, and when he pulled it, a single baritone note blasted outside the vehicle, scattering a flock of sparrows in the canopy and frightening Korden so much he almost fell out the open door onto the pavement far below. After the initial shock wore off, he cautiously pulled the wire again, holding it down this time, and chuckled as the rumble of noise blatted across the forest. The fun ended a few seconds later though, when the siren wound down to a low mutter and then died altogether. Further pulling of the cord produced nothing.

At the rear of the long wagon, a set of double doors stood partially open, revealing a seam of darkness. The hinges were rusted in place. He grunted and pulled at them for several minutes, then closed his eyes and hauled not just with his muscles but with his *mind*, infusing the effort with a burst of artcraft. One of the doors squalled open and separated from its partner just enough for him to climb up and slip through.

The interior stretched away like a cave. He lit a *demno* as he stepped across the dirty metal floor.

A heavy metallic tang polluted the inside of the wagon. Most of the rectangular space lay empty, but the rear was occupied by boxes stacked to the ceiling, made from a thick, brown paper that he recognized as cardboard only from some of the hardback books in Skewtz' library (all of which were, he realized, now burned to ashes, as dead as their owner). Mildew and rot caused this outer covering to disintegrate at his touch.

Inside were smaller packages sealed in a clear wrapper that had preserved them from the elements, like the coating on the map. The label on these read 'Kools'. When he finally managed to peel one open, he found several rows of white cylinders that smelled faintly of tobacco but looked nothing like the plant that Bibb grew and stuffed into his pipe. Korden took a handful of these packs and dropped them into his bag. After determining the wagon held nothing else of value, he left the rest of the cargo and started back out.

Just before he jumped down from the door, a screech drifted through the forest.

Korden paused. That sound—a keening, high-pitched caterwaul—had definitely not been in his head. A few seconds later, it came again, vacillating between higher registers as it echoed among the trees. He thought it originated from somewhere to the southwest.

It seemed to have an angry undertone.

Suddenly, Korden regretted trumpeting the siren in the auto's cockpit.

From deep in the forest to the north, a second cry answered the first.

2

He hurried on after that, putting several more spans between himself and the cargo wagon before stopping for the night. When he did make camp this time, he did it while there was still enough light to see by. An idea had come into his head, and he wanted ample time to experiment with it.

Korden ventured away from the roadside for the first time, but never strayed far enough for it to leave his sight entirely. Again, the fear that he could be lost among these trees forever seemed very real. He searched for another meadow like the one from last night, and settled on a patch of dry earth with a thin roof of tangled branches. Before unpacking, he settled into his usual cross-legged position for faithing, got himself as still as possible, but instead of retreating inward, he reached out with his mind, combing through the forest with fingers of artcraft.

It took only a few minutes to find what he sought: a fat rabbit nestled in its den just a few hundred pargs away from his camp. Korden pressed upon its *mohol* more firmly, invasively, and felt it flinch away from the mental contact. He drew back, but didn't leave entirely. With the creature on the verge of flight, he sent out calm aquamarine waves until its tension drained away, then enticed the rabbit to emerge with the suggestion that it was starving, and a hearty meal lay in this direction.

He realized only an hour before that he needed no bow to hunt, not if he could commune as masterfully as Fortholm. Korden understood the theories behind it—the more base and impassive a life form, the easier its emotions were to influence—but Tash wasn't ready to teach him this discipline. If he wanted to extend his food supply, he would have to learn on his own.

The animal came slowly, hesitantly. Korden never forced his will upon it, just surrounded it with carefully planned emotions and desires, then let it come to its own conclusions. A few minutes after he began, the rabbit trundled cautiously into his clearing and right up to his knee. Korden gave thanks to the Upper before gently slitting the animal's throat.

3

That night, he managed to conjure a tiny flame in a pit bounded by stones, built it into a roaring fire with gathered kindling, then cleaned and spitted the rabbit. While he waited for it to cook, he got out the map he'd found, spread it on the ground, and studied it beside the flickering flames.

The top proclaimed it to be a 'US Road Atlas'. He knew those two letters also: the United States, the nation that existed before the Purges decimated its population. He traced the squiggling edges of the land with his finger, surrounded by water to the left and right, and other countries above and below whose names were not so familiar: the Sovereign Canadian Outlands, and Columbia Prime. Then he looked closer, at the endless collection of labels in all sizes. Some of the larger ones seemed to name the interlocking shapes that made up the country, or even stretch across several of these to designate entire tracts of land. The smallest, which littered the map in the thousands, had to be cities. He wondered which he was closest to. The lay of the land had probably changed much since this map's creation, but if he could at least figure out his location, then he could see where this road went, and what might lie ahead.

Another jolt of annoyance at the men who raised him caused his jaw to tighten. Here was another bit of knowledge the Olders hadn't deemed important enough to tell him. Redfen might not've known, that much he believed, but surely *they* were aware of where they'd settled so many years ago. But instead of practicality, they filled his head with fantasy. What benefit had they seen in keeping so much of the real world hidden from him, especially now that he was out in it?

Was that the Upper's 'divine plan,' Tash? he wondered. *To send me out into the wilderness with nothing more than 'go east' as advice? My choices can't be very true when I don't have enough information to make them.*

He ate blackened rabbit meat until his stomach felt tight, then stripped the remainder from the bones and wrapped it in burdock leaves to have for breakfast. Feeling extremely pleased with himself, he recreated his rudimentary alarm for an even wider perimeter—the process taking him longer this time, as he clumsily attempted to complete parts of the task with only artcraft—and then put down his bedroll and removed his sweat-stained tunic and dungarees. These he hung from a tree to air and sat down to take off his boots and wool socks, which had already developed multiple holes from his trek.

His feet were swollen and red beneath. The blister on his left had turned into a pus-filled crater, soon to be joined by others. He allocated a small portion of water to clean them, then propped them on his carry-pouch to help the swelling go down, just as Feegran always advised for such maladies. With some intense concentration, he squashed the pain down, dulling it in his own head enough so that he could sleep.

But he couldn't ignore them forever. His boots seemed to be the problem; he could've lived with their tight fit a long time back in the village, but usage this constant had taken a fast toll. And they just weren't designed for this level of wear and stress. Already the stitching along the sole appeared to be loose, and the soft spot on the bottom of his left boot had become a full-fledged hole.

Well, it was yet another concern on a long list, and he was too exhausted to fret over it now. He lay back on the ground in nothing but a pair of short breeches, stretched his sore muscles, and dropped into a dead, dreamless sleep as soon as his eyes closed.

4

And then snapped them open again sometime later.

A resonant buzzing filled his head, loud enough to vibrate his nasal cavity.

His bleary mind took several seconds to identify the sound of his early warning system, and then he scrambled to his knees.

The fire had guttered in the night. Only orange and white embers remained. Korden silenced his alarm with a thought and then squinted around his small camp in the darkness, seeking the Incarnate that must have snuck up on him. His hands combed the soil around him for the knife.

Without warning, a reptilian hiss came from his right, just an arm's length away. He leapt back with a cry of surprise, sprawling across his bedroll, and sensed rather than saw something low to the ground come streaking toward him. Korden kicked out on instinct, felt his bare foot connect with slick, plated flesh. His attacker grunted and dodged away. It swung wide around the ashes of the fire and came at Korden again from the side, nothing more than a blurred shadow and two yellow-green eyes that gleamed in the dim firelight.

This time, he had the presence of mind to do more than just react. Korden raised a hand and emitted a blast of art-craft like a thrown punch.

The force sent his attacker tumbling away through the dirt. It hissed again as it regained its feet, watching him with those chartreuse orbs, but seemed to reconsider an attack before launching through the air. The shape—three pargs long and spindly—sprang far over his head in a high arc, latched on to the base of the closest sequoia, and scampered toward the higher branches with the grace of a spider. He lost sight of it amid the dark canopy, but could still hear it rustling up there.

Korden crawled away from the creature that invaded his camp, but somewhere above him came a harsh screech that he instantly recognized.

Whatever had been howling in the distance earlier had caught up to him while he slept.

And it wasn't alone. The noise repeated again to his left, then once more to his right, and then the entire forest came alive around him. A chorus of angry banshee wails assailed him, along with a series of hollow *thoks* and *whaps* that must be his visitors hitting the trees. Branches rattled and leaves rained down on him. Korden got to his feet and spun in a helpless circle.

"*Go away!*" he shouted, covering his ears. The shrieks were loud enough to make his head throb. He opened his mind to probe at his attackers and was surprised to find the treetops filled with furious crimson auras. Hundreds of the small beings bounced and cavorted up there, leaping through the trees or swinging from branch to branch as they screamed down at him. He tried to soothe them as he had the rabbit, but to no avail. Not only were their motivations far more complex and alien than he could comprehend, but there were so many, and their emotions so high, that he would never be able to influence enough of them to make any difference in their overall demeanor.

And, as if his current predicament wasn't bad enough, that strange voice chose this moment to speak in his head again, the words perfectly audible even over the cacophony above him.

KINETIC BATTERY CHARGE TO MINIMUM FUNCTIONALITY LEVELS. POWERING UP! PLEASE STAND BY.

Something struck Korden in the right temple, just above his eye. He staggered, putting a hand to his forehead. The fingers came away wet. A second later, something else smashed into his bare shoulder hard enough to sting. He saw it when it fell to the ground, an acorn the size of his fist.

Then all the creatures in the trees began hurling objects down at him. Sticks and rocks struck him all over, leaving welts on his exposed skin. He tried to dodge them, but there were too many, and he was all but blind in the dark. Korden threw himself to the ground and covered his head with his arms, curling up into a pathetic ball, and shielded himself with a bubble of artcraft. The barrage continued, the missiles clattering against the invisible cover just inches from his body now.

"*Stop it!*" he pleaded. "*What are you, what do you want?*"

BASED ON VOCALIZATION, A 93 PERCENT PROBABILITY EXISTS THAT THE ANIMALS IN QUESTION ARE MONTEELAS.

"*Huh?*"

MONTEELAS: SPECIFIC TAXONOMY UNASSIGNED. ORIGINATION OF SPECIES, UNKNOWN. MOST RECENT ACCESSIBLE DATA INDICATES DNA LINKS BETWEEN GENERA *PAN* AND *BASILISCUS*. BELIEVED TO BE PART OF THE GREAT SPECIES EMERGENCE OF 2039 THAT BEGAN—

"*Slow down, I don't understand!*" Korden cut off the chipper voice, which spouted gibberish at a faster rate than Skewtz when the librarian really got going. Splitting his attention let more and more of his attackers' weapons through his mental force field, but since this voice seemed to understand what these creatures were, he couldn't afford to ignore it. He grabbed his carry-pouch and used it to cover part of his body while he asked, "Do you know why they're doing this?"

AFFIRMATIVE, WITH A 17 PERCENT MARGIN OF ERROR!

Korden waited as more projectiles rained down on him, several hard enough to bruise, but no further answer came. "All right, can you tell me?"

It is certainly within my operating parameters to do so.

A huge tree branch landed in the remains of his fire, spraying smoldering embers across Korden's leg. He cried out in pain. *"Then please tell me!"*

Monteelas are fiercely territorial. Behavioral psychology suggests they will not rest until intruders are driven from their boundaries. The only observed exception to this has been appeasement of the pack leader.

"'Appeasement?'"

Offerings of food have been known to end an assault in the wild.

"Food..."

Still blocking the hail of objects, Korden rolled toward the fire, where the last of his cooked rabbit still lay wrapped in leaves on the circle of stones. He thrust this up in the air with one hand and shouted, *"Here, do you want this? Take it!"*

The barrage stopped all at once. The forest fell silent.

Korden stayed in the same position, holding the pouch over his head with one hand and the meat in the air with the other, until he heard something heavy hit the ground just behind him. A wild, musky aroma assailed his nostrils. He dropped the bag, spilling its contents, then rolled over and peered into the darkness.

That shape from before sat just a short distance away. It moved toward him again, but cautiously this time. After a few seconds, it came close enough to the glowing remains of the campfire for Korden to get a look at it.

Mottled brown, reptilian scales covered the creature, but a layer of coarse black fur sprouted between the plates. While its body was long and sinewy—with a pair of stunted rear legs and a dragging tail that reminded Korden of a gecko—its muscular upper torso sported two lithe arms that ended in a full complement of multi-jointed digits. It moved with these limbs rather than its short legs, plodding quickly along on its knuckles as it approached. The structure of the beast looked awkward to him, more like two animals squashed together.

The monteela stopped and regarded him with squinted eyes. Eyes that might have a sickly bile-colored sheen, but that held unmistakable depth and intelligence. The head on its shoulders looked disproportionately large, with a prominent jaw that seemed to frown at him. A forked tongue emerged between its lips and flicked at the air.

Korden held out the rabbit as his next breath caught. The meat shook at the end of his fingers.

The creature raised a versatile arm and accepted the offering in one lumpy-knuckled hand with surprising gentleness. Korden had never seen an animal with an actual *hand*. It smelled the meat, touched it with that snakelike tongue, and then shoved the whole thing in its maw at once, chewing in great, slobbery bites as it continued to study him.

After it swallowed, the monteela threw back its head and gave a stuttered, grunting shout. A second later, the other creatures mimicked the noise overhead, then came a somber rustling as they moved away through the forest.

The leader of this strange pack issued a final derisive snort at Korden, then turned around and leapt into the night.

5

By the time he calmed enough to think rationally, dawn had settled upon the forest. Korden first tended to his injuries—mostly bruises and welts besides the cut on his scalp, which had already scabbed over—then dressed and set about cleaning up his camp. Once he'd found all of his belongings and swept them into a pile for repacking, he sat on the ground and listened to the cool sounds of the awakening forest. After a few moments, he asked cautiously, "Hello? Are...are you there?"

STANDING BY!

Even though he'd hoped for an answer, Korden still jumped. It was unsettling to have his head invaded by a voice that wasn't his own. He would've thought he was imagining it, if not for the information it gave him about the creatures.

"Thanks," Korden ventured. "I mean, for helping me."

GRATITUDE ACKNOWLEDGED.

"I, um...I thought they were gonna kill me."

AFFIRMATIVE! ODDS OF YOUR TERMINATION IN THE PREVIOUS SCENARIO WITHOUT MY INTERVENTION CALCULATED AT 99.3 PERCENT.

Korden frowned. He'd never heard anyone talk like this. The tone remained upbeat, almost cheerful, but he could barely follow the word choices.

Nevertheless, it felt wonderful just to be talking to someone else again. He hadn't realized how lonely he'd become after only two days until this very moment.

"So...who are you?"

Instead of answering his question, the pleasant voice cut off, and another, much sterner one droned, SAMPLE TRANSACTION LIMIT REACHED. TITLE AND LICENSING AGREEMENT TRANSFER INITIATED. PLEASE STATE YOUR NAME.

"Um, Korden. Korden Bright?"

BIORHYTHMS CONFIRMED. SECURITY VERIFIED. TITLE AND LICENSING TRANSFER COMPLETE. Then the friendly voice returned, saying, Congratulations, Mr. Bright, on your secondhand purchase of a Steinham's Telepathic On-line Network Encyclopedia! S.T.O.N.E: a product of Namenco, Incorporated, bringing you the very best in modern mental conveniences! Visit us on the encoded M-Net, or see an authorized dealer for a complete list of products! All rights reserved, Namenco, Inc. is in no way responsible for product usage.

Korden latched on to only one word among the dense, fast-paced litany: *stone*. Why did that seem so familiar?

You have one new message waiting, sir. Would you like me to play it?

"I...uh...all right..."

And then a new voice filled his head, one that surprised a gleeful laugh out of him.

Hello, lad.

"Bibb!" he exclaimed. "Are you all right?" But the Older continued speaking as though he hadn't heard the question, and Korden realized this wasn't a form of communication, but just some leftover impression, the aural equivalent of the photos he'd found.

If you're hearing this, then Stone is fully charged and blabbing his head off once more. Neural telepathy can be a bit off-putting, but hopefully he didn't frighten you too much. I told you he was no rock, now didn't I?

Korden dug through the pile of items that had fallen out of his carry-pouch until he found the smooth white hunk of mineral Bibb slipped into his palm just before he left the village. He flipped it over and over in his hand, studying it from all angles as he listened to the rest of the message.

As you may've figured out on your own, Stone is a knowledge repository that forms a mental connection with his owner, which is now you. He sees what you see, hears what you hear, feels what you feel, and you can give him orders just by thinking. Models like him were banned pretty much instantly in the old days—mostly because they were designed for idiot kids like me to use in school under their teachers' noses. And, trust me, I never would've passed the seventh grade without him feeding me the answers to every test. My own son played with him for a bit, but he's been sitting idle for a long, long time. Even though his information is likely to be outdated, I figured he might be able to help you survive, or at least keep you from feeling so alone. Take care of him, and yourself. All our hopes go with you.

6

The message finished. Korden sat unmoving until something wet dripped onto his arm. He wiped at the silent tears streaming down his face and then held the rock-like object up to his face. This close, he could see faint lines etched into the surface that were far too straight to be natural. They ran the circumference in a crisscrossing pattern.

"Are you really in there?" he asked.

THIS QUERY IS FLAWED. WHILE IT IS TECHNICALLY TRUE THAT THE COMPONENTS WHICH MAKE UP MY PHYSICAL BODY DO EXIST WITHIN THE PROTECTIVE CASING YOU HOLD, MY INTERFACE—WHICH I INFER TO BE THE TRUE TARGET OF YOUR INQUIRY—EXISTS ONLY WITHIN THE NEURAL PATHWAYS OF YOUR OWN BRAIN.

"Uh…"

CLARIFYING: WITHOUT YOUR CONSCIOUSNESS, I HAVE NO MEDIUM TO DELIBERATE, COMMUNICATE, OR INFLUENCE THE OUTSIDE WORLD. OR, TO GIVE A POPULAR QUOTE FROM THE

NEWSWEEK ARTICLE DISCUSSING THE ADVENT OF TELEPATHIC ARTIFICIAL INTELLIGENCE: *YOU* THINK, THEREFORE *I* AM.

"Yeah, that clarified it. I guess."

MY SELF-DIAGNOSTIC IS 87 PERCENT COMPLETE! IF THIS IS A CONVENIENT TIME FOR YOU, PLEASE ATTEMPT MENTAL COMMUNICATION TO TEST NEURAL LINK.

Korden took a moment to interpret this, then closed his eyes and thought, *Can you hear me?*

AFFIRMATIVE! NEURAL LINK VIABLE, WITH A RANGE OF UP TO 25 METERS. OR 82 'PARGS,' IF YOU PREFER. ALL SYSTEMS OPERATIONAL, MR. BRIGHT! HOWEVER, I DETECT NO WIRELESS CONNECTION TO THE ENCODED M-NET.

It was jarring enough that this gadget could speak in his head, but the fact that it could read his own mind made the small hairs at the base of Korden's neck prickle uncomfortably. This wasn't like reading someone's *mohol* and interpreting their emotions; this was an invasion of his innermost sanctum. He could only liken it to someone moving in to his brain to share the space there, an invisible entity that ensured he would never have privacy again.

ANY INTRUSION IS UNINTENTIONAL, Stone assured him. Which, unfortunately, only served to confirm his fear. WOULD YOU LIKE ME TO SEVER THE TWO-WAY LINK AND ONLY RECEIVE COMMANDS ORALLY?

"No, it's all right," Korden said quickly. He actually felt embarrassed at having been caught thinking this, then realized that 'Stone' undoubtedly knew this now also. "I guess it'll just take some getting used to."

I CAN PLAY MY TUTORIAL IF YOU WISH.

"Er, thanks, not right now." Korden knew he was being ridiculous; after all, it was only a gadget, no matter how much it might seem like a person.

THIS IS TRUE. I AM NOT PROGRAMMED TO TAKE OFFENSE OR PLEASURE AT ANYTHING YOU THINK, AND TO INTERJECT ONLY WHEN I CAN BE OF ASSISTANCE. IN FACT, ANY EMOTIONALITY I EXHIBIT AT ALL IS DUE ONLY TO MY REALEMOTE SOFTWARE PACKAGE, AND IS INTENDED TO MAKE YOU FEEL MORE COMFORTABLE WITH ME. MY PURPOSE IS BUT TO SERVE YOU!

Korden sighed. "All right, so...what kind of things can you tell me?"

MY KNOWLEDGE STORE IS BASED ON THE VAST FILES OF GREGORY STEINHAM'S ONLINE ENCYCLOPEDIA, ELEVENTH EDITION. I CAN LOOK UP ENTRIES ON ANY SUBJECT YOU WISH. BUT BE WARNED, WITHOUT AN UPLINK TO THE M-NET, I HAVE NO METHOD OF VERIFYING INFORMATION. ACCORDING TO MY INTERNAL CLOCK, I HAVE RECEIVED NO SYSTEM UPDATES FOR 287 YEARS, 3 MONTHS, 18 DAYS, AND 5 HOURS.

Korden might not understand every word, but he found the gist easier and easier to get. Two-hundred and eighty-seven years since this mind-reading gizmo last had any contact with the outside world. Could Bibb possibly be so old? He racked his head, trying to figure out what information would be most useful to him now, and his eye landed on the tightly folded paper packet in the pile of objects at his feet.

"Can you tell me where we are on this map?"

MY INTERNAL COMPASS AND PEDOMETER ARE FUNCTIONAL, BUT GPS SYSTEMS ARE ALSO UNRESPONSIVE. I APOLOGIZE, BUT WITHOUT A POINT OF REFERENCE, I CANNOT CONFIRM AN EXACT COORDINATE.

"Oh."

HOWEVER, Stone continued, in his ever-chipper voice, BASED ON VISUAL IDENTIFICATION OF SURROUNDING FLORA—PRIMARILY *SEQUOIA SEMPERVIRENS*—AND CROSS REFERENCING WITH PREFERRED MONTEELA CLIMATES AND MY LAST KNOWN SATEL-

LITE POSITION, AND, OF COURSE, FACTORING IN MASSIVE ENVIRONMENTAL SHIFTS THAT MAY HAVE OCCURRED DURING MY PROLONGED IDLE STATUS, I CALCULATE A 76 PERCENT CHANCE THAT WE ARE CURRENTLY LOCATED WITHIN THE BOUNDARIES OF REDWOOD NATIONAL PARK, AT CRESCENT CITY, CALIFORNIA.

Amid a warm gush of excitement, Korden yanked the map from the pile and spread it back on the ground. He squinted in the dim light as he searched the collection of irregular boxes for the exotic-sounding place Stone named. And, sure enough, he found one labeled 'California' in large, capital letters, a long rectangle with a bend in the middle that took up nearly the entire coast along the left side of the map. He looked closer and even found a tiny patch of dark green called 'Redwood National Forest' isolated all by itself on the edge.

Was that really it? Where he'd lived his whole life, a mere speck amidst this huge expanse? None of the squiggly lines which ran across the map—which Korden now realized must be roads—went anywhere near the place, and he could find no mention of this Crescent City anywhere nearby. Perhaps the gadget was mistaken after all.

THE GEOGRAPHY OF THE LAND MAY HAVE CHANGED SINCE MY LAST UPDATE, Stone admitted, his eagerness becoming apologetic. IT IS ALSO POSSIBLE THAT ANY NEARBY ROADS ARE TOO INSIGNIFICANT TO BE LISTED ON THIS MAP.

Korden started to tell him not to worry, but was interrupted by the sound of more screeches from the direction the monteela pack had gone, followed by a much deeper roar that seemed to rattle the leaves around them.

"Maybe we should get moving," Korden said.

THIS COURSE OF ACTION IS ADVISABLE, Stone agreed.

Relatable Entries

1

The next three days passed in a blur for Korden.

He walked, he slept, he ate, he walked more. He trudged through the forest, which had long since lost its creepiness and foreboding, and actually began to all look the same. The monotony of tree after tree—of having no sign of progress in the unchanging landscape—dulled his senses until he felt like he was asleep as he moved, drifting through a weary dream.

The village seemed further away with each passing day. Not just physically, but mentally. His old routines, his lessons, his home...they all seemed like something he'd read about, the setting for someone else's life. At one point, he was dismayed to find that he could no longer remember his father's face. When he tried, the image in his head resembled one of Tash's paintings; the general shape was there, but the details were fuzzy. The same was true for his *den-so*, and the rest of the Olders, all of it fading from his head after less than a week. And the more Korden tried to hold on to the scraps of these memories, the more they seemed to unravel.

What would it be like in another week? Or an entire *season?*

He had trouble even believing that this new life of his would go on that long. That he wouldn't wake up tomorrow back in his own bed, with his father making breakfast in the other room before they headed down into the village together.

The deeper he got into the forest, the more temperatures dropped into a pleasantly cool range. A heavy ground mist settled between the trees each morning and lay thick across the road, dampening his pants below the knee and then drying up by midday. Once Burning Season truly got underway, Korden knew the mist would turn into dense fog that hung over even the highest boughs, nature's way of sheltering them from the relentless sun. When that happened, visibility would shorten, suspending him in a grayish, eternal void. He intended to be out of the sequoia forest long before then.

Thunder grumbled often from the north, but not a drop of rain fell, to the dismay of his rapidly dwindling water supply. The undergrowth grew wilder and thicker, clinging skilne and clover and ferns encroaching on the road once more, the smaller pine and alder trees increased in frequency until it felt as though he were walking through woods within woods, and the redwood canopy above them became so thick that, at times, it choked off the sunlight entirely, forming a tunnel over the pavement that allowed deep shadows to puddle on the forest floor. As claustrophobic as the Barrier had made him all these years, being trapped in this catacomb of leaves and branches proved far worse. A strange new yearning blossomed in Korden, a need for sky and open spaces that he could only liken to starvation.

And, while the bruises and cuts from his encounter with the monteelas healed quickly, his feet complained ever more fiercely. His boots now felt like cruel torture devices that shrank a little more each day. The blisters cracked open and bled, the muscles along his arches and up his calves became sore and stiffened. But he never once stopped moving. Some of the pain he blocked out by concentrating, and conversation with Stone served to distract him even further.

Korden soon found the little machine (TECHNICALLY SPEAKING, I AM MORE OF A COMPUTER THAN A MACHINE, Stone told him, before launching into a dissertation about the differences between the two) to be an agreeable enough traveling companion, one that kept him from surrendering entirely to this melancholy, even if he (*it?*) did have a tendency to be longwinded. All of the information he offered was useful—his knowledge of edible plants had already stretched the food supply—and he asked a steady stream of personal questions about Korden's life and interests in order to 'calibrate his search inquiries more efficiently.' He seemed particularly excited about their 'quest,' although unsatisfied about the 'lack of input' on how they were supposed to go about it. Korden was thankful for the company, but growing up in a village full of meditational old men had given him an appreciation for silence, a trait that Tash claimed yielded far better results than speech ever could. After a day and a half of having the computer eagerly attempt to answer every question that crossed his mind, no matter how fleeting, Korden felt mentally exhausted. When he stopped midmorning on the second day to eat a bit of jerky and force himself to take a faithing break, he pleaded with Stone to give him thirty minutes of uninterrupted peace.

His irritation must have been apparent, because even when he got back up and continued on, Stone remained uncharacteristically quiet. Korden took the opportunity to get in some practice for the first time since the day after his departure from the village as he ambled along the strip of weed-choked grass beside the road.

Even after such a short break from his lessons, his mind felt sluggish and weak, like an unused muscle trembling from exertion. Tash wouldn't have been happy. Korden could hear him now, saying *That's how we lost tha knowledge in tha first place,* ghammer. *We didn't use it, so we forgot it.* He made a vow to take time each day to faith and practice, no matter what else came.

He'd just managed to conjure and sustain a crackling sapphire flame in the palm of one hand—shaping it into a pine cone-sized sphere and juggling it briefly—when Stone's voice came into his head.

MAY I SPEAK?

Korden closed his hand, extinguishing the fireball. "Sure, go ahead." He'd decided that speaking aloud made the process of conversing telepathically much less strange.

MY LOGIC CIRCUITRY SEEMS TO BE MALFUNCTIONING. THIS DOES NOT COMPUTE.

"Uh...what?"

CLARIFYING: INANIMATE OBJECTS CANNOT BREAK THE HOLD OF GRAVITY WITHOUT PROPULSION, AND COMBUSTION CANNOT BE ACHIEVED WITHOUT FUEL OR CATALYST. THIS DEFIES THE LAWS OF PHYSICS.

The puzzlement in his statements made Korden grin. Nice to know something that Stone didn't, for a change. He levitated a stick into the air and caught it in one hand. "I guess you were switched off long before Bibb started crafting."

THE CLOSEST DEFINITION I CAN FIND FOR THIS BEHAVIOR IN MY FILES IS 'MAGIC': THE POWER OF INFLUENCING EVENTS BY SUPERNATURAL FORCE. MOST PRACTICAL ENTRIES ASSERT THIS PHENOMENON IS FAKE; AN ILLUSION; A TRICK PER-

PETRATED BY SKILLED PERFORMANCE ARTISTS. YET I SENSE
NO DECEIT FROM YOUR BIORHYTHMS.

"It isn't fake!" Korden couldn't keep the indignation
from his voice. He didn't even know why the idea should
offend him so much.

MY APOLOGIES, SIR. I DID NOT MEAN TO CAST ASPERSIONS,
ONLY TO ASCERTAIN IF THIS IS ACCOMPLISHED BY A FORM OF
TECHNOLOGY WITH WHICH I AM UNAWARE. I HAVE BEEN POWERED
DOWN FOR A SIGNIFICANT AMOUNT OF TIME, AND THE NOTED
SCIENCE-FICTION AUTHOR ARTHUR W. CLARKE POSITED THAT
ANY SUFFICIENTLY ADVANCED TECHNOLOGY WOULD BE INDIS-
TINGUISHABLE FROM MAGIC.

"It's not technology, and it's not magic either. It's called
artcraft. Don't you have anything in your *files* about that?"

SEARCHING… 553,968 RESULTS RETURNED. FILTERING FOR
PROBABLE RELATABILITY, CROSS-REFERENCING WITH KEYWORD
'MAGIC'… ONE RELIABLE RESULT RETURNED. *NEW YORK TIMES*
ONLINE HOLO-BLOG POSTED BY MARCUS EVANS, DATED AP-
PROXIMATELY ONE WEEK BEFORE MY LAST M-NET UPDATE.
HEADLINE: *'SO-CALLED 'MIRACLE MAN' OF BOCA RATON NO
HOAX'*. I HAVE AN AUDIO FILE. WOULD YOU LIKE TO HEAR IT?

Korden stopped walking. He had no idea what a 'blog'
or a 'New York Times' were, but he was very interested in
whatever bit of ancient information the computer had dug
up. "Yes, please."

With a soft *bleep*, the computer obliged.

2

The new voice that Korden heard (the voice of someone who died a long time ago, he realized) was deeper than
Stone's, and, towards the end of its tale, trembled with bare-

ly-concealed emotion. The words were measured and fluid, never halting or stumbling, more like someone with a prepared speech. Korden found a nearby tree with a knothole big enough for him to sit in and give his feet a rest, then listened to the story with rapt attention:

> Even as most of Europe succumbs to the Dark Filament's unceasing advance, and the nations of the western hemisphere use the last of their military might to push back the hordes of so-called 'Incarnates' amassing throughout South America, I was recently reminded that miracles can happen in this world.
>
> Maybe you heard the rumors that began leaking out of Florida several weeks ago about a man able to accomplish seemingly mystical feats: levitation, telepathy, elemental control, etc, like some wizard in a fantasy story. If you did, you probably had too many other things on your mind to pay them much attention. Even with their synchronicity of detail, most of these could've been dismissed as cons or urban legends--or even just the mounting hysteria that seems to grip every corner of the country these days--but when I received an email from a former editor in Boca Raton that claimed to have firsthand knowledge of this Miracle Man healing the sick and lame, I knew it bore investigation. After all, if they say these monsters taking over the world can only be killed by those with 'faith,' then why should the second coming of Christ be a surprise, right?

I hopped a NorthTrans to Atlanta last week, which was as close as I could get to my destination with all stratoliners going anywhere filled to capacity. It turned out to be one of the last scheduled flights out before JFK closed its doors for good due to the energy crisis; let's just say, if you were planning to fly any time in the foreseeable future, you better be listed in last year's Forbes 500. And in Atlanta, I found not a single rental skiff, hovertread, or even a ground car available in the entire city, and nearly all public modes of transportation had ceased operation. In the end, I hitchhiked most of the way to Boca Raton, but I'll spare you my apocalyptic version of Kerouac.

In Boca, the streets were deserted, all commerce shuttered. When I met my associate at his home, I learned that most of the city had been abandoned because of a recent Incarnate sighting in Fort Lauderdale that turned out to be completely false. By the time the rumor was squashed, most people had already taken their children and fled west. The only citizens left now were those too old to have anything to fear and no family to protect, turning the retirement-oriented community into a true elderly paradise.

I have known Ben Parsons for a decade, worked under him at the *Herald* for four years, and, in all that time, I have never seen the man without his cane, the result of withered leg muscles from contracting Ferrior's Disease as a child, during the resurgence of '94. Implants were unable to give him back full mobility, but at least he didn't have to spend life in a chair.

However, the Ben that came out to meet me on the sidewalk in front of his house carried no cane, and moved with the spritely step of a twelve-year-old ballerina. I made a point of not commenting on this while we greeted one another.

"I promise," he finally said, glancing at me with uncharacteristic shyness, "that you didn't come all this way for nothing."

"I hope not, because I probably won't be able to get home any time soon."

"It'll be worth it. Everyone needs to know what's happening here. I would've done the story myself, but the few contacts I have left all abandoned their posts. You know, to…to be with their families."

To be with their families. The way Ben said it made it sound as if the whole world had been diagnosed with terminal cancer, but I understood his meaning. My own mother calls me at least once a day for a tearful conversation full of too many goodbyes, as I'm sure most of your loved ones do. The human race has been fighting the Filament for a long time now, and, though they may have just reached America's doorstep, I think most of us started giving up hope right around the time the Russians fell. Now we're all just retreating, closing up shop and turning off the lights, waiting for the Incarnates to get here and sweep us away in a tide of darkness.

But I ignored these thoughts as I pointed at his fully functional legs and said, "I suppose by 'what's happening here,' you mean this."

Ben grinned at me like a dopey teenager. "That, and so much more, Marcus. This could be the start of something big."

I didn't know what to think as he drove me to a nursing home overlooking the coast, a place whose name I will not divulge in order to give its last remaining residents some peace. I could see the evidence of Ben's healed legs, and knew that he wasn't one to be duped by charlatans and infomercials, but at the same time, I just couldn't let myself indulge in a fantasy. I've always believed that a healthy dose of skepticism is the key to true objectivity.

The staff of this assisted living community had left, and the power was out. We walked down dark, stuffy hallways, past rooms from which curious senior citizens emerged to watch us pass. One of them--a feisty old specimen with blue-tinted hair--touched my shoulder lightly and asked,

"You're here to see *him*, aren't you?" Before I could even feign ignorance, she raised her voice and proclaimed, "He's sent to us from the Lord himself! To deliver us from the coming evil! Oh, praise God!" The rest of the old folks murmured their agreement.

I shot a glance at Ben, who only listened to the woman stone-faced. When we walked away, I whispered, "Your guy's got himself the beginnings of a nice little geriatric cult here."

Ben shook his head. "I don't know about all that coming-from-the-Lord bit, but he's the real deal, Marcus. You'll see." He stopped at one closed door from which classical music drifted. Ben raised his fist to knock, but the knob turned before his knuckles could touch the veneered wood.

The door swung open. No one stood on the other side.

"So the magic show begins." I rolled my eyes. If this was the best the Miracle Man could show me, I wouldn't be here long. I started to step through, then realized Ben didn't intend to follow. "What are you doing?"

"You need to see this for yourself, with an open mind. If I go in with you, you'll just be trying to debunk him the whole time because you know I'm watching."

I didn't argue with that, mostly because he might have a point. I just turned away and walked into the room. The power was off in here also, but the curtains on the room's only window had been pulled down and the glass opened to allow sunlight and sea breeze to stream through. A battery operated MP3 player on the sill played that soft classical music I'd heard from outside.

Before I could even address the room's sole occupant, I stood and gazed around at the sketches. I mean, how could I not? They were everywhere, sheets of paper ranging from notebook- to poster-sized and even a few larger, all torn from pads or spirals and tacked crookedly to the walls or taped to every vertical surface and lying in stacks on the dresser and table, like a hoarder that collects art instead of old soup cans. My eye wandered across them, a cornucopia of both color and black-and-white mediums, some of the subjects recognizable--still-life renderings of fruit bowls and glass vases--but others just smeared or scratchy depictions of people whose roughness was either intentional or amateurish. I wouldn't know a da Vinci painting from a five-year-old's scribbling, but my gut told me these would never hang in a museum.

"You can have one, if you like," a voice said over the violin from the speakers. I turned to the hospital bed against the left wall and found a thin, liver-spotted man sitting up against a mountain of pillows. A sketchpad lay across his stomach, and he clutched a charcoal pencil in one fist, frozen in the act of drawing bold black lines as he regarded me.

"You did all of these?" I asked, gesturing around the room.

He nodded. "Three months ago, I'd never so much as drawn a stick figure. Then, one day, I just started sketching. I felt like I had to. Like... my soul needed it. And the more I did, the more I found they helped me to concentrate. To commune."

"*Commune?*" The word choice caught my attention. "Commune with *who?* God?"

He shrugged noncommittally and ignored my question. "Go ahead, take one. Hell, take a dozen."

"Oh, I don't know. They're all so good, I wouldn't be able to pick a favorite."

He rolled his eyes and grunted. "Flattery might get you everywhere, but I find that patronization only gets you a swift kick in the ass."

I laughed.

"So you're the reporter," he continued. "The one from New York. Your friend told me you were coming to meet me. The name's Oliver Truitt." He offered a hand that I shook, but his bony fingers lingered in mine. "Tell me, Mr. Evans…what's it like out there?"

"Bad," I answered. "The Incarnates are sweeping north even as we speak, 'purging' every child in their path, as they put it, along with anyone who tries to stop them. Spontaneous cells have shown up all over the country and even up in the Sovereignty. Overseas, that disgusting black cloud is cutting a line right through Europe and Africa, but a contact in D.C. told me the last estimates indicated we could all be living under it in a matter of weeks." I pulled my hand from his and decided to get to the heart of the matter, without the usual delicacy that I show my subjects. "The people are losing hope, and they're ready to believe in anything. Which is why I've travelled across the country to hunt down Oliver Truitt, the Miracle Man, and see if his abilities are anything more than parlor tricks."

Truitt gave a tired sort of nod, then sighed and settled back on the pillows. "I never wanted attention or publicity, Mr. Evans. I don't ask for money to let folks watch me perform, like some carnival sideshow. All I have done here is try to make life better for my friends."

"Fair enough. But just because you're not profiting doesn't mean your abilities are genuine. There are a hundred other reasons you could be faking, including good old-fashioned insanity, and so far I haven't seen anything to convince me otherwise."

He raised a hand and muttered a quick bit of gibberish that I didn't catch. The MP3 player on the windowsill snapped off, and the sketchpad in his lap rose smoothly into the air, surrounded by a sort of transparent red aura, and sailed just inches in front of me. It floated across the room, the pages flipping shut just before it settled on a stack of pictures like a bird touching down in its nest.

"Well…that was a start," I said. I had seen no wires, nothing other than that light maroon haze, but any magician worth a damn could perform stunts that basic. Hell, there are plenty of flying children's toys that can be controlled through neural telepathy in the same way.

The only difference being, they still have to be *capable* of flight, through a hover engine or magneto-booster, neither of which Truitt's sketchpad were fitted with.

"First of all, they are not *my* abilities," Truitt clarified. "Nor really abilities at all. I am not telekinetic or pyrokinetic or any other label science might wish to place on me. The use of artcraft is a gift."

"Artcraft?" I scrambled in my pocket, digging for my holo-corder so I could begin the interview. Truitt formed a fist in the air and tugged slightly, as though holding an invisible rope. At the same time, I felt something encircle my wrist--just a feather-light band of pressure--and gently pull my hand out of my pocket.

"Please, Mr. Evans, no pictures, no holo-casts. You can go back and tell whatever stories you want to your readers, but, as I said, I'm no carnival sideshow, and I have no wish to become one."

I nodded numbly, rubbing my wrist where that odd pressure had gripped me and racking my brain for an explanation on how such a thing could be done. "Is that what you call it? Artcraft?"

"Yes. It comes from one's will, and is fueled by one's creativity. Not skill, mind you, nor talent, but rather, the raw need to express one's self." His fist still hung in the air. He opened his fingers at this point to reveal a tiny flame dancing on his palm.

"But you just said it's not an ability."

The flame danced in his hand, weaving between his fingers. "And it is not. I merely channel the artcraft as it flows through me, and bend it to my will."

"How did you learn to--?"

"I can't tell you what you want to know," Truitt interrupted me, blowing the flame out like a candle. "I don't know how I learned to do this. I didn't watch a self-help vid or bump my head and wake up with superpowers. If truth be told, I suspect this is something mankind knew how to do in its earliest days, and then forgot. As for me, one day, a few weeks ago, I simply woke up and could feel His presence."

"God?" I asked again. "Is that what this is about? The saving of our souls after the Incarnates get through with the rest of us?"

Truitt smiled dreamily and shook his head. "Not God. The Upper."

"Upper? Upper what?"

Truitt held out both hands to me this time. "It's time for a true demonstration, Mr. Evans. Something not even you can doubt. I suspect that's the only way I'll ever get you to leave me in peace. Come closer, if you would."

I hesitated, suddenly not wanting to give him any further opportunity to amaze me. I never could stand to feel gullible, but, at the same time, I had come too far to turn away now. I approached the bed and bent down. Truitt put his hands on the sides of my face like any two-bit faith healer and rested his thumbs gently on my eyelids, forcing them closed. I heard him muttering again, that strange, broken language, and then...

(it was here that the calm, measured demeanor of the speaker broke down, and each word grew heavy with confused emotion)

I...well, I guess...the only way for me to describe what happened next is for you to imagine a door opening somewhere in my mind...or maybe a dam is more accurate, a wall that I never even knew existed, and instead of water...it was holding back this...this raging river of...hell, I still don't know what it was. But this feeling--this...*energy*--flowed through me, setting my nerve endings on fire. And I don't mean in a painful way. Not at all. In fact, it was a comforting presence...one that made me feel both happy and safe.

Like I wasn't alone.

All the same, I jerked away from Truitt as if he had just tried to open my throat with a razor.

"What...what did you do to me?" I gasped.

"Gave you a glimpse," the old man said simply. "Opened the conduit to the Upper in your mind. That was artcraft you felt flowing through you. If you're a creative type, and you keep at it, you might be able to harness it, too."

"No. No, that's...impossible," I said. And then, looking at him with what I'm sure must've resembled horror, "What are you?"

"I don't know," he said thoughtfully, "but I don't think I'm the only one. I can sense others out there. People who are waking up to this power. Some of them want to help, just like me. Others...not so much."

"Help *what?* Are you talking about the Filament? Can you...can you really stop them?" I felt ashamed at the sudden excitement that surged through me. Not because it showed how deeply I had already bought into Truitt's story, but because, for the first time, I realized how sure I was that I would be dead some time in the very near future, that--just like all those people who had gone *to be with their families*--my life had become about killing time until the Incarnates finally got here.

Truitt said, "I don't think so. Not by myself, certainly. But soon, I'm going to leave here, to try and find those others. If we marshal our power, then...who knows?"

The stifling air in that room suddenly felt too thick to breathe. I turned and lurched away from Truitt's bed, out into the hallway, and past Ben, running away before he could catch me. I needed time to think, to process, and I had to be alone to do it.

The following day, I returned to the retirement home with a list of questions for Truitt, only to find the man gone. The other residents told me he had left in the night, the blue-haired lady proclaiming that he left to 'smite the face of evil.' That made me think of David and Goliath, for some reason.

I post this now from a motel in Orlando--one of the few that still has M-Net access--as I search for anything that might be able to get me home again. From what I hear, the Incarnates have broken through the battle line at the Panama Canal and are chewing their way up through Central America, and a cell in Montreal has begun to gain ground, like a tumorous growth. Cities around the country are in chaos. The carefully constructed walls of civilization are tumbling down around us.

But even with things so bleak, I find myself smiling. Oliver Truitt seems to have ignited a spark in me--so much like the tiny dancing flame in his palm--and now, I would like to do the same for you, by spreading word of his existence. I may not know why he can do these amazing things any more than he does, but I do believe he is, as my associate said, the real deal.

All we can do now is wait to see if he--and the others like him--can pull off the biggest miracle of all.

3

WAS THIS ENTRY HELPFUL? Stone asked.

Korden took a while to answer. "I guess so."

ARE YOU CERTAIN? I DETECT BIORHYTHMIC INDICATORS OF DEPRESSION. IF THIS ENTRY IS IRRELEVANT, I CAN FLAG IT IN MY DATABASE.

"No, it's not that." While Korden understood very little of the details in the recorded message—'stratoliners' and 'editors' and 'nursing homes' were as foreign to him as any image in the book of fotos had been—but he certainly recognized that feeling the speaker described, the one like a raging torrent of energy ripping through your veins. This had been a story about one of the first Olders. He wondered if he could find this 'Boca Raton' on the map. "It's just...I guess they weren't able to do much. To stop the Incarnates, I mean. And if they couldn't...how will I?"

THIS IS THE CAUSE OF YOUR DISTRESS?

"A little. I just wish I knew more about what happened. Can you find anything else about this man Oliver Truitt?"

SEARCHING… 3,679,014 RESULTS RETURNED. NONE SUGGEST RELATABILITY WITH KEYWORDS 'ARTCRAFT' OR 'MAGIC'.

"What about the Dark Filament?" Korden asked, suddenly excited. How had he not thought to ask before? "What do you know about that?"

SEARCHING… OVER SEVEN TRILLION RESULTS RETURNED.

74 PERCENT SUGGEST RELATABILITY. WOULD YOU LIKE ME TO BEGIN LISTING THEM?

"No, that's all right." There might be useful information buried in Stone's files, but it would probably take forever to find it.

IF YOU WISH, I CAN BEGIN COMPILING AVAILABLE DATA FROM MY RECORDS ABOUT THIS 'DARK FILAMENT' IN AN EFFORT TO FORM A COHERENT PICTURE OF THE TOPIC UP UNTIL THE POINT OF MY COMMUNICATION SEVERANCE. BE WARNED: THIS PROCESS WOULD TAKE SEVERAL HUNDRED THOUSAND COMPUTATIONAL CYCLES. NORMAL OPERATIONS COULD EXPERIENCE LAG.

"Does that mean you won't be able to talk as much?"

AFFIRMATIVE.

"Stone...do whatever you have to."

4

During the early afternoon on the third day—five days after leaving the village—a cloud of mosquitoes and gnats descended upon Korden and set about chewing him to pieces, buzzing about his face so thickly he could barely keep his eyes open, and reduced him to a state of constantly swatting misery. An hour later, he found out why. The road took a sharp turn to the north, the trees along the right side vanished, and he found himself on the shore of the vast lake he'd glimpsed from the high ridgeback.

Before this, the largest body of water he'd ever seen was the shallow, scummy pond to the west of the village, just inside the Barrier, where he learned to swim, and it looked nowhere near as beautiful as this. The surface was a glittering reflection of sky and as flat as a plate all the way to the rocky far shore, which appeared to be several spans away. The redwoods there grew on another slight upgrade, the tops high enough to hide the shadow of the Filament on the horizon. To the north, the lake followed the steep curve of the road, stretching beyond his view. Korden marveled for several long seconds while waving gnats out of his face, basking in the sun after so long hemmed in by the forest, then abruptly dropped his belongings, stripped out of his filthy clothes, hobbled down the rock- and shell-littered beach naked, and dove into the lake, despite Stone's cautions. The sun had warmed the water, but on his bitten, bug-ravaged skin and sore feet, it felt heavenly. Fish followed him in a cloud through the clear blue pool, completely unafraid, crappie and huge trout that made his mouth water.

Korden bathed as best he could, then swam so far out from shore that Stone's voice faded to a distant whisper in his head. He never imagined it could feel so good just to move through the water without his toes touching bottom. He laughed and splashed about until his muscles trembled and his breaths rattled in his chest.

For the first time since watching everyone and everything he loved be destroyed, he felt happy.

He'd dreamed of freedom like this for so long.

That's great, Kord…but was it worth the cost?

A flush of guilt warmed his cheeks. Even though he knew he would gladly give this experience up in a heartbeat to have his father back, the splendor of the moment was ruined.

Back on the shore, he cleaned all his clothes, wrung them out, and hung them in the trees on the opposite side of the road to dry. When the mosquitoes found him again, he took Stone's advice and smeared a thin layer of mud on his skin. He refilled his water skin from the lake only after holding some of the liquid on his tongue, so that Stone could 'use his receptors to test for potability'. The computer even found an entry with step-by-step instructions for catching fish, and, by the time the sun sank into the tree line at his back, Korden had built a rudimentary net out of branches, coaxed several of the larger trout into it, and fried them up on a flat rock for supper.

He was beginning to understand how technology could make life easier…and that insight scared him. If Tash was right, then reliance on computers and machines would only lead him farther from the Upper. He spent the next hour faithing as twilight fell, each star emerging along with its twin painted across the surface of the lake, then wrote in his journal until it was too dark to see the pages anymore.

As he put the leather-bound book away, his hand brushed against the hard cylinder of the gun. Korden pulled it out and held it in his lap, running a finger along the curves. He had no inkling about how to care for such a weapon. His father mentioned oiling the piece, but now he would never be able to show Korden how to do it.

SPRINGFIELD M1911 .45 CALIBER SEMI-AUTOMATIC PISTOL, DISCONTINUED FOR MILITARY USE IN 2104 IN FAVOR OF HIGH-DENSITY PLASMA WEAPONRY, BUT REMAINED THE MOST POPULAR HANDGUN ON THE CIVILIAN MARKET. I HAVE ENTRIES WITH COMPLETE INSTRUCTIONS FOR DISASSEMBLY AND CLEANING.

"Oh. That's good."

CONTRARY TO YOUR ASSERTION, BIORHYTHMS INDICATE THIS DOES NOT PLEASE YOU.

"No, it does. Really. It's just…Redfen…my father…he gave me this. Right before he died. I keep seeing his face… how he looked at the end…"

YOU ARE SAD.

"Well, yeah."

MY APOLOGIES FOR YOUR LOSS, MR. BRIGHT. WOULD YOU LIKE ME TO LOOK UP ENTRIES ON COPING WITH GRIEF, OR PERHAPS RUN MY POCKET PSYCHIATRIST APPLICATION?

Korden gave a tired smile. There had been no noticeable decline in the amount of the computer's conversation. "That's all right." When he moved, uncurling from his cross-legged position, pain spiked in his feet. The faithing break had used up the last of the concentration his exhausted brain could muster; there was none left to keep the sting at bay. He barely had enough artcraft flowing through him to light a *demno* and hold it close to his extremities to examine them.

The blisters—raw and weeping blood and clear pus—had spread along both soles now. He prodded at a couple and winced.

THIS POSES A SERIOUS HEALTH RISK, Stone advised gravely. THE CHANCE OF CONTRACTING GANGRENE OR OTHER BLOOD-BORNE INFECTIONS WILL RISE EXPONENTIALLY WITHOUT TREATMENT.

Korden sighed. "I know, but what do you want me to do about it?"

FINDING ADEQUATE FOOTWEAR MUST BE A PRIORITY, Stone told him. His nagging might not be spelled out the same as Redfen Bright's, but the spirit was the same.

"Trust me, it's at the top of my list."

I HAVE ENTRIES ON HOW TO MANUFACTURE YOUR OWN, USING ONLY AN AWL, PLIERS, ONE POUND OF FIRE-GLAZED RUBBER, AND SEVERAL YARDS OF TREATED LEATHER.

"I'll keep an eye out for all of that."

SARCASM ACKNOWLEDGED. IN LIEU OF FOOTWEAR, I RECOMMEND A REST PERIOD TO ALLOW HEALING.

"That will take days, Stone." Korden stretched out on the ground. The moment his head touched the bedroll, his eyelids seemed to gain ten pounds. "We can't afford to stop for that long. We have to keep moving."

The computer remained silent for several seconds, long enough for Korden to think he might have given up for the night. Then, hesitantly, MAY I QUERY?

"I think you just did."

ERROR. THAT IS NOT PERMISSION.

"You don't have to ask if you can ask me something, Stone."

NEW BEHAVIORAL INSTRUCTIONS IMPLEMENTED. MY APOL-OGIES IN ADVANCE FOR ANY PERCEIVED IMPUDENCE—IT IS NOT MY INTENT TO QUESTION MY OWNER'S MOTIVES, ONLY TO HAVE A BETTER UNDERSTANDING OF THEM WITH WHICH TO SERVE—BUT IS THERE A TIME LIMITATION IMPOSED ON OUR TRAVEL? WHERE, EXACTLY, ARE WE MOVING *TO*?

"No time limit, but Incarnates could be coming for us at any time. For now, let's just try to get out of the forest."

IN THAT CASE, THERE IS ANOTHER TOPIC I WISH TO DISCUSS. ACCORDING TO MY PEDOMETER, WE HAVE TRAVELLED APPROXIMATELY 150 KILOMETERS TOGETHER—OR 31 SPANS, BY YOUR MEASUREMENT—IN A STEADILY SOUTHEASTERN DI-RECTION. THIS IS IN ADDITION TO ANY DISTANCE YOU TRA-VERSED FROM YOUR VILLAGE PRIOR TO MY REACTIVATION.

"All right."

ACCORDING TO MY CALCULATIONS, WE HAVE TRAVELLED FARTHER THAN ANY KNOWN DIAMETER OF THE REDWOOD NA-TIONAL FOREST.

"Could you explain that?" he asked exasperatedly around a yawn. This seemed as though it would be another night where he had to order the computer to quiet down so he could sleep. At least he didn't have to set up a perimeter anymore; Stone made for an excellent sentry, using Korden's own sense to keep watch.

Clarifying: we should have left the confines of the forest by now.

Korden felt himself yanked back from the edge of sleep. "So…we're not where you thought we were on the map?"

Negative. Further examination of terrain, wildlife and climate have only served to confirm my previous calculation.

"Then what?"

The park preserve appears to have grown in size.

He took a deep breath to steady his nerves and closed his eyes once more. "It *has* been almost three hundred years, you know."

My calculations considered this possibility. However, according to my knowledge of growth patterns for *Sequoia sempervirens*, this level of forestry spread would require a considerably longer amount of time. I believe the disparity could arguably be a symptom of the "Evolutionary Gap Phenomenon" first observed by Doctors Daniel Goener and Phalak Singh in 2058, which attempted to connect rising ecological anomalies occurring across the world, such as the Great Species Emergence.

"That's all well and good," Korden said. He never thought he would actually be bored by stories about the past, but Stone had found a way. "Except the forest *does* have an end, I promise you. I saw it for myself. We'll get there eventually. Now please, be quiet for a while and let me get some sleep."

Affirmative. Watchdog mode engaged.

The nighttime sounds of the forest—more familiar than frightening now—provided a soothing lullaby as Korden dropped into an exhausted slumber.

The Cost
of Shoes

1

"What does it mean?" Korden asked. He felt like this was a question he asked a lot recently.

Searching... Stone replied. His responses to queries like this had been taking longer and longer to return since he began the mysterious process of 'compiling data' on the Dark Filament from his files.

The road followed the sweeping curve of the lake for another two days before veering off again into the forest to the northeast. Korden had been reluctant to leave the water. His time on the shore was a happy experience on this otherwise dismal journey, with plenty of fresh food and clean water with which to fill his belly. And, of course, access to sun and sky. When the trees closed in over him again, a hand of fierce panic squeezed his chest with cruel fingers, setting off a bout of as-mah. His breathing became so labored he had to stop for half an hour until he could calm down. Eventually his lungs loosened, but the spell left him feeling dizzy and unbalanced for hours afterward, as though the beat of his heart had become irregular. A quick medical check by Stone found nothing out of place.

This day began like any other—faithing and writing before another hike through the endless tract of sequoias on feet that pulsed feverishly with every step—but by mid-morning they came to a place where the road went through the center of the biggest redwood he'd ever seen, a titanic monster whose lowest branches began somewhere above the canopy. The middle of its trunk had been bored straight through to allow the road to pass, but a twisted network of roots sprouted within the interior and was now in the process of closing the gap at a snail's pace. Korden tried to imagine the axe blows required to carve through its meat. Inside the tunnel, he ducked under the dangling root tips and ran his fingers over the ringed inner core. He thought about the history that Tash said was written into these trees, the long millennias that this stoic sentinel had stood watch over.

On the other side, he found the sign.

It stood on rusted metal poles that looked ready to dis-integrate at any moment, the corrosion causing one side to lean. The board itself was carved from a solid sheet of red-wood that had once been overlaid with paint, most of which had weathered away except for the deepest crevices between the upraised letters. Even so, he could still easily read the words they spelled.

YOU ARE NOW LEAVING REDWOOD NATIONAL FOREST! COME BACK SOON!

"Guess you were right," Korden told Stone. He looked beyond the sign, but could still see no end to the trees. If the forest once ended here, then how much further could it possibly be?

He went around to the other side of the sign to look at the back. The message here was different—WELCOME TO

REDWOOD NATIONAL FOREST! HELP KEEP OUR PARK CLEAN!—but it was the sharp, spiky words scrawled across the carving that concerned him.

In faded black writing, someone had defaced the sign with the cryptic phrase, BEWARE MOAMBATI.

For some reason, the words sent a chill creeping up Korden's spine. He stared for several long seconds before asking Stone about them. Now, the computer's answer finally came back.

1,923,711 RESULTS RETURNED, 83.3 PERCENT OF WHICH SEEM TO RELATE TO A SINGLE TOPIC.

"Which is?"

MOAMBATI INDUSTRIES. THEY APPEAR TO HAVE BEEN THE LEADING RESEARCH AND DEVELOPMENT COMPANY IN THE AREA OF CEREBRAL TECHNOLOGIES THROUGHOUT THE TWENTY-FIRST AND TWENTY-SECOND CENTURIES.

"A technology maker?" Korden asked. "Why would someone say to beware of them?"

INCONCLUSIVE. IT IS PROBABLE THAT THIS WARNING IS UNRELATED TO THE TOPIC, OR IS, PERHAPS, NONSENSE ALTOGETHER.

Korden agreed, but only with the most logical parts of his mind. Those words—so big and urgent across the sign's original face—didn't feel like nonsense at all. Someone wanted them to be seen.

SUPERSTITION OFTEN LEADS TO IRRATIONAL BEHAVIOR, Stone told him, sounding smugly casual.

Korden countered with a favorite phrase of Tash's about common sense:

"And if the Upper wanted us to have fewer fingers, Stone, He wouldn't have given us the instinct to keep them away from fire."

2

That evening, one of the threatened rainstorms finally descended upon them from the north just as they were getting ready to stop for the night. For the first few minutes, Korden could hear it rattling against the canopy, but the natural shield prevented the downpour from reaching the forest floor until it could saturate the leaves and work its way through. Korden had just enough time to make a shelter before a drizzle of fat, thumb-sized drops began to fall. He settled on a slab of mossy granite jutting from the ground at a shallow grade beside a thick, full pine tree. Following instructions from Stone, he built a tiny camp in the narrow space beneath the rock from a thick layer of branches, brush and his coat, then crawled beneath, too exhausted to even lay out his bedroll. The ground was damp, but the makeshift walls blocked the worst of the wind and rain. After stripping out of his wet clothes and warming the interior with a turquoise flame between his palms, the shelter became rather cozy.

Even if he'd been willing to go back out in the deluge and search for food, game had been scarce since leaving the lakeside. His stores had been replenished with dried fish, and, as he sat against the rock listening to the hiss of the rain, he made himself eat an entire filet before daring to remove his shoes.

The swelling was so severe now that he could barely tie the laces of his worn leather boots. The thin fabric of his socks stuck to the weeping sores, forcing him to peel them away like banana skin. It looked like a wild animal had been at the flesh beneath. His blisters had combined to form one raw wound across both heels, and the soles of his feet were cracked and bleeding. They were hot to the touch, and stung so much the slightest pressure set them ablaze. A foul odor wafted from them, noticeable even in the damp air. Korden was used to being sick, but this was an entirely new kind of debilitation. If only he'd paid more attention to Feegran's healing wordspells and potions…

Maybe I should just walk barefoot, he thought. *I used to do it at home all the time.*

THIS COURSE OF ACTION IS INADVISABLE. ALLOWING FOREIGN MATTER TO ENTER THE WOUNDS COULD HASTEN IN-FECTION. YOU MUST—

"Not now!" Korden moaned, flopping back onto the ground. He couldn't stand to be lectured again when he felt this awful. "Just…sing for me, will you?"

It wasn't singing exactly, but he'd found that Stone could play music the same as Bibb's gadget. They were never the entire song, only half-minute excerpts that Stone called 'samples,' but they'd become a welcome distraction. So far, he'd been unable to find the beautiful melody he heard in the village, and his attempts to hum the song for Stone to identify had also failed.

I WILL NOT, Stone answered matter-of-factly.

Korden sat back up, almost banging his head against the heavy chunk of granite suspended over him. The computer had never refused a request.

Stone's voice dropped from its upbeat whistle down to an anguished register. MY APOLOGIES SIR, BUT MY BASE PRO-TOCOLS ENSURE THAT I CANNOT ALLOW ANY HUMAN TO COME TO HARM THROUGH INACTION, ESPECIALLY MY OWNER. YOUR DECISIONS HAVE BECOME IRRATIONAL, AND COULD POSE A HAZARD TO YOUR HEALTH.

A grin slowly worked its way up Korden's face. "Does that mean you're *worried* about me?"

I AM UNABLE TO EXPERIENCE 'WORRY,' Stone answered, and for someone that claimed his emotions were fake, he certainly sounded miffed.

"All right, I appreciate the concern, but it's my problem, and I'll deal with it."

NOT ONLY DO MY PROTOCOLS REQUIRE ME TO ATTEMPT TO SWAY YOU, BUT IT IS ALSO IN MY OWN BEST INTEREST. UNDER CURRENT CONDITIONS, MY SURVIVAL IS DEPENDENT UPON YOURS.

Korden remained quiet as he considered this. *Best interest*, Stone said. Apparently everyone had those, including tiny telepathic bits of wire and circuitry. The vulnerability made him see the computer in a whole new light. He might have been conversing with Stone for days, but for the first time Korden felt as though they were really *talking*.

And suddenly, the realization that another entity in this world depended on him—even one who wasn't technically alive—made this journey feel a little warmer and less lonely. Which is undoubtedly what Bibb intended all along. Korden made a resolution to be more patient with the computer's constant chatter.

PLEASE LISTEN TO REASON, Stone prodded gently. YOU MUST ALLOW YOUR WOUNDS TO HEAL WHILE WE DECIDE ON A NEW COURSE OF ACTION.

"One more day," Korden negotiated. "Just give me one more day of good walking without bothering me about it, and then we'll stop for a while, all right? But if any Incarnates catch up to us, I'm going to make sure they get *you* first."

The bargain seemed to please Stone. He gave a happy chirp and said, I AGREE TO THESE TERMS.

Korden wished that, if they were going to stop, they'd done so at the lake, but nevertheless, the prospect of a respite eased his mind. Just one more day, and they could work on a solution together.

But they came to the dead, crumbling town the next day, and what happened there made him forget all about such trivial problems as blisters.

3

The first building loomed out of the gray morning mist all at once, shrouded one second and popping into existence the next. After so long with only the irregular shapes of the forest to look at, Korden's eyes had trouble processing the boxy silhouette. At first he thought it must be a mirage or hallucination, no different than distant shimmers of water on a hot day. Then the road widened drastically as he limped closer (on feet that now felt slick with blood, pus, or both), taking on a second lane to either side separated by a white line rather than a yellow one, and an upraised crete lip along the edges. When he finally reached it, Korden stood in the middle of the cracked and pitted street and examined the square building.

Despite the obvious lack of artcraft in its construction, it appeared to be far more durable than anything the Olders had built. But whereas they used natural elements in their structures—working with the environment instead of against it—everything about this particular building looked artificial and synthetic, all the way down to its most basic components. Thick walls made from reddish stones compressed into perfect rectangular shapes (BRICKS, Stone informed him helpfully) and a roof that looked like a conglomeration of plastic and steel, all built upon a foundation of the same crete material that the old world seemed to love so much. He surmised that the wall facing the street had once been long plates of glass, but was now just a frame to which a few yellowed shards still clung. The single room inside couldn't be more than ten pargs deep. He could see a floor covered in a layer of muck blown in by years of wind and rain, and a row of rusted, waist-high metal boxes along the rear wall. Each one had a small circular window that opened onto its guts.

"What was this place?"

EVIDENCE INDICATES IT TO BE A LAUNDROMAT.

"'Lon-dro-mat,'" Korden repeated, savoring the word as he did all of the language of the past. "What was it for?"

PEOPLE BROUGHT THEIR CLOTHES HERE AND PAID TO WASH THEM.

"Paid? You mean with money?"

AFFIRMATIVE.

"The Olders told me about money," Korden said, circling around the building. "I never really understood why they wanted pieces of paper so much. Why didn't they just give each other what they needed?"

PERHAPS YOU WOULD ENJOY MY FILES ON KARL MARX WHEN WE STOP FOR OUR FURLOUGH.

Even with such sturdy construction, the forest was doing its best to reclaim this parcel of land. Several large, gnarled pines grew right at the edge of the slab behind the Laundromat. They leaned forward with their branches pressed against the outside, as though trying to exert enough pressure to shove the whole thing over. Vines as thick as his fingers climbed the sides in clinging sheets, their tendrils seeming to actually grow *into* the bricks, pushing them out of place so that the whole wall looked warped. In a few short years, he figured there would be nothing but a collection of oddly shaped rocks to mark what once stood here.

The place was a crumbling pit, but he still couldn't help feeling a small measure of excitement at seeing this trace of the world from which the Olders had come. It made him think of the explorers in some of the books he'd read, men who entered forgotten temples looking for adventure and riches. The latter was another concept lost on him, but he understood the craving for the former all too well. For that reason, he was tempted to go inside and poke around, but knew it would be a waste of time, done merely to satisfy his own curiosity.

And if the laundromat got him excited, then ten minutes later he stood absolutely dumbfounded when he reached the rest of the town.

The road came to an intersection with another, smaller avenue, and beyond it, the green canopy disappeared and an endless field of crete replaced the forest floor: crete underfoot everywhere he looked, crete walkways and stairs and even a few big empty lots where the ground had simply been paved over, as though the inhabitants went out of their way to ensure they would never have to see a single blade of grass. All of Tash's diatribes about mankind's disregard for the natural world suddenly made sense to him now.

More buildings of all shapes and sizes marched across the brightening horizon, poking out of the mist like an uneven row of teeth in a jawbone. Some of them were taller even than the *hangala* back home, the biggest and most elaborate manmade constructions he'd ever seen. Autos sat here and there, lumps of dull metal rusting in the street, along with more of the huge cargo wagons. He wondered if any of the cars could fly, like the vehicles in the fotos.

Ahead, Korden could see even more roads branching off from the one he'd followed to get here…and he suspected that those must lead to still more within the town…and those to even more…and he just couldn't imagine how many people must've lived here, or how any of them could ever find their way around in a place this big. His entire village could've fit within the first few square sections of this grid. When Stone told him there had once been cities that would dwarf this township, the sheer size of the world suddenly made him feel dizzy.

One of the buildings closest to him—an austere, gray-and-navy-blue edifice—had scratched and faded lettering across the front that read FIRST NATIONAL BANK OF EMMET. Korden dug in his bag and retrieved the map, then squatted in the street to unfold it.

It took him only a minute to find the tiny dot with the same label. It stood alone, a mere fingernail's width outside the dark green border of the redwood forest.

"You think that's where we are?" he asked.

THE PROBABILITY IS ALMOST ABSOLUTE. I WILL RECALIBRATE MY PEDOMETER AND INTERNAL MAPS. IF WE CAN REACH ONE OF THE LABELED ROUTES AND RECONFIRM OUR POSITION, I SHOULD BE ABLE TO KEEP A CONTINUOUS TRILATERATION OF OUR POSITION.

Korden continued steadily east as the morning wore on, weaving up the middle of the abandoned hamlet through what seemed to have been a commercial district. The empty buildings—some of them sitting alone in the middle of their barren lots, others pressed together in a long string, so much like wide-eyed faces as they peered down at him from either side—should've frightened him perhaps, but he found them lonely and a little sad. He could close his eyes and see what this place looked like when still new and full of people, with the growl of autos filling the air instead of just his echoing footfalls.

At each intersection, he stopped to take in the scenery and study each structure, to read the jumble of faded signs (FREE CAR WASH WITH STATE INSPECTION! NO RIGHT TURN ON RED! TWO FOR ONE McRIB DEAL, LIMITED TIME OFFER!) that seemed to shout at him from all directions. Here, in a place so foreign to him, the benefits of having a telepathic encyclopedia truly became apparent. Information from Stone came so fast and naturally now, Korden was surprised to find that he could identify much of what he saw, that the labels and names he needed and the purpose of each store were simply there in his head, waiting for him to access them.

"That's a place where you could buy clothing, right?" he asked excitedly. "And over there, that's a coffee shop! Dillish used to talk about how much he missed coffee! But he always called it 'star-bucks.' And those up there…they told the autos when to go and when to stop, right?" He pointed at a yellow box with three circles down the middle, suspended above the next intersection. The one on the bottom flashed an emerald green color at irregular intervals, buzzing loudly whenever the lights came on. "I read about those. And that tower, is that for electricity?" This time he indicated an intricate construct of metal poles that rose up behind one of the buildings to his left.

INCORRECT. BY EARLY IN THE 22ND CENTURY, EVEN TOWNS THIS SMALL CONVERTED AWAY FROM THE ELECTRICAL GRID TO RECEIVE THEIR POWER DIRECTLY FROM THE ACCELERATED ION NETWORK. THE TOWER YOU INDICATED IS AN M-NET BROADCAST STATION. THESE SUPPLY FREE WIRELESS M-NET ACCESS TO THE ENTIRE COUNTRY, AS MANDATED BY THE FREEDOM OF KNOWLEDGE ACT OF 2047. I STILL DETECT NO VIABLE SIGNAL, EVEN AT THIS RANGE.

Korden stopped beneath the traffic light and watched as its lone bulb stuttered to life once more. "So...does that mean the electricity...I mean, the *ion...power...whatever...* does it still work here?"

THE AIN WAS DESIGNED TO FUNCTION WITH MINIMAL HUMAN INTERACTION, BUT IF THERE HAS TRULY BEEN NO ROUTINE MAINTENANCE IN APPROXIMATELY THREE-HUNDRED YEARS, THE INFRASTRUCTURE WOULD BE SEVERELY DEGRADED. IT IS LIKELY THAT NO MORE THAN A TRICKLE OF ENERGY IS ABLE TO REACH REGIONAL CONTACT NODES, WHICH WOULD THEN BE DISPERSED FURTHER TO FUNCTIONAL SUPPLY DEPOTS IN TOWNS SUCH AS THIS.

As much as there was to marvel at, Korden couldn't help noticing how hard the forest worked to bring Emmet crashing down. The damage was worse at the edges of the city, where thick grasses broke the crete streets and sidewalks into chunks that seemed to be sinking into the earth itself. But, as Korden progressed deeper, he could see further evidence to support Stone's theory that the woods had begun a more recent growth spurt. Moss and vines swept over cars and covered entire buildings in creeping vegetation that dismantled them piece by piece. Trees—mostly pines, but even a few young redwoods—had busted through the foundation of the town like the fingers of a drowning man clawing at the water's surface. They thrust their branches through walls and toppled storefronts, while some grew straight up in the middle of buildings to explode through the roof. A sequoia lorded over a pile of rubble and twisted steel that had once been a grocery store, as though proud of its victory. The process seemed violent, as if the forest fought a slow-motion war to rid itself of an enemy.

An awful thought crossed Korden's mind.

What if the forest grew even now? What if the edge he saw from the hillside days ago was now even farther away and getting farther by the second? Suddenly, he thought he could feel the trees sprouting up whenever his back turned and then pausing when he looked, like the game several of the Olders taught him as a child. That uncomfortable bubble of claustrophobia expanded in his chest once more.

"What do you think happened to all the people?" he asked Stone, in an attempt to distract himself.

I CALCULATE A 97.2 PERCENT CHANCE THAT THE TOWN WAS SIMPLY ABANDONED.

"Why though? Why would they all leave?"

But the very next corner provided the answer before the computer could.

4

A long, two-story building stretched along the entire next block, brown brick and high, narrow windows set at regular intervals down the side. A large archway stood in the middle, atop a short set of stairs. Rusted iron letters above it read, 'Hargrove Elementary'.

A school, Korden thought in amazement. Children once came here to learn. He wondered if the classrooms within would look like his own.

The damage inflicted on this structure quickly stole his attention. A rash of small holes peppered the exterior; bullet holes, according to Stone. One entire end bore signs of a fire that left the surrounding wall blackened and charred from ground to roof. But the most extensive damage by far was where the long rusted tube of a school bus jutted from one wing of the building. Korden could see where it rammed straight through the wall when it still had wheels, bringing down a hail of bricks and wreckage. More of these buses were parked across other doorways to form makeshift barricades. One of these still had a grinning skeleton propped in the driver's seat.

A marquee mounted on a high post in front of the school had its letters arranged to spell:

INCARNATE SHELTER
ALL CHILDREN INSIDE BY SUNDOWN

THEY ATTEMPTED TO DEFEND THEMSELVES HERE, Stone told him. ACCORDING TO MY ONGOING RESEARCH, SUCH SHELTERS WERE A COMMON PRACTICE, ESPECIALLY IN SMALLER TOWNS THAT COULD EXPECT NO MILITARY DEFENSE. MANY WHO LIVED AWAY FROM THE LARGE METROPOLITAN AREAS DID NOT BELIEVE THE INCARNATE MENACE WOULD EVER REACH THEM.

"So that's what happened? Incarnates…attacked them?" Korden gave a nervous look around the empty street as he asked this. He sensed no other presence besides a scrawny crow perched on a canted stop sign, watching him with glassy black eyes, but in this giant, spread-out place, his perception couldn't reach more than a few blocks.

THERE IS A MUCH HIGHER PROBABILITY THAT THE AGGRESSORS WERE SIMPLY MARAUDERS. IN EITHER CASE, THE TOWN WOULD QUICKLY BECOME UNSUSTAINABLE WITHOUT AN INFLUX OF FRESH SUPPLIES. THE SURVIVORS OF THIS CONFLICT—IF ANY—WOULD HAVE BEEN FORCED TO LEAVE EVENTUALLY.

"And go where?"

UNKNOWN. COMPILATIONS FOR MY FINAL REPORT ON THE TOPIC 'DARK FILAMENT' SHOULD BE COMPLETED IN APPROX-

IMATELY 150 HOURS. I MAY BE ABLE TO PROVIDE FURTHER INFORMATION ABOUT POPULATION MOVEMENTS AT THAT TIME.

Korden took one last look at the school, trying to envision the battle, and then continued up the street.

5

At Stone's urging, the first building he entered was a fueling station somewhere close to the middle of town, mostly intended for vehicles that ran on ion but also carrying gas for older autos. Korden walked past the star-shaped pumps sitting isolated away from the store under a FINA banner and stepped through the shattered front door. A bloated, ten-legged spider sat in a web just on the other side, so close that Korden's nose bumped into it before he could pull away. The ugly creature seemed just as terrified of him as it emitted a high-pitched squeal and ran for the ceiling, disappearing through a crack in the plaster. Korden ducked under the web and went further inside.

The interior had been ransacked long ago, but he did find an overturned shelf with a few medical supplies, white pills that rattled in their plastic containers, bottles with greenish residue caked inside and metal tins of bandages. Stone had him take several of the latter, then directed him to a stack of tubes labeled 'Antiseptic Cream'. Korden unscrewed the caps on these one at a time. The contents were dried to a crusty powder except for one, which, after squeezing the container until his fist ached, oozed a last dribble of opaque gel onto his finger. Korden dropped it into his bag.

He ate lunch—the last of the dried fish—on a bench facing a playground full of equipment to swing on, dangle from, or crawl through. When he finished, he climbed to the top of the slide, sat down the way Stone instructed, and hurtled down it, laughing uncontrollably by the time he reached the bottom. He did this three more times before deciding to move on.

The last of the morning's mist had burned away by now. He could see farther up the street, to another large block of stores that would soon be on his right. On the way, he would pass a large, vacant lot on the other side of a low wrought-iron fence. It seemed to be one of the few areas in the town not smothered by crete, host instead to a layer of scraggly, weed-choked grass. But his interest truly peaked when he got close enough to see inside the yard.

Rectangular metal plates were set in the ground in long, uniform rows, mostly hidden by the high grasses. He leaned over the fence to look at one. When he saw the name and numbers embossed there, he didn't need Stone's input to know what it was.

"This is a graveyard," he said quietly. "A dead person is buried underneath each of these, aren't they? That's what Tash said they would do with...with my father." He had a vivid—and blessedly brief—mental flash of Redfen Bright sealed up in a grave like this, down in the dark where light would never touch him. That's what he thought he wanted at the time, but now it felt obscene, a victory for the Filament somehow, and made him want to go racing back to the village to pull the man's corpse out of whatever hole they'd stuck him in.

He didn't like to think about his father reduced to no more than a plaque with his name and age on it. What good did that do, anyway? Once everyone who knew you was also dead and gone, then such a monument just became a vain reminder of your existence to the generations that came after.

My apologies for intruding on your reflection, but would you please look up and to your left, along the fence line?

Korden did, on the verge of asking why before remembering that his own senses were the sole means of input for the computer. When he turned his head as indicated, he saw immediately what Stone wanted to examine.

Several rows up, one of the graves next to the fence had been exhumed. A shallow hole in the ground revealed the open lid of a black casket with tarnished brass inlays. The cloth covering on the inside of the lid was rotted to tatters. As Korden moved closer, he braced himself for a glimpse of another skeleton like the ones in the abandoned auto. But the interior of the box was empty except for a film of mud on the bottom which had been there for so long, grass sprouted on it, forming a soft green bed.

"Someone took the body."

And several others as well.

Korden scanned the cemetery. The graves ran up a gentle hill and disappeared over the other side. But, just on the portion that he could see, he counted seven other low mounds of dirt marking unearthed plots. "Why would anyone want a dead body?"

The most common cause of grave robbery is monetary. Stone paused and then said, with uncharacteristic hesitation, However, there are other reasons. But telling you about them would violate my decency protocols.

Korden read the headstone beside the open grave. "Daryl McKenzie, 2094-2102." He gave a sharp glance back at the coffin and realized how small it was, barely four feet long. "Curse, this is a kid's grave! When do you think it happened?"

Korden shuddered inwardly. "I never thought I'd want to be back in the forest, but I'm ready to leave this place."

6

This location turned out to be a shop in the middle of a long string of stores called a 'mall.' The faded sign across the front read 'ZAPATOS SÓLO,' but Stone assured him this meant shoes.

A wonderland waited inside. This store was still mostly intact compared to the fueling station, and Korden walked up and down the dim aisles, stirring up a haze of grit that coated every surface and sent him into a sneezing fit. He gazed at the items on display, dusty shoes and boots and sandals in a garish array of styles and colors, made from canvas and rubber and leather and more materials he couldn't identify. All were in bad shape, their padded interiors rotted and soles coming unstitched or unglued. But Stone directed him to a rack at the rear of the store, sitting beneath a sign with a single symbol on it, a sweeping checkmark.

One lone black box waited on the shelf. Korden took it down, knelt over it in the floor, and blew the dust away. The word 'Infierno' was written on the lid in a flaming script. The letters glittered as he shifted the box back and forth in the weak sunlight from the store's front windows. He pulled the top off and moved aside paper so thin and old it disintegrated when he touched it.

Nestled inside was a pair of jet black 'sneakers,' footwear of such sleek design that the eye rolled along their curves without ever finding a place to stop. There were no laces on these, just a leathery outer shell of orange and red shaped to look like twisted flames racing up the top and sides. He removed them from the box and inspected them from all angles, brushing and scrubbing away every speck of dust until they were pristine.

RECORDS INDICATE THESE WERE THE FASTEST SELLING SHOE IN THE 13-24-YEAR-OLD DEMOGRAPHIC EVERY YEAR AFTER THEIR RELEASE. ARE THEY SATISFACTORY? A trace of nervous hope could be heard in the question.

"Yeah," Korden breathed. *Satisfactory* didn't quite cover it; they were gorgeous. It scared him that he could want anything this much.

He sat on a bench right there in the store to remove his boots from his swollen feet. Stone made him smear some of the antiseptic cream on his wounds and cover them with the bandages from the gas station, although the adhesive on the square pads wouldn't stick. He even found replacements for his threadbare socks, in vacuum-sealed bags beneath the cashier stand, in as perfect condition as the day they were sewn. Korden put several pairs in his bag and pulled one carefully over his wounds before finally sliding his feet into the sneakers.

At first, they seemed like they would be far too big. Disappointment crushed him. But as his heels touched the bottom, they produced a soft whirring noise, and the insides of the sneakers plumped and reshaped themselves, conforming perfectly to the contours of his feet.

The Upper will provide, he thought.

When he stood up, the relief was immediate. Compared to his boots, these were like walking on a pad of goose feathers. He gave a few experimental bounces, shifting his weight back and forth, then tore his eyes away from his new shoes long enough to realize that someone stood watching him from just a few feet further up the aisle.

7

Korden gave an involuntary yelp of surprise. He took a quick step backward and encountered the rear wall of the store, next to the cashier stand. His hand drifted toward the knife, still in its sheath against his hip, but before he could pull the blade, the hunched shape between him and the door clapped its hands together in delight.

"Oh Aged be praised, Aged be praised!" it cried in a high, quivery voice. "A boy, a real *live* boy! I knew it must be when I saw him!"

The figure shuffled forward a few steps, enough for Korden to get a good look in the shafts of dusty light slanting steeply through the storefront. An old man stood in front of him. Well, not as old as the Last Fathers, but one that clearly had several decades on Redfen Bright. His pale cheeks and loose jowls were carved with wrinkles, a web of vivid purple veins clawed at the sides of his nose, and a tangled nest of frizzy hair the silvery color of fish scale floated around his head. He wore crude, hand-woven clothing, little more than a shapeless burlap bag with ragged holes for arms and head. Beneath that, however, his body was even more oddly formed than Bibb's wobbly, pear-shaped frame: dumpy and rounded at the hips, with a disproportionately broad chest that pushed awkwardly at the breast of the roughspun blouse, and arms from which pockets of doughy flesh sagged.

His murky green eyes bounced in their sockets as he scuttled even closer, roaming over Korden eagerly. His mouth flapped open in a rather vapid expression of awe and disbelief. Korden shrank away, but had nowhere to go; his back was against the wall, in the most literal way. He sensed no hostility in this man's *mohol*, just the vibrant indigos of intense interest, but being the subject of such scrutiny made him uncomfortable. The old man raised his hands and placed them on the sides of Korden's shoulders, just as his father had done countless times. He kneaded the flesh there briefly before moving them upward, pawing at the boy's neck and face with embarrassing intimacy. Korden turned his head as the stained fingers swiped at his lips and squeezed his cheeks painfully.

"Real, he is!" the man declared at last in his shrill, trembling voice, taking his hands away and clasping them to his own bizarrely lumpy chest, where two enormous bulges sloped off his shoulders. Bibb's overabundance of weight caused his breasts to plump and sag, but they'd never looked as full as this. "An *actual* child! Not a haint, nor 'lucination! And who might this young man be? Tell ol' Merise your name, now!"

"Um...m-my name is Korden, sir."

The old man—Merise, presumably—squealed and clapped his hands together once more, making the bags of loose skin under his biceps jiggle. The twin globes hanging off his bosom heaved perilously. "Korden, is it? And what a proper gennelman he is! By the good Aged Lord above, I ain't seen a child in nigh on...thirty years? C'n that be right?" He threw back his head and gave a loose-tongued cackle. "Then again, I ain't even seen another human bein *period* since my husband up and died, and that must be twenny-one years ago next Bloom!"

The word *husband* stuck quivering in Korden's mind like an arrow, although at first he couldn't understand why. He reexamined the person in front of him with new eyes. A warm gush of realization hit him at the same moment in which Stone summed up his thoughts perfectly.

I BELIEVE THIS 'OLD MAN' IS ACTUALLY A FEMALE.

A woman. The first woman he'd ever seen in his entire life. Suddenly Korden was just as fascinated with her as she was with him. Her *mohol* had given no clue to her gender, but now he understood the difference in her body shape, the swelling hips and mountainous breasts and the subtle softness of her facial features that no amount of aging could hide. She was female all right, but she certainly didn't inspire the same feelings in him as the pictures in the car, the dizziness and the pleasant tingling in his groin. He wouldn't have admitted it to anyone, but he had been more than curious about what those women looked like under their strange garments. The thought of the elderly, overweight body lurking under Merise's filthy dress just made him a tad queasy.

"Where did you come from, young Korden?" Merise asked, as she resumed her prodding. She took his arm and turned him gently in a circle, the same way he had his new shoes. Her pudgy hands paused at the knife belted to his waist before spinning him back to face her. "Tell me...

be there more young 'uns with you?" She craned her neck around at the rest of the store, as if she expected more children to pop their heads over the top of the aisles.

"No, sir. I mean…ma'am." He felt as odd using the title—known only from books—as he would *king* or *queen*. "I'm the only one. I came from…" Korden stopped himself on the verge of telling her about the Last Fathers. None of the Olders requested that he keep the existence of the village a secret, but they'd made a point of keeping themselves isolated long before he and Redfen came along. "Somewhere else," he finished. "Somewhere far away."

"*Else?*" Merise's face darkened, the vacant grin falling away. "There is no *else*, dearie. There is only right here, this godforsaken town, in the middle of this godforsaken forest." Her eyes glazed over. She lowered her voice conspiratorially. "I tried to get out several times, you know. Walked and walked for days until I ran out of yummies and had to come back. It wouldn't let me go, you see? Infects my dreams, it does, tries to lure me out there where it can steal my soul." Upon concluding this cryptic warning, Merise seemed to come back to herself. Her head whipped around and stared at the door while her hands squeezed at one another.

I CALCULATE A 65.7 PERCENT CHANCE THIS WOMAN SUFFERS FROM SOME FORM OF MENTAL DEFICIENCY.

"A few wheels shy of a cartload," Korden agreed, using one of Allin's favorite phrases for the Olders who slipped into senility.

"What was that, dearie?" Merise asked, turning back to him with eyes squinted suspiciously.

"Oh, uh…nothing. Just…talking to myself." He'd gotten so used to bantering with Stone, he'd completely forgotten to think his response while in the presence of another person.

Merise frowned at him for another moment before barking more laughter. "I understand talking to oneself all too well, yes I do!" She trudged a few steps back up the aisle, toward the door, then stopped and beckoned to him. "Come now! You come with ol' Merise!"

"What? Come where?"

"You'll see! I have things to show you! Yes, yes I do!"

Korden hesitated. Eddas and Tash's warning to stay away from other people burned in his brain. "I...I can't. I have to leave."

"No! No *leavin!*" she bawled, and came rushing back toward him. "I must feed you! A growin boy needs his yummies! Have a bite of my delicious stew before you go your way!"

"Thank you, really," he said apologetically. He could remember how lonely he felt during his first few days in the forest, before Stone activated, and could only imagine how awful it had been for this poor woman to spend so many years on her own. "I'm sure the stew is great, but I need to be somewhere..."

"You can't, you-you...you must at least pay for your shoes!" she sputtered.

"Pay?" Korden looked down at his newest possessions, the beautiful reflective flames that seemed to be engulfing his feet. "But I thought—"

"That they was free? I assure you, *nothin* is free, young man! Ol' Merise has been this town's only resident for many and many years, therefore everything in it belongs to me! And the cost of these shoes is you comin with me *right now!*"

Is that true? Korden asked Stone.

A legal case could conceivably be argued under some abandoned property laws.

I don't think there have been any laws like that for a long time.

Acknowledged. However, it might be useful to see if she has information about the forest and what lies beyond this place.

Korden reached out with the artcraft once more. The woman's *mohol* was still purple, now with veins of yellow impatience, but he still sensed no deceit or harm in her.

Maybe it wouldn't be so bad to keep this woman company through one meal. After all, Sheriff Protector always helped the weak and downtrodden.

Merise eyeballed him throughout this silent exchange.

"Well…all right. But only for a quick meal, and then I really have to go."

"Come, come! Not a moment to waste!" She grabbed his wrist in her pudgy fingers and marched toward the front of the store, giving Korden just enough time to snag his carry pouch before she dragged him out behind her.

8

The large woman let go of him only once they were back outside the store. She hurried down the grassy sidewalk toward the closest intersection, looking back at him every few steps to see if he followed. He did, reluctantly at first, and then picking up his pace when it seemed she might come back and latch on to him again. He wondered if all women were this pushy.

She moved quickly for such a big person—waddling hunched over, with nervous glances left and right all the time—

and Korden had trouble keeping up with her. His feet still hurt, far too much to run after her, but the new shoes were a drastic improvement over the boots. If there truly was a price to be paid for them, he decided he would pay it, and gladly.

Merise led him away from the main street up the middle of town, down one of the branching smaller streets, then turned again onto another avenue two blocks up, then immediately onto a curving lane that circled around a moss covered building called a 'city hall,' with a rounded dome and ornate columns in front. Two of these had bowed to the pressure of an angry spruce that sprang from the crete between them; they'd toppled into the building's front lawn, leaving behind only splintery stumps. Merise went on without stopping, taking a right at the very next intersection. Soon they'd left behind the stores and restaurants with their many signs and entered an area full of structures that could only be dwellings. Korden feared he would never find his way back to the road, but Stone assured him he was mapping every inch of their route.

They were on another sidewalk beside an apartment complex (he identified this with the influx of information flooding his head courtesy of Stone, but was still fascinated by the series of homes stacked on top of one another in double rows) when Merise turned abruptly and darted into a narrow alley choked with vines. The tendrils, some of them wrist-thick, grew between the walls in a network so tight Korden didn't think they could get through. But the woman grabbed hold of any greenery blocking her path and tore them down in a frustrated display. The severed vines bled sticky fluids until her fingers were stained a dark olive color.

"Curse them, Aged *curse* them," she muttered under her

breath. "It grows everywhere. Faster and faster. Won't be happy until it covers the entire town, and ol' Merise with it!"

With her forced to slow down as she fought her way through the tangles, Korden was able to catch up. "Ma'am, what you said earlier, about the forest…"

She spun on him, jabbing one finger to her lips and grabbing his with her other hand, squishing them closed. "SHHH!" Merise told him, eyes wide and panicked. She leaned closer to him, close enough for those fleshy bags on her chest to squash against his shoulder, and hissed in his ear, "Not outside dearie, *never* outside! This forest…it's alive, you see? It has eyes, and ears…and a heart, yes, so it does. A heart so cold, it sucks the very life out of everything it lures into its embrace. One would be foolish to leave the road and go mucking about in these woods. Do you understand?"

THE ODDS OF MENTAL DEFICIENCY HAVE NOW INCREASED TO 87.9 PERCENT.

She still had hold of his lips, so Korden just nodded.

Merise let go and resumed her blundering progress through the alley. On the other side, she crossed another intersection and then stopped long enough to point ahead.

"*There*. There is where we go. My home."

Merise's 'home' was the largest building Korden has seen thus far, taking up the entire corner it sat on. A rectangular structure made from dark slate stone, it had a peaked turquoise roof mostly given over to rust, and spires that reached toward the sky on every corner, high enough to rival some of the tallest redwoods. At the roof's apex, a long, white lowercase T was held aloft by an enormous alabaster sculpture of a shirtless man with feathery wings sprouting from his back.

The sign in front of the building read, CHURCH OF THE ANGELIC REDEEMER.

A hangala, Korden thought immediately. He knew a place of worship when he saw one.

"Most holy," his new companion remarked, clasping hands to her bosom as she gazed lovingly up at the statue. "A shrine to our good Aged Lord above."

"Aged Lord?" Korden asked cautiously, waiting for his lips to be squashed closed again.

But this time, Merise answered him without hesitation. "He watches over all the elderly of the world, the bodlas and crones alike. Sent his own son to lead mankind into sin, so that the Incarnates would leave us be once we reach free age. I pray for him to smite the Dark Filament and bless us all with children again."

Korden said nothing. Tash had told him there were other religions in the world, but he never expected anything like this. They walked on.

The building looked to be in good shape, especially compared to the rest of the town. Merise had obviously done everything she could to keep rot and forest growth from taking the place over. She approached the grand staircase in front that led up to a set of magnificent arched doors, with more winged people to either side. Water damage created dark stains in every crease and crevice of these ghostly white figures, and ran down their cheeks like tears. Korden wanted to stand and study them, but Merise hurried up the steps.

He thought she would open the large archway with its double doors, but instead she turned left at the top of the stairs and scurried along a narrow walkway that ringed the church. Further down the wall, close to the corner, was another, more humble metal door. Merise tugged on the handle and held it open, allowing him to slip past her.

The sunlight didn't reach more than a few feet over the threshold. He stood just inside the entrance, blinking to get his eyes to adjust. The room he now found himself in was small and bare, no more than a vestibule, with an opening on the opposite side that seemed to let onto a whole suite of chambers beyond this one. Under his feet was a mosaic of black-and-white, diamond-shaped tiles that reminded him of a chess board. A musty, earthen odor hung heavy in the air, irritating the inside of his nose. Merise came in behind him and closed the door, sealing out the sun and leaving them in pitch darkness. A few seconds later, he heard a click. Brilliant white light—not unlike the illumination of a *demno*—poured down from above. Korden looked up and found a row of long, covered bulbs flickering into existence. He gaped up at the display in delight.

Merise noticed his interest. "Ah, not seen such light before, have you? There is still Power here, just enough for ol' Merise to see and cook by! Come, must get you ready for yummies!" She grabbed hold of his carry pouch without warning and had the strap halfway off his shoulder before he snatched the bag away. She pulled her hand back as though he'd slapped it and looked at him sternly. "Now, now, dearie, just leave it here while you eat and you can pick it up on your way out! Your knife as well! I'll not have armed young men traipsin about in here! I keep a civil home, yes I do!"

Korden hesitated another moment before lowering his bag to the floor beside the door.

THIS COURSE OF ACTION IS INADVISABLE. Artificial or not, that anxious note returned to Stone's voice.

It's just for a few minutes, Korden assured him. *I'll eat, see what she can tell me, and then we'll get back on the road.*

He unclipped his knife from his belt and set it down on the leather flap of the bag, then turned and followed Merise deeper into the building.

9

She made Korden sit at the head of a long, glass table in a room lavishly decorated with paintings and fancy furniture, like the 'museums' Skewtz had described to him. The clean, white bulbs along the ceiling were switched off here; the illumination came instead from shaded vases sitting out on pedestals that cast gauzy bands of colored light on the walls, creating a somber atmosphere. Though the décor was nice, there was no real order to it, as though she'd simply carried these things here from all over the town just to have them in this one room. High-backed chairs and great, padded benches lay scattered across the floor in no discernible pattern, and the artwork festooned the walls in an overbearing collage, some of them hanging crooked. Korden thought of Oliver Truitt, with his feverishly drawn collection of sketches. He looked around at the artwork while she went into an adjoining room to get his meal, but without the stream of information from Stone, he had no idea what any of them depicted. Oddly enough, he found he missed his disembodied companion. His head felt empty now without the computer's cheerfully droning voice.

By far, the most exciting moment was his discovery of a small bookshelf in the corner, packed with tomes he didn't recognize, and several pieces of thinner reading material full of more fotos, with titles like *PEOPLE* and *NEWS-DAY*, their slick paper remarkably preserved. One of the latter had a picture of the Shroud on its cover, taken from a great distance but still closer than he'd ever seen it, a cloud that reached to the sky at the edge of the foto. The murk seemed to roil even in the still picture, a darkness that, like the Incarnate's aura, made him feel slightly queasy just to behold it. The black shadow it cast upon the land bisected a wondrous city overflowing with tall buildings, the kind called 'skyscrapers,' built along the shore of a blackish-green thread of water. Some of the buildings were ablaze in the photo, with columns of dark smoke swirling into the air to mingle with the artificial cloud. Those in the shadow of the Shroud had been all but gobbled up, only the merest outlines still visible.

In huge, bold, red letters across the picture loomed the caption, "SHANGHAI FALLS!"

After a few minutes, Merise returned with two steaming, crystalline bowls. Korden reluctantly left his inspection of the books and joined her at the table. The meal—a dark stew full of carrots, potatoes, and a stringy meat—looked no different than any he might've gotten back home, but the first bite proved to be flavored with strong spices. A gush of saliva filled his mouth; he'd never tasted anything so wonderful. He swallowed another heaping spoonful of stew, savoring the taste, and wiped a dribble of broth from his chin.

"See?" Merise beamed from the corner of the table closest to him, over her own bowl. She looked like she'd tried to clean herself up some. Her wild mane of silvery hair had been tamed to some degree, and the grime was scrubbed from her droopy face, leaving her cheeks a healthy pink. "Ol' Merise always says a growin boy needs his yummies! Dinty Moore that is, still as fresh as the day it was sealed! And if you eat all of it, there might be a bit of dessert waiting for you!"

Korden didn't need the incentive to wolf down the rest of this heavenly concoction, but he was suddenly overcome with the need to find out what delicacy she might present him with next. As he ate, he remembered his reason for being here. Steering clear of talk about the forest so as not to upset her all over again, he instead asked, "How long have you lived here then? In the town, I mean."

This question seemed to please her. She cradled her head with one hand and replied, "My husband and I—dear ol' Jaffer, Aged rest his soul—found this place...oh, it must've been thirty years ago. Found a supply of canned food from the old world, enough to last us a lifetime. A good thing, too; Jaffer never was one much for the hunt. Couldn't hit an elephsaurus from a parg away, that one! Yes, we thought this place was Aged-sent. Until the forest began growin up around us, that is, and callin to us in our sleep. Then we tried to leave again, but..." She frowned and shook her head, as if trying to dislodge these thoughts.

"What about before that? You must've come from somewhere else too. Can you tell me what's *beyond* the forest?"

"That was a long, long time ago. We lived up north, in another colony, close to the Rim. Everyone there had children. Oh, what a fine place it was! We thought the troubles of the world had forgotten about us. Jaffer and I...we had our sweet, sweet Pips. Only one year old, and I swear that boy could already sing like a nightingale." She halted and frowned, then laid her spoon down on the table and spoke to her lap in a voice that had gone rough. "But the Incarnates found us, just like they always do. Demanded the children. We fought, yes, of course we did, but we weren't a fortress, we had no real defenses. They...they slaughtered everyone who stood against them. They took my Pips away and...

and..." She raised a blubbery arm and swiped it across her eyes.

"I'm very sorry," Korden said solemnly. His heart truly ached for her loss, and yet a sudden yawn sprang to his lips. He stifled it before it could escape, not wanting to seem rude. He blamed it on the fact that his stomach hadn't been this full in a long time. "They came to my village also. A lot of my friends died."

"So much is taken from us in these dark days," she agreed, then looked up from her lap. He expected to see tears and indeed her eyes were brimming, but a brilliant, shining smile lay on her puckered lips as she added, "Sometimes though... our good Aged Lord gives back as well."

Korden started to ask what she meant by this, when he suddenly realized there were two Merises now, sitting side-by-side to his right.

His vision. Something was wrong with it. Korden shook his head, but that only made the problem worse. The inside of his skull felt fuzzy.

"Oh, careful now, dearie," she cooed, reaching for his arm. "Wouldn't want you to fall out of your chair!" Her words seemed to come from leagues away.

His eyelids drooped. Korden slumped over his food. He struggled to straighten back up, but his spine had turned to jelly. His arms felt like two dead lumps at his side.

Just before his head hit the table and his eyes closed for good, he heard her say, "You see? Not all our prayers fall on deaf ears..."

10

Consciousness returned in jagged pieces, each of Korden's senses contributing their part. He heard humming first, a merry, jangling tune full of flat notes, and smelled something thick, creamy, and naggingly familiar drifting through the air. His eyelids felt stuck together. When he managed to peel them apart, the light arrowed through his skull.

He lay on his back, stretched out on some cold, smooth surface. Above him, he recognized the ceiling of the *hangala's* many chambers. One of the bright electric torches burned just overhead, a line of hard white light running parallel with his body. The discordant humming seemed to originate from somewhere to his left.

Korden tried to move. At first he thought his limbs too numb to work properly, but after a few seconds, he realized he could feel his fingers stroking the slick surface beneath him. Then, as sensation returned, he felt the tight bands of pressure on his legs and the texture of rough cord against the bare flesh of his arms, and understood.

He was lashed down.

His head was the only part of him still free. He raised it off the table instead—groaning at the bolt of pain that shot up his neck and tried to split his brain in half—and peered along the rest of his body. Through his blurry vision, he could see a gleaming steel surface beneath him, a table that held him aloft, and the ropes tying him to it looked like braided leather. They wrapped around and around him countless times, all the way down to his bare ankles, just above the tops of his sneakers. The bonds were so tight, he barely had room to take a full breath, like a simulated asmah attack.

Nauseating pain pulsed at his temples. The effort of keeping his head up proved too much. He dropped it back against the metal with a hollow thud and let it roll to his left.

A large man—no, *woman*; Merise, her name was Merise—stood nearby with her back to him, close enough to touch if his arms weren't tied. She purred that happy, tuneless melody as she huddled over a square panel that jutted from the wall like a legless table. The surface of this panel looked like flat black glass, but a metal pot sat on top of it, from which a thin pall of steam rose. Korden could hear a rapid bubbling echo from the interior, and realized that the panel was somehow heating the contents of the pot enough to boil them. Even confused and sore, he still appreciated the ingenuity of the old world's technology.

The woman glanced around, still wearing that shiny grin. "Oh, dearie, you're awake! Such a good boy you are! I thought I would have to disturb your nappy!"

"N-nappy?" he repeated. His tongue felt bloated in his mouth. It took all the concentration he could muster just to string words together around the fog in his brain. "I don't remember what—"

"Shhh, hush now," she told him gently. "Just lie still while I get your dinner all ready!"

Korden did as asked, because to do anything else would probably make his head explode. He closed his eyes again, tried to think. Something was wrong here, but the darkness behind his eyelids was just too cool and inviting, like the waters of the forest lake. He drifted and dreamed and when he finally opened them, Merise was humming again as she lifted the pot off the black heating panel by its handle. He caught another whiff of that rich scent from before, a cloying odor that made him gag far back in his throat. From a cabinet above her head, she produced a clear bottle that looked to be made of plastic and began pouring the contents of the pan into its mouth.

A watery, white fluid filled the container, floating a head of foam on top. Now he recognized the scent, even though he hadn't smelled it since the last of the village's goats died years before.

Milk. Several of the Olders loved to drink it warm before bed, claiming it helped them sleep. Korden himself had been weaned on it, continued to drink it as a young boy, but lost the taste for it right around the age of five. After that, the odor alone had been enough to sicken him.

Merise filled the bottle to the brim, then took down a cap that she screwed onto the opening. A yellow nipple stuck out of its top, like the ones he distantly remembered from his infancy. Once she had this in place, she turned the whole thing over in one hand and squeezed it gently over her opposite wrist. A few fat, white droplets dotted her skin. She nodded once, as though satisfied, and licked the fluid away.

"Here we go!" She approached him, holding out the sealed bottle with its rubber nipple. "I knew this day would come! I told your father you would return to us, but ol' Jaffer never listened! Thought I was foolish, he did! But I kept my motherly juices flowin, just in case! And now, here you are, my sweet boy, ready to pick up right where we left off!"

Korden felt more confused than ever, even though his head cleared by the second. He did, however, have an awful suspicion about what she planned to do with that bottle. "Merise, what are you talking about?" He squirmed in the ropes. "Can you please untie me?"

"Now, now, those are for your own good," she chided. "And you know better than to call me that, dearie. My name...is *Momma*."

With that, she turned the bottle upside down and jammed the nipple into his mouth.

Korden thrashed. The bindings held him firm. He tried to turn his head away, but Merise slid a blubbery arm beneath his neck and cradled him in the bend of her elbow. She squeezed the sides of the bottle in her other fist. Warm stickiness filled Korden's mouth. The slightly sweet flavor made his stomach clench.

"That's it, take it down, dearie," she urged. "I'm sorry I fed you that other rubbish, but it was just to get you gentled down. Momma knew this is what you *really* wanted!"

Korden tried not to swallow, but Merise's relentless pressure forced the fluid down anyway. He spluttered and gagged as it coated his throat, flowed up the inside of his nose. Hot rivulets traced down his cheeks. He tried to use artcraft to shove her away, but he couldn't find the conduit to the Upper in his fuzzy mind.

Just when he began to think he might drown in the gummy liquid, she pulled the bottle from his mouth. He hacked and coughed, spewing milk from his lips in a frothy geyser. "Looks like that didn't go down very well, did it, dearie? Might need to burp you!"

Potent anger kindled in his chest, surprising him with its ferocity. It was an emotion he'd never needed much in his life, not until the Incarnates came. But now, a bolt of pure fury galvanized his muscles. It seemed to be another person entirely that gathered the remaining milk in his mouth and spit it into the crone's face.

For a moment, Merise gave no reaction as the white spittle ran down her long jowls. Then she calmly reached over, took a towel from the counter, and wiped it away. "That wasn't very nice, Pips," she said flatly.

"I am *not* your son," he told her slowly. "Let me go. *Right now.*"

She stood up and came to the edge of the metal table next to his head. He tensed, waiting for her to jam the bottle back in his mouth, but she only grabbed hold of the table and began to push. The room slid away on either side of him. Korden realized the table was actually a cart on wheels.

"When the Filament took you, it was the worst day of my life," Merise said, in that same somber tone, as she wheeled Korden through more unlit chambers. "Jaffer tried to convince me you were dead, but I couldn't give up hope. Not for my precious boy."

Korden let her jabber while he took a deep breath, steadied his mind, and tried again to touch the Upper. He strained until the pulse at his temples felt like a bull trying to bash its way out of his brain, but couldn't find that inner state of perfect focus amid his muddy thoughts. A cork had been jammed into the conduit's opening, damming the flow of artcraft.

How did she fool him in the first place? He'd seen no malice in her aura, no intent to harm him.

Beware, ghammer; not everyone wears their true emotions so readily. Though Tash never actually said this to him, Korden had no trouble imagining the advice in his voice. *Her insanity is a mask; she doesn't believe that she* is *harming yeh.*

"I prayed," Merise said. "Prayed every day to the Aged. Sometimes for hours. I knew if I prayed hard enough, then He would have to send you back…"

The foot of the cart hit something. Korden raised his head—which no longer hurt as much—and saw that they'd come up to a set of wooden double doors like the ones at the front of this *hangala*. They swung open as Merise pushed. The table wheeled into a much larger room, with a ceiling that stretched overhead into darkness. Roosting birds cooed softly from the rafters.

"After a time, I 'spected that maybe He just couldn't hear me…"

Korden craned his neck, trying to see this new place. He got an impression of a wide, carpeted aisle whispering past below the cart's wheels, with rows of pews to either side. It looked like a much bigger version of the Older's worship room.

"I needed a way to make sure He listened, that my prayers rose above all others…"

The bench seats ended. Merise guided the cart into a wide, open space at the front of this auditorium. They came to a stop. Korden lay in tense silence for what felt like an eternity, staring into the gloom. When Merise spoke again, her voice echoed from somewhere across the room.

"Jaffer provided the answer to that. He said all I needed was a ten-ah, like those old metal towers outside. A direct line to the big man upstairs, he said. I 'spect he was funnin me…but I also believed he might be right…"

A beam of electric light blazed on far above Korden's head. It slanted at a steep angle over his prone body, a wide band of illumination aimed directly at the pulpit in front of him. He rose up again to see what it had been cast upon.

And gasped.

In front of the cart, in the middle of the circle of light, stood another giant wooden 't' like the one on top of this building.

But this one sat at the center of a bizarre sculpture made from bones.

They were old, yellow, brittle-looking things, wired together in a rigid spiral made from interlocked femurs and spines and pelvises. They coiled around the wooden 't' and then formed dangling fingers that curved from the top in all directions, a shape that reminded him of the rampant vines outside. The bones were such a random collection of pieces, he might've thought they were animal in origin, but then he spotted the row of human skulls lined up along the bottom, and their tiny size revealed the truth.

These had once been the bodies of *children.*

The ransacked graves came back to him.

"You see now, don't you?" Merise stood next to him again, having crossed the room while he stared at her hideous centerpiece. She gazed at him lovingly, then reached down and stroked his forehead. "You see what a miracle you are, dearie? How hard I worked to bring you back? And now that I have you, I promise to love you and hold you and never let anything bad happen to you again!"

A gout of bright blue flame burst from the palm of Korden's right hand.

Throughout her diatribe and the horror of the bone altar, he'd continually tried to clear his head enough to channel the artcraft. When the cork plugging the conduit finally popped free, it surprised him every bit as much as Merise. The conjured fire was his largest creation by far, the backwash of heat enough to singe his exposed face. Blue flames licked at Merise as she screamed and fell away from the table. Korden kept it going, and turned the full force upon the leather straps binding him to the table. The tongue of fire licked at his lower half, burning straight through his dungarees to sear his leg, but he gritted his teeth against the pain and didn't stop until the ropes went slack.

Korden rolled off the cart. His legs felt wobbly, almost buckling beneath him; he redirected his will to bolstering them. Then he faced the horrible shrine, Merise's *ten-ah* to her god, and pushed outward with his mind while muttering a string of Craften. The entire altar burst apart at once, bones clattering against the walls and pews.

"You're...you're one of *them*..." Merise picked herself up off the floor, and stood looking at him with nostrils flared in piggish disgust. "One of those...those filthy 'bominations! No child of mine would ever use that witchcraft! Straight from the Stranger it is!" Her voice became higher and more strident with each sentence. She hooked her fingers into claws and swiped them through the air at him "Get out! Leave my home, and *may the forest eat you alive as you go your way!*"

At that moment, Korden would gladly have taken his chances with the redwoods. He moved past her in a wide, wary circle and ran up the aisle toward the doors they'd come through, ignoring the low throb in his feet and the pain from his burned flesh. As he left the auditorium, he heard Merise sobbing behind him. He didn't look back.

His knife and pack were still by the exit where he'd left them. Stone's voice returned before he could get the strap over his head.

Did you learn anything of use?

"Yes," Korden said, wiping crusts of dried milk from his face. "That I should really listen to you more often."

He unlocked the door and stepped out into the afternoon.

THE ENEMY OF SURVIVAL

1

Even with the specter of Merise still fresh in his head and the forest once more lording over him on all sides, the next few days on the road turned out to be surprisingly pleasant ones for Korden, as he rushed to put distance between himself and the disintegrating town of Emmet.

His feet—along with the self-inflicted burn on his thigh—healed rapidly, the sores disappearing so fast that Stone relented from their agreement to take a furlough. Each night, Korden rebandaged and rubbed more of the healing salve on the wounds, and, when the tube ran out, he cut the top off and scraped out the dried leavings within, then used some of his water to mix a paste. He wondered if the amazing substance was anything like the artcraft-infused ointments Feegran created.

He couldn't discount the contribution of his new shoes, either. The flaming red sneakers were a vast improvement over his boots. Even before the blisters made life such a misery, he'd only been able to walk for a solid few hours at a time and then everything below the knee throbbed horribly until he took a rest. Now, he felt like he could walk for the rest of Burning Season and never get tired. He got into a nice rhythm of rising with the sun, faithing and practicing, and then taking to the road until dark fall, even eating his meals as he walked. Stone confirmed that the amount of ground he covered each day had increased by 31.8 percent.

And still there was no end to the forest in sight.

The experience in Emmet weighed on his mind. He found that, with time and distance, his anger at Merise softened once more into pity. She would likely be trapped in the abandoned town until she died or the trees succeeded in knocking it down, no doubt rebuilding her altar and praying for her long dead son to return, too afraid to venture into the forest. If she hadn't poisoned him, tied him up, and forced him to suckle like a newborn babe, he might've attempted to convince her to come with him.

If she even agreed to accompany him, that is. The look of disgust on her face when he revealed his ability (*filthy 'bominations…straight from the Stranger…*) wasn't lost on him. He'd never heard of her 'Aged Lord,' but her reaction to artcraft made him think of what Redfen told him about his mother, how some of the townspeople refused to live with her. Korden wished there had been more time to ask the man about this now.

Could Crafters really be so despised? And, if so, why had he never been told? Tash warned him that people might view him differently because he was a child, but not because he was a Crafter.

The old man had been away from the world for a long, long time, Korden realized. Maybe *too* long.

Merise's insane ramblings and superstitions swam through his thoughts occasionally. Mostly at night, just before he plunged into sleep. They were nonsense, he *knew* they must be. Certainly these woods were growing at an abnormal pace, but that didn't mean there was anything malevolent or supernatural in it.

Nevertheless, he was more careful than ever to stay close to the road when he camped.

So Korden continued on his way in this fashion, rededicated to reaching the end of the forest, and as happy as he'd been at the lake.

The only worry which marred this otherwise content existence was the continued decline of wild game in the area. By the second night after his escape from Merise, when Korden quested outward with his mind, he could find not a single *mohol* blazing in the woods around him, less even than he sensed in the town.

As if every living creature had vanished.

2

Five days out from Emmet, Korden awoke from a fitful sleep—the result of a strange dream where his name was whispered repeatedly through the forest; more unsettling than terrifying—and went through his new routine: a solid hour of faithing, a few scribbled pages in his journal (more adventures of Sheriff Protector this morning), and then concentrated artcraft practice until he got good and hungry. The problem with the latter was, he'd just about reached the end of the exercises he could dream up for himself, and resorted to fine-tuning some of his worst.

For the first time, he missed Tash's surprise tests. They were frustrating, and he failed them more often than not, but at least they provided structure to his lessons, and new approaches to the discipline that kept him interested.

Training himself had begun to feel like a chore, with minimal improvement. He still couldn't recapture that state he'd achieved back at the village, where his will had been all-consuming and the artcraft flowed through his veins like a rampaging river. Try as he might, he couldn't even conjure a flame equal to the one that freed him from Merise.

Tash told him that giving his emotion too much influence over his will would make his abilities unpredictable. He needed to calm down and keep practicing if he ever wanted his artcraft to be reliable.

Stone learned to leave him alone throughout this regimen. Only as he prepared breakfast did the computer greet him.

WOULD YOU LIKE SOME MUSIC WHILE YOU EAT? OR PERHAPS AN ENTRY FROM MY FILES? I HAVE SELECTED SEVERAL TOPICS YOU MAY BE INTERESTED IN.

"Not this morning," Korden grumbled. His head ached from the old world knowledge he'd been cramming into it lately.

He dug his food stores out of his carry pouch. His water jug remained half full, but unless he found game, he figured he had only another two days of jerky left, and only if he supplemented it with whatever greens he could find.

IF YOU LOOK UP AND TO YOUR RIGHT, I BELIEVE A PATCH OF FULLY DEVELOPED *PORTULACA OLERACEA* IS GROWING JUST A SHORT DISTANCE AWAY. THOUGH SOMEWHAT SOUR, THE LEAVES ARE ENTIRELY EDIBLE.

Korden wasn't in a foraging mood, but the need to preserve his rations spurred him to try anyway. He set the jerky aside and crawled on his hands and knees to the small plants with the yellow blossom that Stone indicated. He harvested them by the fistful and brought his collection back to camp. They smelled tart, enough that his appetite actually grew. He popped a few in his mouth.

The taste that assailed his tongue wasn't sour, but acridly bitter. He grimaced. "Ugh! Stone, these are hor—"

WARNING! the computer squawked. DO NOT SWALLOW!

Korden twisted his head and spat the wad on the ground, swished water in his mouth until the taste faded, then spewed this as well. "What was that? You said they were edible!"

IT APPEARS THIS PARTICULAR PATCH HAS BEEN POLLUTED. MY ANALYSIS OF YOUR SALIVA CONFIRMED A HIGH TOXICITY. PERHAPS A CONTAMINANT IN THE SOIL OF THIS REGION.

Korden gazed around at the trees. They looked no different to him, but the forest had been eerily silent for days now. And he still could sense no life, not a deer or rabbit or snake or even an insect. The isolation made him feel as though he'd lost one of his senses, no different than going blind or deaf.

After a minute, he ate a few bits of jerky to quiet his stomach, and got moving.

3

Just after noon, the tree line ahead thinned, allowing a screen of watery sunlight into the otherwise dismal woods, bars of illumination so bright they stung his eyes. Excitement carried him forward, the fervent hope that he had at last reached the end of the redwoods. A low, constant roar built in the air as he approached. Korden ran toward the sound and then emerged all at once from the forest to find himself on the high banks of a narrow river flowing from left to right past him. The road continued straight ahead, interrupted briefly by an iron bridge that spanned the green waters.

It wasn't so much an end to the forest as a brief reprieve; on the far side, the sequoias resumed their kingdom in a regal, unbroken line. Korden's hopes sank so hard and fast they almost dragged him to his knees on the crete. He covered his eyes with one hand to cut the sun's glare and studied the curve of the opposite bank as far as he could see in both directions. At no point did the march of redwoods falter. They looked defiant to him, ready to rip loose from the soil and stampede across the river.

"Are we even still going *east?*" he asked. The sun floated too high overhead for him to tell.

AFFIRMATIVE, EAST IS STILL OUR DOMINANT DIRECTION. HOWEVER, THE ROAD HAS TURNED STEADILY NORTH OVER THE LAST 36 HOURS. I DID NOT FEEL THE DEGREE WAS STEEP ENOUGH YET TO ALERT YOU.

"But that's not good. We need to keep heading east." Korden gnawed on his lower lip, then asked hesitantly, "Do you think you could guide us if we left the road on the other side and cut through the woods?" His stomach performed a queasy flip-flop at the idea, but the forest edge he'd glimpsed days ago lay directly to the east, he was sure of it. His desire to reach it—to escape his colossal wardens—was quickly becoming a raw, unceasing need that eclipsed all else.

MY COMPASS IS IN PERFECT WORKING ORDER, Stone confirmed, BUT IN A SURVIVAL SITUATION, LEAVING A MANMADE TRAIL OF ANY SORT—LET ALONE A ROAD—IS TYPICALLY INADVISABLE.

Korden fidgeted, dragging the flaming toe of one sneaker across the pavement. That phrase 'survival situation' gave him pause, even though he supposed that's what this journey had been from the beginning. Up until this point, he could pretend that the dwindling food supply wasn't dire, but it seemed to him, somehow, that talking about it like it was a problem would be the best way to make it one.

Of course, escaping the forest wouldn't guarantee a solution either; Korden just figured it would be a step in the right direction. In any case, he refused to worry about it, because, well...

The Upper will provide, he thought.

AND PERHAPS HE WILL, Stone agreed cheerfully. OR PERHAPS, LIKE CERTAIN OTHER DEITIES, HE TENDS TO HELP THOSE WHO HELP THEMSELVES.

Korden sensed an insult lurking somewhere in this statement. "What's *that* supposed to mean?"

MY APOLOGIES, NO OFFENSE IS INTENDED, the computer rushed to add. BUT I DO CALCULATE YOUR ODDS OF SURVIVAL AS 35.9 PERCENT HIGHER IF YOU DO NOT PLACE YOUR FATE IN THE HANDS OF SUPERNATURAL ENTITIES.

"'Supernatural?'"

CLARIFYING: POTENTIALLY NON-EXISTENT.

Korden was baffled. He'd never asked Stone for his opinion on the Upper, had just assumed he would take the Great Spirit as fact, if for no other reason than his owner did. "How does that have anything to do with my situation?"

Stone sounded like he regretted speaking in the first place. IT IS BELIEVED—NOT BY ME, YOU UNDERSTAND, BUT BY CERTAIN PHILOSOPHERS AND EXPERTS ON THE SUBJECT— THAT RELIGION CAN BREED COMPLACENCY. AND COMPLACENCY IS THE ENEMY OF SURVIVAL.

A spark of anger shot through Korden. "Curse Stone, we made it this far, haven't we? I haven't gone hungry, we found shoes and medicine when I needed them, and I escaped from Merise. What more do you want? Can't you have just a little faith?"

AFFIRMATIVE. IN YOU. IN OBSERVABLE DATA. BUT TRUSTING IN INTANGIBLE LIFE FORCES IS BEYOND MY PARAMETERS.

"You wouldn't say that if you could feel His presence, like I can." Korden frowned. "Wait, you're in my head, you can read my thoughts! Don't you sense anything when I commune? Can't you...I don't know...feel the conduit open?"

DURING THE MOMENTS YOU CLAIM TO BE ADMINISTERING THIS 'ARTCRAFT,' I DETECT ONLY A SHARP BRAINWAVE ACTIVITY INCREASE IN YOUR FRONTAL LOBE, THE TYPE USUALLY INDICATIVE OF INTENSE CONCENTRATION. WHILE YOUR POWERS INITIALLY DEFIED THE BOUNDARIES OF MY LOGIC, I HAVE CHOSEN TO PLACE THEM WITHIN THE REALM OF PARAPSYCHOLOGY; TELE- OR PYROKINESIS, FOR EXAMPLE.

Korden sighed and shrugged. He didn't know what these labels meant, but he recalled Oliver Truitt denying them. Anyway, it suddenly felt superbly pointless to be arguing with an electronic gadget about matters of religion and faith.

Instead, he cut away from the road and moved to the crumbling edge of the embankment. A short drop separated him from the sandy shoreline leading to the riverbed. He climbed down and walked to the water.

The surface looked relatively calm from the road, but now that he neared, he could see how fast it moved. Tiny whitecaps in the center flowed by too fast for the eye to follow. The very edge of the bank was shallow and clear enough to see the mossy collection of stones at the bottom, but, just an arm's length from where he stood, the water got deep quickly, the turgid emerald color taking on undertones of muted black. Over the years, this flood had carved a harsh, narrow channel through the valley. He wouldn't want to try swimming across, but if he had a boat, he might consider floating downstream for a while.

The vantage also gave him a better view of the bridge. A simple metal deck with thick girders running in a blocky arch on top and a network of support cables strung just beneath. Its length couldn't have been more than 80 or 90 pargs from one end to the other.

After allowing Stone to test the water quality and pronounce it potable, Korden refilled his bladder from the river and drank all his belly could hold. The water was icy, much colder than the lake. He followed its course to the north in his imagination, to some frozen wasteland of the kind that a man named Jack London had once written about, where melting glaciers formed the head of the stream. He wondered if the Incarnates would follow him that far. For all he knew, they might be waiting when he got there.

Once the fantasy ran its course, he used artcraft to sift the river, searching for fish he could lure close to shore, but the water was just as devoid of life as the forest had become over the last few days. Finally, after running out of reasons to linger, he climbed back up the bank and rejoined the road just before the cracked crete met the steel of the bridge.

The structure was barely as wide as the road, but in remarkably good shape compared to any of the buildings in Emmet. The forest had yet to encroach on it, and only a few patches of rust could be seen, most of these high in the girders overhead. Korden started across without pause, listening to the way his feet clanged against the metal surface and savoring the sunlight.

He'd almost reached the halfway point when Stone's strident voice wailed in his head.

Warning! Auditory sense scans detect approaching life forms!

Whatever sound the computer heard was too distant for Korden to perceive, but he reached out and found four *mohols* rushing toward them from the far side of the bridge, the first sparks of color in his mindscape for some time now. Two of these were simple and base; he recognized them as belonging to horses. But the other two ...

They were blacker than the darkest night.

"Incarnates!" he whispered. His muscles hardened until he felt he'd become a statue.

What could he do? He certainly couldn't fight them, and outrunning them wasn't an option. But he couldn't just stand here and wait for them to ride him down either.

Eddas' claims came back to him, that Incarnates would have only a general idea of his location. Perhaps if he could hide...

Korden forced himself into motion, spinning to survey the bridge. The area was completely open unless he retreated to the girders at the entrance, and he thought the Incarnates would clear the tree line long before he made it there.

He was caught.

I calculate a 92.1 percent chance of impact survival from jumping into the water.

Korden ran for the closest side. The guardrails along the edge were made from a single steel beam with what looked like a solid sheet of metal beneath connecting it to the deck. Only up close did this reveal itself to actually be a tightly woven mesh, giving him a view of the river rushing by through the hundreds of small gaps.

He leaned over the rail and peered down. The drop didn't look that far from the banks, but up here, it seemed eternal. And even if he survived the fall, as Stone claimed he would, he didn't relish the idea of treading those swift, chilly waters.

Dread caused his breath to drag; he couldn't bring himself to leap.

His eyes caught on an iron rivet as big as his fist that jutted from the outside of the guardrail. If he used it as a handhold, he could probably reach the first of the support cables running under the structure, just visible beyond the lip of the deck. Without stopping to ponder, he threw a leg over the rail, stretched out on his stomach, repositioned his carry pouch so it wouldn't throw him off balance, and—using artcraft to steady his nerves and strengthen his muscles—he eased both legs out into space and lowered himself down the side of the bridge as fast as he dared. Just as his head dipped below the guardrail, he saw two huge horses burst from the far tree line at a mad gallop.

After that, Korden concentrated on nothing but the task at hand. He hooked his fingers around the rivet and lowered himself further, until his legs dangled in midair beneath the bridge. Wind—no more than a mild breeze when he stood safely up top, but what now felt like a surging hurricane—knifed through his clothes and whipped his long hair into a frenzy around his face. Gooseflesh crawled across the back of his neck and down his sides. The last of his wheezing breaths stopped altogether. There came a panicked moment where his feet couldn't find the cable, but then it appeared beneath his toes, a cylinder of taut steel that fit snuggly in the arches of his sneakers. He could feel it wobbling in the wind, but it steadied him just enough that breath could creep back into his aching lungs. He clung to the rivet with his cheek pressed against the cold mesh beneath the guardrail and listened to the ringing thunder of the horses' hooves as they started across the bridge.

Go on, he willed them. His arms already burned from exertion; he concentrated harder on bolstering his strength. *Just hurry and go past…*

The rhythmic clatter of the horses slowed as it approached him.

Korden's heart muscled its way into his throat. He opened his eyes and peeked through the mesh.

One of the horses came to a stop just abreast of him. A towering golden-brown stallion, twice the girth of the elderly Mulder, with a matted, dingy white mane. The huge animal snorted and pawed uncomfortably at the bridge while its rider sat unmoving in a worn saddle. This man looked more or less normal—average-sized, a bit pale perhaps, bare-chested and wearing only leather breeches and boots—but even if his *mohol* hadn't been the color of midnight, the dark tinted goggles over his eyes would still have marked him as an Incarnate.

The other horse, a malnourished white mare, ran on a few paces before the rider reined up hard and wheeled around in a tight circle. Korden could tell nothing about this one. A dark longcloak hid every inch of its body, the garment so expansive it hung down to the horse's front knees, and clamped to its head was a featureless black mask that completely covered its face except for a tiny window across the eyes; a welder's mask, according to his new store of knowledge. When it spoke, Korden was surprised to hear traces of femininity in its guttural voice.

"Why do you hold?" she demanded. The snarling words were barely audible over the whistle of wind along the side of the bridge and rush of water below.

"There is Light close by." The male Incarnate moved at last, craning his head back so that his goggled eyes gazed up at the sky. Korden could see his nostrils quiver. There was something hungry in the movement. "A single flame, I believe. Do you not feel it?"

The female used one arm—covered by long sleeves and gloves—to throw aside the longcloak and point into the forest from which Korden had come. "I feel nothing but the pull of those that lie ahead. So let us ride and get there. The more we linger, the better chance we will be late to the slaughter."

"Your bloodlust makes you overeager, wasteling," the male snapped. The horse beneath him gave a nervous whinny. "What would Regent Torgas say if he knew we left a Lightbringer alive?"

"Regent Torgas is undoubtedly far too busy explaining to the Deadfather how such a large group of children suddenly appeared in his keep overnight."

Tash, Korden thought jubilantly. *They're talking about Tash and the others! They're still alive!*

The male said nothing, just continued to stare at the sky, until the woman growled, "We've been riding for days now. If we don't catch the dispatch battalion, it was all for naught."

The other Incarnate looked down from the sky at last. "Once the larger group is extinguished, we will only have to return here to hunt down this one. We will deal with it now." He dismounted his horse with a heavy thud. Korden was horrified to see him turn and stride toward the side of the bridge to which he clung.

I CALCULATE ONLY A 63.6 PERCENT CHANCE OF ESCAPE IF YOU ARE SEEN.

Would you shut up, that doesn't help!

Korden lowered himself further, putting more weight on the cable, and let go of the rivet to dig his fingers into the very bottom of the grating where it met the deck, but he couldn't get a solid grip. His pack shifted on his shoulders without warning, dragging him backward. Just before he would've plunged away, sudden inspiration struck.

Paste. Back home, Tiller brewed homemade paste for various uses around the village, a sticky concoction that could seal just about any two surfaces together. And, while he didn't have any of it now, Korden fixed the idea of the glue in his mind—the yellow-white look and gooey, snotlike feel of it—and then imagined his hands coated in the stuff. He focused, pushed, *willed*, and felt his palms adhere to the metal as solidly as if he'd been welded to it. Suddenly, he no longer needed to maintain a grip on the side of the bridge. The muscles throughout his arms and hands shuddered in relief.

If not for the demons lurking above, he would've laughed in delight at this bit of fast-thinking creativity. It seemed like the exact sort of scenario Tash had prepared him for.

From this new position, he could no longer see what was happening on the bridge. He heard the Incarnate's footsteps halt. Korden tried to shrink into the steel. When the creature spoke again, it sounded directly above him.

"It is close. Frustratingly so. But what is it doing so far out here?"

"Probably some sin cow who thought they could hide their brat by living alone in the woods." The woman barked laughter. "We will show them how wrong they were."

The man grunted. "If so, they picked a good place. There is an odd power at work in this forest. Something ancient.

Primal. Its aura is so strong, I nearly overlooked the Light amid its pulse."

"We should report it when we return. If the Regent finds it valuable, we might be rewarded."

The Incarnate above him said nothing for so long, Korden thought he must've missed the sound of it moving away. He shivered against the bridge for another few seconds, closed his eyes, and when he opened them again, he found a goggles-covered head thrust over the guardrail, leering at him from a foot away.

"This bridge appears to have a rodent problem," the Incarnate said.

4

"Leave me alone!" Korden told him.

The Incarnate sneered. "Or else what?"

Korden peeled one hand away from the bridge, pointed his palm at the demon's face, and tried, with all his might, to conjure the spout of blue fire.

A few sparks and one sputtering flame appeared, not even enough to cook a hank of rabbit over.

The Incarnate laughed as he reached over the guardrail, seized the offered wrist, and pulled. Korden's feet slipped off the beam, the stickiness faded from his other hand as his concentration lagged, and he found himself dangling by one arm in the Incarnate's grip, like a freshly hooked trout at the end of a fishing line. The bones in his arm ground against one another under the pressure. Upper help him, these creatures were so much stronger than they looked. He struggled, kicking and thrashing, as the Incarnate lifted him up until he could stare directly into the smoky lenses of its goggles.

"Maybe we will bring you along," it told him. "Your screams will amuse us as we ride."

If he couldn't rely on the mystical, he would have to go with the practical. Korden drew his knife from the sheath at his waist and stabbed the Incarnate through the forearm. The blade sank to the hilt in the pale flesh and protruded from the other side; there was a vibration as it scraped against bone. The Incarnate's face registered only a flicker of pain, but the hand holding Korden's wrist unlocked.

Time ratcheted to a halt. For one moment, he seemed to be lighter than air, floating on the wind currents.

And then he began to fall.

The Incarnate scrambled to snatch at him again. Its fingers twined through a few locks of his hair, yanking his head back before the strands tore from his scalp. The sudden jerk pulled the Incarnate off balance. Korden caught one fleeting glimpse of the demon tumbling over the guardrail after him before the world spun too crazily to make sense of it.

He hit the river upside down, the impact hard enough to jar his brains in his skull, but that was quickly forgotten as the freezing water enveloped him. The shock rocketed through his body, numbing his extremities and leeching away his strength. He sank into murky darkness, too stunned to swim. The current snatched him up, rolled him until he couldn't tell which way was up. A moment later, the river bottom rushed to meet him. Jagged shards of rock scraped against his side, his lungs felt ready to burst, his carry pouch became an anchor around his neck, and Stone bleated a stream of frantic warnings and instructions directly into his head, which did nothing to help his confusion.

Korden shook off the daze and kicked hard, propelling himself away from the riverbed with a burst of artcraft.

Once he'd broken free of the undertow, he rose quickly. His head breached the surface; he gulped at the air. Stone continued wailing, something about severe oxygen depletion in his bloodstream (*no duh*, as Allin had been fond of saying), but Korden ignored him while he gagged out the last of the water in his lungs and then paddled in a circle to get his bearings.

Trees flashed by on either side as the current carried him swiftly along. He caught sight of the bridge, already a surprising distance away and receding even as he watched. The tiny figure of the female Incarnate was visible at the guardrail and then the river swept him around a sudden bend and a copse of pine trees hid the road from view.

Korden turned and swam toward the eastern bank, his limbs unbearably heavy.

The water in front of him erupted as the other Incarnate shot from the depths.

Its goggles had been swept off its head in the trip downriver, but it came at him regardless, with eyelids squeezed shut and roaring wordlessly. Korden saw his knife still jammed through the creature's forearm just before its hands found his throat. It shoved him below the water again before he could get a breath, putting all its weight on his shoulders to drive him deep.

He pried at the fingers locked around his windpipe. They wouldn't budge. Black spots swam through his vision. His flailing hands landed on the handle of his knife where it protruded from the demon's arm. He twisted sharply. A cloud of oily blood exploded into the water.

Somewhere above him, the Incarnate shrieked. The pressure on Korden's throat slackened, but the creature's weight kept him beneath the water. It brought a knee into his side that the carry pouch blocked. The strap on his overloaded pack snapped. The weight around Korden's neck disappeared and, a heartbeat later, Stone's panicked voice faded from his head.

His sight narrowed to a pinhole. His lungs were burning coals in his chest. In another few seconds, he would lose consciousness, and it would all be over.

Then, without warning, the river shallowed. Pebbly sand grazed his knees. With the last of his strength, he planted his feet and shoved upward, lifting the Incarnate up enough that he could get his head above the surface for a breath that felt far too short.

The demon grappled with him, trying to force him back under, but its blindness, injured arm and Korden's solid footing gave him the advantage. The training Eddas put him through—once used in a sport called 'wrestling' which he said was mostly for show, but Allin swore was entirely real—took over, as thoughtless and automatic as drawing breath. He used his shoulder to roll the Incarnate aside, wrapped an arm around its leg to give him leverage, and then, somehow, *he* was on top, practically sitting on his enemy. The Incarnate squirmed, but its strength could do nothing to help it in this position. Korden placed a knee on its chest, both hands on its forehead, and held it down. He could hear someone screaming—a sound of savage triumph and fury—and realized it was himself.

Beneath him, the creature's flailing movements slowed. Until then, Korden hadn't known if they even needed oxygen to live, but he supposed they were bound by the same weaknesses of the flesh and blood bodies they inhabited. Perhaps even more so, with their sensitivity to light. As long as one had faith, you could apparently kill them in any manner.

Through the water, he could see the glow of its red eyes fading. Heeding Eddas' advice, he jerked his knife free of the Incarnate's arm and shoved the body away just as a geyser of black smoke squirted up through the water. It hung in the air for several heartbeats, a miniature storm cloud, before dissipating on the breeze.

The corpse bobbed to the surface, spun in a lazy circle, and floated downriver.

Error 147

1

"*Stone!*" Korden shouted, shivering as the chest-deep water flowed around him. He knew he should be silent with another Incarnate so near, but the idea of losing his only friend panicked him as much as his near-drowning. "*Stone, where are you?*"

He paced anxiously back and forth on the sandbar that saved his life. Even in the shallows, the water was much too dark to peer through. With as fast as it moved, his belongings could already be a span away. He probed the river with his mind, trying to figure some way to use artcraft to track the computer. Just when he was ready to give up, he heard a screeching siren in his head, broken momentarily by a distant cry of, ALERT, ALERT! ASSISTANCE IS REQUIRED!

"I hear you! Tell me where you are!"

I AM UNABLE TO GUIDE YOU TO MY LOCATION WITHOUT EXTERNAL SENSORS! SIGNAL STRENGTH SHOULD PROVIDE A GENERAL DIRECTION!

The computer's voice sounded slightly louder when he moved toward the front of the sandbar, so Korden dove back into the freezing river, fighting against the current to swim upstream. Stone continued to speak and blast his siren, both of which grew stronger as Korden went deeper beneath the water. Flotsam loomed out of the murk, and then his fingers brushed against fabric. The carry pouch lay tangled in a web of rotted logs on the river bottom. The wailing siren cut off at last as he pried the pack loose and resurfaced with it under his arm.

THIS IS FORTUNATE. EVEN BROADCASTING AT FULL CA-PACITY, I CALCULATED ONLY A 23.2 PERCENT CHANCE THAT YOU WOULD LOCATE ME. OF COURSE, THAT FACTOR TAKES INTO ACCOUNT A 17 PERCENT CHANCE THAT YOU WOULD SUR-VIVE THE BATTLE WITH THE OTHER COMBATANT.

"That just...shows you...how reliable your numbers are," Korden gasped as he waded ashore. His chest burned with the effort.

BE THAT AS IT MAY, YOUR ASSISTANCE IS APPRECIATED. NOT EVERY HUMAN WOULD RISK THEIR LIFE TO SAVE AN AR-TIFICIAL INTELLIGENCE.

"Yeah, well, if I didn't have you around, I wouldn't be able to stand the silence."

SARCASM ACKNOWLEDGED. I BELIEVE AN APPROPRIATE RESPONSE WOULD BE, 'HARDY HAR HAR.'

There was no beachhead on the eastern bank of the river. Instead, brambles and thick, almost impenetrable undergrowth crowded the shore right up to the edge of the water. Korden blundered through it, snapping small branches and tearing away from clinging burdocks and thick blades of skilne grass that clutched at him until he reached the tree line, then collapsed in the first clear space of forest floor. He lay on the ground with his eyes closed and concentrated on nothing but drawing breath until the tense knots in his chest eased and the sun warmed him enough to halt his shivering.

I INFER THAT THE MAN WHO ATTACKED YOU WAS ONE OF THE INCARNATES.

"You infer correctly." Now that he was warm, Korden could feel every ache and pain the encounter left him with: various bruises and scratches caused by his tumble in the river and subsequent fight with the Incarnate...the bloody rip on the back of his scalp where his hair tore away as he fell from the bridge...and an uncomfortable pressure in his throat from the throttling that made him think about those finger-shaped marks on his father's neck.

HE SEEMED TO HAVE AN ABILITY TO SENSE YOUR LOCA-TION, ALTHOUGH I AM UNABLE TO CITE A MECHANISM FOR THIS. MY LOGIC CIRCUITS SUGGEST A KEEN OLFACTORY DE-TECTION, BUT YOUR PROPIONIC ACID PRODUCTION DOES NOT SEEM SIGNIFICANT ENOUGH TO PRODUCE BODY ODOR.

"If you're trying to tell me I don't smell bad, thanks, I guess." He winced as he pressed the tail from his dripping wet tunic to the wound on his scalp. "Anyway, they might sniff a lot, but I'm pretty sure the way they sense children has nothing to do with their noses."

Stone pondered this and let him rest another moment before saying, WE SHOULD CONTINUE MOVING. THIS LOCATION MAY BE UNSAFE IF THE INCARNATE'S COMPANION ATTEMPTS TO TRACK YOU.

"I know. But maybe she won't. She did seem pretty impatient to get to..." His eyes flew open as he sat up. "The Olders! Curse, we have to get back to them!" He reached for his sodden pack.

FOR WHAT PURPOSE? Stone inquired.

"To warn them, of course! That the Incarnates are coming for them!"

THAT COURSE OF ACTION IS ILLOGICAL.

"How so?"

From what you have told me, the ones you call 'Olders' intended to create a diversion to draw the Incarnates away, giving you easier mobility for as long as possible. It seems as though their ruse is working. Therefore, warning them of something they already know would serve no purpose.

Korden's mouth worked as he tried to counter the argument. He briefly wondered if this was another reason Bibb had given him the computer, to motivate him, to keep him moving forward, no matter what happened. "They're my family," he managed. "My *only* family. I can't just let them die."

Even if your intervention was guaranteed to have some discernible effect on the outcome, I see no viable scenario in which you could reach them in time.

Korden sank back to the ground, overtaken not by grief, but by helplessness that quickly bred a futile anger. Stone was right; Tash and the others were on their own. Korden could accept that, would probably have come to that conclusion himself, given time. He was just sick of being told that everything he wanted was wrong, that his life was beyond his control.

In some ways, he never left the Barrier.

2

When his anger faded, it left him weak and trembling. But he got up again—just as he always did, no matter what befell him—and looked into the shadows of the deep forest.

Extreme caution is advised in returning to the road, in case the other Incarnate is searching for you.

"Then we probably shouldn't follow the river." That wouldn't have been an issue anyway, Korden realized; the banks held some of the thickest vegetation in the forest so far. They were far too overgrown for him to traverse all the way back to the bridge. "Point me in the right direction."

Stone oriented him by degrees, putting the river to his back. THIS NORTHEASTERLY HEADING SHOULD CONNECT US WITH THE ROAD SOME DISTANCE AWAY FROM OUR POINT OF DIVERGENCE, HE PROMISED.

But, four hours later, as the color bled out of the canopy and shadows crept from their holes, they still hadn't found the crete path. Korden might have been more apprehensive if he'd been alone, but Stone assured him that, past the bridge, the road probably turned further to the north, widening the distance between them and it. Not only that, but the lushness of the forest forced them to make constant detours to the east, the redwoods growing closer together and the spaces between them filled with scraggly alders, wild brush and vines like the ones that had been so prevalent in Emmet. At first, Korden hacked through these collections with a machete made of artcraft, sharp slices of his hand that cleaved right through even the thickest branches, but, before long, his mind became just as exhausted and used up as his body.

Stone remained confident they would rejoin the road early the next morning. Korden, on the other hand, couldn't help recalling what Merise said, about it being foolish to go mucking about in the woods.

Only when they'd stopped for the night and set up camp did he go through his waterlogged carry pouch. The books he brought were thoroughly ruined, but the road atlas' slick outer coating saved it from a similar fate. Other than that, none of the damage seemed irreparable. He mended the bag's broken strap, then laid out his clothes and the thin pad of his bedroll to let them dry, and hastened the process by channeling warmth through his palms.

The chore directed his thoughts back to the encounter on the bridge. Making his hands stick to the steel had been a great trick, but his inability to conjure a flame frustrated him too much to take pride in it. He still had a lot more work to do on his focus.

Are you sure these failures are from lack of focus, *or lack of* faith?

Korden sat for a moment, gnawing at his lower lip as he considered this, along with Tash's advice on the subject. He believed in the Upper, believed with all his heart…but he also had to admit that, out here, on his own, he'd learned how doubt went hand-in-hand with fear.

In the last strangled rays of sunshine, Korden used strips cut from the bottom hem of his dungarees to fashion a tiny leather harness for Stone's physical casing. He slipped the pebble-like device inside, tightened the knots around it, and then attached it to a loop of rawhide, which he hung around his neck.

"There. You won't get lost anymore," Korden told him. The computer's response overflowed with gratitude.

Korden dared not light a fire, in case the female Incarnate—or perhaps others—were still combing the area. Instead, he ate half of his meager stash of jerky while sitting in the dark. The silence in the empty forest was so deep now it seemed to press against his eardrums, like the air before a storm. If not for the ability to reach out with the artcraft and confirm for himself that no living thing existed anywhere close to him, he might've believed he'd gone deaf.

After eating, he faithed for several hours, communing with the Upper as intensely as possible, seeking reassurance that he hadn't been abandoned. The conduit opened as easily as ever, and the idea of doubting the Great Spirit's existence seemed entirely silly. He could feel that comforting presence right there, on the other end of the umbilical in his mind. In moments like these, the universe felt whole and centered, with not a shred of uncertainty to torment him.

It was just after coming back to himself that a very different sensation hit him: a strange tingle that swept across his back and neck, then worked its way up to prickle at his wounded scalp. The same feeling he used to get all the time when he gazed at this forest from the confines—and safety—of the Barrier.

He was being watched. The feeling seemed to come from everywhere and nowhere at once, yet the woods were just as empty as ever.

After tasking Stone with guard duty, Korden stretched out and drifted into an uneasy sleep.

3

The morning found him as tired as when he went to bed. He lay in his bedroll while the sun lightened the dense woods, stomach growling for a breakfast he couldn't give it, and tried to figure out why he still felt so weary.

Stone finally said, YOUR HEART RATE AND BREATHING WERE ELEVATED THROUGHOUT THE NIGHT, BOTH INDICATORS OF UNCONSCIOUS BRAIN ACTIVITY.

Korden frowned. Unlike the dream yesterday in which his name was whispered through the forest, he couldn't remember the content of any nightmares, just a vague smear of unease and dread. They must have been long and bad though, because his chest hurt like it did whenever he ran too much.

"Can't you see what I dream? You must read my mind while I'm asleep too."

Negative. One of the founding protocols of telepathic AI is a forbiddance to intrude in human thought stream once a certain level of delta brainwave activity is reached, due to this state's susceptibility to suggestion. But if you wish to tell me the details, I can research the psychoanalytical symbolism.

"That's just it. I can't really remember any of it. Tash says most dreams aren't meant to be held on to."

Once he'd packed up the camp, he ate the last of his jerky, which did nothing to assuage his hunger. He took a few minutes to hunt for edible plants again, but the only ones he found were just as bitter as the blossoms he'd picked the morning before, no matter what the species.

Poison ran in the veins of every branch and leaf and blade of grass in this part of the forest, it seemed.

"All right, point me in the right direction," he said, trying to keep the fear from slipping into his voice. Not for Stone's benefit, who would surely read it in his thoughts anyway, but for himself. "I want to be back on the road as soon as possible."

If I turn our course back to the west by a margin of three degrees, I calculate we can reach it within the hour.

"Do it," Korden ordered. Just the sight of that hard, black canal through the forest would do much to elevate his mood.

Orienting himself to Stone's heading, he set off.

4

THIS DOES NOT COMPUTE, Stone insisted, the latest in a long string of such declarations. Each refrain became a little more frantic. This time, he added, EVEN IF THE ROAD TURNED COMPLETELY BACK ON ITSELF BEYOND THE EASTERN RIVER BANK—A COMPLETELY ILLOGICAL ASSUMPTION—ALL CALCULATIONS USING ANY VARIABLES STATE THAT WE SHOULD HAVE AT LEAST ARRIVED BACK AT THE RIVER ITSELF BY NOW.

Korden would've shrugged in response, but he didn't have the energy. They'd walked all morning, nearly three hours according to the computer's chronometer. Which was all they had to go on; the canopy entirely shut out the sun now, leaving the forest suspended in an eerie, eternal twilight and him with no way to tell time.

Other than his hunger, of course. That growing discomfort kept him painfully aware of how long had passed since his last meal.

But mostly his exhaustion was caused by the roughening terrain. They travelled steadily uphill, and encountered increasing patches where the foliage grew rampant. To Korden, these spots looked less like forest and more like descriptions of tropical jungles that he'd read, complete with colorful, fragrant blossoms of a variety that even Stone could not identify. The air became muggy and damp, the ground perpetually moist, so that it sucked at his sneakers and made just lifting his feet an effort. They could've tried detouring around these places again, but Korden refused to deviate from the most direct path back to the road. At first he used artcraft again to cleave a path through the vegetation, until the constant concentration taxed his mind to the point that the conduit was drained dry. Then he pushed and clawed and sometimes even crawled, despite Stone's admonishments that he would only tire himself faster. Mud coated his hands and sneakers, his muscles quivered, and sweat poured off him in salty rivers that saturated his tunic and made the inside of his dungarees feel slimy.

ERROR 147! ERROR 147! Stone suddenly screeched, startling Korden so much he stuck his hand in a bush full of thorns. The computer's voice climbed a full octave higher than normal. IRRESOLVABLE LOGIC FALLACY DETECTED! PLEASE SEEK ASSISTANCE AT AN AUTHORIZED NAMENCO, INCORPORATED REPAIR FACILITY!

"Stone, calm down!" Korden snapped. His patience had been stolen by the muggy air.

The computer's pitch lowered, but his panic did not. MY APOLOGIES, BUT I MUST BE EXPERIENCING CIRCUIT DEGRADATION! FURTHER ATTEMPTS AT SOLVING THIS PROBLEM COULD RESULT IN FATAL RETURNS!

"Then just don't think about it anymore, all right?" He stopped to pull a long thorn from the meat of his palm and brushed the blood away. After allowing himself a single swallow of water from the bladder—which emptied at an uncomfortably fast rate even with his rationing—he surveyed the rest of the hillside. "Look, there's sunshine just at the top of this rise. If the forest is opening up, maybe that means we're almost there."

But the clearing turned out to be no more than a wide, rocky fissure in the ground from which no trees could sprout, creating a break in the canopy through which they could see the sky again. Instead of being disappointed, Korden stood in the tiny oasis and tried to be grateful just to have light on his face, but that too withered when he realized which direction that light came from.

"Uh, Stone? If we're still going northwest, then why is the afternoon sun *to our right?*"

The computer said nothing for several seconds, just issued a series of low beeps in his head. THE ONLY CONCEIVABLE EXPLANATION IS THAT MY INTERNAL COMPASS IS MALFUNCTIONING, he replied timidly.

"So we've been going the wrong way this entire time?"

NEGATIVE. WE CAN CONFIRM BY THE MORNING SUN THAT WE BEGAN MOVING IN THE INTENDED DIRECTION, SO THE ACTUAL POINT OF DEVIATION IS UNKNOWN. ON A POSITIVE NOTE, THIS DISCOVERY DOES RESOLVE MY LOGIC FALLACY.

"That's great." Korden kicked an exposed tree root hard enough to send a flash of pain all the way up his knee, then plopped to the ground and picked strands of sweaty hair out of his face. "At least you'll be in perfect working order when I die of starvation out here."

IF IT IS ANY CONSOLATION, I CALCULATE YOU ARE AT LEAST 13 DAYS AWAY FROM CATASTROPHIC ORGAN FAILURE DUE TO NUTRIENT LOSS. DEHYDRATION SHOULD BECOME AN ISSUE LONG BEFORE THEN.

Korden dropped his chin into his chest and closed his eyes. "You're really not helping. At all. Just tell me how this happened."

MY APOLOGIES, BUT ALL OF MY FAIL-SAFES RELY ON EXTERNAL DATA FOR CONFIRMATION, SO I WAS UNAWARE OF THE MALFUNCTION. Stone sounded miserable. AND I STILL CAN FIND NO REASON FOR IT. IF THERE IS A MAGNETIC DISTORTION OF TRUE NORTH IN THE AREA, I SHOULD THEORETICALLY BE ABLE TO DETECT IT. UNLESS MY DETECTION PROGRAMS ARE ALSO MALFUNCTIONING. I WILL RUN A COMPLETE DIAGNOSTIC IMMEDIATELY.

"Hold on." The computer's excuse rang a bell in Korden's head. For the first time, he thought about what he'd overheard while he clung to the side of the bridge. Most of the exchange had been washed away by the flood of adrenaline from the fight, but now it all came back with crystal clarity. "The Incarnate…he said there was a power here, remember? Merise said pretty much the same thing, except she called it a heart. Could that be screwing up your compass?"

UNKNOWN. I DETECT NO ENERGY ANOMALIES THROUGH YOUR BIOMETRICS.

Korden sighed heavily, but the growling of his stomach drowned it out. This was exactly what he'd been afraid of since he started out, getting lost in the woods. "So what do we do? Turn around and see if we can find the road?"

THIS COURSE OF ACTION IS NOT ADVISED. I HAVE NO DATA TO PLOT SUCH A ROUTE AND, WITH NO RELIABLE METHOD TO DETERMINE DIRECTION, OUR PATH WOULD CERTAINLY CONTINUE TO MEANDER.

A pang of pure, burning panic slowed Korden's breath to a syrupy trickle. He brought one fist up and smashed it down against his leg to jumpstart his lungs. He couldn't do this now, couldn't let fear overtake him, not when the forest itself seemed to be against them.

And how do you know it's not?

The thought distracted him from his impending attack. He raised his head and took another look around, at the ocean of trees surrounding this island of light. The feeling of being watched had never really left, just become so routine he didn't think about it anymore.

UNDER THESE CONDITIONS, THE MOST UNOBSTRUCTED PATH WOULD OFFER THE GREATEST CHANCE OF SURVIVAL.

The way they'd been heading all this time—south, apparently—continued uphill and remained rife with clinging vegetation and underbrush. In fact, the only direction that offered easier passage seemed to be east. True, this was the way he wanted to go, but it was also the same direction they'd been forced to detour each time the path became too rough.

As if, he realized, the forest had guided them.

5

The canopy robbed Korden of light long before sunset, forcing him to stop for the night when he could see no more than a few pargs in front of him. His artcraft supply still hadn't recovered from heavy usage throughout the day; a mere trickle of energy reached him through the conduit now, not even enough to conjure a *demno*. Just as well. The going became easier since he turned to the east, but he still felt weak and shaky from hunger. If he didn't give himself time to recover, he could imagine getting sick too easily in these moist conditions.

He huddled on the ground with his knees pulled up to his chin, without the will to even try lighting a regular fire. What would be the point; he had nothing to cook over it. So his mind turned to thoughts of his favorite meals from the village and the laughter that always filled the social hall and the warmth of his father's embrace. He thought about worship service on Seventh Morn, and Bibb's trunk full of treasures and the beautiful song from his iBod and, when the realization hit him all over that he would never experience any of these things again, he began to sob. Since the first night after leaving on this wretched journey, he cried until his eyes were sore and his nose ran.

Stone fretted and did his best to console, but Korden only lifted from his grief when the computer finally said, YOU MIGHT BE INTERESTED TO KNOW THAT MY COMPILATION ON THE TOPIC 'DARK FILAMENT' IS NOW COMPLETE. I AM READY TO SUMMARIZE MY FINDINGS AT ANY TIME.

"Yes," Korden said, with tears still drying on his cheeks. A vein of dull fury pulsed at his temple like a war drum. "Tell me everything you know about the Dark Filament."

6

BEAR IN MIND, MY FINDINGS ARE BASED ON RECORDS AVAILABLE AT THE TIME THE ENCODED M-NET CEASED BROADCAST. MANY OF THESE WERE SUBJECT TO CONJECTURE. HOWEVER, THE FOLLOWING IS A BRIEF TIMELINE OF THE EVENTS THAT SEVERAL NOTED EXPERTS OF THE DAY REFERRED TO AS 'THE DARK FILAMENT EPHEMERIS':

THE FIRST EVIDENCE OF THEIR EXISTENCE CAME IN THE LAST DECADE OF THE 20TH CENTURY, ALTHOUGH ALL WERE RECOGNIZED AS SUCH ONLY IN HINDSIGHT. AROUND THE WORLD, A WAVE OF VIOLENCE DIRECTED AT CHILDREN EMERGED, KIDNAPPINGS AND MASS SHOOTINGS—PARTICULARLY AT SCHOOLS—BEING THE MOST PREVALENT. THE PERPETRATORS ARE WIDELY BELIEVED TO BE THE FIRST INCARNATES, TRAVELING ALONE TO AFFECT DEEP SOCIETAL INFILTRATION. HOWEVER, AS MOST ARE KILLED BEFORE THEY CAN BE TAKEN INTO CUSTODY, THERE IS NO PROOF TO SUPPORT THIS.

"I know about that," Korden interrupted softly, but he was mostly speaking to himself. This story was being told to the topmost part of his mind, but, beneath it, deep down on a barely conscious level, Stone pumped in a steady stream of pictorial concepts and definitions to help him make sense of it all. Still, that word 'ephemeris' lodged in his brain like a fly mired in tree sap. According to Stone, it meant a table or journal that detailed celestial positioning; star charts, in other words. It seemed too pretty to be paired with something so ugly. "Well, some of it. Tash told me. But what *are* they? Where did they *come from?*"

UNKNOWN. IF THIS THEORY IS CORRECT, MANY OF THESE EARLY INCARNATES BEGAN AS NORMAL, LAW-ABIDING INDIVIDUALS WHO TURNED TO VIOLENCE WITH SEEMINGLY NO EXPLANATION OR WARNING. THE CAUSE FOR THIS CHANGE, ALTHOUGH WIDELY DEBATED, REMAINS A MYSTERY.

"My father always said they were demons. They take over your body and…and you can never get free of them." Allin, his eyes glowing fiery red, face twisted in murderous rage.

THIS WOULD EVENTUALLY BECOME A POPULAR THEORY. BUT, AS THESE INCIDENTS CONTINUED WELL INTO THE 21ST CENTURY, THE PUBLIC ATTRIBUTED NOTHING OVERTLY SINISTER TO THEM, VIEWING THIS TENDENCY TO 'SNAP' AS NO MORE THAN A PRODUCT OF THE TIMES IN WHICH THEY LIVED. AT MOST, THEY SPARKED RENEWED INTEREST IN WEAPON CONTROL LEGISLATION. HOWEVER, THERE ARE SOME THAT BELIEVE—AGAIN, ONLY IN HINDSIGHT—THAT THE GOVERNMENTS OF THE WORLD, PARTICULARLY THE UNITED STATES, WERE FULLY AWARE OF THE INSURGENCY OF THE DARK FILAMENT AT THIS TIME, AND WERE WAGING A WAR AGAINST THEM IN SECRET.

"Why would they do that? If they knew, why wouldn't they tell people, to warn them?"

LOGIC SUGGESTS THEY MIGHT HAVE BEEN UNAWARE OF THE EXTENT OF THE THREAT, OR PERHAPS DID NOT WANT

TO CAUSE A PANIC. OTHERS BELIEVED A MORE SINISTER AGENDA. IN ANY CASE, THE GOVERNMENTS OF THE 20TH AND 21ST CENTURIES WERE NOTORIOUS FOR THEIR SECRECY.

Korden shook his head in disappointment. He might be fascinated with that lost civilization, but he didn't know if he would ever fully understand the people who lived in it. "Go on."

THE NAME 'DARK FILAMENT' ITSELF FIRST APPEARED IN PUBLIC FORUMS AROUND THE TURN OF THE MILLENNIUM, MOSTLY ON VARIOUS CONSPIRACY-THEMED WEBSITES AND IN-TERNET COMMENT THREADS. MUCH OF THESE REFERENCES WERE OBLIQUE, NO MORE THAN THE PRODUCT OF WHISPERED RUMORS ABOUT WHAT WAS BELIEVED TO BE A DEVIL-WORSHIPPING CULT WHICH BRAINWASHED SLEEPER AGENTS INTO DOING THEIR BIDDING. THERE ARE SEVERAL DOCUMENTED CASES OF INDIVIDUALS CLAIMING TO HAVE EVIDENCE OF THEIR EX-ISTENCE, THE MOST FAMOUS OF WHICH IS THE STORY OF A MAN WHOSE DAUGHTERS WERE KIDNAPPED BY AN INDIVIDUAL ON A MURDER SPREE IN THE STATE OF SOUTH CAROLINA IN THE YEAR 2006. BUT, FOR THE MOST PART, THE PEOPLE OF THE WORLD REMAINED BLIND TO THESE FIRST RIPPLES OF DISCORD.

HOWEVER, IT IS AT THIS TIME THAT THE FUNDAMEN-TAL FABRIC AND NATURE OF THE EARTH ITSELF BEGINS TO CHANGE IN WAYS TOO EXTREME TO GO UNNOTICED.

UNNATURAL WEATHER PATTERNS AND OFFSEASON MIGRA-TIONS SET THE SCIENTIFIC COMMUNITY ABLAZE. NEW ANI-MAL CLASSIFICATIONS ARE DISCOVERED WITH A REGULARITY TOO DENSE TO BE COINCIDENTAL; THIS MOVEMENT WILL EVENTUALLY BE CALLED THE GREAT SPECIES EMERGENCE, BUT THE FOREIGN NATURE OF THESE CREATURES' DNA WILL GO UNEXPLAINED.

BY FAR THE MOST SIGNIFICANT CHANGE COMES AS AMATEUR ASTROLOGISTS ALL OVER THE WORLD BEGIN CLAIMING THAT THE RECOGNIZED ASTERISMS ARE NO LONGER IDENTIFIABLE. THEN, ON MARCH 18, 2044, THE WORLD IS SHOCKED WHEN THE NATIONAL AERONAUTICS AND SPACE ADMINISTRATION ISSUES A REPORT CONFIRMING THESE FINDINGS, STATING THAT THE STAR ALIGNMENTS HAVE INDEED SHIFTED IN MINUTE INCREMENTS, A PHENOMENON THAT HAS NEVER OCCURRED IN RECORDED HUMAN HISTORY.

"The stars?" Korden looked upward instinctively, thinking again of that word 'ephemeris,' but the forest canopy created a black ceiling overhead, without a single point of heavenly illumination visible. "The stars…changed?"

AGAIN, THE EXACT REASON FOR THIS IS UNKNOWN. THE MOST POPULAR THEORY STATES THAT THE EARTH'S AXIS HAD BEEN DISTURBED, BUT SUCH A CHANGE WOULD BE ACCOMPANIED BY CATACLYSMIC EARTHQUAKES AND TIDAL SHIFTS, NONE OF WHICH WERE OBSERVED.

EACH OF THESE EVENTS, THOUGH REVOLUTIONARY, REMAINED ISOLATED UNTIL 2058, WHEN THE EVOLUTIONARY GAP PHENOMENON THEORY WAS PUT FORTH AS A MEANS TO CONNECT THEM. DOCTORS GOENER AND SINGH POSTULATE THAT THESE CHANGES ARE A SIGN OF SOME COMING GLOBAL TRAUMA, AN IDEA LAUGHED AT BY A MAJORITY OF THE SCIENTIFIC COMMUNITY, BUT WHICH CAUSES MASS HYSTERIA AMONG THE PUBLIC. WHILE MANY WILL POINT TO THIS HYPOTHESIS 70 YEARS LATER DURING THE DARK WARS, IT IS STILL NOT KNOWN IF THE THEORY HAS MERIT OR IF ANY OF THE EVENTS ARE INDEED CONNECTED TO ONE ANOTHER.

Korden sat up straighter at the mention of the battle in which Tash's son lost his life, but he said nothing to interrupt the narrative.

AT APPROXIMATELY 12:00 AM UTC+12—THE TIME ZONE WHICH DENOTES THE INTERNATIONAL DATE LINE—ON JANUARY 1, 2121, THE NATIONAL WEATHER BUREAU ISSUED A NOTICE THAT A BLACK CLOUD HAD APPEARED OVER PARTS OF ANTARCTICA. THIRTY MINUTES LATER, THIS DARKNESS STRETCHED FROM ONE POLE TO THE OTHER ALONG THE INTERNATIONAL DATE LINE, LYING IN AN UNNATURAL, STRAIGHT-EDGED FORMATION. FORTY-FIVE MINUTES LATER, COMMUNICATIONS WERE LOST WITH A CHAIN OF INHABITED ISLANDS IN THE SOUTH PACIFIC, AND THE BLACK CLOUD BEGAN SPREADING WEST IN A UNIFORM LINE TO COVER THEM.

"The Shroud." Korden's aching belly groaned as fear tightened his insides. Looking at the dark mass in the sky his whole life had been bad, but he could only imagine what it must've been like to actually live through its appearance.

CORRECT. OVER THE NEXT TWENTY-FOUR HOURS, THIS CLOUD CONTINUES TO SPREAD WEST ACROSS EVERY UNINHABITED PIECE OF LAND FALLING IN SEQUENTIAL DISTANCE FROM THE DATE LINE. THE MAJORITY OF THE WORLD IS UNAWARE OF ITS EXISTENCE. MANY GOVERNMENTS WISHED TO KEEP IT FROM THEIR PEOPLE, BUT WHEN SOME BEGIN ALERTING THEIR POPULACES FOR PURPOSES OF PREPARATION, IT QUICKLY CIRCLES THE GLOBE.

"What did the people do?"

THE INITIAL RESPONSE IS CONFUSION AND DISBELIEF. MOST SEE IT AS A HOAX. THEN, AS THE FIRST IMAGES OF THIS CLOUD ARE BROADCAST ACROSS THE M-NET, CONFUSION TURNS TO PANIC AND CHAOS. SOME BELIEVE THE INVADERS TO BE EXTRATERRESTRIAL IN ORIGIN; SOME THAT AN ARMAGEDDON BASED ON THE JUDEO-CHRISTIAN/ISLAMIC PROPHECIES IS UPON THEM. RIOTS, LOOTING AND MURDER ARE RAMPANT. MANY COUNTRIES, INCLUDING THE UNITED STATES,

ARE PLACED UNDER MARTIAL LAW UNTIL COOLER HEADS CAN PREVAIL.

DURING THIS TIME, MASSIVE ARMIES OF INCARNATES EMERGE FROM THE CLOUD EACH NIGHT AND DESCEND UPON ANY POPULATED AREAS IN THEIR PATH. THIS IS THE FIRST TIME THE WORLD SEES THEIR ATTACKERS, THROUGH LEAKED AMATEUR VIDEO AND NEWS HOLO-CASTS, AND IT CAUSES A FRESH WAVE OF TERROR. THEIR APPROACH—WHICH BECOMES KNOWN AS THE PURGES—IS ALWAYS THE SAME: THEY MASSA-CRE ANYONE UNDER THE AGE OF 18, LEAVING THEM IN THE STREETS TO ROT. OTHER THAN THIS SELECT GROUP, THEY SLAUGHTER ONLY THOSE WHO STAND AGAINST THEM. ANYONE THAT COOPERATES IS ALLOWED TO LIVE. ONCE THEY HAVE ROBBED THE POPULACE OF ITS YOUTH, THE BLACK CLOUD SPREADS BEHIND THEM TO COVER THE CONQUERED REGIONS, WHICH ARE THEN BEREFT OF POWER AND COMMUNICATIONS.

NEW ZEALAND FALLS QUICKLY, AND RUSSIA'S VASTLY UNINHABITED EASTERN TUNDRA IS AN EASY VICTORY FOR THE DARK FILAMENT. RUSSIA, JAPAN AND THE AUSTRALIO FEDERATION ARE AMONG THE FIRST TO MOBILIZE THEIR ARMIES AND ATTEMPT EVACUATIONS OF THEIR PEOPLE. AS THE INCARNATES CONTINUE THEIR WESTWARD MARCH, SMALL SKIRMISHES BREAK OUT ACROSS THE HEMISPHERE.

THESE EARLY BATTLES ARE, AT FIRST, CONSIDERED A SUCCESS. THE INCARNATES HAVE SEEMINGLY ENDLESS NUM-BERS, BUT LITTLE TECHNOLOGY. THEY RELY ON BRUTE FORCE AND HAND-TO-HAND COMBAT, SWARMING THROUGH EACH AREA IN A MANNER NOT UNLIKE LOCUSTS. AIR STRIKES AND HEAVY ARTILLERY ARE EFFECTIVE AT HOLDING THE FILAMENT'S ARMIES AT BAY. HOWEVER, IT SOON BECOMES EVIDENT THAT SUCH ATTACKS ARE LARGELY A WASTE OF RESOURCES. THE ENEMY RECOVERS FROM SETBACKS QUICKLY TO MAKE UP LOST

GROUND. SOME FIELD REPORTS SUGGEST THAT THEY CANNOT BE KILLED BY LONG RANGE WEAPONRY.

"They didn't have faith," Korden interpreted.

Stone either didn't hear or, more likely, chose not to comment. IN THESE EARLY DAYS, THE UNITED STATES REFUSES TO GET INVOLVED. THE DARK FILAMENT'S WESTWARD-ONLY EXPANSION PLACES THEM IN THE LEAST DANGER, ALTHOUGH THE WESTERN SEABOARD IS HEAVILY MONITORED IN CASE THE SHROUD SHOULD START SPREADING THE OPPOSITE DIRECTION. MUCH OF THE WORLD FOLLOWS THEIR EXAMPLE. CHINA, RECOGNIZING THE IMMINENT THREAT TO THEIR OWN DOMAIN, SENDS REINFORCEMENTS TO BOTH JAPAN AND RUSSIA, FORGING A BOND THAT WOULD BE THE BASIS FOR THE INTERNATIONAL COALITION. WITH THEIR HELP, A WALL IS HASTILY CONSTRUCTED ALONG THE LENA RIVER FROM THE ARCTIC OCEAN DOWN THROUGH MONGOLIA AND INTO BEIJING. A SIMILAR WALL BISECTS THE AUSTRALIO FEDERATION. THE DEATH TOLL AT THIS POINT IS ESTIMATED AT CLOSE TO 400,000. FOR THE NEXT DECADE, THESE MANNED BARRIERS SERVE AS A BUFFER TO REPEL THE INVADING FORCES, AND THE REGION SETTLES INTO AN UNEASY GUARD.

"Didn't the rest of the world do *anything* to help?"

NOT AT THIS TIME. THE WEST WAS LITTLE AFFECTED BY THE INVASION, AND LIFE CONTINUED AS BEFORE. NOW THAT THE INITIAL SHOCK HAD WORN OFF, MOST VIEW THE FIGHTING HAPPENING ON THE OTHER SIDE OF THE GLOBE AS NO MORE THAN ANOTHER FOREIGN WAR THAT HAS NOTHING TO DO WITH THEM. FAMILIARITY MAKES THE UNKNOWN NATURE AND ORIGIN OF THE INVADERS LESS OF A CONCERN. IT IS NOT UNTIL LATE IN THE YEAR 2132, WHEN CELLS OF INCARNATES SPONTANEOUSLY APPEAR IN COUNTRIES AROUND THE WORLD, THAT EVERYONE COMES TO TERMS WITH THE DANGER.

ALMOST OVERNIGHT, NATIONS THROUGHOUT EUROPE, AFRICA, AND THE CENTRAL EAST FIND THEMSELVES AT WAR WITH THE FILAMENT IN THEIR OWN BACKYARDS. NO ONE UNDERSTANDS HOW THE ENEMY IS CAPABLE OF MOVING SUCH VAST AMOUNTS OF TROOPS UNDETECTED, OR WHY IT HAS TAKEN THEM SO LONG TO DO SO. SOME OF THESE INCURSIONS ARE PUT DOWN; OTHERS GAIN GROUND. RUSSIA AND CHINA—WHO SOON FIND THEIR WALL USELESS AS THEY BEGIN TO FIGHT ON TWO FRONTS—BEG THE WEST FOR ASSISTANCE. AFTER AN INCARNATE CELL IS DEFEATED IN ONTARIO, A UNITED NATIONS TREATY FORMING THE INTERNATIONAL COALITION IS QUICKLY RATIFIED.

2133 SEES THE LARGEST COORDINATED WAR EFFORT IN HUMAN HISTORY. IT IS ESTIMATED THAT 96 PERCENT OF ALL NATIONS WITH A STANDING ARMY CONTRIBUTE FORCES, AND THOSE WITHOUT SEND AS MANY VOLUNTEERS AS THEY CAN MUSTER. THE FIRST MASSIVE BATTLES OF THE DARK WARS ARE WAGED AT STRATEGIC CHOKE POINTS SIMULTANEOUSLY.

"And they failed...didn't they?"

AFFIRMATIVE. BOTH MILITARY AND CIVILIAN CASUALTIES ARE MASSIVE, NUMBERING IN THE HUNDREDS OF MILLIONS. GROUND FORCES EVERYWHERE BEGIN TO REPORT, AS YOU CLAIM, THAT 'ONLY THOSE WITH FAITH CAN KILL AN INCARNATE,' A VIEW LARGELY DISCREDITED BY GOVERNMENTAL LEADERS. HUMAN FORCES ARE STEADILY PUSHED BACK AS THE DARK WARS CONTINUE FOR ANOTHER TWO YEARS, DURING WHICH PLANETARY LIFE AND RESOURCES ARE SEVERELY DEPLETED. THE SHROUD CONTINUES TO SPREAD, BECOMING AN UNOFFICIAL LINE OF DEMARCATION BEYOND WHICH ALL LAND AND SOULS ARE CONSIDERED IRREVOCABLY LOST. CIVILIANS ARE EVACUATED WHERE POSSIBLE; ANY LEFT BEHIND FIND THEMSELVES AT THE MERCY OF THE FILAMENT AND THEIR

FATES UNKNOWN. WAVES OF REFUGEES RUSH WEST ACROSS THE CONTINENTS, BUT SOON REALIZE THEY HAVE NOWHERE TO HIDE.

IN 2134, AUSTRALIO AND JAPAN GO DARK.

IN 2135, CHINA, RUSSIA AND MOST OF AFRICA AND THE CENTRAL EAST GO DARK.

BY MID-2136, EUROPEAN FORCES CONTINUE TO FIGHT AS CONCENTRATIONS OF INCARNATES APPEAR ON SHORES THROUGHOUT SOUTH AMERICA.

IN NORTH AMERICA, SOCIETY COLLAPSES LONG BEFORE THE INCARNATES CAN REACH THE LAST OF HUMANITY'S NATIONS. MOST OF THE POPULACE OF THE UNITED STATES AND THE SOVEREIGN OUTLANDS BEGIN A WESTWARD TREK WITH THEIR CHILDREN, LEAVING BEHIND VACANT CITIES.

AND, ON MAY 15TH, THE M-NETWORK CRASHES, WHICH IS WHERE THE LAST OF MY FILES COME TO AN END.

7

"That's it?" Korden asked. "It took you this long just to tell me *that?*"

Stone made a noise that could only be categorized as an indignant squawk. THIS SUMMARY WAS COMPILED FROM OVER SEVEN TRILLION RELATED ENTRIES. THE TERM 'DARK FILAMENT' WAS THE MOST REPEATED AND SEARCHED M-NET TOPIC IN HUMAN HISTORY. I REDUCED OVER 500 YOTTABYTES OF INFORMATION INTO A FORMAT THAT YOU COULD DIGEST WITHIN YOUR LIFETIME. BUT I SUPPOSE YOU COULD HAVE DONE BETTER.

"No, probably not," Korden admitted.

I CAN, HOWEVER, ELABORATE ON ANY ASPECT YOU WISH TO KNOW MORE ABOUT. SO TELL ME, WHAT IS IT YOU EXPECTED TO LEARN FROM MY RESEARCH?

"I...I just thought that...I don't know..." But that wasn't true, he knew exactly what he hoped to get from the computer's story: the chink in his enemy's armor. Detailed footnotes on what he should do to destroy them, to defeat the Filament once and for all.

The solution to his problems wrapped up like one of his birthday presents, and presented to him with a bow on top.

As I stated, these files are merely the collective knowledge of the world at the time of the M-Net's collapse. No definitive explanation for the Dark Filament had been discovered; therefore, I have only theories to offer. If more information has surfaced since, I have no way to access it.

"I know, I'm sorry. It's not your fault." He lay back on the bedroll and instantly felt sleep threaten to overtake him.

It is curious to note that, after such rapid initial advancement, the Shroud has spread no further in three centuries. Extrapolation suggests that these Incarnates should have accomplished their goal by now.

"Someone is holding them back," Korden said around a yawn. "At least, that's what Tash thought. And whoever it is, we're going to find them."

A comforting thought, a last hope to cling to, but, of course, it was dependent upon them finding their way out of the forest first.

And, for the first time, he began to believe that might not be possible.

HEART OF THE FOREST

1

Korden ran through the dark woods, carefree and laughing. All around him, the sequoias whispered his name, calling to him in a thousand voices, urging him on. He seemed to remember thinking those murmurs were creepy at one time, but not anymore. They were beautiful and ethereal, a warm blanket that he wanted to wrap himself in.

Something ahead caught his attention. It looked like a doorway standing between two of the mighty trees. And not just any doorway; as Korden drifted closer, he recognized the entrance into the *hucté* where he lived most of his life, a rectangle that canted to the right a little more each season from the sagging of their roof. And, even though there were no walls on the other side, nothing but more forest, a faint light spilled out across the threshold.

He paused in front of it. Tried to peer inside. The voices pleaded with him to move on, but Korden stepped closer, into the doorway. He'd passed through it so many times, he knew every inch by heart, every ding and scratch and chip, most of them made by him during one of his childish flights down to the village. As he passed through the opening, he stretched out one hand and let his fingers trail across the hardened mud. The jamb felt exactly as he remembered.

On the other side, the forest was gone. He stood in the common room of his home, just as he left it, but the details seemed dim and unimportant, because in the middle was their supping table, and sitting at it with eyes downcast, as he had been on the morning Korden came sneaking in after breaching the Barrier, was—

"*Redfen!*" Such excitement gripped Korden, not even the sudden suspicion that this was a dream could dampen it. He wanted to run to his father, but he seemed to be stuck in place, unable to move closer. The man lifted his eyes and took in his son with a gaze both wistful and a little sad. "Is this real? Are you really here?"

"Only you can answer that," Redfen Bright said slowly. Almost mechanically. He seemed to fade in and out of focus, the details of his face blurring and sharpening. "And what you decide is of the utmost importance. So tell me...do *you* believe I'm real?"

Korden gave the strange question serious consideration. His father raised an eyebrow apprehensively as he waited for the answer. That worried face—one he knew so well—convinced him. "Yes! Of course I do!"

As soon as the words were out of his mouth, Redfen's features jumped back into sharp contrast, the scar on his temple so vivid it seemed to float in front of his face. Korden realized he hadn't forgotten what the man looked like at all. Redfen appeared immensely relieved as he nodded. "Good. That's very good. That means we can talk honestly, without *him* interfering."

"Him?" Korden repeated. The emphasis on the word sent an unpleasant tingle along his neck.

Redfen didn't answer, just gestured at the seat on the other side of the table, closest to his son. Korden slipped into it and sat with his hands in his lap, staring across at his father. "I miss you so much," he said. Tears welled in his eyes, spilled down his cheeks. "I just wanna go home, I don't wanna be in the forest anymore."

"But you're so close," Redfen told him matter-of-factly. "You've almost reached the end of these dreary woods, but the worst is yet to come."

"What…what do you mean?" Now the tingle spread and deepened into dread.

"You got lost," Redfen told him, and grimaced. "That isn't good. If you'd stayed on the road, I think you would've been all right—roads can be an anchor, to keep both the body and the mind from wandering—but now…"

"It's not my fault, there were Incarnates and—!"

"Hush, son." The interruption was swift and stern. "We don't have much time. You are in his grasp now, and he is drawing you to him even as we speak."

"Redfen…who are you talking about? The Filament?"

"No. This has nothing to do with the Dark Filament. And yet they are responsible for it, as with most things wrong in our world." His father drew a deep breath, and seemed to take an eternity to speak again. "I say 'he,' but I don't think this entity has any more gender than a clod of dirt. If the Incarnates are parasites, then he is a scavenger. A hitchhiker. A side effect." These terms meant nothing to Korden without Stone to translate them, but he thought he understood the gist. "He has been trapped for long, gathering what power he can, extending his reach through the forest as he searches for someone who can set him free, someone just like you. And now there is no choice but to face him, not if you want to escape this place."

"I still don't understand!" Korden insisted. Something was happening to this room. It seemed to be collapsing in on itself, as though they were inside a bubble that some giant hand was squeezing.

"Just remember, he can't force you, only coerce you. And he will know exactly what to say, because he lives where you play." Even though Redfen still sat just across the table, he seemed to be growing farther and farther away. The next words in his odd poem were no more than a dying echo. "He eats what you dream and drinks what you fear, and the only way past him is the truth."

"Don't go!" Korden pleaded. "Please, I need you!"

"I can't stay, and neither can you, because it's time for you to w

2

—AKE UP, SIR! REPEAT, WAKE UP! KORDEN BRIGHT, PLEASE RETURN TO CONSCIOUSNESS IMMEDIATELY!

Korden's eyelids peeled apart as Stone's voice dragged him from the depths of sleep. For just a moment, beneath the computer's fear laden warble, he thought he could once again hear his name repeated in countless different voices, all of them as airy and light as a gentle breeze. Then he realized what he was seeing, and confusion drove all other thoughts away.

He could clearly remember stretching out on his bedroll last night, but now, somehow, he was standing. No, more than standing; he was *moving*, walking swiftly and easily between the trees as though he knew the route by heart. Korden looked down, amazed to watch his limbs working without his consent, then ordered his legs to stop. He almost expected them not to listen, to find that he was now a helpless passenger in his own body, but, with a sort of crisp mental *snap*, they instantly became his own again. The disorientation caused his knees to buckle, spilling him into the damp forest floor. He sat in the mud, shivering, and gazed about him.

"What...where...?" Dewy tendrils of golden sunlight filtered through the canopy, barely enough to see by, but still bright enough to dazzle his tired eyes. There was no sign of his bedroll or the camp he'd made. "H-how did I get here?"

YOU APPEARED TO BE SLEEPWALKING, ALTHOUGH YOUR BRAINWAVES WERE INCONSISTENT WITH THIS PROGNOSIS. I HAVE BEEN ATTEMPTING TO WAKE YOU FOR THE PAST TWENTY-THREE MINUTES.

"I...*I walked here?*" He couldn't understand the computer. Not just the message, but the individual words themselves. His head seemed to have gained ten pounds during the night, and all of his thoughts were coated in molasses. Every cupit of his body felt sore.

He knew this feeling. He was getting sick. A fever. Possibly worse. As he tried to shake off the lethargy, another shiver wracked him so hard his teeth chattered.

YOUR REST WAS FITFUL, THEN, WITHOUT WARNING, YOU STOOD UP AND BEGAN WALKING ONCE MORE. IT IS FORTUNATE THAT YOU WORE MY CASING AROUND YOUR NECK, SO THAT I COULD ROUSE YOU BEFORE YOU INJURED YOURSELF.

"Yeah...fortunate..." Korden had suffered many ailments over the years, but sleepwalking had never been one of them.

Pieces of his dream resurfaced. The joy he'd felt from the brief reunion still warmed his chest. In the dream, he'd been so *sure* the man was his father—hadn't he even said as much?—but now, armed with waking logic, he saw this Redfen Bright for what he truly was: a representation cobbled together from deepest memory. The real man was never so cold or mechanical, and he certainly never spoke in rhymes and riddles.

But that didn't mean the dream was complete nonsense either.

You are in his grasp now, and he is drawing you to him even as we speak.

This could've been a bit of paranoid nonsense inspired by Merise…and yet *something* had compelled him to get up while he slumbered and start walking.

Toward whatever power haunted these woods. He felt sure of that much, if nothing else.

May the forest eat you alive…

He shook his head. There were too many voices in there, vying for his attention. Most of the actual exchange from his dream had now slipped away, except for that last cryptic warning: *He eats what you dream and drinks what you fear and the only way past him is the truth.*

Korden climbed to his feet, using a nearby sequoia to steady himself. A wave of lightheadedness made him stumble again. He leaned against the broad tree trunk and closed his eyes. The rough bark seemed to tear at his sensitive skin through his tunic.

WARNING: YOUR BODY TEMPERATURE HAS RISEN ABOVE 100 DEGREES IN THE PAST HOUR. YOU APPEAR TO BE SUFFERING FROM AN EXHAUSTION-DERIVED FEVER, MOST LIKELY COMPLICATED BY STARVATION.

Korden waited until the dizzy spell passed and pushed away from the tree. "Do you know how to get back?"

Affirmative. I plotted your route visually so that I could guide you.

It took them twice as long to return to the camp, and not only because of Korden's growing illness. The landmarks Stone memorized were still present, but he insisted that the forest had grown in the short amount of time since they passed. What was a clear path before had become almost impassable.

Because we're going the wrong direction now, Korden thought. *As long as we keep heading east, the way it* (he) *wants us to go, the forest will stay out of my way.*

The thought made his skin crawl. The feeling of those invisible eyes on him continued to gain strength.

He moved carefully, deliberately pushing through the dense foliage, too exhausted to manipulate the artcraft to ease his passage. By the time they reached his belongings, he bled from dozens of scratches. Sweat poured down his face and neck, yet he felt freezing cold and shivered uncontrollably. He changed into the warmest set of clothes from his carry pouch, and even pulled on his coat, then forced himself to drink the last of the water from his bladder. As he rolled up his bed and packed it away in preparation to move on, Stone spoke up.

This course of action is not advised. Further exertion could worsen your condition. A lengthy period of rest and recuperation is recommended.

"And just what am I going to eat while I'm recuperating? What am I going to drink?"

Stone hesitated for the barest fraction of a second. I concur, this is a dangerous drawback, but I calculate—

"I don't care about your calculations!" Korden shouted. The outburst startled the computer into silence. "I don't care about anything except getting out of this cursed forest, and I won't stop until I do!" He lifted his head up and took in the canopy, whose leaves, in his overheated mind, seemed to have arranged themselves in the shape of a smirking mouth directly above him. "DO YOU HEAR ME?" he screamed. "I'M LEAVING, *AND YOU CAN'T STOP ME!*"

This burning will was the only thing that saw him through that day, one of the longest in his life, and even it could only take him so far. His hunger faded, but a gnawing thirst replaced it, one that made the inside of his mouth feel like sand. The pools of stagnant, muddy water he passed looked ever more appetizing. After another hour of walking (this time back to the east, and, sure enough, the plants cleared him an easy path), he developed a wet cough to go with his fever. By noon, his vision wavered whenever he tried to focus on anything, and each exhalation came out as a shuddering, reed-thin wheeze. An hour after that, his shaking reached the point where he was doing more stumbling than walking.

With half an afternoon of useable daylight still left, he finally found a dry spot and sank to the ground.

"I'm going to die here," he rasped. "Aren't I?"

Stone remained silent.

Korden coughed, a rattling bark that filled his throat with fluid. His skin was boiling hot and slick with sweat, and still he shivered. As many times as he'd been sick in his life, he'd only felt this miserable once before, during the illness that bestowed him with as-mah as a parting gift. "I just don't understand what it was all for. If I had a destiny...like Tash said...then why is the Upper letting this happen? Maybe... maybe you were right about that, too. Maybe He only helps those who help themselves."

Or He never existed at all.

This idea had the power to shame him even now.

WITH YOUR PERMISSION, Stone said solemnly, I WOULD LIKE TO REGISTER MY LICENSE AS OPEN USAGE AND SWITCH OVER TO STANDBY MODE TO PRESERVE BATTERY LIFE. THE CHANCE OF SOMEONE FINDING ME, EVEN BEFORE MY PHYSICAL COMPONENTS DEGRADE IN 30,000 YEARS, IS SLIM, BUT THIS WOULD SKEW THE ODDS OF SURVIVAL .000001 IN MY FAVOR.

"Go ahead," Korden waved a hand. "Everyone else deserted me. Why shouldn't you?"

MY SINCEREST APOLOGIES, IT WAS NOT MY INTENT TO MAKE IT SEEM AS THOUGH—!

"Stone…it's fine. I'm not mad at you. You've been a good friend. I never would've gotten even this far if not for you."

The computer gave a pleased—but still somehow melancholy—chirp. AND YOU HAVE BEEN AN AGREEABLE OWNER. I REGRET THAT WE WERE UNABLE TO COMPLETE YOUR TASK.

"Me too. If you do get found, tell whoever it is what I was trying to do. Maybe that's what I was meant for. To inspire someone else to stop the Filament."

AFFIRMATIVE. IT IS AGAINST MY PROTOCOLS TO ASSIST ANY HUMAN WITH SELF-INJURY, BUT UNDER THE GUISE OF THEORETICAL INTEREST, I COULD, IF YOU WOULD LIKE, RECOMMEND SOME PAINLESS WAYS TO…

Korden shook his head. "No, that's all right. I just want to sit here and think about my father. I hope…I hope I get to see him again." *For real this time.*

AS DO I. SHOULD YOU NEED ME, JUST SQUEEZE MY CASING TO BRING ME OUT OF STANDBY MODE. FAREWELL, KORDEN BRIGHT.

There was a soft, dwindling hum in his head, and the computer's presence faded away.

Alone again, Korden leaned back against a thin alder tree with his pouch beside him, and settled in to die.

3

He wasn't sure how many hours passed. The next time he opened his eyes, night had fallen, yet the forest wasn't dark. A pure white glow like that of Merise's electric torches spilled out between the trees from somewhere ahead, an explosion of light bright enough to throw crisp shadows away from it in all directions. Korden raised a shaking hand to shield his eyes and found that he barely had any strength left to hold it there.

"H-hello?" His voice was a dry puff of air blowing over chapped lips. Sweet Upper, he was so *thirsty*. "Is anyone t-there?"

korden

His name came from everywhere and nowhere, whispered by a multitude of voices. Their cadence was soft, soothing… but the hairs along the back of his neck still stiffened at the sound.

"Who said that?"

korden come to us we need you save us give yourself surrender

The voices talked over and around one another, each adding their own sentiment to the message. His overheated brain had to work to sort out one from the next. "W-what do you mean? Who are you?"

This time there was no answer, but that glow coming through the trees remained, pulsing in slow, steady beats, as though beckoning him. He tried to scan the forest for signs of life, but his well of artcraft remained bone dry, his connection to the Upper a tenuous thread. Not surprising, considering his willpower felt like mush.

Korden stood on legs as brittle as dead twigs. He could feel the sickness sitting in his chest now, a hot, sloshing weight that made each breath a misery. Sweat poured down his brow and cheeks. Every part of him ached; skin aflame, muscles cramping, even the pads of his feet sore atop the sneaker soles. He gathered his carry pouch, falling again as he did, and then limped on through the silent forest.

The light ahead cast everything in harsh tones of black and white. Between each blink of his eye, the poisoned woods seemed to part a little more in front of him, the trees and vines and plants all drawing back to create a smooth pathway.

He only walked for a minute before he saw the first small lump beside the path, a shape that could've been a rock except for the fat, bushy tail curling off its rear. When he realized it was the first wildlife he'd seen in days, his stomach gave an involuntary rumble.

Until he got closer, and then the notion of eating what he'd found made him instantly nauseated.

The body belonged to a dead squirrel. Its corpse was shriveled, so drained and dry as to be mummified. But the head of the creature truly horrified him. The back of the furry crown appeared to have collapsed inward, leaving a clotted crater with scrambled matter inside. One tiny, dried-up eyeball stared out at him from the hole.

That dread welled up in Korden again, a slow, caustic fear that ate at his insides like acid.

He wanted to run, to go anywhere except forward, but when he turned away from the glow, he found that an impenetrable barricade had sprung up behind him, made from stunted, skeletal pine trees wrapped in blackish vines. They seemed to press closer, like the trees in Emmett, ushering him forward. He did as they bade and moved on, feeling out of control of his own body again. The fever heat lent the world a sheen of surreality.

Now more animals lay strung along both sides of the path and caught in the underbrush like leaves, dead chipmunks and beavers and rabbits and birds and snakes. All of their heads caved in like the squirrel, cataclysmic ruptures that left their skulls flattened and deformed. Some of the bodies were so old they were no more than bleached bones gleaming in the bright light, and even on these he could see where the craniums had fractured into pieces.

A heart so cold, it sucks the very life out of everything it lures into its embrace.

Where had he heard that? He just couldn't remember anymore.

The bodies grew in number as he drifted on through this nightmare, piles of ancient corpses stacked everywhere like cordwood, and now there were bigger animals as well, a deer with most of its pulped brain matter dangling out of its mouth in a vomitous string, a wolf whose muzzle was the only part of its head intact, and even the skeleton of a gigantic elk draped across a fallen log, its antlers reaching for the sky above a shattered skull.

This was where the missing creatures of the forest had all gone. They'd been drawn here, much like the rabbits he coaxed out for his own meals.

Now *he* was the one being coaxed, and he was powerless but to obey.

As he drew closer to the glow, Korden made out a sheer

rock face rising through the trees ahead, a craggy mountainside that burst up through the canopy. He headed in that direction, following the path the forest carved for him, until a coughing fit seized him. Each hack caused a burst of stars across his vision.

He fell to one knee, the world spinning around him. There would be no getting up this time, he suspected; the forest could direct him all it wanted, but, short of a miracle, he just couldn't go on. He would finish his journey right here and that would be the end of him.

"Oh, come on now, pardner," a gruff voice said suddenly, startling Korden so much he fell back on his haunches. "I've been waiting on you too long to watch you poop out on me now."

A figure strolled out from the field of trees ahead. It stood with its face turned just enough that the glow washed across it, and, even though he'd never laid eyes upon this person, Korden instantly recognized that chiseled jaw and the rugged features above it.

Sheriff Protector put his fisted hands on his hips in a regal, dramatic pose as he regarded Korden. "Besides...don't you know a true hero never gives up?"

4

"You...you can't be real..." Korden murmured from the ground.

"Course I can," the Sheriff proclaimed. He stood as big as Korden had always described him, at least six pargs tall and as broad-chested as a bear, with bulging arms and legs that put even Eddas to shame. He wore a crisp, one-piece garment perfectly tailored to his hulking form. In the all-consuming white light, it was impossible to tell the exact color, but Korden still knew it was a dark, midnight blue; when he'd written about it, he called it a 'uniform'. Cinched around his midsection was a thick belt overflowing with tools and weapons, an item for every occasion or purpose. A polished metal star twinkled from dead center of the man's breast to top off the ensemble. "I'm standing right in front of you, aren't I?"

"B-but I created you!"

The large man broke his akimbo pose and held up a callused finger. "Hey now, that don't make me any less real! After all, someone created *you*."

Actually, you might be surprised, Korden thought, and felt the sudden urge to burst into hysterical laughter. He searched for some sign that this was another dream, but it all seemed too real. The strobing light stung his eyes if he looked directly at it, and the earth squelched with dampness beneath his hands.

The Sheriff squatted in front of him. He unhooked a dented metal canteen from among the many objects on his uniform belt and held it out. "You look a tad thirsty, slick."

Korden snatched the container and put it to his lips, guzzling the contents until they coursed down his chin. The water was cool and soothing on his sore throat. He still felt terrible, but at least the world stopped its drunken spin enough to keep unconsciousness at bay. When his thirst abated, he tried to hand the empty canteen back, but it slipped from his grasp.

Sheriff Protector watched it tumble across the dirt to land beside the corpse of a ramlar with its head just about turned inside out. "I know all this is a lot to take in, so I'm gonna cut to the chase. I need your help, buckaroo."

"My…help?"

"Yep. We gotta save someone's life, just the way heroes are supposed to." The Sheriff held out his large hand again, empty this time. "But first, let's get you back on your feet. Whattaya say?"

All Korden ever wanted was to help Sheriff Protector. To join him on his never-ending adventures. But he made no move to take that hand. There was something wrong here, but he was just too disoriented to figure out what.

The Sheriff reeled back in his arm and stood up. From this vantage, the man seemed as tall and imposing as one of the redwoods. A huge, friendly grin spread across his wide jaw…but his eyes harbored a hard glint of anger. "Well, what do you wanna do then? Sit there all day?"

Korden shook his head dazedly. "This is some sort of trick. It *has* to be."

"Ya know, for a kid that just met his own personal hero, you seem downright ungrateful." He waited, but when Korden didn't respond, he sighed heavily. "I don't have time for this, pardner. I said I needed your help, and I meant it. A friend of mine is in trouble, and we gotta come to the rescue. Just like in all those stories you wrote about me."

"Wait. Trouble?" He couldn't help anyone, *he* was the one who needed help. "What do you want me to do? I'm… I'm really sick…"

"We'll get you all fixed up. Don't worry, it's simple." His smile tightened into a knowing smirk. "And you're gonna wanna meet this person, trust me. All you gotta do is come with me just ahead, where you see yonder light." He turned and pointed further up the path, toward the hypnotic glow.

With some difficulty, Korden drew his gaze away and looked out at the carpet of animal corpses around them, with their skulls popped like ripe grapes. "W-what happened to all of them?"

The Sheriff lifted one shoulder in an embarrassed way, the sort of gesture that Allin had once accompanied with an *aw, shucks.* "People gotta eat," he said sheepishly. "And my friend's got some…specific dietary needs, I guess you'd say. These critters here, they weren't much of a meal, but it was all my friend had for quite a while." The Sheriff held out his hand once more. "Now…are you gonna come with me? We'll get you fixed up and then, if you help my friend outta this jam, the world is gonna be your oyster. Anything you can dream up, it's yours. You wanna be my sidekick? Done. We'll travel the land, fighting evil and righting wrongs."

This time, Korden hesitated for only a moment. If he'd been feeling better, this would have been one of the most exciting things that ever happened to him. As it was, his curiosity burned as hot as his fever.

And really, since the alternative was staying right here to die, what choice did he have?

5

The big man felt surprisingly solid to be a figment of Korden's imagination. Once Korden stood with his pouch securely around his neck, Sheriff Protector clapped an arm around his shoulders to steady him.

"C'mon, li'l buddy. It ain't far at all."

He didn't lie; the path took them only a few more steps through the sea of dead wildlife, past the last of the trees separating them from the cliff, but Korden had to lean against his creation just to make it that far. He could see now that it wasn't an actual mountain ahead, just a titanic wedge of rock thrusting up from the forest floor, like the prow of some massive, sinking ship. A cave opened into the base of this monolith, a tunnel into the earth itself, and the white glow emanated from here in those gentle, rhythmic waves.

"My friend's right inside there." The Sheriff's voice rang with excitement. Or was it eagerness?

A few natural steps were carved into the stone leading up to the cave mouth, where the field of furry bodies came to an end. Korden didn't have the energy to climb one, let alone three, but the huge man carried him up. When they reached the top, the Sheriff placed him back on his own feet and gave him a gentle shove forward. The white glow got brighter as Korden shuffled through the entrance, blotting out his vision with searing whiteness, forcing his eyes closed...

Then it ebbed, and he opened them again.

To find himself standing in a cheery kitchen filled with sunlight, warmth, and the smell of fresh baked blueberry pie.

Korden turned in a slow, confused circle. Sheriff Protector was gone. So was the cleft in the rock he'd just come through, replaced by a solid wall decorated with drawings of colorful fruit. He stood on a shiny, black-and-white checkered surface now instead of rock, glossed so highly he could see his reflection. Sparkling white countertops ringed the room, with cabinets above and below, and a line of shiny gadgets atop them. A bank of long windows above the sink looked out on rolling green lawns and blue skies.

He knew this place. This was a room that, until now, had only existed in his mind. An ideal amalgam of all the stories he'd read and the ones the Olders told him of the way they once lived. A slice of the world from before the

Filament ground it to dust, taken from his mind and made reality.

Only one thing didn't belong here, a single piece of the picture that he didn't recognize. On the other side of the room, in front of the tall doubled-doored cabinet that Korden believed was called a 'frij', stood a narrow oval archway made of rough-hewn stone that seemed to sprout right out of the checkered tile, a gateway leading to nothing. It looked as out of place here in this gleaming, sunlit room as the elk carcass from outside would have.

"H-hello?" he croaked. Speaking tore at his raw throat, caused his vision to waver. "Sheriff Protector?"

"I'm so glad you came."

The voice issued from behind him. He turned.

A woman stood in the corner of the room, although where she came from, he didn't know; there were no doors or entrances into this place. She was tall and beautiful, the complete opposite of Merise, with warm blue eyes and flowing golden tresses, wearing a long, regal yellow gown that matched her hair. Even if she hadn't been the spitting image of the person he'd built up in his head for the past sixteen years, Korden would've known her by the wild rose nestled amid her flaxen locks.

She held her arms out to him. "Come to me, my sweet child."

6

"Mother?" he whimpered, inching hesitantly toward the woman.

"Yes, it's me. I've missed you so much, Korden."

Hearing his name from her lips broke something inside him. He leapt forward, falling into her embrace, and felt tears spring to his eyes as she enfolded him. The safety of her arms wiped away all worry and doubt. How long had he dreamt of this moment, almost *exactly*?

Long enough it made no difference that he knew this woman had never been real, that the image he'd held of his mother all these years was just part of a story his father told him to keep from facing the truth.

"Son, please listen to me," she said, gently but firmly pulling away. He had to refrain from grabbing hold of her again. "I need your help. I've been locked in here for such a long time."

"Locked up by who?" he demanded.

"Bad people. Bad people that want to keep us apart."

"Sheriff Protector, he can help us, he can—!"

"No, my love." She laid a hand on his cheek. "Sheriff Protector got you here, now you have to do the rest."

Korden's hands curled into determined fists at his side. "Tell me. I'll do anything."

"Good. That makes me so happy." She took him by the shoulders and turned him around, to face the arch across the room. "Do you see that?"

He nodded.

"All you have to do is walk through. If you do that, then I can leave here and stay with you. Forever and ever."

As much as he wanted that, Korden didn't see how walking through an arch could possibly change anything. "But… what is it? What does it do?"

"It's what's holding me here. And only you can free me, Korden. Only you can be my hero."

The words were the sweetest he'd ever heard. Korden would've walked into fire for her at that moment. He started across the slick tile, circling around to approach the rock arch from the side. The ring itself was only cupits thick, the hole through the middle perhaps six pargs tall and two across, barely wide enough for his shoulders to pass through without turning sideways. As he drew closer, he noticed a series of scratches in the stone frame that looked far too regular to be random. He continued forward and choked back a cry of surprise when he realized what they were.

Craften symbols were carved into the oval. Some of them he recognized, but most were beyond his level of comprehension. The loops and swirls ran up the length of the arch in a narrow script.

A spell had been performed here. Something far more complicated than his capabilities, an incantation that required a physical component to be left behind, to hold the artcraft in place long after the Crafter departed.

Korden came around to stand in front of the arch. Before, he'd been able to see right through the stone oval, but at close range, this was not the case. Something shimmered between the narrow walls, growing more opaque as he approached. It looked like liquid suspended in the air, but it was a rich, velvety bluish-purple, a heart-achingly beautiful color ripped from a sunset such as the world had never seen. Staring into it, Korden received the impression of vast distance, as though he were actually looking into an ocean of unfathomable depth.

A single spark as big as his fist sat in the middle of this, an ember floating on that cerulean surface.

The thought of touching it disgusted him for some reason. He halted.

Without warning, those disembodied voices filled the room, their whispers echoing over and through one another in a confused jumble.

yes yes come inside help us we need you

He stepped back in sudden terror.

"Don't be afraid, Korden." His mother said. She sounded as eager as the Sheriff now. "Just go through. You want to help me…don't you?"

yes korden save us only you can free us

"Yeees…" Those murmurs sounded so forlorn and desperate. They purred inside his mind, made the blood rush in his ears. He couldn't think straight.

His mother urged him again from behind, but now the warmth left her voice. "Do it. Go through. You can have anything you dream of. Anything you desire."

anything all your fantasies just surrender

He stared at the spark, at the bed of gorgeous violet around it. "I…I don't…"

"Then maybe *I* can convince you."

Korden wheeled around. His mother had disappeared now too, and in her place was another face he knew. The girl from the photo stood before him, wearing her alluring half smile and the outfit from his dream, the one that bared her long, smooth legs. He swallowed a sudden mouthful of saliva as she padded across the cave floor on bare feet and began circling around him.

"I know what young men want." She came to his side, easing closer until their bodies touched, just as he'd wanted. The curved mounds on her chest—so much more delicate than Merise's—rubbed against either side of his shoulder. At the contact, an electric tingle shot through him. Her hands caressed his back and chest. She rested her chin on his shoulder and breathed into his ear, "I can be yours. All you have to do is pass through." The hand on his chest slipped down toward his waist and what lay below. Korden shivered. He was so dizzy and confused. "Or, if I'm not good enough, just tell me what you wish, and it can be yours."

yes we'll give you anything anything *just set us free*

Anything he wanted. Well, if that was true, there was only one thing he would wish for.

"I want to see my father," Korden whispered.

7

The girl jumped away from him so fast, his request might've grown arms and slapped her. The teasing smile on her lips fell away. A ripple of transparency ran through the kitchen so that, for just a moment, he could see something darker beneath. At the same time, the confusion in Korden's head cleared. His mind suddenly felt as sharp as the knife on his belt.

"If you can give me Redfen Bright," he challenged, "and have *him* tell me to walk through your arch, I'll do it."

The girl snarled, lips peeling away from her teeth in a primitive display of fury. She continued to back away, toward the stone oval. All around them, the walls of this room were fading, revealing the true interior of the cave: yellowed limestone walls and a furry carpet of moss that squelched beneath Korden's sneakers. Vines grew everywhere, sprouting from chinks in the stone to form a haphazard lattice of vegetation. To his right, the jagged entrance to the cavern reappeared, shimmering into existence like a heat mirage. With the false sunlight gone, the inside of this hollow was lit only by the glowing spark inside the arch.

"But you can't show me him, can you?" Korden pressed. "Because he was real…and you're *not*."

"Believe me, child, we could've been real enough for you." The girl's voice turned husky and deep. Her face seemed to be melting, the structure rearranging and elongating, skin turning black. But he couldn't look for long, because she slipped into the shadows on the far side of the cave, where he lost sight of her.

"No." Korden shook his head. Understanding burned through the last of the fog in his brain like a lighthouse. His request (*the truth, the only way past him is the truth*) had broken whatever spell had been placed on him. Suddenly he felt much better, the awful heat and weakness and pressure in his chest subsiding. And the conduit stood wide open once more; he could feel artcraft flowing into him like floodwater replenishing a spring. "You, my mother, the Sheriff…you came from my imagination somehow. Because of *that*." He looked to the arch, where that single spark floated. For the first time, he saw how much it looked like a hideous, gigantic eye. He addressed it directly for his next question. "Who are you? *What* are you?"

"We have no name. Not one that you could comprehend, anyway." The violet murk suspended in the arch bulged grotesquely before resettling, but the guttural voice came from the dark on the far side of the cave, where the girl had disappeared. "Once we were called Loathe, by a people far, far from here. That 'spark,' is merely a vessel. We have no physical presence."

Korden thought of his mother's embrace, the nameless girl's hands running down his body. "You felt pretty physical to me."

"Liked that, did you?" Korden could hear the smugness in that gruff voice. "I assure you, they were avatars only. Manifested from your own mind."

"But it's not just them, is it? Everything…the forest moving, Stone's compass failing, even my sickness…they only happened because I was *scared* they would happen." He suspected that was why the Redfen in his dream insisted that Korden say he was real; it had been the only way he—or whoever had been using his form to communicate—could get a message through without this creature intercepting it.

"Oh my my my, so clever as well as creative." The floating spark—Loathe—gave an excited flutter. "You really are quite a find. We've been trying to lure someone, *anyone*, to us for nearly two centuries, but we never expected to snare such a tasty morsel."

Fear prickled the small hairs on Korden's arms. *He eats what you dream and drinks what you fear.* Imagination didn't just give this creature form, he realized; it *sustained* him. The idea seemed more horrible and perverse than if it merely hungered for his flesh.

"That's right, child. Now you understand," Loathe confirmed, reading his mind as easily as Stone. "Since time untold, we have moved from host to host, mindscape to mindscape, following in the Filament's wake as they tear holes from one plane of existence to the next. We have dined on the most inventive minds the allverse has to offer. Made even their most extraordinary fantasies a reality."

"You...you mean people wanted you to...?"

"I am kind to those who are kind to me," Loathe purred.

Something dark flitted through the shadows along the cave's periphery, circling behind the arch to move between Korden and the only exit. He moved in the opposite direction, searching the darkness with both eyes and mind and finding nothing with either. He raised one hand menacingly, ready to defend himself. "Stay back! I'm warning you!"

A wet chortle bounced around the limestone walls of the cave, coming from everywhere at once. "Maybe you're not as intuitive as we thought. We *feed* on imagination, which is the very essence of your pathetic magics. Anything you throw at us would only make us stronger."

Korden's immediate instinct was denial. There had to be *some* way, some creative new spell that would thwart—

"Sweet child, it took thirty of your ilk to find a way to subdue us, and you have nowhere near their discipline."

This caught Korden's attention. He recalled the symbols carved into the stone. "That's not a vessel, is it? It's a prison. You're trapped inside that arch. Crafters put you there."

"*Crafters.*" Loathe snorted derisively. "Nothing but self-important pretenders using borrowed power. When they couldn't destroy us, they created a pocket between dimensions to hold us. But you know what that's like, don't you, child? To be hidden away, forgotten, desperate to escape? You had your Barrier, but this cave is ours. And the fools that put us here hoped we would simply wither away if starved long enough." The laughter sounded sly and haughty this time. "But animals have imaginations, too. We called to their subconscious just as we did yours, lured them here one by one. They provided more than enough nourishment. And with their dreams of the forest, we were able to expand our influence throughout these woods, to seek out a new host."

Korden swallowed a lump of fear. "Is that what you would do to me? Suck out my brain?"

"Oh, you're much too fine a meal to gorge on." The spark gave another excited pulse. When it spoke again, Loathe's voice became a vicious growl that made Korden's heart feel encased in ice. "We will be together for such a long time, you and we. But it doesn't have to be a bad thing, child! Just as we said, you can have your desires fulfilled as we savor every wish, nightmare and fantasy in your expansive head. But first…you must free us from this prison."

Korden at last caught sight of a shape prowling the darkness on the far side of the arch, a silhouette hunchbacked and misshapen. He hurried to keep the arch between him and Loathe's new form.

"But you can't force me to do it. I have to go through the arch on my own. That's why you tried to trick me."

Two red orbs appeared amid the darkness, the color of an Incarnate's eyes. Korden's breath caught. "Yes, that is the terms of the curse. No mandate of such magnitude can be given without an equal measure of mercy."

"I'll never do it," Korden declared.

"So you say. We tried to persuade you nicely…but that doesn't mean fear and pain won't work just as well. When we're finished with you, you will *BEG to release us!*"

Something barreled across the room at him, a hunched shape on all fours. Korden leapt out of the way of its charge before he could get a good look at it. He landed in a sprawl and rolled away with his carry pouch clutched to his stomach, then scrambled back up. Claws scratched against the stone floor as the creature turned to come at him again.

The cave mouth lay just ahead. Korden ran through it without looking back.

8

Outside, the first rays of morning trickled through the treetops. Korden leapt down the stone steps without touching any of them, his carry pouch banging against his side. Using the sun's direction, he turned east again, plunged into the forest, and kept running.

A blood-curdling howl pierced the quiet.

This devourer of imagination wasn't finished with him yet, apparently.

Korden pelted through the forest, dodging through the trees in whatever direction offered the least resistance. His flaming sneakers carried him over brush and fallen timber. Several of the smaller pines seemed to reach for him, moving dry branches into his path, but he ducked beneath them and sprinted on.

After a few seconds, he chanced a look over his shoulder.

A shaggy, red-eyed beast larger than any wolf loped in his wake, its slavering jaws snapping at the air.

The monster from his nightmare.

It's not real, it's not real, he told himself. Perhaps so, but just because this creature came from his own head, that didn't mean its teeth wouldn't tear his flesh. So Korden fled, with terror blotting out all other thought. He was barely aware of it when his breath turned to syrup in his windpipe. His sole focus became running while the sounds of the beast at his heel drew closer. The tree trunks blended into a dizzy brown blur around him.

The sound of its growls seemed to come from right beside his ear. He had no idea how many seconds and days and seasons and years he'd been running, but his chest ached and black spots bloomed in front of him and he knew he couldn't go on much longer.

Then Korden burst through a last stand of sequoias and came to a halt at the edge of a road running immediately in front of him, just like the one he'd found on the morning of his birthday, except this one was twice as wide.

What he saw on the other side made him gasp out the last of the air in the very bottom of his lungs.

A group of strangely-dressed men stood in front of a small wooden building. They looked at him in surprise, but it was not them that caused his shock.

This had to be another of Loathe's trick. It *had* to be, because he wanted it too badly for it to be anything else.

Beyond the building, the redwood forest came to an abrupt end in a panorama of dazzling blue sky so bright it burned his retinas to look at it.

The people across the road continued to stare at him. He raised a hand and tried to say 'help,' but couldn't get the word out.

Korden's eyes rolled back as he fell across the crete.

Hidden Glen

THE TRADE
SHACK

1

It was sheer happenstance that Winstid faced the newcomer as he charged out of the forest.

Because of this, he was first to notice the boy over the leather-clad shoulders of Clan Triker's deliverymen. Things spiraled out of control quickly after that, but, when he had time to think back over events, Winstid would see that this morning could've gone very differently if not for that tiny advantage. His mind didn't amount to much more than mush these days—or so he was fond of saying—yet just a mere few seconds was all he needed to grasp the implications of their visitor and calculate the effect his arrival would have on the five men gathered in front of the trade shack.

The kid ran so fast, you would've thought the Stranger himself had descended from that ugly stain in the sky to give chase. He seemed to burst into existence all at once, materializing from the grim shadows of the morning forest. He was rail thin, a sickly-looking specimen, wearing rough, homespun clothing and carrying a satchel over his neck. Mud caked his entire body, a layer of filth so thick it hid his skin color. Maintaining that breakneck pace, he winnowed through a tight grove of alders with the grace of a young buck, hurtled a long bed of sword ferns growing in the cool shade of the last sequoias, and came to an abrupt halt at the crumbling edge of Old Five Road right across from them. He stood there with one foot in the far lane and gazed around with a wondering, slack-jawed expression.

It was a toss-up as to which was greater: Winstid's shock at seeing a child come out of Big Woods, or his shock at seeing *anyone* come out of them. Dreams were haunted along this stretch of gigantic forest. Folks said that the trees moved when you weren't looking. Everybody knew you didn't lose sight of the crete when you travelled close to Big Woods, lest you hear the call of the spookie who dwelled within. Winstid—a paunchy blackened man with a helmet of tight gray curls and a rash of pebbly dark bumps across his brow and temples, a common affliction among blackenfolk that his mother had called 'elderskin'—had never seen anything out of the ordinary here himself, but he sure wouldn't spend the night anywhere within a good span or two.

To either side of Winstid, Becks and Jakel caught sight of the boy a half second later, but only Jakel was fool enough to call attention to him. A soft exclamation of surprise escaped him. Winstid could've smacked the man for such an unchecked reaction, but, then again, he hadn't exactly prepared either of his Peacekeeps for such a situation. The most they dealt with back in Hidden Glen was the occasional dispute over stray livestock. He could scarcely look away from the filthy figure himself as it raised one limp hand toward them. The boy gasped and hitched, as though choking on the air itself.

Heater's men stood in front of the Glen trio, their backs to the road. Both were dressed in the one-piece, faded gray leather *jhaken*s their clan favored, as opposed to the denim pants and embroidered cotton tunics worn by the Glenners, Winstid's overlaid by a stately deerskin vest. The transaction with the trikers had been close to complete. In another two or three minutes, they would've been astride their floating machines and roaring back to whatever dank hole they called home, thereby relieving Winstid of the dilemma he knew was coming.

Dostey, the larger of the two, realized something was amiss before his partner did. His pitted face clouded over as he followed Winstid's gaze. He spun. One hand dropped to the handle of the shortshooter tucked into one of the many holdout pockets of the *jhaken*'s cape, a reflex as automatic as breathing; just a potent reminder that Heater's minions might look heavy of brow and smell like three-week-dead poccoon, but they were a savvy bunch when it came to dealing death. He caught sight of the boy just as his eyes rolled back in his skull. The sound of the kid striking the hard roadway was a heavy thud that made Winstid's sixty-four-year-old bones ache.

"Well…I'll be cursed," Dostey muttered, his thick accent producing the last word as 'coarsed'. "Where in hells did *he* come from?"

"Out tha forest, I seen 'im come runnin!" Jakel said excitedly, his rheumy eyes bulging out of his skull above his vein-covered nose. The man possessed a dog's eagerness to be of assistance. Winstid shot him a fierce glare that only Becks seemed to catch.

"'Zat a kid?" Cloonan asked. The other triker wore a swatch of black cloth around his forehead, to hold back the greasy blond tresses spilling off his head. He looked to be in his mid-forties, the youngest man here by a good decade. "Fer *true?*"

Dostey had already started across the band of cracked crete by this point. He moved cautiously, hand still hovering above his weapon, boot heels clacking. His shaven head was on a swivel, eyes scanning the forest. When he was satisfied this was part of no ambush or trick—a possibility Winstid remained undecided on, although he couldn't begin to guess who the perpetrators would be—he dug the thick toe of one boot under the boy's arm and flipped him over with a grunt.

"He's breathin," the triker called. He knelt and gave the prone figure's cheek a rough slap. "C'mon, wake up, boy."

"Cursefire, I ain't met nobody under thirty-fi' since that fur trader's daughter in Yellit, and that was four years ago!" Cloonan gave a grin that displayed his tobacco stained teeth. He turned back to the Peacekeeps and nodded at the kid sprawled across the Old Five. "So you don't know who dat is?"

This time, Jakel wisely waited for Winstid to respond. "Never seen him," he said, opting for the short and simple. A terrible, sinking feeling dragged at the pit of his stomach.

"You sure 'bout that?" Dostey demanded suddenly, squinting hard at him from across the road, where he crouched over the body. Winstid could only guess what wild suspicions were going through his head.

He nodded.

"Then where you think he come from?" Cloonan asked his partner.

"Don't know. Don't care. But it sure looks like we caught ourselves a bonus." Dostey motioned to his partner. "Get over here and help carry 'im."

Winstid stepped forward. At a scant five pargs, he wasn't an imposing figure, but he did his best to straighten his spine and suck in the sagging pooch beneath his vest. He put all the authority he could in his voice as he asked, "Steady on there, what're you doing?"

As if he didn't know. As if he hadn't known things were headed here as soon as he realized that the person emerging from the forest was under that magical age of 18.

"What's it look like? We're takin 'im with us." Dostey picked up the satchel and dropped the strap around his own neck. He put his hands under the boy's shoulders as Cloonan hurried to grab his feet.

"Yeah, but why?" Winstid pressed.

Now Becks shot *him* a look. Winstid's stoic second tended to speak little in the presence of strangers. He had close-cropped salt-and-pepper hair and a rigorously trimmed beard, which only made the fact that his right ear was little more than a stump even more apparent.

Dostey and Cloonan lifted the boy by arms and ankles and started to carry him toward their vehicle, parked in the weeds just a little farther up the road. "You funnin? You know what an honest-to-god *child* is worth to the right people? Curse, you could probly get three seasons worth of venison and ramlar at the outpost in Skor, and that's if you didn't barter first."

"You sure 'bout that? Who would want the risk?"

"Oh, there'll be *someone*. Believe on." Dostey's chapped lips spread into a devious smirk. "Or hells, maybe Heater'll wanna keep 'im around for a while. Have a little fun. His cheeks are bound to be softer than the rest of us saddle sore motherhangers."

Cloonan brayed obnoxious laughter at this.

Winstid walked after them, and, after a beat of hesitation, Becks and Jakel followed. "Just...stop and think on for a minute. That's a lotta trouble to pull down on Heater's head. Suppose he's not so 'preciative when you show up with a big Incarnate target? There's surely some of 'em tracking that boy even as we speak. Mayhap that's who he was running from in the first place."

"All the more reason to put some spans between us and here."

Winstid stopped and sighed. Reasoning would get him nowhere with these men.

Don't get involved. It was the single guiding philosophy that Hidden Glen lived by, that allowed them to survive while so many other tenuous settlements folded up or tore themselves apart as the average age of their citizenry climbed. No one from the outside world knew where they were located; very few even knew they existed. The various trade shacks strung along the roadside of Old Five were where they met contacts they trusted enough to exchange goods with. And it had been a long, wary process to set up an agreeable market for Heater Kay's unique goods, but everyone felt the arrangement was more than worth it.

As Winstid pulled the longshooter from the sling strapped to his back and aimed it in Dostey's direction, he wondered if he was throwing it all away for someone he'd never even met.

Not just someone; a kid.

That fact probably made what he was about to do even worse.

2

Dostey halted, causing Cloonan to jam the boy's head into his midsection. The triker gave Winstid a glare that could freeze water. "Old man…" he said slowly, although Winstid couldn't be more than a handful of years his senior, "You point a shooter at me, you best be prepared to have it jammed down your frammin throat. Now, what the hells are you doin?"

"What the hells *are* you doing?" Becks murmured beside him, low enough for the trikers not to hear.

"Can't let you take him," Winstid said evenly, holding Dostey's gaze over the tapering iron barrel of the rifle. The irony that the weapon and its ammunition had been manufactured by Clan Triker did not escape him, but considering the things misfired more often than not, he didn't feel too guilty about it.

Dostey glanced down at the body dangling between himself and Cloonan, then back up at Winstid. "I see. Got greedy, did ya? Relax, bodla. Fair is fair. You helped find 'im, so I'll make sure you're cut in for whatever we get."

"No thanks. We got all the meat we need."

"You lied then," Cloonan growled. "You *do* know 'im, don't you?"

"Nawp, wrong again."

The trikers exchanged a look of utter bafflement over their unconscious captive. "Then what business is it of yours?"

The question almost broke Winstid's resolve. His throat locked, preventing him from answering.

And then he thought of Cheree, young and glowing, with a belly just beginning to bulge from the life inside it, and forty years of festering guilt and regret crashed down on him all at once.

"I just can't stand by and watch you carry a child away to do god-knows-what with him."

Dostey snarled, "Is that worth breakin your trade with

Heater? Cause that's what you're doin. You'll never get so much as another popshell outta us. Those shooters won't be good for much else than scratchin your asses."

"If that's what Heater wants to do, that's on him. We got along before him, we'll get along after. Now put the kid down and go your way in peace."

Dostey didn't move, but Winstid could see his body tense, like a coiled snake. If his hands hadn't been full with the boy, Winstid suspected the triker might've gone for his shooter anyway, covered or not. After a moment, he looked over at Cloonan and nodded. The two of them bent in unison and lowered the boy back to the pavement.

"The bag too." Winstid kept his weapon trained on Dostey as he removed the satchel, dropped it on the ground, and straightened up at a pace that snails would've envied.

Too late, Winstid realized he was being distracted.

Cloonan turned and drew while his attention stayed on Dostey.

The motion was no more than a blur, but that probably had more to do with Winstid's poor eyesight than the other man's speed. The devil power inside his weapon ignited with a hollow boom. Winstid felt the heat of the shot as it grazed by his curly pile of gray hair; a single cupit to the right and the crete would've been decorated with his brains. Then he was moving himself, diving into the knee-high skilne growing beside Old Five. This was more action than his elderly body had seen in many a season. The impact pulled something hard in his shoulder; pain flared all along his left side. A second later, Jakel hit the ground beside him, and covered his head with his arms.

More shots cracked above him. Winstid rolled over to find Becks had remained stubbornly on his feet. His own shooter was in his hand, pulled from the oiled leather holster at his hip. One finger squeezed the trigger in rapid succession.

Cloonan took one of the wild rounds in the neck. He clutched at the wound, blood oozing between his fingers, then went down. Beside him, Dostey scrambled to draw his own weapon.

"You're covered by three shooters right now!" Winstid cried, ripping free of the clutching grass and raising his weapon up enough to be seen. It wasn't true exactly—Jakel still lay with his head covered, uttering a string of whimpers—but the triker had no way to know that. "You better get your hand off'n that piece, 'less you think you can take us all!"

Dostey considered, then reluctantly hoisted his hands into the air.

Winstid stood (his side screamed in protest as he did; that tumble might just've cracked a rib) and made Jakel compose himself while he continued to cover Dostey with Becks. The three of them cautiously moved toward the trikers.

Cloonan lay unmoving beside the unconscious boy, face snarled in pain, a pool of blood spreading on the crete around him. The bullet had laid his throat open to the bone. Winstid grimaced at the sight.

They'd killed one of Heater Kay's men. It was like a nightmare that wouldn't end.

"Go on then," Dostey barked. Some of Cloonan's blood dotted the side of his bald head. "Kill me. Get it over with."

Winstid reached over and plucked the pistol from the man's pocket. It didn't make him feel any safer; the triker probably had five more hidden on him somewhere. Now that the violence was over, Winstid's hand picked up a nasty tremor that he did his best to hide. "We're not gonna kill you."

"Then you're even stupider than I thought."

"The wife says that same thing just about daily. If she ain't shamed me, you sure won't." Winstid twitched the longshooter's barrel past him. "Just go, Dostey. We'll help you take this'n's body, if you want."

The triker snorted, reared back, and spat a greenish yellow wad of phlegm on the road at Becks' dusty boots. "He made the mess. He can clean it up."

They turned the big man around and marched him back to his trike at shooterpoint, while forcing him to keep his hands up. The rusted metal machine had been built for only one rider, but a second, mismatched saddle seat was welded behind the first to carry a copilot. Baskets of vegetables, bread, and cured meats were strapped along the vehicles long, narrow body; payment for today's delivery of ammunitions. Beneath these loads, two strange words were emblazoned across the metal: Harley Davidson.

Dostey slung a leg over the front saddle—the seat of his leather *jhaken* stretching enough to give him clearance—and punched buttons on the tiny console beside the steering bars. Something in the trike gave a wheezy screech before the whole contraption rose two pargs into the air. It hovered on a cushion of blazing yellow light emitted by three half-spheres that jutted from the undercarriage. One of these buzzed and began to blink rapidly as the landing skids folded, causing the trike to tilt forward before the light evened out and the vehicle righted itself. Clan Triker may have learned to use these fantastic vehicles from the old world, but Winstid suspected they had no idea how to repair the things.

"Tell Heater the truth 'bout what happened here," Winstid urged over the crackling hum of the trike. "Tell him this ain't what I wanted, it's just something that had to be done. If he can see his way past it, leave word at the shack and we'll continue our arrangement."

"That ain't gonna happen." Dostey glared at Winstid from his seat astride the trike. "Heater don't forget and he don't forgive. You'll pay for what you did today." With this promise, he grabbed the steering bar, flipped another switch, and the trike roared away up the road, backwashing the three Peacekeeps in a strong, acrid wind.

3

"You sure 'bout letting him go?" Becks asked as they stood on the faded yellow line running up the middle of Old Five, watching the hovering vehicle dwindle in the distance. "I hate to say it—"

"Then don't."

"—but if we'd just killed him, it might save us a lotta trouble down the line."

Winstid turned to study his second, trying to determine if the man was serious. "And just how would that look if Heater found out?"

"Prob'ly no worse'n when he finds out about this." Becks' gestured to Cloonan's body a few pargs away.

"Lies have a way of catching up with you," Winstid said. "As it stands, the situation was murky, at worst. We start slaughtering unarmed men who've already surrendered, no amount of talking would justify it. Not to them, or us."

"I doubt Dostey's overly grateful for the mercy."

"Mayhap he will be, once his blood has cooled."

Becks gave a disappointed shake of his head to convey his disagreement. "Can't afford to be naïve on this, Win.

You don't really mean to meet them again if they say all's forgiven, do you? Like as not, we'd be walking right into a trap."

"Nawp. I think our dealings with Heater Kay and Clan Triker are over. Fact, it might be best to abandon this trade shack altogether, give them no connection to us. So let's not dally." Winstid turned to Jakel. "Get the shot loaded up in the saddlebags. We'll grab the boy."

Jakel looked up from wiping grass off his knees and exclaimed, "We're takin 'im with us?"

"You think we went through all that just to leave 'im unconscious in the road for Dostey to come back and collect? Or worse?" Winstid gave a nervous glance over his shoulder at the forest as he added this last. "Now mind me and get going."

Jakel nodded and ran to do as told, shirttail fluttering. Winstid approached the kid again, stepping wide around the crimson puddle that had leaked from Cloonan's savaged throat. He knelt at the boy's side and gently brushed locks of crusty brown hair out of his face.

Underneath all that grime, he was...thirteen? No, closer to fifteen. It'd been so long since Winstid had seen such young features, he couldn't really gauge. The kid's clothes—a tightly-woven green tunic and patchy black leather dungarees that engulfed his gaunt, emaciated frame—looked like the sort of simple fashion favored by some of the hill clans to the north. All except his shoes, that was. Winstid had never seen footwear as fancy as these flaming, thick-soled short-boots. A wickedly-honed knife with a hilt of polished bone hung from his belt. Perhaps strangest of all, around his neck hung a rock in a leather sling. *Prob'ly the totem for some pagan god*, Winstid reckoned. Not everyone worshipped the

God of the Aged, after all; some of the more isolated settlements still clung to that ancient Saint of Christ hooey, with all its many rituals. Winstid gave the boy a cursory examination for wounds and found none other than minor scratches and bruises, and a scabby hole on the back of his scalp where a chunk of hair was missing.

Where did he come from, for the Lord's sweet sake? Where on earth could a child survive to this age without the Incarnates hunting it down?

"You there. Boy." Winstid patted the smooth cheek with considerably more care than Dostey. "Can you tell me who you are?"

The kid's eyes fluttered briefly. He mumbled a string of nonsense before sinking back into unconsciousness, of which Winstid caught only two words. One was 'dream'.

The other was 'monster.'

A cold tingle stiffened Winstid's neck hair.

He reached over, opened the flap of the satchel, and rifled through the contents. More clothes, a thin bedroll, a water-stained book, more odds and ends and junk of the sort that would only matter to a child. Nothing to indicate where the boy had come from. The forest simply opened its dark maw and spit him out.

At the bottom of the bag, Winstid's hand touched something heavy and hard wrapped in a scrap of blanket. He pulled it out and unwrapped the cloth in his lap.

Inside lay a gleaming hunk of metal that he could easily identify as a shooter, even if he'd never seen one to equal it. It was a menacing work of art, all sleek, smooth parts and aesthetic design that—like the boy's footwear—spoke of the long gone world of industrial manufacturing, with a comfortable, hand-conforming grip and multiple moving parts.

Winstid couldn't even figure out how to tell if it was loaded. Their own weapons—pieces cobbled together by Heater's clan, the only projectilers Winstid had ever seen—were crude things, all rough wood and clumsily welded metal.

How much would the boy's worth have gone up if Dostey had known he carried this on him?

"Been a long time since I had to kill somebody," Becks said distractedly. He stood over Cloonan, rubbing his gnarled ear as he stared down at the triker's blood-smeared death grimace. Winstid wrapped the shooter back up and jammed it into the satchel before he could see. "Since before I came to the Glen, anyway. Never used a shooter on nobody neither. What a frammin mess."

"You didn't have a choice," Winstid told him.

"No, I didn't." Becks turned a heavy gaze on him. "You made a play, and I had to back it."

The words—and the accusation behind them—stung. "You think it was a mistake."

"Didn't say that. But there are certainly people I would've preferred to piss off before the man who builds deadly weaponry for a living."

"Then what should I have done?" This wasn't a challenge from Winstid, but a sincere inquiry. "Let those perverse, slaving roughrods have him?"

Becks shrugged. Usually his detached coolness was a comfort to Winstid, but right now he wanted to shake the man out of it. "Done is done, and no use lamenting. Plenty of time for that when we're back to hunting with bow and arrow by the end of the season." He looked up in the direction of the trade shack, where Jakel had disappeared to load up their horses, then hunkered beside Winstid. "But taking this little Lightbringer with us only complicates an already frammed-up situation. The Glen won't care about your reasons for doing it. It's not our way to get involved with anyone, let alone a child. *You* know that better than most."

"Not everyone in town agrees with that philosophy," Winstid said quietly.

"Well, Neller does. And when he finds out—"

"Neller's not gonna find out."

Becks' eyebrows shot up on his forehead. "So what, you wanna *sneak* him in? Without Council say-so? Win…besides the fact that we're Peacekeeps, you know what the punishment could be for something like that."

"You don't have to help. You and Jakel can claim ignorance of the whole thing."

"That's not what I'm saying." The other man sounded stung. "You know I'd stand by you no matter what, but even aside from Council repercussions, the same as you told the trikers applies to us: he'll be a candle flame attracting every Incarnate moth for a thousand spans. Just a matter of time before they get to him."

"Curse Becks, I'm not planning to let him live there! I just wanna make sure he's all right and send him on his way!"

"Yes, and then he'll know where we are. Think on, Winstid. A perfect stranger, and we'll have handed him the keys to the kingdom." He ran a hand across the ruins of his right ear again. The unconscious gesture was the surest way to tell when he was truly upset. "Hells, maybe this is all just someone's ruse to find the Glen in the first place. Get us to bring a spy right into our midst."

Here was one possibility Winstid hadn't considered. He glanced at the kid again, who still appeared to be unconscious, but without any sign of what was physically wrong with him. Then he thought of that shooter in his bag, a deadly relic from a lost age. "We'll take precautions. Blindfold him on the way back. Keep him locked up until we decide how to handle it."

Becks sighed and said nothing.

"He's our responsibility," Winstid insisted. "We can't just—"

From the forest along the western side of the road came an angry, warbling shriek that caused both men to jump.

"Fine, let's just go, before we're all breakfast for that monteela," Becks said.

"That was no monteela, it sounded more like…" Winstid trailed, because the next words out of his mouth would've been laughable, even to himself.

Winstid spent his own boyhood within the walled city of Phoenix. The fortress—which some said had been built up out of a great metropolis of the same name that existed in the days before the Purges—was secure and well-armed enough to repel even the large Incarnate forces that came marching out of the east, a bastion of freedom and hope whose legends drew desperate mothers and fathers from across the land that begged protection for their children. But not even the highest walls kept the town from falling to disease and famine when Winstid turned nineteen. Life had been a rough struggle for survival in the years after he set out north from the ruins, but before that, he'd grown up in relative security and comfort.

His mother loved telling stories to Winstid and his younger brother. Jarrol that had been, a sweet, towheaded boy who starved to death before he turned thirteen. One of the stories they requested over and over again was the tale of the giant Grendelis, who kicked in houses in the middle of the night and ate children while they slumbered. The woman had a way of describing the deformed monster so that Winstid could almost see it.

One stormy night, long after he and Jarrol were put to bed, the shriek of the wind had kept both boys awake. After one particularly strong gust, Jarrol insisted that it was actually Grendelis coming for them. Winstid assured his brother it wasn't so, and told him that the giant made a very different sound before it attacked. This was an embellishment to his mother's tale, and so, when Jarrol demanded to know the creature's call, Winstid opened his mouth and let loose with a keening wail from deep in his throat that woke the whole barracks. He hadn't thought about that night in more years than he could count, and yet...

That was what just came drifting out of the forest, he was sure of it. A noise he made up himself, an imaginary cry from an imaginary monster.

"Win?" Becks asked, raising an eyebrow at him as he stared into the forest. "You square?"

"Yeah." Winstid pulled the satchel strap over his head. "Let's go."

"What about him?" Becks nodded toward Cloonan's body.

"Less you feel like digging a grave this morning, leave him for the crows."

Together they lifted the boy—Winstid's side screaming in protest—and carried him toward the trade shack.

THE ONE IN CHARGE

1

Korden sat bolt upright before even opening his eyes, arms flailing and heart hammering. The beast, the one from his nightmare, it had come to life and was snapping at his heels and...

He stopped himself just short of another hyperventilation and gazed around. This wasn't the forest. Or the cave of the creature who called itself Loathe. He was definitely indoors though, a building whose construction wasn't quite as sturdy as the brick-and-mortar ruins he'd found in Emmett, but not quite as simplistic as the *huctés* of the village.

Beneath him was a metal bunk covered by a thin straw mattress, the top smeared with grime that had apparently come from Korden himself. The room itself was small, barely long enough to accommodate the length of this cot, and its width could be spanned by stretching his arms to either side. The floor, ceiling and three of its walls were made from rough, knotty timber set in neat rows, the crevices between filled by a hard, black material. The fourth, the one he faced as he turned and swung his legs off the bunk, was nothing but crude iron bars reaching floor to ceiling, sealing him into the tiny space.

Korden reached out and grasped one of them, as if testing its reality. His filthy hand shook as he did; he might not feel feverishly sick anymore, but still weak with hunger and thirst. The bar felt cool to the touch, and firmly seated.

Prison, he thought. But not like the restraint of the Barrier, which he'd always bemoaned so piteously; this was *real* prison, the kind one went to for...well, for breaking the law.

Or it could be a trick.

Perhaps he really *was* still in the cave after all, and this was another of Loathe's illusions, designed to get him to pass through the arch.

But as he pondered this further, he realized how unlikely it was. Beside the fact that the stone arch was nowhere in sight, if all this had been plucked from his mind—something he'd made up or envisioned during his daydreams of the old world—surely he would recognize it, as he had everything else.

He turned his attention to the space on the other side of the bars. He could see another area the size of his common room back home, one with wide glass windows through which sunlight streamed, and a splintery wooden door opposite his cell. The timbered walls were decorated by oil paintings on stretched animal skin. Even with his unease growing, Korden recognized the talent of these portraits would've made Tash envious. They were nature scenes, one depicting a babbling brook, another purple wildflowers, one a long rolling meadow with a lonely willow tree in the middle, all so startlingly real that Korden thought, at first, he was looking at more photos. Alongside these hung a pristine sheet of red and white metal, the colors somehow actually engrained in the gleaming surface, so that they shared the same gloss. On it, in flowing, curvy script, was the curious phrase, *Enjoy Coke!*

The rest of the room was sparsely furnished, only a dark mahogany desk and three chairs clustered around it, the former covered with nicks and scars.

Beyond this desk, Korden spied his carry pouch sitting in the floor. He realized, for the first time, that his knife no longer hung from his belt.

His hand stole up to his neck to feel for Stone. The false rock and its leather sling were both missing.

He placed his hands on the bars again and pulled, then pried at them with all the artcraft he could muster. Which, he was pleased to see, was replenished and flowing rapidly. The bars still wouldn't budge, didn't even rattle, but now he could see where they opened on the left side of the cell, and the lock that kept them closed. He reached inside the keyhole with his mind, exploring the interior to try releasing the mechanism, but it was far too intricate for him to manipulate.

Finally, he reached an arm through the bars toward his pouch and concentrated. If he couldn't escape, then at least he could retake his belongings and hope his knife still waited among them. The contents shifted as the bag inched across the wooden floor toward him.

Then the door to this room swung open, and in walked a man with the darkest skin Korden had ever seen.

2

His visitor halted abruptly in the doorway when he saw Korden staring back at him. Redfen had told his son about blackenfolk, and Korden had read about them (*negroes* they were called, in most of the books Skewtz assigned him, along with a few other derogatory names that felt dirty on the tongue) but before this moment, Santo's deep olive skin tones were the darkest he'd ever seen. The unfamiliarity made it hard to judge this man's age, but Korden believed him to be older than Redfen, closer to Merise's age, although in considerably better shape. He was slight of frame, barely five-feet-tall, and skinny everywhere except for his sloping gut, which hung low over his belt. His clothes were clean and ornate, rich blue denim pants and a white tunic stitched with beautiful gold patterns down the arms, overlaid with a brown-and-white deerskin vest that strained at its single button. Over his right shoulder he wore a sling of some sort, from which jutted a blocky wooden handle that Korden thought must be some club or mace, although this man didn't look like the type to wield such a brutish weapon.

He carried a flat tray on which rested a steel mug and a plate heaped with steaming food.

"You're awake," the man observed. His boots clomped against the wooden floor as he resumed his entrance. "That's good. Now I won't have to chew up your dinner and spit it down your throat."

Behind him, another head poked around the edge of the doorway. Red-rimmed eyes goggled at Korden as their owner asked, "Want me to watch your back?"

"Reckon I can handle it," the blackened man told him. "You just stay put till Becks gets back. And *nobody* comes in, you hear?" He started to close the door with his hip. The person outside moved with it, straining to keep the occupant of the cell in view. All at once, Korden recalled seeing these men right before he'd passed out, in front of that gorgeous strip of open sky. Did that mean he was inside the building he'd glimpsed across the road? It hadn't looked this big from the outside.

The newcomer faced the cell. Korden watched him without speaking, and the other man returned the favor. After a few seconds, he tilted the tray forward to display its contents.

"You want?" His accent drew out his words, with the kind of drawled vowels that Allin spoke with, but without the clipped-off word endings or twangy undertone.

Korden gave no reply, thinking again of Merise, and Tash's mandate. Avoiding other people hadn't been as easy as his *den-so* made it sound.

"God-be-good, I know you must be hungry. You looked half-starved when we found you, and that was before you slept the day away."

Korden's stomach gave a confirming rumble so loud there would be no use denying it.

His visitor came forward with the offering, to the other side of the bars, and placed the tray on the floor in front of the cell. Korden got a look at the object strapped to his back as he did: long and slender, with a metal tube visible at the bottom of the sling. "Go ahead, have a bite. It's left over from midday, but still fresh enough."

On the plate sat a hunk of steaming meat clinging to a delicate bone, most likely bird of some sort, surrounded by small potatoes in white gravy and a phalanx of some stringy greens Korden had never seen before. The mug brimmed with crystal clear water, so cold a film of frost formed on the lip. His stomach gurgled again when the roasted smell of the meat hit him.

Still, he hesitated. The last time he shared someone else's food, he'd ended up strapped to a table and force-fed breast milk.

He looked up at the man on the opposite side of the bars and opened the conduit. His *mohol* glowed calm turquoise tinged at the edges with intense orange curiosity. Not a hint of malice or deceit, although Korden now knew that didn't always mean anything.

But what could he accomplish by drugging me that he couldn't while I was unconscious?

This logic decided him. Korden reached through the bars for the mug and put it to his lips, taking a few experimental swallows, then wiped his dirty fingers on one of his tunic's few clean spots and gingerly tore a strip from the meat. It was rare and juicy, with a smoky flavor. He went back for more, then snatched up the bronze fork that came with the meal and began to shovel potatoes into his mouth.

"Easy on, boy. At least chew." The man grabbed a chair from the desk, brought it in front of the bars, and sat down with a grunt.

"How—" The word caught in Korden's throat. He swallowed a mouthful of greens and washed it down with more of that heavenly water. "How long was I out?"

"So you *do* speak. Beginning to think you might be a mute. Or worse, a Mex." This must've been a joke of some sort, because one corner of his mouth jerked up in a distracted half-grin. "Nigh on ten hours you been down. Managed to stay winked through the whole trip while tied to the back of a horse. A pretty kye trick, especially considering we couldn't find a thing in the world wrong with you."

"I have as-mah," he explained, and then, at the questioning look the other gave him, "I can't breathe. Sometimes it's so bad I pass out. I'm not usually out this long, but..." He shrugged and filled his mouth with food so he didn't have to do so with words.

"I see," the man said softly. His bushy white eyebrows climbed his forehead as though he wanted to say more on the subject. Korden avoided his gaze, letting his eyes wander to the windows, through which only clear sky showed. This prompted his visitor to tell him, "In case you didn't know, you're in a town called Hidden Glen."

"Town?" Korden frowned as the implications of this set in. "Then...are we truly away from the forest? I didn't dream it?"

"You mean Big Woods? Well, we're not exactly a lifetime away, but the closest edge is a little piece off from here, yes. That a good thing?"

Korden nodded, unable to stop a big, dopey grin from widening his mouth. *I made it. I really made it.* He knew his journey was far from over, but just escaping the forest felt like an incredible accomplishment.

He dug into the food again, trying to ignore the watching eyes of the man outside the bars as he ate. The other let him get most of the way through the meal before he finally spoke again. "Name's Winstid. Winstid Crane. I'm the head Peacekeep here in the Glen."

"Peacekeep?"

"Yes sir. Just like it sounds. I keep the peace and make sure everyone stays safe and happy."

"Like a..." Korden stopped himself just short of *sheriff*; that word would never feel the same to him. "A police officer?"

Winstid inserted a finger into his nest of gray curls and scratched behind his temple. "Well, I suppose you could call me an officer of sorts, but *poleese* is a new one on me."

Korden didn't know if he should be excited or not. Police officers were supposed to be trustworthy, honest, and helpful, but this man didn't look like the descriptions he'd read, the ones that fused in his mind to birth Sheriff Protector. No uniform, not even a badge, and he certainly didn't appear able to chase down lawbreakers.

Plus, the only person he has locked up is me.

Korden gulped down the last of the cold water and put the mug and fork back on the tray. Fresh energy coursed through him, making him feel better and more alert than he had in days. He pushed away from the bars, scooting back on the bunk until his back touched the wall, and decided not to skirt the matter. "Did I do something wrong?"

"Not that I know of."

"Then why am I in here?"

"It's just a precaution."

"Against what?"

Winstid Crane sighed and moved the tray away from the bars with his foot. Korden kept a careful watch on his aura as it faded through hues of discomfort. "As I said, I'm a Peacekeep. In a town where the average age is sixty-eight, that's not too hard a job. Mostly I just keep the bodlas who elected me from knocking each other senseless over totala disputes." He sat up straighter in the chair and crossed his arms. "But it also means keeping the community safe from outsiders. That's why the location of Hidden Glen has been a secret for close to thirty years."

Korden nodded. "I understand. We did the same thing in my village."

"Oh. Did you now?" Again those raised eyebrows, as threads of deep violet suspicion wormed through his *mohol*. The Peacekeep leaned back, his arms still folded above his protruding belly. Korden shifted uneasily under his scrutiny. "Well, it *is* the safest way. Too many bandits and brigands roaming the countryside who would very much like to take everything we've built. We have little contact with the outside world. Nobody leaves without permission, and nobody comes in without permission."

"I don't want in," Korden told him. "I just want to go on my way."

"Great. That makes me happy to hear. The only problem is, you're inside the Glen right now. You know where we are."

"But...I don't know anything," Korden protested. "I don't even remember how I got here or where here is."

Winstid took a long, slow breath. "Hopefully that's true. We blindfolded you to get in, and we'll do the same when you leave. But just so you know, we took a pretty tough trail to get back to the Glen. If you were counting on friends to rescue you after they followed us here, they're probably lost now."

Korden blinked at him as understanding slowly dawned. This man thought he was partaking in some ruse to learn the location of their town. His skepticism when talking about Korden's unconsciousness made sense now: he thought it all a sham.

"I don't have any friends," Korden said. "And I don't want anything from you. Just let me go, and I'll leave."

Winstid said nothing, nor did he move.

Korden couldn't keep the frustration out of his voice when he spoke again. "If you didn't want me to know where you lived, why'd you bring me here in the first place?"

"That was for *your* protection."

"I don't need any protection!"

"Oh really? And I suppose you were running pell-mell through the forest until you fainted for fun?"

Korden's indignation fizzled.

"What was after you?" Winstid pressed. "Incarnates?"

"No. There was…something else. Something in the woods."

"I got news for you, son, there's plenty *out* of the woods, too. You were 'bout three seconds from becoming the property of some very unsavory folk when my men and I stepped in, and it cost us dearly. Bringing you here was the only option I could come up with in case you…" He stopped, furrowed his brow, and sucked at his dark upper lip. "In case you really are what you appear to be."

Korden looked at his mud-crusted sneakers, dangling from the front edge of the bunk. He wanted to trust this man, but panic kept him wary. Those iron bars seemed to press in on him. "So I'm a prisoner."

"Absolutely not. I have every intention of letting you go."

"When?"

His brown eyes searched Korden's face. "When I'm satisfied you don't pose a threat."

"All right," Korden waved a hand impatiently. "How do I do that?"

"For starters, how 'bout telling me your name?"

"Korden Bright."

"All right. Now we're getting on." Winstid nodded, genial once more. "Korden. I like that. Now Korden, can you tell me where in the world you came from?"

"I…I can't do that."

"And just why not?"

"I just told you, my village is hidden the same way yours is."

"No." The Peacekeep shook his head adamantly. "That's a lie."

The indignity of the accusation shocked him. "It is *not!*"

Winstid uncrossed his arms and rested them on his knees as he leaned forward to bark, "There is no place hidden from the Incarnates, boy. They would've started tracking you the second you were born and not stopped until they found you. I don't believe you grew up in a village or town or anyplace stable. The only chance of survival when you're under free age is to keep moving, and even that's a slim one."

Korden leapt forward, to the edge of the cot, and wrapped his hands around the bars. "That's why you have to let me go! Every second I'm in here is another second they catch up to me!"

This seemed to break the man's hard façade for just a moment. A crease etched across his brow as a bolt of yellow-greenish fear shot through his aura. His mouth quivered briefly before it set in a hard, firm line. "Believe on, I don't want you in there anymore than you do. Last thing I need is a host of those devils on my doorstep making demands and threatening to burn my town to the ground unless I hand you over. So give me something I can work with. What were you doing in Big Woods?"

"Trying to get to the other side," Korden answered as if this were obvious, thinking of a joke Bant loved to tell about a chicken.

"And where are you headed?"

"Somewhere else."

"So Korden from nowhere, going somewhere else." Winstid nodded and sucked at his lip again. "All right. If you don't like those questions…" He rose from his chair, walked behind his desk, and opened a drawer. "Then maybe you can explain this."

He held up Redfen's shooter.

"It's called a gun," Korden told him.

"I know that much." Winstid said, rolling his eyes. "We may not have ones this fancy around here, but that doesn't mean we're ignorant. What I want to know is, what are you doing with it?"

"It was a gift."

"Some gift. Thing looks like it could chew a hole straight through someone's chest. That what you came here to do?"

"I don't even have any shot for it!"

Winstid laid the pistol back on the desktop and leaned over it. "I want to believe you, but look at it from my point of view. You happen to show up right where we are, in the middle of nowhere and armed to the teeth, and then just keel over so we have no choice but to bring you with us or leave you for the spookies. Now you're being defensive and uncooperative and feeding me a bunch of nonsense."

Korden squeezed the bars in his hands again, frustration and claustrophobia combining to make him feel desperate. "Police officers aren't supposed to lock people up that haven't done anything."

"If I ever meet one, I'll tell him that."

The conversation had become fruitless. Korden couldn't tell this man about the Olders or the Barrier and he certainly wasn't comfortable admitting his destination. The disgusted look on Merise's face when she'd found out he was a Crafter still haunted him. So he closed his eyes, communed with the Upper to still his fluttery heart, and said nothing.

"All right then. We'll leave off for now." Winstid stood up from the chair and looked down at him. "But I guarantee you, if any Incarnates show up here before we get this worked out, it'll go a lot worse for you than it does for m—"

As if to punctuate this sentiment, the door to the room opened again, swinging far enough around to crash into the wall.

3

Without even having to turn, Winstid knew it wasn't Incarnates busting into his Keep, but the horrified look on the boy's face told him that the mysterious Mr. Bright certainly thought so.

No, a pack of those glow-eyed demons would mean considerably less trouble for Hidden Glen's head Peacekeep than who he suspected had just arrived.

"Miss'um, I said you cain't go in there!" Jakel bawled from outside.

The voice that answered was feminine and pretty, but with an edge of fire-hardened steel. "Jakel, you old curse, take your hand off'n me this instant, or I will see to it that every meal you eat for the rest of your miserable life has fur and teeth in it. Even your desserts."

"It's fine, Jake," Winstid said, staring up at the splintered ceiling beams. No reason to get mad; a twenty-man posse couldn't have kept his wife out of a place once she'd set her mind to get in.

He turned to find her breezing past the other Peacekeep as she jabbered. "Winstid, Tanda saw you sneak that food out'n the storehouse, now you tell me what's..." A gasp escaped her as she caught sight of the boy in the cell. One set of knuckles flew to her gaping mouth.

Cheree Crane had celebrated her sixty-first birthday only last season, but Winstid still thought she looked as good as on her thirty-first. She stood a full parg taller than him (a consequence of him being oddly short as much as her being oddly tall), with long brunette hair kissed by gray at the temples, and porcelain white skin that glowed in the moonlight and had taken on only the barest of wrinkles around her eyes as she entered the twilight of her life. Today she wore sandals and an ankle-length denim skirt that showcased the swell of her hips, and a silken purple blouse that she'd stitched herself from material he'd traded steeply to get for her. That shirt had been the source of envy with many a crone in the Glen, so she wore it often. Around her neck, a pearlescent opal hung suspended on a fine link chain.

"Oh my Lord," she said, the words barely a breath. "Oh my good Aged above, where did he come from?"

"Cheree." Winstid put a hand on her elbow to turn her back toward the door, where Jakel still stood gawking. "Step outside so we can talk."

She pulled free without even looking at him and crossed the room to the cell, which had, up to this point, only been occupied by a handful of individuals from town too sunk on mead and apple wine to stumble home from the Pavilion on Sixth Eve. Winstid put his hands on his hips and watched, helpless and interested in spite of himself. The boy stared raptly as Cheree sank to her knees just inches from the bars. He appeared to be utterly enthralled as he studied her, eyes wide and bouncing around in his skull, as though taking in every part of her.

Aha, Winstid thought. *Wherever you came from, my friend, it sure didn't have any wombies, did it? I know that much about you now, at the least.*

"What is your name, dear one?" Cheree asked softly, gazing in at him.

The boy gave her the same answer to this as he had Winstid, albeit in a more reverent tone.

"I'm Cheree. I have the misfortune of calling myself that blubbergut's wife." She jabbed a thumb over her shoulder at Winstid as she said this. "How old are you, Korden?"

"Sixteen."

She sucked in air with a sharp hiss. "Sixteen! You've made it so far! Free age is just around the corner! You must be excited!"

He shrugged and nodded.

"And where did you come from?"

The kid hesitated, eyes straying to Winstid. "A village far away from here. On…on the other side of the forest."

"The other side of…? Surely you don't mean to say you came through *Big Woods?* I didn't know there *was* anything on the other side! Weren't you terrified walking through those dark trees?"

"Some," he admitted.

"How long did it take you to get here?"

"Weeks. Several weeks. I can't really tell you any more than that, ma'am."

Cheree didn't question or push, just tilted her head back and loosed one of her peals of tinkling, merry laughter, the ones Winstid loved so much to hear. "Lord, I haven't heard *ma'am* since my grandmother used to say it! I don't know how they do things on the other side of the forest, but if you want to fit in around here, you'd best use *miss'um!*"

"Oh." He blinked several times. "All right."

She giggled once more. A tentative smile crept across the boy's face, utterly transforming it. He was a good-looking youth, Winstid noticed, high cheekbones and piercing golden-green eyes beneath his unkempt hair. He needed some cleaning, grooming and fattening up, but once upon in a time, in a very different world, he would've had his choice of all the young ladies.

"Now, what about your parents, Korden?" Cheree asked. "Where are they?"

"Uh…well, they're both dead."

Parents, Winstid thought sourly. *Can't believe I didn't think to ask about his parents.* How could he, when he was so busy accusing the boy of infiltrating the town as the vanguard for an army of murderers and thieves? Winstid felt woefully out of his element just being in the youth's presence. They might speak the same language, but he still needed an entirely new mindset just to converse, one that his wife seemed to be adapting to with much greater ease. *Should've let* her *question the kid; she's gotten more out of him in a minute than I did in twenty.*

"I'm so sorry to hear that," Cheree told him solemnly. "Are you…all alone?"

Another nod.

"You poor thing. Yes, of course you are. I should've known just by the state of you."

She licked the tip of her slender thumb and then reached through the bars. Winstid opened his mouth to tell her to stay back, then closed it again. He watched as his wife cupped the boy's chin and rubbed at the crust of mud on his cheek. With all the rest of his filth, this was the equivalent of using a table knife to chop down one of those towering redwoods he claimed he'd travelled through, but she didn't give up until the skin beneath his eye showed through healthy and pink. Korden stiffened at her touch, but allowed himself to be groomed as he continued to study her in that intense way. It was strange; his eyes moved as though he were reading a book, like the kid could see something around her that Winstid couldn't.

"Korden," Cheree began carefully, "would you like to come to our home? You can clean yourself up, take a meal with us, even stay the night if you're of a mind."

"Now hold on, Cheree—" Winstid said, and was summarily silenced by one raised hand.

"Say on, Korden. Would you like that?"

Glancing up at Winstid again, Korden said, "Yes, miss'um."

"Bring the key, please, Winstid," his wife said over her shoulder.

"I will not," Winstid answered. The door hung open from when Cheree busted in, and he could sense Jakel standing just behind him, absorbing every word. "Woman, listen to me, no one knows he's here, and I'd like to keep it that way. Not only that, he could be dangerous. We don't know the slightest…"

He trailed as his wife straightened to her full height in front of the cell bars and then rounded on him with dreadful slowness. Her eyes blazed with an awful, angry heat that he'd only seen one other time during their marriage, and that last time had almost been the end of them. Another flush of warm guilt spread through every corner of his body, like blood from a picked scab.

Shouldn't have brought him, it was a mistake. Our good deed was done when we saved him from those two rough-rods. No one could've faulted us for leaving him there by the side of the road afterward.

No one except himself, of course.

"Winstid Crane," she said, her musical voice lowering a full octave. "Fetch me the key. This boy is not spending the night in a cell."

Winstid looked from her, to the boy, to Jakel, and back again. "Yes, miss'um," he agreed.

4

Korden waited anxiously while Winstid produced the cell key from his desk and surrendered it to his wife. *Wife*; another alien word for him to get used to. He knew the barest basics of the ritual called marriage, but what exactly did that entail, being one's 'wife'? Judging from these two—who were physically as different as night and day—it seemed to mean that you were the one in charge.

Aside from that, the woman named Cheree fascinated him. Not counting Loathe's false avatars, she was only the second female he'd ever met, and far more pleasant than the first. It was hard to determine the exact nature of his feelings for her. He wasn't attracted to her, like the nameless girl from the photo, yet his cheek still tingled from where she'd cleaned it with such gentleness. Her demeanor was so comforting—her aura a soothing yellow he'd never seen before—that he'd been willing to tell her just about anything she wanted to know. No, more than that; it made him want to curl up and put his head in her lap.

Was this what having a mother was *really* like?

Cheree inserted the key in the lock, twisted it, and pulled the cell door open with a rusted squall. He stood there uncertainly until she beckoned to him. "Come out. It's all right."

Korden edged out of the cell, expecting to be pushed back in at any second. He took care to keep Cheree between himself and Winstid. The Peacekeep wore a scowl on his face, yet his *mohol* turned a teal shade that Korden could only interpret as amusement.

Then, to his surprise, Cheree put an arm around his shoulders, pulled him close—soiling her pretty purple blouse in the process—and planted a kiss at his temple. "Oh, don't worry about that grump. If my husband knows what's good for him, there'll be no more terrorizing today."

One corner of Winstid's mouth twitched upward. He rolled his eyes. "Come on, then. If Tanda told you, she's told everyone by now. Let's get him home before the rest of the Glen moseys up this way to snoop."

Cheree released Korden, giving his hand a squeeze. She started to lead him through the door, but he stayed put and pointed at his carry pouch. "May I have my things?"

Winstid handed him the carry pouch by the strap, then held up the pistol and his knife. "If it's all the same to you, I'll keep these here until you leave."

Korden shrugged, knowing it would do no good to argue unless Cheree sided with him. On this matter, she stayed silent, one hand fiddling with the bauble at the end of her necklace.

"But...I suppose there's no harm in you having this." Winstid reached into his drawer again and drew out a small bundle which dangled from his fist by a strip of leather hide.

Korden just barely managed to conceal his glee as he accepted Stone. As soon as the computer fell into his palm, he squeezed the hard outer casing between his thumb and forefinger.

Rebooting... Calibrating to current conditions... Mr. Bright? Sir, I am confused, what has transpired to—Soft, rapid chimes sounded in Korden's head as the computer searched through his recent memories and then proclaimed, This is an unexpected turn of events.

As usual, that's an understatement.

THIS CREATURE YOU ENCOUNTERED, LOATHE—

Not now, we can talk about that later. I want away from here before they decide to lock me back up.

"Ready?" Cheree asked. She and Winstid were both watching him with matching puzzled expressions as he exchanged mental transmissions with Stone.

Korden nodded and slipped the leather necklace back over his head. After Winstid leaned through and asked the man outside if the 'coast was clear,' Korden followed Cheree through the door, where he got his first look at Hidden Glen.

5

Outside, the afternoon sun glowed hot and bright just a few degrees to the left of center sky, throwing a blanket of cheerful light across the land. The last time Korden had truly seen it like this was days ago on the bridge, just before falling into the river. After so long hemmed in by the endless trees, the sight of it made him want to find a place to sit and write an ode to its beauty, but he had too much else to take in.

A short fence surrounded Winstid's prison house, one whose pickets were not but bark-stripped branches strung together with twine. Two horses milled in the yard beside the door, beautiful, well-fed palominos with glossy white and brown coats. They stamped impatiently at the ground as Korden and the others emerged.

The structure stood atop a gentle rise that allowed an unimpeded view in all directions, the location undoubtedly chosen for this very reason. Korden saw no sign of the forest, no way at all to tell where they'd brought him from or how to get back to the road, which, besides the sun and the Shroud, was his only real point of reference in the world.

The front of the prison overlooked an open plain of verdant Bloom grasses smattered with wildflower patches, like paint on a palette, the most flat, open landscape he'd seen since leaving the village. A sprawling settlement stretched across this meadow, comprised of timber buildings like the one behind them (LOG CABINS, Stone clarified, OF THE TYPE USED IN SETTLING THE AMERICAN WEST), in all shapes and sizes, interconnected by worn footpaths and tamped dirt lanes. Smoke drifted lazily from stone chimneys, carrying the scent of roasting meat and baked bread. There were only a few people out and about, all of them too far away down the hill for Korden to see clearly, but more horses roamed everywhere, grazing in the field or lashed to posts in front of several buildings. At the far end of the settlement, he could see the red roof of a large octagonal structure rising above the other buildings. Music drifted from that direction, a raucous, upbeat tune full of fiddles and banjos and other instruments that Korden couldn't identify.

A pang of homesickness punched him in the gut. The panorama reminded him so much of the village, even though this community had to be ten times bigger. And, though the whole of Hidden Glen could've fit inside just a few blocks worth of Emmett's paved avenues, the fact that it was alive and breathing and filled with people made it feel larger than even that abandoned town.

Cheree, standing beside him, noticed his awe. "I take it the place you come from isn't quite this big?"

"No. It sure isn't."

"This is just the proper, you know. A full third of us have ranches or farms scattered on the outskirts. We produce all our food, with plenty left over to trade."

"How many people live here?"

"Just shy of two hundred."

"Two *hundred?*" Korden exclaimed. The biggest crowd he'd ever been in numbered exactly forty-two, counting himself; he couldn't conceive of so many people in one place, had never even thought so many people could be left in the entire *world.* "And you let men and women live together?"

"Of course!"

"But aren't you afraid they'll make babies?"

Cheree's smooth face fell. She looked away from him, out over Hidden Glen. "That was a concern, once," she said stiffly.

Before he could think on that, Winstid rushed to interject. "All right, this ain't a tour, son. We're pressing our luck just standing around out here. Let's go if we're going." It was the third time he'd mentioned that Korden's presence here was a secret. "Cheree, you take Jakel's mount, and the boy can ride with me. We'll head south, get away from town, then circle around toward home."

The Peacekeep named Jakel had been standing on Winstid's other side until now, still gawking indiscreetly at Korden with his eyes bugged out. He didn't even look away as he asked, in his much thicker accent, "Ya want me ta stay here and mind the Keep, boss?"

Winstid shook his head. "No, get over to the pavilion and give Becks a hand. People are gonna think it strange enough that Cheree and I aren't there for Sixth Eve festival; no need for us all to be missing."

"It's Sixth Eve?" Korden asked. He'd completely lost track of the days during his travels.

Cheree had to be helped up on her horse, sitting sidesaddle to accommodate her skirt. As he and Winstid turned to the other animal, Korden examined the land to the left of the prison house door; west, judging from the sun. In this direction, the meadow ran on and on, sloping steadily down toward the base of a towering dirt embankment that ran north and south parallel to the town as far as he could see in either direction. The cliff face had to be a hundred pargs high, and looked much too steep and soft to climb. It was as though the earth had split in two, and the side on which Hidden Glen rested sank far below the other. In an hour or so, the sun would disappear behind the top of this ridge, and the whole meadow would be cast in its shadow.

Winstid reached out and ran a finger through the air, down the length of the bluff. "The ground trembles constantly along it, sometimes so bad you can feel it for spans around. Strangest sensation. The animals hate it, and it's caused a building or two to cave, but at least it helps discourage visitors."

FAULT LINE, Stone declared. I BELIEVE WE ARE TOO FAR EAST FOR IT TO BE THE SAN ANDREAS. PERHAPS THE ROGERS CREEK FAULT.

Winstid patted the neck of the palomino, who lowered his head as though bowing, much to Korden's delight. "This is Starry. You sit in front, I'll take the rear. Might be a little cozy, but it won't be for long."

He offered a hand, but Korden, who'd ridden Mulder many times until he got too heavy for the plow horse's bowed back, swung up onto the long saddle easily. Starry twisted his neck around to look at him suspiciously. Korden ran a hand through the horse's slick white mane, which seemed to placate him. Winstid mounted and squeezed onto the back of the saddle, wrapping an arm around his side and hissing in pain as he settled.

"What's wrong?" his wife asked.

"Nothing. Ran into some trouble at the exchange." From a saddlebag draped over the horse, he removed a round-topped hat with a diamond-shaped brim and pulled it over his coiled hair. Then he reached around Korden to take the reins. "All right boy, hold on tight."

They left Jakel still gaping after them as Winstid led the way behind the Keep, through a gap in the fence, and down into the lush prairie. He urged their mount to a trot that Cheree matched. The sounds of the Hidden Glen proper were lost behind them as they entered a sea of skilne that came up to the horses' chests. Their pace slowed as the long blades reached for the animals, drawn to their body heat. Starry grunted and huffed as he pushed through, tearing some of the grass out of the ground roots and all.

"I've never seen skilne this thick," Korden remarked.

"Gotta have a horse to get through it when it's like this," Winstid told him. "Man on foot would be suffocated."

After only a few minutes of plowing onward, they veered sharply to the east. The skilne grew sparser, revealing a landscape that remained flat enough to see across for several spans, all the way to the edge of another forest, this one consisting of only green pines and squat, jolly firs. It looked much less dense and foreboding than the sequoias, almost friendly in comparison. Korden wondered if it was the same one he'd seen from the high hillside when he first set out. If so, Hidden Glen must lie in a clearing nestled somewhere between the two woodlands. Several lonely, flat peaks rose above the trees far in the distance, reaching toward the sky, where bulbous gray storm clouds blotted out the Shroud.

The ride didn't take long, but the shadows had deepened and spread by the time he realized the meadowland had been replaced by neatly plowed rows that stretched out to their left and right, from which sturdy green corn stalks sprouted.

They were approaching a low house built in the midst of this tilled earth, a tidy log structure with an olive green roof, white shutters on the windows, and deep eaves across the front that formed a shaded porch beneath. A rounded red dome hunkered in the field beyond. Three strange beasts with black and white hides grazed serenely in front of it.

They came to a stop in the yard and dismounted. Cheree offered Korden her reins, but she looked defiantly at her husband as she said, "There's a trough just behind the house. Would you mind tying the horses up so they can drink?"

"Yes, miss'um." He accepted the reins and turned to take Winstid's. The Peacekeep glared up at his wife for several seconds before grudgingly surrendering them. Korden led both mounts through the yard, to the corner of the house. When he looked back, husband and wife still stood locked in silent, staring combat.

6

Winstid waited for Korden to round the house—a hard enough task itself, allowing the boy out of his sight, where he could easily jump on one of those horses and ride for the horizon—before he even attempted speaking to his wife.

"Cheree, sweetlove…I know you don't wanna hear it, but we know less'n nothing about him." He pushed back the pointed brim of his hat just so he could look up into her eyes. He loved her long, slender legs with a passion that could still make his pants tent, but cursed if it wasn't hard to be imposing when they gave her such height over him. "The way we ran into him was suspicious on its own, and that story 'bout coming through Big Woods has gotta be cursepucky. Becks is convinced someone is using him to get to us. Not only that, but—"

"I'm so proud of you," she interrupted gently, reaching to caress his stubbled cheek with one of her silky smooth hands. Winstid expected fire; he was so surprised by this, he nearly flinched away. "Proud of you for bringing him here. It was the right thing to do. But I don't care about the rest of it. Not where he came from or what he wants or what you had to go through to get him here." The rigidness went out of her spine then; she seemed to age a decade right before his eyes. "He's a child, Winstid. A *child*. That has to still mean something, even with the world this broken. It has to because I believe it does, even if you don't."

"I didn't say—"

"So we are going to help him," she continued, still in that tone barely louder than a whisper but heavier than a mountain. "We are going to give him whatever he needs and let him stay as long as he wants and send him on his way with our blessing whenever he wishes. I don't care what it costs us. Not...not this time."

Those last three words stung more than anything she'd ever said to him in all their many seasons and years together. He'd believed—or maybe fooled himself into believing—that the old grudge had healed with time, been buried beneath a landslide of love, but now he saw that it lay just as close to the surface as his own guilt.

At least she hadn't stated what was so plainly obvious: that if he denied her this...stood in her way...the love she held for him would most likely wither and die, like a crop deprived of rain.

Because that scared him more than anything else he could imagine—more than anything the town Council could bring down on his head—Winstid gathered his tall wife in his arms, pulled her down so he could plant a kiss on her lily forehead, and vowed to do as she asked.

The Customer is Always Right

1

Dostey Trullo roared through the front gate of the clan compound on his hovertrike without slowing, almost running down the sentry before he could leap back into the guard box. When the man shouted something angry after him, Dostey twisted around on the vehicle's saddle and held up his small finger. The framming asshole better feel lucky all he got was an obscene gesture; with the mood Dostey was in, he would gladly go back and stomp the man's throat into paste. The long ride north on Old Five—through abandoned towns and burned out fortresses, past the old, rusted sign welcoming him to a long-forgotten place called 'Oregon'— had not cooled his blood, as Winstid Crane hoped, but given it time to simmer into a murderous stew.

Across a barren asphalt lot sat the long, blocky building that served as Clan Triker's base of operations. Bluish-gray walls rose high on all sides, forming a massive rectangular edifice whose sharp corners slashed at the sky. A pre-Purge structure, all steel and crete, the kind of design you rarely saw outside the ruins of the old cities, if you were brave enough to venture in. This one had been in remarkably good shape when Heater Kay discovered the wonders contained within, structurally sound and little weather damage. Best of all though, it still received a trickle of power from wherever such energy was created, enough for them to turn on lights and work some of the machinery. The Clan—back then just a handful of nomads on horseback, raiding fishing villages along the coast—moved into the structure and made it livable within weeks.

All along the flat rooftop, powerful search beams blazed down on the paved wasteland around the compound, controlled by the men on watch. One of them turned theirs on Dostey as he steered his trike toward the gigantic steel shutter in the middle of the building's face, bathing him in blinding light until they could verify his identity. Security wasn't a priority at the compound; the idea of someone attacking them here was laughable. He gunned the vehicle's engine angrily and shot ahead of the beam.

The shutter stood halfway open. Light and music and the whining, discordant sounds of electrical machinery drifted out through the gap beneath. As demand for their product increased, work continued around the clock.

Just above this door, the sigul of Clan Triker was displayed in runny black paint: a pair of crossed longshooters big enough to be seen from a span away. But behind that, in faded red letters, the moniker of the people that once claimed this building was still visible as well. Dostey couldn't read the words, but Heater had told him what they said.

FARRELLY MUNITIONS.

He cut the trike's propulsion and ducked his head as he coasted beneath the steel shutter, the *jhaken*'s waist length cape flapping behind him. On the other side, a cavernous bay ran for hundreds of pargs. A ceiling of naked steel girders stretched overhead, ringed with catwalks and rusted chains, and crisscrossed with tracks for the suspended cranes that once moved heavy loads onto trucks for delivery. Clan Triker's output wasn't quite enough to necessitate such measures...yet. Heater envisioned a future where their influence continued to spread until they were shipping goods far and wide across the land. 'Resurging the economy,' he called it, one of those curious phrases that often spilled from his thin lips, no doubt obtained from the many books he read from the old world.

Charging pads for the hovertrikes lined the left wall. This is where they'd found the vehicles that would give their clan its name, amazing machines that travelled ten times as fast as a horse, and allowed them to make deliveries to places that would take weeks to reach otherwise. They'd just been sitting here in the dark, fully charged and waiting for their new masters.

Dostey pulled onto the number six pad and powered down. The landing skid in front gave a protracted creak as it shuddered into place. He hopped off the saddle and punched the button on the console that recharged the vehicle's batteries from the shimmery platform below, a process that still seemed like magic to him.

Eight of the other pads were empty, their riders out on delivery runs. Another four showed bright green light from their control readouts, indicating a fully charged trike. But all the others housed vehicles that either never worked, or had fallen into disrepair since the clan took possession of them. Try as they might, they couldn't comprehend the technology enough to get them running again. Dostey figured his ride would be joining the scrapheap sooner rather than later.

A menagerie of workstations took up the rest of the bay, where the firearms were assembled. Hammers rang out, drills whined, welders threw streams of sparks into the air. Over it all, speakers high in the rafters piped in amplified music direct from the machine in Heater's quarters, some tune with multiple male voices singing in harmony about hanging tough and being rough. Heater loved his collection of audio chits, but Dostey never understood what the hells any of them were talking about.

These workstations used to be manned by Trikers, but the days of the Clan having to perform the labor themselves were long over. Instead of *jhakens*, these people wore rags and manacles, most of them shackled to the tables where they worked. The clan did a lot of community outreach to find new customers, but if they deemed a settlement too small to have anything to offer in trade, its citizens were 'forcibly enlisted to the people's labor force.' Another favorite phrase of Heater's, always said with a knowing grin.

All of these crewmen were male; no females were ever taken. In Heater's opinion, wombies were only good for raping and killing, and not necessarily in that order. Keep women around men too long, and love would inevitably blossom. And love was a useless—not to mention dangerous—luxury these days.

Dostey snapped at two of the slaves as he strode across the bay. "Get my trike unloaded before I cut off your frammin toes." All of the food from his deliveries would be added into the compound stores, perishables distributed at upcoming meals, the rest stockpiled. He didn't wait to see if they obeyed as he passed through the door from the bay that led to the rest of the compound.

A maze of hallways lay beyond. Dostey navigated them quickly, passing crew bunks and huge storage rooms that held enough raw materials and pre-fashioned parts to build hundreds of thousands of projectilers. It took them two seasons to interpret the design blueprints to know what each one was for. The models they finally managed to cobble together were crude, but they did the job. Their biggest breakthrough came when they finally perfected their own mixture of devil powder, powerful enough to fire a popshell but not so much that the weapons outright exploded in their hands.

Only when he reached the stairwell leading to the top floor of the building did he encounter resistance. Pim and Big Weryl stood guard on the landing, just outside the door to Heater's quarters.

"*He's got comp'ny!*" Pim shouted over the music reverberating through the stairwell. He threw an arm riddled with infected needle marks across the door.

"*Move!*" Dostey growled.

"*Don't wanna be disturbed! Said he'd have another job for you and Cloonan in the mornin!*"

"*Cloonan is dead! Get the fram outta my way unless you wanna join 'im!*"

Pim still hesitated, terror in his glassy eyes as he tried to decide who scared him more. Big Weryl shook his head and rumbled, "*Let 'im through!*"

"*Fine! But it's* your *hole on the line, curseface!*" He withdrew his arm but it still wasn't fast enough for Dostey, who grabbed the stick thin appendage and pressed a thumb into his weeping jinko sores as he did. Pim squealed as Dostey shoved him aside and pushed through the door just as the song changed, the male voices now belting out that someone had the 'right stuff.'

2

Heater's quarters had been created from one long chain of rooms, complete with their own still-functioning toilet, something Dostey had never even seen before coming to this place. Ornate rugs covered the cold crete floors in a mismatched carpet. The walls, once drab gray plaster, were hung with the finest cloth they could scavenge, steal or barter, rich silks and satins that cascaded across in a variety of cool, muted colors. They seemed to lead the eye down the length of the chamber, past gauzy curtains that served as barricades between each room, toward a huge, luxurious bed at the far end festooned with sheer nets and heavy draperies. Heater said the style was supposed to be 'Arabian,' but Dostey found the hazy, dreamlike effect of the man's bedroom unsettling.

Luckily, he didn't have to go that far to find their leader. Heater Kay sat at the terminal just inside the door. The bank of switches, dials and glowing screens allowed him to make announcements, play his precious music, and control most of the electrical systems in the compound. At the moment, he sat reclined in the swiveling chair, naked from the waist up, his hairless, muscled torso gleaming with old scar tissue and blood ink tattoos. One of the crewmen knelt in front of him, head bobbing up and down in Heater's lap.

"Dostey." Heater greeted him with a lazy grin. From the pinkish hue to his otherwise dark eyes, Dostey figured he was cruising the jink himself. The man wasn't an addict, but he did use the gritty plant extract now and then, injecting himself with makeshift needles. His speech even slurred when he spoke again. "Have a seat, brother. You gotta try this one out when I'm finished. He's...*uh*...very talented."

"Those motherhangers killed Cloonan, Heat."

Most men in such a state would've needed time to sober up, but the transformation on Heater's lean face was instantaneous and drastic. His coal eyes cleared between blinks, the glaze replaced by a glint of cunning, catlike intelligence. He sat up and whipped one hand across the control board, flicking a switch that killed the music. The crewman on his knees looked up fearfully for a moment and then quickly went back to work. "What are you talkin about?" Heater said evenly. "Who did?"

"That Crane fram and 'is goddamn Pacemakers, or whatever the hells they call themselves. Drew on us, then gunned down Cloonan when we tried to defend ourselves."

Heater sat still and silent for so long, Dostey thought he might have gone to sleep with his eyes open. Then he brought one clenched fist smashing down on the console, scattering a stack of his beloved music chits across the floor. "Son of a rotted womb!" he exclaimed through clenched teeth. He shoved the crewman away hard enough to tumble him over backward, then rose to his full six parg height with his member still standing stiff and proud from the leggings of his *jhaken*.

The leader of Clan Triker looked to be somewhere in his early-fifties, but not even he knew for sure; like a lot of people, he hadn't bothered to keep track of the years after surviving to eighteen. His hair was raven black to match his eyes, falling in lank curtains over his shoulders, where it framed the thick, coarse beard he'd been growing his entire life, the end of which reached to his exposed navel.

He took a look around at the mess of chits and the cowering crewman as if he couldn't understand how they'd gotten there, then grinned and held out his arms. "Sorry. That's embarrassing. Can't restart civilization when we're acting like animals, now can we?" His wilting cock caught his eye; he tucked it carefully back into the tight leather covering his crotch. Then he leveled one finger with no nail at Dostey. "Let's try this again. So what you're tellin me is…you let a buncha elderly farmers steal our delivery."

"No, no. They paid for the shot."

"Then why would they—"

"There was a boy," Dostey cut in, before the man could get himself worked up again.

Heater's eyes narrowed to dangerous slits. "Speak on, Dostey. And know that I'm gettin impatient, so choose each word carefully."

Dostey already intended to do just that, if only to insure he wasn't blamed for this colossal fram-up. "We delivered, they paid. As we were finishin up, this Incarnate bait comes runnin outta that big ass forest they're all so scared of."

"How old?"

"I dunno. Fifteen, sixteen. Closer to free age than not. He had some kinda fit right by the side of the road, fell over cold. We asked Crane if he knew the kid, he said no. So Cloonan and me picked 'im up to bring 'im back here to you."

"And why, pray tell, did you think I would want him? That's why there ain't no women on the compound, so I ain't gotta deal with shit like that."

"I-I just figured," Dostey began, unsure of his reasoning for the first time, " that if we didn't have 'im on hand very long…kept on the move and got him to a post…maybe he'd fetch a good price."

Heater thought about this as he ran a hand down the scraggly length of his beard, and then waved at him to go on. "What happened then?"

"Then Crane drew. Said he couldn't let us have the kid. We jawed back and forth, Cloonan opened fire, and one of Crane's men shot 'im. Then they took my piece and marched me outta there at shootpoint." Dostey snorted. "Said to tell you they didn't want it this way, that they still wanted to trade."

"Oh, we're gonna trade all right." Instead of being furious, Heater sounded excited. Which was far, far worse; the leader of Clan Triker killed far more people with a smile on his face than a scowl. He left the console and strode over to grab Dostey by the shoulders. "Now, listen on, brother, cause this is *very* important: did they take the kiddo with them?"

Dostey flinched, expecting a blow—or worse—at any moment, but was careful not to pull away. "I...I don't know, I figure so..."

Heater released him and clapped his big hands together once. "Round up some men. Big Weryl...Morn...maybe the Scummer, if he's back. A couple more. I want everyone ready to ride in an hour."

"What, *tonight?* Heat, no, what's the point? I can head out with some guys in the mornin..."

Heater shook his head and moved past him toward the door, his bare feet slapping against the rugs. Dostey rushed to follow. "No, we're goin right now."

"But we don't even know where their town is. We'll have to keep a watch on their shack and hope they're dumb enough to come back. Just...just let me handle this, and I promise you—"

Heater paused at the door long enough for Dostey to catch up, and slung an arm around his shoulders. "You know Dostey, there's a sayin. The customer is always right. By that logic, you're as much to blame for this situation as they are. You started a fight with some of our valued customers over somethin you really had no business takin in the first place. A fight, I might add, that I'm gonna have to finish for you." That huge, beaming smile spread his thick lips again, and the skin on Dostey's bare scalp began to crawl. "But that's okay, because there's a bigger opportunity now. See, we got somethin really incredible goin here. Somethin no one else really has: a successful business. We've made a name for ourselves, just like in the old days. But it's also a *delicate* business. Because the product we manufacture and distribute, that so many people want…well, essentially, we're stockpilin all of our customers with everything they need to become our enemies. Get enough of them together, they'll march in here and push us out. America made that same mistake over and over again in its foreign diplomacy."

Dostey frowned. "Who's *America?*"

Heater sighed. "Curse brother, you really gotta learn to read." He waved a hand. "It ain't important. What *is* important is that, when a customer turns our own product against us, we gotta deal with that curse swiftly and harshly, before anyone else starts gettin the kinda ideas we don't want 'em to get. So while some men might say that you frammed up and lost us a customer…" He patted Dostey's cheek here hard enough to rattle his teeth. "…I'm just gonna think of this as an opportunity for us to flex a little muscle, bolster our reputation, and remind our clientele just who they're dealin with."

"Sure," Dostey nodded eagerly, all arguments done. "Sure, I understand all that, it's just…how are we gonna find 'em?"

Heater winked at him. "I'm glad you asked."

3

He led the way back out onto the landing, where Pim and Big Weryl waited, then down the staircase to the first floor of the compound. Dostey kept a wary distance, still awaiting some sort of punishment for today's loss. But Heater only hummed happily as he continued past the first floor, into the sub level.

Under the compound stretched a vast, dank bunker whose ceiling was supported by a grid of crete pillars. Endless shelves packed this space, and steel boxes containing tools or weapon parts the Clan hadn't been able to use. This included racks of hollow tubes with fins mounted on the sides, which their experts claimed could be packed with devil powder and flung at enemies hundreds of spans away. The lights didn't work down here; the only illumination came from reflective patches on every fourth pillar, which gave off an eerie green glow whenever someone approached. Dostey had ventured into this underground warehouse only a handful of times since they'd taken over the building; the enclosed space made him feel as though he'd been buried alive.

Heater—still stripped to the waist, the upper half of his *jhaken* hanging behind him—navigated the narrow aisles with confidence, but Dostey was lost after a few minutes. The patches lit up as they neared, then powered down again as they passed by, leaving them adrift in a sea of darkness on a raft of green light.

Soon they reached a wall, although Dostey couldn't have said which one. A set of double doors interrupted the smooth crete. Heater took a dangling key from a nearby shelf and used it to unlock them.

"I was saving these for a special occasion," he said, the green lights making his teeth appear to glow and turning his beard into a mossy nest. He pulled open the doors and stepped through.

Dostey came in and stood beside him. The space on the other side of the doors felt small, but was far too dark to see in. He tensed, sure that this is where he would receive his rebuke. "Heat, I don't—"

Something moved in the darkness ahead. Tiny red lights flared into existence, projecting halos of ruddy illumination across the room. Dostey caught a flash of something reaching for him. He gasped and tried to back away, only to be stopped by Heater.

"Relax brother, they're locked up," he said.

The assurance did little to comfort, but Dostey stared into the maroon glow ahead, waiting for his eyes to adjust. This room was no more than a handful of paces deep, but a cage of some sort took up the back half, with parallel bars running from wall to wall and floor to ceiling. A vault. But whatever the creators of this building needed it to protect was long gone. Trapped inside now were three cadaverous forms, their eyes awash with a hellish inferno as they thrust their arms through the bars and clawed at the air.

"*Release us, sin cow!*" one of them rasped.

"Holy hells," Dostey murmured. This time he shoved past Heater in his haste to get out of the room. "Why the fram do you have Incarnates in there?"

"You like 'em?" Heater asked proudly from the door. The conflicting lights painted one side of his face red, the other green, like the old holiday Dostey's grandfather told stories about. "I came across these three beauties two weeks ago, just wanderin down the road about eighty spans from here. They were in bad shape, too weak to fight me off, so I roped 'em and brought 'em back. Figured they might come in handy."

Dostey made a fist in the air. "You have to let them out, Heat! Curse, we'll have a whole army of those things outside the fences!"

"*They come for us already!*" one of the Incarnates confirmed. Dostey wasn't sure if it was the same one who'd spoken before; all their voices sounded like they had a mouthful of broken glass. "*They'll tear this place apart and flay you all until you beg for death, they'll—*"

"I don't think so," Heater told them casually. "I mean, yes, if they knew I was keepin you penned up, they'd prob'ly be pretty pissed. But I have a theory. I think that you cursestains can smell a brat on the other side of the world, but you wouldn't be able to sense another of your own kind if you were standin on top of him. Ain't that right?"

The Incarnates didn't answer, just continued to watch him with those burning holes in their heads.

"Not to mention," Heater said, sidling closer to the cage, "that every year, it seems like there are less and less of you assholes around. Maybe it's from whatever's been holdin up your Shroud for so long, or maybe it's because of those crazy new stories I'm hearin from the far side of the Valley of Bones, but…your numbers are dwindlin almost as fast as ours. Naw, I'm thinkin if I kept you down here in the dark… away from that mean, awful sunlight…you'd be my little pets until the end of time."

One of them swiped out at his face with fingers curled into claws. Heater sidestepped, grabbed the demon's arm, and brought it crashing against the bars all in one fluid motion. After a sharp snap and a noise like ripping cloth, Heater stood holding the creature's severed limb. The stump of the appendage dribbled oily black fluid onto the floor as the Incarnate pulled it back inside the cage.

"Your time is up, my friends." Heater tossed the severed hand at Dostey, who leapt out of the way and let it fall to the floor. "I don't know what's happenin out east, but here on the west coast, us humans are makin a comeback in a biiiiig way, and Heater Kay intends to be on top when we do. But...if you're willin to play nice...I'll make you three a deal for your freedom."

The Incarnates looked at one another, then back at Heater. "What is it you would ask of us?" one of them inquired, sounding sulky.

Heater looked back at Dostey with a triumphant grin, then stepped even closer to the bars, as though daring them to come at him again.

"I just want you to do what you do best." He tapped the end of his nose. "Sniff out a kiddo for me."

Burning Out

1

"I didn't really think there would be. He said something about following the Filament, so he probably wasn't around before then to even be in your files."

Korden spoke in hushed tones while he washed himself by lamplight in the Cranes' dented metal bathtub. Cheree heated the water for him in her kitchen on an ancient cast-iron wood stove much like the one in the social hall back home, then left him alone in a separate, tiny bathing chamber after taking all of his clothes to clean. The warm water felt wonderful, but it turned black as soon as he sat down in it.

 Stone sounded almost respectful.

"He's just as much a parasite as the Incarnates. He uses people's hopes and dreams and fears to manipulate them, then attaches to them and sucks out their brains. At least he's stuck in that arch until he tricks someone into walking through." Korden frowned as he scrubbed at the dirt under his fingernails. "Poor Merise. I think Loathe's been working on her for a long time. He's just about driven her insane."

You say he uses people's dreams, yet it was a dream that warned you of him.

"That was different. It wasn't really a dream, more of a...a message. One that came in the form of my father, so Loathe couldn't use it against me."

But who could have sent such a message? Besides the unproven existence of such a method of communication, you were the first person to chance upon him in the two-hundred years he claimed to have been imprisoned. Who else would be aware of the situation in order to warn you?

"Tash used to say that dreams were the head's way of interpreting what the heart already knows. Maybe my undermind just took what Merise said and everything that I saw happening around us and figured it out. Or maybe..." He stopped, not wanting to spark another debate with the computer, but, of course, this was already far too late for a companion that could read his thoughts.

You believe the Upper to be responsible.

"Yes," Korden answered. "I do."

Stone didn't argue, just went back to praising the terrible creature that tried to consume Korden. The range of his illusions is unprecedented. He not only made you believe you were ill, but created entire settings with tactile representation as well as visual. The height of hologram technology could not achieve such realism. He was even able to deceive my systems.

"Because I don't really think it is an illusion," Korden clarified. "He can make anything we imagine real, *actually* real, not just for his host but for everyone. It's really not too different from artcraft, just on a larger scale. Think about the forest. He somehow used the imaginations of all those animals he ate to grow those trees, just so he could extend his reach and search for people he could lure to him." The scrub brush slipped from his hand and sank into the filthy bathwater as a sudden realization struck him. "With a creative enough mind, he would pretty much have control over reality itself."

But you were able to halt his use of your mind by focusing on something real, something you did not have to imagine. In this case, your father. This is an important weakness to note.

"We don't need to note it. Because we're never going to see him again. He can rot in that forest another two-hundred years for all I care." Korden stood and grabbed the threadbare towel Cheree provided him to dry off and pulled it around his shoulders. "Right now, I'm more worried about these people."

Do you believe them to be dangerous?

"No, not at all. They seem really nice. I think they're more scared of me than I am of them."

It is fortunate—however improbable—that they found you when they did.

"Yeah. Now we just need to convince them we don't mean any harm. It'll be best for them and us if we get out of this town before any more Incarnates catch up to us."

Agreed. If they can provide us with our current location relative to the map, we should return to the closest identifiable road and plot our course from there.

Korden nodded. Though he knew they truly did need to move on, Korden felt a sudden, surprising pang of sadness at the idea of leaving Hidden Glen.

2

When he finished drying, he tried on the clothes Cheree gave him to wear until his own were ready. They were Winstid's; another embroidered tunic, this one a light blue, and more denim pants with intricate stitching up the seam. After rolling up the cuffs, the pants fit him fine, but the tunic ballooned out in front where the Peacekeep's sloping belly would hang. Korden tucked the excess cloth into the pants and stepped from the bathing chamber into the common room.

The interior of the Crane home was constructed from a dark timber, and smelled pleasantly of cedar and fresh flowers. A skylight and wide windows would've let in a stream of sunlight during the day, but now, with twilight upon the world, the majority of the illumination came from lanterns around the room and crackling flames in a fireplace to his left, in front of which two sturdy oak rocking chairs waited. Shelves and a heavy supping table took up the rest of the room, the latter already set for three, with plates made of highly glazed porcelain and more copper silverware. No sign of his hosts, but Korden could hear a low sizzling from the kitchen on the opposite side of the room.

Hung on the walls were other paintings like the ones in the Keep, hyper-realistic portraits of rivers and trees and sunny meadows, and one above the fireplace that looked like the same view of Hidden Glen Korden saw from the Keep's dooryard. He stood admiring it for long moments, imagining what it would be like to live there, until a door squeaked behind him.

"Don't you look a handsome devil?" Cheree proclaimed as she emerged from the kitchen, accompanied by the tantalizing aroma of cooking meat. "Everything all right in there, dear? I thought I heard you talking to yourself."

"I was?" He gave a laugh that sounded too nervous. "Um, maybe. Sometimes I don't even realize I'm doing it." He gestured toward the painting. "Someone from the Glen painted this?"

"Oh yes." Cheree stood with her hands clasped primly in front of her waist. "That one is actually my favorite. Took me an entire Burning Season and most of Harvest to capture just the look I wanted. By then, the grass had all died for the year and I didn't have anything to use as a reference."

"*You* did these?" Korden asked, looking around at the other paintings with new appreciation.

Cheree nodded shyly, a flush of color rising briefly in her milky cheeks. "I know they're not very good…"

"They're fantastic!"

"That's kind of you to say. Winstid doesn't really see the point. He says if he wanted to look at a flower or a river, he would just go outside and do it. Have you ever tried to paint, Korden?"

"Some. I like to write more."

"Really now? A writer?" She beamed. "That's a rare skill indeed. My grandmother taught me to read, but I so seldom have anything new to practice on. Seems like there are too few books left in the world. I would love to read something of yours."

Korden shrugged uncomfortably and went back to looking at the painting over the fireplace. Just being this close to such skill made him feel inspired, the well of artcraft inside him brimming over. A few seconds later, she joined him.

"I've always loved to create. I don't even know why, it just...it makes me feel like I'm part of something larger. Soothes the soul. Like praising our good Aged Lord."

He stared at her as a sudden suspicion gripped him. "Do you...do you know artcraft?"

The question confused her. She squinted and frowned. "*Artcraft?* Dear, whatever do you m—?"

"He's talking about those witch people."

Winstid stood in the cabin's entrance, a bundle of firewood in his arms. A gust of wind sighed around the blackened man, blowing out one of the lanterns; the storm they'd seen while riding to the house was almost upon them. He frowned at Korden over the logs and said, "There hasn't been any of those Upper-worshipping loons in these parts for a long time. What do *you* know about them?"

"N-nothing!" Korden said quickly. "I just...heard stories."

"Stories." Winstid carried his load across the room and put it down beside the hearth, grimacing as he straightened. "That's all anyone knows about them anymore. My ma told me small covens of them would come 'round every once in a while when she was a girl, using their magic tricks to try and rouse the people up against the Filament. But as soon as the Incarnates started going out'n their way to hunt them down as well, they all turned tail and ran north into the Rim. Probably still up there now, freezing their noses off while they paint and sing and hold hands and wait for a sign from their heathen god."

"So...you've never even met one?" Korden kept his disappointment from showing.

Winstid's brow—stippled with those dark bumps—bunched up as he thought. "There was another boy in the fortress where I grew up. I don't know if he was one of these…whattaya call them, Crafters?…but he could make things float. Not very high, just a few cupits, and nothing heavier than a water mug. But that was enough to get him and his entire family tossed out on their rears when the governors found out." The Peacekeep poked Korden in the chest. "You'll find that Crafters aren't a very popular topic among civilized folk. Even less than mysterious, secretive children."

"Stop funning the boy," Cheree chided.

"Who's funning? He sure ain't very popular with me at the moment."

"But no one ever said you were civilized, either."

Korden heard none of this good-natured exchange; he was too busy reflecting on Winstid's story. Even with what Redfen told him about his mother, he still had trouble believing that the rest of the world viewed the men that raised him as charlatans and cowards. Would these nice people cast him out of their home this very instant if they knew he could not only 'float' most of the objects in it, but burn the place to cinders as well?

He suddenly wondered if the Olders' seclusion was as self-imposed as they always claimed.

Winstid studied him. "You cleaned up nice, boy. Those my clothes?"

"Yes sir."

He nodded and gave Korden a clap on the shoulder. "Well, not everyone can wear them as good as me. C'mon, let's eat."

3

At the Sixth Eve feast on the Pavilion, they would be serving racks of roasted lamb ribs, river frogs stuffed with carrots and barley, celery pie for those with weaker stomachs (a great deal of the aging population, in fact), cranberry wine, and the last of the flanks from the chicara pod Becks and a few other men had hunted down several weeks ago, a feat that would've been impossible with only bow and arrow. Winstid hated missing it, but the dinner that Cheree prepared—a slab of grilled t-bone from the Vickery ranch's last culling, and turnips smothered in wheatmilk gravy—was delicious enough. From the way the kid ate the meat—cutting deliberately, inspecting each piece, then chewing as carefully as though he expected it to come to life in his mouth—Winstid figured he'd probably never had steak. Or anything else that came from a cow, for that matter. Even though he'd just eaten a couple of hours before at the Keep, he showed no sign of slowing down on this meal.

Winstid also noticed that his wife put out the good plates for the occasion, the glazed beauties he'd given her for their first anniversary, which they'd carried with them throughout all their wanderings before settling Hidden Glen. He had no doubt that if they possessed a silk pillow, Cheree would've wanted the boy to sit on that as well.

She babbled as they ate, telling Korden about her own youth and their farm and Hidden Glen (more than Winstid would've liked on the latter) while outside the wind groaned like some great, dying beast. The boy listened, spellbound, asking questions about everything, but Winstid noticed his eyes flicking to the longshooter, still in its holster and dangling from the empty fourth chair across the table.

When they lingered a third time, Winstid said, "You wouldn't be trying to work out how to get your hands on it, now would you?"

The kid looked at him with such genuine bewilderment, Winstid knew he'd been wrong. "What?"

"My rifle. You keep looking at it. And I know you can't be as fascinated by it as you seem to be by everything else, because you have one of your own that puts this slipshod junk to shame."

"I…I've never shot it," Korden said quietly, his words lost in the first rumble of thunder from the approaching storm. "And also…I was told no one even *had* shooters anymore. I'm just surprised to see another one."

Winstid gave a grudging nod as he forked turnips into his mouth. "Well, you weren't lied to 'bout that. Before last Stilling, the closest I ever came to a shooter were some old, cracked plastic things that looked like toys, being peddled by a clubfooted bodla who claimed they used to shoot deadly beams of light. *Light*, if you can believe it. Then, late last year, one of our trading contacts told us about some group from up north that was visiting every settlement they could find on flying machines and saying they knew how to build shooters."

The kid froze in the act of spearing a piece of meat. "*Flying machines?*"

"Yeah, figured you'd like that'n. Didn't believe it myself 'til I saw them. They don't so much fly as hover, but they're still kye little things. And faster'n sin. There was one out by the side of the road where we found you." He lifted a shoulder. "Too bad you passed out and missed it, huh?"

"Who are these people?"

"They call themselves Clan Triker, but they're nothing but a gang of glorified brigands who lucked into some pre-

Purge tech. We put the word out through our traders that we were interested in meeting them, and before long I found myself out at the trading shack face-to-face with their leader, a bizarre man named Heater Kay." Winstid suppressed a shiver at the thought of the man with his long, waggling beard and the huge grin that never touched his eyes. "He kept going on and on about the *economy* and *supply and demand* the whole time we negotiated. Big words that don't mean anything. Fella thinks he's gonna singlehandedly revive the old world."

"I'd really like to meet him!" Korden exclaimed.

Winstid pointed at the boy with his fork and snapped, "Don't you dare say that. They're some of the most dangerous scum I've ever met, and believe me, that's saying something. His men were ready to snatch you up and take you to be sold. Or worse. We had to shoot one dead just to save you."

Cheree gasped. "You killed a triker?"

"I tried to tell you that earlier woman, and you didn't wanna listen." He turned back to Korden. "Their weapons aren't much, but they sure changed our lives. Made hunting easier, and gave us some security. I worked for weeks to reach a deal with them, traded honestly for three seasons, and then you came along and mucked all that up. Not to mention that Heater's boys will no doubt be searching for us from now on, so maybe you can understand why we have to be so careful about who comes and goes from this town."

Cheree swatted a hand through the air at him as the other worried the pendant dangling from her neck. "That's not his fault and you know it!"

But Winstid had said his piece, and went back to eating with angry jabs at his plate, guilt already making him feel like a jackass for snapping at the boy. The table lapsed into uncomfortable silence, broken only by the sound of rain tapping against the windows and hissing in the fireplace. The kid stared down at his half-finished meal and said nothing.

"Korden," Cheree began, speaking deliberately, "we want to help you. We really do. It's just that we don't know how. We understand you don't want to tell us where you come from, of course we do, but maybe you could just tell us where you're going. Or do you even know?"

The kid considered this for a moment before looking up from his plate. "East. I'm heading further east."

His answer caused her to give Winstid a startled glance. "How far east?"

"As far as I can. To the Shroud, if possible."

Winstid snorted. "After centuries of everyone—below free age and above—hightailing away from the Dark Filament, this kid says he's going *toward* it. Now I've heard everything."

Cheree frowned at him, a hush-up face if ever he saw one. "Korden, dear, you understand what you're saying, don't you?"

"Yes miss'um."

"Then what business could you possibly have going east?"

This time, Korden took even longer to give an answer. "To stop them," he said simply. A single bolt of lightning struck outside, flushing the interior of the house with brilliant white light and revealing the hard determination on his young face. "To find a way to stop the Dark Filament."

His answer—not so much the words, but their delivery—sent a chill rippling up Winstid's spine. He forced himself to laugh. "And just how are you gonna do that, boy?"

"I don't know yet. But you asked how you can help me. You can help by giving me some idea what lies ahead. I have a map…" He turned to his satchel, hanging from the back of his chair.

"Now, just hold on a moment." Winstid put down his fork. Why did everything this boy did only serve to frustrate him further? "You can't very well drop a boulder like that on us and then just skip merrily past it. Who put such an addled thought in your head?"

"It doesn't matter. It's just something I have to do."

"Well, I may never have been more than three hundred spans east of where we sit right now, but I can tell you what you'll find out there, and it sure isn't a way to stop the Filament. *If* you make it to the Shroud—and that's a very big if—you'll run into more Incarnates than you can shake a stick at."

"I don't care," the kid said stubbornly.

"Then what's the point of even going?"

"Someone has to try."

"People *have* tried! What, you think you're the first one to ever have the brilliant idea of fighting the Filament? People have tried, and they've died, every last one! If you're one of the few unlucky enough to get born into this world, the best thing to do is keep your head low, stay alive 'til you turn eighteen, and then make damn sure you don't inflict the same curse on anybody else!"

He waited for a response from the boy, but was surprised by the one he got: an exasperated snicker.

"What?" Winstid demanded. "What's so funny?"

"You just sound like my father."

"Then he must've been a smart man."

"He was. But he was also selfish. He survived, just like you said, and he wanted to make sure that I did too, and that was all he cared about. He never saw beyond his own situation, just like you."

Winstid leaned forward, glowering over the tabletop. Before, he'd merely been frustrated by the kid's ignorance. Now he was insulted and furious at his presumption. "Really now? And just what should I do different? Take up sword and shield and ride off to throw my life away on a windmill like Sir Dawn Quick-Toe?"

Korden shook his head, still maddeningly calm. Winstid tried to remember if he'd ever been this cocksure in the long forgotten years of his youth. "Children are what the Dark Filament is trying to eliminate. If we stop making them, then we're just hastening whatever work they're here to do. Everyone should all be having *more* children, not less. As many as we can."

"Oh ho, then here's the problem with that plan, smart fella: we're all too old. There's not a single woman in this town that could still bare a child. In fact, I'd be willing to bet you'd run into that same problem pretty much ev—"

Across the table, his wife gave a broken sob as she pushed away from the table. "Excuse me," she cried, and ran for their bedroom with a hand over her face.

The door slammed. Winstid closed his eyes and silently cursed his own name.

4

"What happened?" Korden asked timidly. The fleeting impression he'd caught of Cheree's aura as she fled the room revealed a deep well of heartbreaking sadness. He knew his baby plan was stupid and childish—Tash had told him as much and Winstid certainly seemed angry about it—but he hadn't thought it would upset anyone this much. "I didn't mean to—"

"It wasn't you." The words were borne on the crest of a melancholy sigh. Winstid opened his eyes and let them rest on the door behind which his wife had disappeared. "That was because of me. Cursehead that I am."

Korden remained quiet. Even if he wasn't responsible for whatever just happened, he still felt like he'd said more than enough for one day.

Winstid got up as well, his movements slow and labored. He skirted the table and went to a cabinet across from Korden, then lifted a panel and slid it back into the unit, revealing several tall, skinny bottles and shorter glasses. He grabbed one of the former and two of the latter, then seemed to think again. "You ever taken drink, boy?"

"Drink?"

"Devil water. Alcohol."

"Oh. Redfen—my father—he used to let me have a cup of mead with dinner sometimes. But only one."

"One sounds like a good number to me. A lot of men would have a lot less to regret in their lives if they lived by that rule. C'mon."

Winstid carried the bottle and glasses over to the fireplace and slipped into one of the sturdy oak chairs. Korden came around and sat in the other. He watched as Winstid filled one glass from the bottle—a reddish liquid much thinner than the syrupy golden mead back home—downed the entire amount in three quick swallows, then poured more into both and handed the fresh glass to Korden. "Cranberry wine. Just sip now. Might be stronger than what you're used to."

And was it ever. He could smell the contents before the glass reached his lips, and the wine itself burned his throat bad enough to make him gag as it went down. An analysis by Stone informed him that this flaming mixture was CLOSE TO THIRTY PERCENT ALCOHOL BY VOLUME.

Winstid grinned at his reaction as he set the bottle on the wood floor between them. "You'll find that the older you get, the less time you have to waste with anything. And that includes getting drunk."

He leaned forward, grabbed a log, and tossed it onto the fire to produce a fresh roar of heat and light. Then he sat quietly, sipping from his glass and staring into the flames. Korden did the same, his head growing heavier with each tiny swallow of the wine. Outside the house, the brief squall had already begun to die down.

"We were careful." The Peacekeep spoke suddenly, without preamble, eyes still fixed in the flames, but Korden saw his thoughts were somewhere far beyond that. "When we first married, I mean. We agreed that having children… well, there was still a few folks back then optimistic enough to try, but we told ourselves it was just heartache we didn't need.

"The years were hard. Food was scarce. We travelled a lot, alone or with other groups, from one endless string of towns and outposts and fortresses, looking for a place to call home. Then someone we were with had the idea to build our own community, away from the rest of the world. Nine times out of ten, a venture like that would fail, but we had the right resources, the right group of people, with the right set of talents, and, well…Hidden Glen is the result."

Winstid trailed off, lost in memory perhaps, as many of the Olders used to do. Korden didn't prompt him, just observed the man's *mohol*—a lonely, sad shade of wintergreen—and waited for him to start up again on his own.

"We worked hard, and we were proud when this place started to come together. Course, we needed to be selective 'bout who we took in. A lot of them were couples our own age, so we had to be firm 'bout the rules, too." He held up a hand with the fingers and thumb forming an open-ended rectangle, as though framing each of his next words. "Absolutely. No. Breeding. Allowed. We would *not* compromise this place. The punishment for seeding was—and still is—expulsion. No exceptions."

"That's why you couldn't let anyone know I was here," Korden deduced.

"That's right." The light from the flames flickered against Winstid's dark face, turning the tiny black bumps across his brow into a broken terrain of shadows. "Not everyone agreed with it, but enough so it remained in force. And there were a few that had to leave this town for that very reason. I escorted them out myself, forbade them to return as long as their child was with them. Most of them called me a coward. A few spit on me. One couple even came back, after giving up their baby to Incarnates out on the road, but they left again after a season. Couldn't look at any of us the same again. But I ignored it all. Clung to my righteousness. I knew I was right, and that was that. So it shouldn't have been a surprise when the good Aged Lord above chose to swell my own wife's belly."

It took Korden, with his alcohol-laced thoughts, a moment to process this. "You mean Cheree was *pregnant?*" he blurted loudly, and then clapped a hand over his own mouth.

Pregnant; what did that really and truly mean? For all his talk on the subject, he realized he actually knew little about the process after the man put the baby in there. For instance, how in blazes did it get back *out* again? One of the many photos he'd found came briefly to mind: the woman in a bed with strange machines all around her, looking sweaty and exhausted, with a wrinkled infant curled up on her lap. Stone offered to fill in the holes of his knowledge with a brief discourse on the subject, but Korden declined for the moment.

"When she knew for sure, she changed overnight." Winstid's lips spread in an absent grin. "Suddenly, babies were the most important thing in the world. They had to be loved and protected. All our agreements and vows and pacts meant nothing in the face of the life growing inside her. She was happier than I've ever seen her…and more beautiful, too." He took in a single shuddering breath and held it. "I was desperate to make her see what it meant for us. For weeks I told her how we would have to leave here, take to the road again on our own, and all the while most of the town waited with breath held to see if we would go on our own, without causing a fuss. She didn't care. When I threatened to stay here and make her leave by herself, she told me to do what I had to do, with a look of…such disdain. The only thing that mattered to her was the baby. I remember thinking it was like some sort of madness, that babies must infect their mothers with it to ensure they get born. She only began to listen when…when I described what it would be like to have that child ripped from her arms by those monsters, like so many other mothers before her."

Winstid tilted his head back and drained the rest of his second glass, his Adam's apple working. Then he looked over at Korden with eyes that were glazed and jittering.

"I convinced her that nothing we did would matter. Not in the long run. There was nowhere to run, nowhere to hide. In the end, our child would die, either from Incarnates or the ever-abundant cruelty of the world, and if we fought, we would just die with it. I told her that the most merciful thing would be...to end its life ourselves, before it could ever be born."

"No," Korden whispered. A hard ball formed in his stomach, one that tried to work its way back up to his mouth and bring his dinner with it. The idea of such an act horrified him. "H-how is that possible?"

"There are ways," was the only answer Winstid offered. "Some of them dangerous. Cheree finally understood, finally saw it my way...except, I don't even know if I did, not truly. I think now I was just scared. Scared to take responsibility for something I didn't know if I could protect. But she agreed... and we did it...and our child came out of her such a bloody, lumpy mess you couldn't even tell if it was a..." He broke off abruptly, gave his head a hard shake, then put a thumb and forefinger in the corners of his eyes and squeezed there. "And that was that. Life went on. It took a long time for Cheree's body to heal, longer for her mind, and longer still for our marriage. She held me responsible, and, as always, I convinced myself I'd done the right thing. But sometimes I wondered what that child would've been like..."

The thought of drinking any more wine made Korden ill. He set the glass on the floor beside the bottle and leaned back in the chair, feeling hollow. He recalled Tash saying how awful the world had become even before the Dark Filament showed up to claim it, how people had done most of the Filament's work for them.

It seemed that much hadn't changed, at least.

"I don't know if your plan would work, boy. But I know it would produce a lot more lambs for the slaughter. So maybe, rather than restarting the fire, it's best if what's left of humanity just quietly burns out." As if to illustrate this, Winstid glanced at the fireplace, where the flames were already guttering again. "There are some spare blankets in that cupboard if you wanna stretch out in the floor. Tomorrow we'll figure out what to do with you…unless you're gone in the morning, that is. I'm not gonna stay up and guard you all night, so there's nothing to prevent you from slipping out and stealing one of my horses. Come to think of it, maybe that wouldn't be such a bad thing."

The Peacekeep stood up and started across the room toward the door Cheree had slammed. Korden asked after him, "Do you regret it?"

Winstid didn't turn around to give his answer. "I'll tell you this: I love my wife above all else. I would do anything to keep her from being hurt…but I probably hurt her worse than anyone ever could."

He collected his shooter, then disappeared into the bedroom and closed the door behind him.

5

It was still early in the evening, but Cheree was already in bed. Winstid couldn't tell if she slept or just pretended. Either way, she was done with him for the day. He watched her for a bit, lying beneath the covers with her face hidden in the crook of one elbow, then changed into a pair of night breeches to join her. He'd only just lifted back the covers when the churn of horse hooves outside set his nerves jangling.

Their bedroom had a separate door that let out on the porch. Winstid grabbed his weapon and a lantern, then barreled outside, wobbling a bit from the wine still coursing through his veins. His eyes were near useless in the dark, but he made out the shape of the approaching animal and its rider clopping through his muddy fields and aimed his shooter in their direction.

"*Halt!*" he bellowed. "*Identify yourself!*"

"It's me," a voice hissed out of the darkness. "For Aged Lord's sake, don't fire. We can't afford the ammo."

Winstid dropped the rifle's business end with a sigh of relief as Becks dismounted and walked the rest of the way to the house. When he entered the lamplight, Winstid saw the man's clothes were soaked from riding through the storm. "What happened? Everything at the feast go all right? Did Jom get after Hurlett about that damn fence again?"

Becks waited until he finished. "It went fine. Except everyone is buzzing about the mysterious prisoner you brought to your house."

"Tanda," Winstid muttered.

"Tanda," Becks confirmed, then shook his head in disgust. "What in hells were you thinking, Win? Bad enough we snuck that kid into town in the first place, but bringing him way out here with only the two of you as wardens? I expected to find both of you gutted."

Winstid waved a dismissive hand. "It's fine. He ain't dangerous, he's just a kid passing through."

"Oh, that's great," Becks said, his words dripping with uncharacteristic sarcasm, "I'm so glad you cleared him, but I was more worried about the legions of bloodthirsty demons that could show up for him at any moment." He scowled. "And for sweet Aged's sake, you were all about to just bed down without even keeping a guard, weren't you? Living here has made you entirely too soft, my friend."

Winstid looked around before answering, studying the night beyond the porch. "Tomorrow we'll take him to the edge of town and cut him loose, and this will all be over."

"I wouldn't make plans so fast, less'n you intend to go with him."

"Curse man, what're you spouting now?"

Becks' hand went up and rubbed furiously at the stump of his ear. "The Council's up in arms 'bout you bringing someone into the Glen without approval. If you'd left him in a cell—like I thought we agreed to do—we prob'ly coulda called it Peacekeep business and gotten away with it, but, even you gotta admit, bringing him to your house sure don't look good. Neller grilled Jakel and me, demanded to know who it was and why you did it."

"Ah hells," Winstid groaned. "You didn't tell him it was a kid, did you?"

"I didn't tell him anything. But him and the rest of the Council want our guest presented to them first thing in the morning, or…'measures will be taken'."

Winstid leaned against the porch rail and bowed his head. "Hasn't this just become a fine mess?"

"Good deeds have a way of doing that," Becks said quietly.

What Comes Next

1

A sharp crack awoke Korden on the floor of the Crane common room. At first he thought it was a concentrated burst of thunder, but the morning sky looked clear and sunny through the windows. He sat up in alarm when the sound repeated twice more in rapid succession, then slowly faded away.

I calculate an 87.4 percent chance those were gunshots.

He jumped up from his bedroll, hitching at Winstid's baggy clothes before they could trip him. The door to the bedroom opened and Cheree emerged, clutching at the neck of the white sleeping gown she wore. Her eyes were wide as she told him, "Winstid's gone!"

Korden ran for the front door of the cabin, transported back to his mad dash toward the burning village. Early morning sunlight momentarily blinded him. He hurried out into the flat planting fields that surrounded the house and gazed around until he spotted Winstid's short form in the distance, at the far end of the crop rows, his diamond-billed hat pushed back on his head. The Peacekeep stood with the stock of his longshooter against his shoulder and the barrel aimed at something on the ground in front of him. He turned as Korden approached and held up a hand.

"Stay back," he ordered. The man looked haggard, his eyes bloodshot and hair a mess. "I wanna make sure these things are good and dead before we get any closer."

"What are they?"

Winstid hesitated, then said, "Incarnates. Three of 'em."

Korden's breath caught. He edged closer to Winstid until he could see the forms sprawled on the ground. All three were male, wearing little more than filthy rags and goggles over their eyes. They looked emaciated and pale, except for small patches of sallow skin like bruises. Two lay face down, the third on its back and staring up at the sky. This one was not only missing an arm below the elbow, but the top of its head as well, where Winstid's shot had sheared it away. Both wounds looked raw and fresh, but only the one on its crown bled, leaking a congealed black mess onto the ground.

"Saw 'em coming from the porch," Winstid said, without looking away from the corpses. "Scrawny things. Unarmed and in bad shape, too. But they definitely knew you were here. Threatened me, then, when they saw I wouldn't budge, they tried bargaining for you. I shot 'em before I could even hear what they were offering. Thank god I was up most of the night or they'd of caught us in our sleep."

"You killed them. But I thought you had to..." *Have faith*, he almost finished. Saying it would only bring up questions about the Upper that he couldn't answer. And besides, Tash never said what you needed to have faith *in*. Perhaps the Aged Lord they worshipped was enough.

Winstid watched him with narrowed eyes. "Had to what?"

"Had to leave them alone," Korden finished. "You could get in trouble. They slaughter anyone that defends a child."

"I know that," Winstid snapped irritably. "How's that for gratitude? Next time I'll just let 'em have you."

Korden ignored him and turned in a circle, scanning the parcel of flat land in all directions. He reached out with his mind, but the area was just too big for him to search. He thought he could feel eyes on him, just as in the forest, but it could be his imagination this time. "There could be more."

"Oh, I'm sure there are some comin, but these three were probably just rovers."

"Rovers?"

Winstid glanced at him and lowered his weapon, satisfied the creatures were dead. "I've seen raiding parties and even entire armies of these things on the march; armored, well-supplied and mounted. Nobody seems to know where they come from, where they disappear to, how they coordinate, or who leads them. But unless you have something they want—which is to say, someone below free age—those sightings are rare. More often'n not, you get some like these three. They wander the land, slowly rotting away until they find a new host or fall to pieces. Maybe they're scouts. Or deserters. Either way, most folks just call 'em rovers."

In that case, it was most likely 'rovers' like this that killed Redfen and slaughtered most of the village, Korden realized. He couldn't imagine facing an entire army of such creatures, but even the one that stole Allin's body had assured him there were tens of thousands more.

He thought again of the conversation he'd overheard on the bridge. Two Incarnates who'd spoken of battalions and quadrants and someone named Regent Torgas.

From the house, Cheree's high voice called out, "*Is every-thing all right, boys?*"

"*Just some pocoons nosing around the crops!*" Winstid waved his hand high above his head at her and then said to Korden, "Do me a favor, and keep this between us. I have to dispose of these monsters before she sees them. You go inside and change your clothes, then we'll go back to the Glen."

"What for?" Korden asked suspiciously, imagining more time in one of his prison cells.

"To get the rest of your things. Maybe we'll even take a look at this map of yours. But then I want you out of my town before anything else comes looking for you."

2

The boy said his goodbyes to Cheree in the cabin. She wrapped her arms around him and squeezed him until Winstid thought his guts would squirt out his mouth. "Next time you visit, I expect to get to read some of your writing."

"Yes miss'um," he agreed, his voice muffled against her breast.

"You take care of yourself, Korden Bright," she commanded as she released him. Tears strained at the corners of her eyes.

"I will. Don't worry about me."

"You're a very brave young man." Cheree cupped his chin gently in both palms and searched his face. "You know, I almost believe if anyone could rid us of the Filament once and for all, it would be you." She turned to Winstid then, with a hand still on the boy's shoulder. "Remember what you promised."

This time, Winstid embraced his wife in a constrictor's grip, and lifted her off the ground. His hurt ribs ached in protest, but it was worth it to hear her high, girlish laughter after last night. "I remember. Whyn't you have some lunch ready when I get back and we'll go for a picnic down at that spot you like."

"It's a plan, Peacekeep."

At the door, something made him turn back and look at her once more. She grinned and blew him a kiss, and, as simple as that, he knew everything was all right between them again. Winstid tipped his hat and followed Korden outside.

"What did you promise?" the boy asked.

Winstid let one corner of his mouth slide up into a wicked grin. "That I'd make sure you left town with all the fingers, toes, and brains you came in with. But I don't have to worry on too much about the latter, now do I?"

<h1 style="text-align:center">3</h1>

He rode Starry and let Korden take Jakel's mount. The boy handled the animal easily. They followed the same trail as before, looping south through the overgrown skilne fields to approach the Keep from the rear. Hidden Glen was awake and bustling—or as bustling as a town of two hundred elderlies could get—but since most folks were attending Seventh Morn services at the Church of the Aged Redeemer, Winstid thought he could get the kid in and out quietly, before anyone noticed. If Neller and the rest of the Council wanted to strip him of his title for defiance, so be it; that would be far better than trying to explain why he'd brought a child into their midst.

Mostly though, he was just too tired to care.

Behind the Keep, where they would be hidden, two other saddled horses were tethered to the fence. One of them was

Becks' mean-spirited bronco. Winstid pointed at the other, a smaller gray mare. "That'n's yours."

"Mine?"

Winstid nodded. He'd asked Becks to barter the animal from one of the ranches on the far side of the Glen and have it ready when they got here. "To speed you on your journey. Wherever it is you're going."

"You…you really don't have to. If you'll just point me back toward the road…"

"Oh, stop. We got enough martyrs around here, boy. Besides, we'll have to take you there ourselves." He pointed at the high dirt embankment several hundred pargs away which bordered the east side of the proper, where the land trembled unendingly. "You can't see it from here, but there's a narrow canyon that opens down there and leads up to Old Five. There's so many offshoots and dead-ends along the way though, you'd never find your way out."

Jakel and Becks waited inside the Keep just as Winstid had instructed. When the door opened, both men leapt to their feet with matching expressions of guilt.

"Settle on, gentlemen," Winstid told them, then, to Korden, "You met Jakel yesterday. And this is Becks. We make up the entirety of the Hidden Glen Peacekeep force. Say hello Becks, and leave the gawking to Jakel."

"Nice to meet you," Korden ventured.

Becks gave a single curt nod, but kept his mouth shut.

Winstid hung his hat on a peg and hurried behind his desk. "You bring what I asked you to?"

Jakel hefted a burlap sack sitting under the table beside him. "Three water skins and all the meat, bread and cheese I could lay hand to." He offered this to Korden as though he thought the kid might take his hand with it.

"Thanks." The boy met each of their eyes in turn with a sincerity and forthrightness that most of the grown men Winstid knew wouldn't have been able to muster. "For everything. It means a lot."

"Not everybody you meet will want something from you." Winstid retrieved the boy's knife and fancy shooter, and handed them over as well. "Just most of us. Now, show us this map of yours."

Korden moved to the desk, dug through his satchel. A few seconds later, he spread a long rectangle of paper across the scarred desktop, one that showed a tapestry of irregular boxes in various shades of brown and green, all of them crisscrossed with a tangle of lines that ran every which way. It looked like a puzzle to Winstid. Writing sprawled everywhere, hundreds of tiny labels for what were presumably long gone cities and roads. Each of the boxes seemed to have their own strange name as well, emblazoned across the map in bold, capital letters that Winstid could probably sound out if he tried hard enough.

Jakel gave an appreciative whistle. "Jee*zum*, that's gotta be worth somethin. You ever see anything like that?"

Winstid shook his head. "Saw a hand-drawn map of the settlements down around Phoenix when I was a kid, but it didn't have near this much detail, nor cover so much land. A map this expansive hasn't existed for a long time. Course, most of it's probably wrong by now anyway. I wouldn't even know where to start."

"I can help with that," Korden said. "From what I figured out, I came through this forest over...*here*." He took a homemade charcoal pencil from his bag and used it to circle a splotchy green section of the map on the far left side, just beneath a bold capital 'R' in the tongue-twistingly long word 'CALIFORNIA'.

"That makes sense." Becks swiped a line with his fingertip from Korden's circle to the left—and nearest—edge of the map, where the mottled green of the land met a hard edge of uniform blue. "I don't think anyone here has seen it, but we know the ocean is to our west. Never heard it called a 'pack-if-ic' before."

"*Pacific*," Winstid corrected him quietly. It had been one of his mother's fondest wishes to see this mythical place before she died; a wish that was never fulfilled.

"And look right there!" Jakel tapped a tiny symbol they all leaned forward to see, Winstid so far his nose almost touched the paper. Red and blue, and shaped like a shield, with a bold 5 in the middle. It was printed several times next to a long, squiggly line running north and south across the paper. Winstid recognized it immediately. The same symbol appeared on rusted signposts all along the road where they met the boy. "You reckon that's the Old Five?" Jakel ran his crooked finger up and down the length of the line.

"I'll be cursed," Winstid muttered. "It sure is. Hidden Glen has gotta be somewhere along it, just to the east." It felt strange and disorienting to see this new perspective of the place he'd lived most of his life. As though, if he peered close enough, he might be able to see a tiny version of himself studying this very map.

"Do any of you know how far away the Shroud is?" the kid asked.

Becks shook his head. "Gotta be a long, long way. Never even met anyone that claimed to've seen it up close. Don't know anyone who'd want to."

"Don't get him started on that," Winstid cautioned.

Korden shot him a look. "Then what about just further to the east of here? Can you tell me what I might find?"

Winstid spoke up before the others could. "More forest, for a while, but not nearly as thick as what you've already been through." He put a finger on the map to indicate another narrow band of green, then moved it slowly eastward, where the green gave way to brown close to the border of the next shape in the puzzle, a rectangle with a pointed bottom called 'NEVADA.' "Then you're gonna run into a vast, dry desert, one that stretches south all the way past the fortress where I lived when I was your age. Remember how I told you I've never been more than three hundred spans east of here? The Valley of Bones is the reason why."

"It *is* passable though," Becks added. "Trade caravans cross it, but you're gonna need several weeks worth of food and water if you try. More than you could carry on that little filly we got for you."

"Or you could trek on north around it!" Jakel put in eagerly. "Reckon it'd take you an extra season or two outta your way though…"

Winstid waved his hands for silence, then tapped the map again on the far side of the desert, past the boxes of NEVADA and UTAH, and into the mythical land of COLORADO. "Either way, if you make it to the other side, this is where your journey ends, my young friend."

"Why?" Korden demanded. "Incarnates?"

Winstid looked around at his fellow Peacekeeps and saw the same dread reflected in their eyes.

"Moambati," he said.

4

The word—pronounced out loud for the first time as 'Mo-am-bah-tee'—grabbed Korden's attention, but it wasn't until Stone reminded him where he knew it from that the shock truly set in.

Winstid read the surprise on his face. "You already know."

Korden shook his head. "No, I just saw it painted somewhere. 'Beware Moambati.' What is it?"

"That we can't tell you. All we know is, it's been on everyone's lips for the past year."

"Then tell me what you *do* know."

"Bits and pieces. Stories and rumors from the folks we trade with. What we know for sure is this: past the desert is a long ridge of mountains. *This* ridge, I believe." He pressed a finger against the map again, running it down each of the letters in a label that spelled out ROCKY MOUNTAINS. "You might be able to go around the Valley of Bones by heading north, but judging from this, you couldn't avoid the mountains even if you went all the way into the Rim. From what I understand, they're rough terrain, nigh impassable during Stilling. But the land on either side holds some fertile valleys, and there have always been settlements and fortresses strung up and down the foothills. Farming communities and even some major trading posts at the passes." Winstid looked up from the map, his brow a grim line across his spotted forehead. "Until a few seasons back, when they started disappearing one at a time."

"Disappearing?"

"Well, not the towns themselves, just the people." He snapped his fingers. "Gone, just like that."

Becks said, "There's a story that one rider heading west stopped in at a trading depot, found it alive and bustling. He rode out from there, pitched a camp that night, then realized he'd left behind some supplies. When he went back the next morning…the place was empty. Everybody vanished overnight. And scrawled in the dirt on one of the windows was that word—Moambati."

"Since then, pretty much all travel through the mountains has stopped. So far as we know, no one's had word or trade with anyone to the east in almost two seasons, and no one from the west who attempts any of the passes has come back."

"The Filament," Korden suggested. "How do you know it's not the Filament that—"

Winstid was already shaking his head. "The Filament doesn't take people. They *slaughter*. They leave behind carnage and corpses. No, this is something else. Something that's taken up residence in those mountains and divided the land right in two."

Korden said nothing, just bowed his head and stared at the map. Disappointing enough just to see what little distance he'd gone, and how much farther he had to go. Now they were telling him he had something else in his path to fear besides the Filament. Maybe he really should go north as Jakel suggested.

THIS DEVIATION WOULD TAKE A CONSIDERABLE AMOUNT OF TIME; I CALCULATE AS MUCH AS A YEAR, BASED ON RATE OF TRAVEL BY HORSEBACK AND PREDICTED WEATHER OBSTACLES. NOT TO MENTION THE FACT THAT WE ARE ILL-EQUIPPED FOR SUCH TEMPERATURE EXTREMES.

"The only good part about all of it," Becks said, "Is that we think it's affecting the Filament, too."

This reclaimed Korden's attention and pulled him from his despair. "What do you mean?"

The Peacekeeps looked at one another, trying to decide who would answer. "In my lifetime," Winstid finally began, "The

Shroud has never moved. It's been hovering far to the east, beyond even these mountains. For hundreds of years, they say. But the number of Incarnates on this side of the..." He gestured at the map, fumbling for the right word. "*Country*...it's only grown. When I was a boy, the fortress where I lived was only attacked once every few seasons. The chances of successfully rearing a child to free age were much better. But the patrols increased, and the odds got worse with time."

"My father told me that, too."

"Well, if your father's been hidden away in this village of yours for the past sixteen years, he might not know what's been happening the last few seasons. The number of Incarnates has been *falling* again. Not a lot, certainly not enough for anyone to think we're free of 'em, but enough for folks to notice. Less coordinated patrols, and the ones you do see are in bad shape. Most of the ones I've come across the last few seasons have only been rovers. That's probably why this town hasn't already been overrun with creatures looking for you."

"I don't understand," Korden said. "What's the connection?"

Winstid tapped the map for the last time. "Whatever has seized control of these mountains has cut off all the Incarnates on the west side from the Shroud—and their reinforcements—on the east side. The ones over here are trapped, and slowly rotting away." He leaned back, crossed his arms, and stared at Korden. "Now, if they can't get through, I don't see how you fare too much better of a chance."

Korden shrugged, but the bravado was as much for his own benefit as theirs. "I'll worry about that when I get there. And from the sound of it, this *Moambati*—whatever it is—has made it much easier for me to at least reach these mountains." Not only that, but Tash told him to find whoever was complicating the Filament's plan; perhaps this was them.

"No, son." Becks shook his head. "Don't hear us wrong: if you're dead set on heading east, there will still be plenty of Incarnates between here and there. You'll need to fight them or outrun them. I know you can't do the first, so you'll have to find a way to do the second."

"The Prophet," Jakel mumbled, his first contribution in several minutes. Then, louder and more excited, "Yeah, the Prophet! The Prophet could tell 'im how to avoid those bastards!"

Winstid and Becks groaned in unison.

"Who's the Prophet?" Korden asked.

Winstid rolled his eyes. "Don't worry on that. There are stories—like this business of Moambati—and then there are crone's tales. The Prophet falls squarely into the latter category."

"It does *not!*" Jakel said indignantly. "He's real! Camber said his brother's wife's uncle heard him talkin with his own two ears!"

"Sounds like supreme bullcurse to me," Becks muttered.

"*What* does?" Korden insisted.

Winstid nodded at Jakel. "You're the one brought this nonsense up, you explain it."

Jakel seemed only too happy to do so. "There's a settlement called Ida a few days' ride south of here. Trading post close to this big lake they call…uh…"

"Tay-ho," Becks put in.

"I'm tellin it!" Jakel cried. "Yeah, Tay-ho. Anyway, I ain't never been there, but the way I hear it, the people in charge of the place have this…this box. And the Prophet, he speaks to them through it!" Jakel finished his explanation and beamed proudly at Korden.

"But…who is he? What does he tell them?"

"Oh, well…nobody knows who he is. But he tells them all sorts of things! Predictions and the like. He warns them when storms are coming, or raiders, or even where Incarnates are patrolling! I bet he could tell you the same thing!"

"Even if any of that were true," Winstid cut in, "it sounds like Crafter magic to me."

That was the last incentive Korden needed. "Can you tell me how to get to this place?"

Before any of them could respond, a high, nasally voice from outside shouted, "Winstid? Step out here, please."

5

Winstid bowed his head as Jakel ran to the window and peeked out. "It's Neller!" he squeaked, telling them what Winstid already knew. "Looks like he brought half the town with 'im!"

"We know you're in there, Winstid!" the head of the Hidden Glen Leadership Council hollered. "If'n you intend to keep your title, you best come out right now and answer to your constituents!"

"Oh fram, what's a con-stitch-eent?" Jakel moaned.

Winstid looked at Korden. "Get your stuff packed and be ready when I call you. Depending on how this plays, we might have to leave in a curse-all hurry." He rose, came out from behind the desk, and started toward the door.

Becks hurried to get in front of him. "Let me take the blame for this."

"That's not gonna happen. When they boot me outta this job, you're the only one capable of taking over. No offense, Jakel."

"But Win—"

"*No*, Becks. Now get outta my way."

The Peacekeep stood aside with a grunt, and Winstid walked out.

Half the town wasn't outside the Keep, as Jakel claimed, but Winstid figured there were a good sixty or seventy people just beyond the dooryard, clustered around the short fence. Many of Hidden Glen's oldest and most vocal residents were here, he saw, with Neller's blubbery form hunkered in front of the gate like a mushroom, and several other Council members with him. All were dressed in Seventh Day finery, denim dresses and deerskin suits and peaked caps, a sure indication that they'd left from worship to come directly here.

Winstid stood in the dooryard, trying not to let all those eyes ruffle him, and said, "Good Seventh Morn to you, Neller. What can I do for you fine folks?"

"Don't play on with me," Neller snapped, his swollen, froggish lips flecked with saliva. He was a squat man, barely five pargs yet still close to 250 stone of weight, with a girlish voice that didn't seem like it belonged to him. Cheree always made sure that Winstid's tunics were tailored around his ample gut so that he still looked fashionable, but the finery worn by Hidden Glen's mayor— an aqua-colored blouse and black denim pants bedecked with silver thread and smooth river stones—strained at every seam. White hair stood up in a wispy fan from his brow no matter how much he tugged and smoothed it down. "We know you brought someone into town yesterday without consulting the Council, and then took them to your home to hide them from us. And we know this person is inside right now."

"That's good puzzling," Winstid said admiringly. "Maybe *you* should run for Peacekeep next time."

Neller scowled and, even though his next words were meant for Winstid, he turned to the rest of the crowd as he announced, "We demand to see this person for ourselves, and know why you chose to deceive us. Outsiders are a detriment to Hidden Glen, as you well know. I'm not saying you didn't have reasons, but—"

"Oh for Aged's sake," Winstid groaned. Neller Laman loved the sound of his own voice, but Winstid didn't have the patience for grandstanding today. "Just hold your water and I'll bring 'im out so you can see for yourselves."

6

Korden waited just inside the door with his bursting carry pouch over his shoulder as Winstid spoke to the angry man in the too-small clothing. Raw anxiety twisted his guts. He looked through the window at the group outside, which was so large, intimidating and emotionally turmoiled that when he checked the color of their collective aura, the brightness of its rainbow momentarily blinded him.

"Don't worry." Becks put a hand on his shoulder. "They won't be mad at you. Not really. They'll just want you outta this town as fast as the nearest horse can carry you."

"But what about Winstid? And Cheree? Will they get in trouble?"

Becks didn't answer.

A second later, the head Peacekeep stuck his head back inside and said, "C'mon, just smile and act innocent." Then, under his breath, "And remember, not a word about our visitors this morning."

Heart pounding (and ignoring Stone's strange advice to

imagine the crowd in their underclothes to assuage his fear), Korden stepped through the door and stood beside Winstid.

A general gasp went through the assembled people of Hidden Glen, a part awed and part shocked sound, with a healthy dose of disgust thrown in. He even heard a terrified scream come from somewhere in the crowd. Korden stood still and tried to smile as Winstid had advised while the elderly residents all began to talk and shout at once.

"*Aged Lord, save us!*" one woman that looked as old as Tash cried.

"*He'll bring doom on us all!*" another man with rubbery jowls proclaimed.

The fat man that Winstid called Neller used one hand to wave for the crowd's attention and the other to tug at the untamed strands of hair snarling off the top of his head. When the townsfolk quieted, he said, "Winstid, what's the meaning of this? Who is this...this *child*, and what is he doing here?"

"Steady on, folks." Winstid's tone remained easy and light. He put an arm around Korden's shoulders. "This young man's name is Korden Bright, and he's just passing through. I was on my way to escort him right back outta town when you all stopped me."

A great gasp of relief went up. "*Yes, yes, he must leave!*" several people agreed eagerly. Korden denied the urge to tell them that was all he wanted also.

Neller wagged a finger at Winstid. "You're not getting off that easy, sir. We want to know why you brought him here in the first place. The way I see it, you have abused our trust and outright lied about—"

"I told you last night he wasn't trying to hide anything!" Becks stormed out of the Keep and took up a position beside Winstid. Jakel slunk through the door as well and tried to hide behind Korden. "You better watch what you say or *you'll* be spending the night in the cage, Neller!"

"And now they threaten me with unjust detainment!" the fat man said to the crowd, huge lips spread in a smirk. "Hidden Glen, it would seem as though our Peacekeep force has been corrupted!"

"Stay outta this," Winstid ordered Becks from the side of his mouth.

Korden noticed a commotion on the edge of the crowd to his right. Someone forced their way through the throng. A slender woman sporting lank grey locks and a denim dress with white frill at the ankles made it to the front of the crowd. "Now, just wait here!" she shouted, her voice raspy and cracking, the exact opposite of the fat man's.

"There's no time to wait, Molinda," Neller told her. "Every second that boy is here puts us all in danger."

"Does it now?" the woman asked. "Cause it seems to me we would do well to *open* our eyes this time, steada squeezin 'em shut."

Several voices in the crowd shouted out for her to be silenced...but Korden also heard more than a few insisting that she be allowed to speak.

"All right," Winstid called out. "It may change come tomorrow, but for now, I'm still the head Peacekeep of Hidden Glen, and everyone in this town has just as much cause to be heard as anyone else. Molinda, speak your mind."

Molinda nodded at him gratefully, then addressed the crowd, but with much less pomp than Neller. "Everyone, take a look at what you see before you. How old is this boy? Fourteen? Fifteen?"

"Sixteen," Korden said respectfully.

"Sixteen years old!" Molinda exclaimed, her dry voice like the whisper of falling sand. "Think on, now: when was the last time you saw a child so old? That is to say, one that survived so long?"

A few grumbles came from the group, along with one excited cry of "*Years and years!*" Neller said nothing.

"The danger is less now, we all know that. Here this boy has been in our town for an entire day, and we've seen nary even one Incarnate!"

Korden started to look up at Winstid, until the man gave his shoulder a hard squeeze.

"It's a sign!" a man near the front of the mob yelled.

"That's…that's ridiculous," Neller blustered, and then was immediately drowned out by a surge of boo's and shushes, some of them from the very people that were just urging for Korden's departure. Now Korden did glance up at Winstid, and saw that the Peacekeep looked just as confused by the turn of events.

Molinda's cheeks were flushed as she spoke again. With determination, according to her *mohol.* "It's been so easy for us to live here in this town and forget about the outside world and its problems, because we've insured those problems would never touch us. We built Hidden Glen from the ground up. This has been a wonderful, peaceful place to spend our lives, but let me say what I know many of you have already thought: in ten years, half of our population will be gone. In twenty, the rest will follow. There's no denying it. Everything that we've built stands on the brink of ruin. I don't know about you, but that makes me question what it was all for."

Several people actually began to cheer at this, and more followed with clapping. Neller looked around uncomfortably. It was as though this minority only needed a voice to bring out their confidence.

"We're too old to start having our own children," Molinda continued. "No, that ship has sailed. But that doesn't mean we can't help and harbor those who can. People who can carry on our traditions and keep this town going long after we're all gone."

"This...this should be addressed at a township meeting," Neller mumbled, but Molinda's next words drowned him out, along with her support from the crowd.

"Maybe...maybe this boy *is* a sign, from our Aged God on High! A sign that times are changing, and we must change with them! A sign that the great fount of life has been renewed! A sign that...that things are going to get better!"

"Well, maybe not for everyone," a new voice boomed. The crowd, along with Korden, turned its eyes away from the Molinda and toward the left side of the Keep, where a figure emerged, a much younger man than anyone else Korden had seen in Hidden Glen, perhaps even younger than Redfen, wearing a one-piece outfit of tanned leather and with an unkempt black beard down to his chest.

"But for me," this newcomer said, "times just got absolutely *fantastic*."

RENEGOTIATIONS

1

Winstid kept trying to find a place to inject his thoughts into the argument, but he had no idea what to say even if one presented itself. Besides, Molinda seemed to be doing a fine job on her own. He couldn't believe his ears as the crowd turned on Neller. Perhaps this was years of regret bubbling up in his fellow Glenners, along with an optimism they'd kept hidden all this time.

Or maybe there really was something special about this boy. Something people could sense on a subconscious level.

Something that gave them hope.

But Winstid's amazement came crashing down a moment later as Heater Kay himself strolled around the side of the building, as easy and cocksure as if he belonged there, with Dostey and four other men trailing along behind him like scavengers following a predator. At the sight of Clan Triker's leader standing in his dooryard, thrilled grin from ear to ear, Winstid felt the bottom drop out of his stomach.

Another shocked gasp ripped through the crowd. This many outsiders had never been in the Glen in its entire thirty year existence, much less on the same day. And these visitors—all of them carrying shooters—were no children. The Glenners strained their necks and stood on tiptoes to get a better look at the newcomers.

"That's the kind of entrance a man could get used to," Heater proclaimed. He turned toward the four people gathered on the Keep's doorstep and approached, jovial and light of foot. Winstid never trusted that good humor; it seemed to mask an innate hunger for cruelty. His men stayed in a tight group behind him, glowering around with their hands on their weapons. "Peacekeep Crane! Great to see you again! And this must be the kiddo I heard so much about! Put 'er there, dude." He held his hand out flat, with the palm up, which Korden only stared at in confusion. Heater reached up and ruffled his hair instead. "That's cool, we'll work on it."

A voice in Winstid's head screamed for him to speak, to try to get ahead of—and hopefully defuse—this situation, but a terrible numbness turned his muscles to ice. At the trade shack, his thoughts had been razor sharp, able to predict action and outcome, but here, on his home grounds, there were too many variables, and he felt extremely vulnerable. Beside him, he could sense Becks tensing up as well.

"W-who are these men, Winstid?" Neller asked from the other side of the fence. He no longer sounded as boisterous and belligerent as when discussing Korden.

"The great Hidden Glen!" Heater cried, ignoring Neller as he turned to face the crowd. He threw his arms out wide, as if to embrace the whole town. "Quite a secret you've all been keeping here, but now I understand why! This place is *beautiful!* You don't see too many settlements this well maintained anymore. I might have to come visit more often." He threw a wink over his shoulder at Winstid. "You know… now that I have the address."

How? How in hells did you find us, you bastard? Winstid wondered. He went back over the events at the trade shack in his mind, searching for the mistake they must've made.

"S-see here," Neller stammered. Winstid gave the little toadstool points for bravery; even if he didn't know who he spoke to, these six men looked rough enough to use him for outhouse paper. "This t-town, it's…it's private property! You need an invitation to enter. You gentlemen will…j-just have to leave."

Heater walked over to the fence, the short holdout cape of his *jhaken* fluttering behind him. He about-faced, slung an arm around the fat man's neck and pulled him into a friend-ly, side-by-side embrace, forcing him to lean over the fence posts. Neller's eyes widened into round, shocked circles, but he smiled hesitantly, unsure what to think. "And who might you be, my tubby friend?"

Neller tried to look as dignified as possible while intro-ducing himself with his head in Heater's armpit. "My name is Neller Laman. I'm the mayor of Hidden Glen."

"The *mayor?* Wow, I'm honored, sir! I'm sort of a mayor myself. Heater Kay, they call me, head of Clan Triker." His eyes came up to meet Winstid's, and in them was the same manic callousness that had been there the only other time they'd met. "And, incidentally…I'm also the man who just framming murdered you."

Heater's hand dipped to his belt, too fast to follow, and came up with a serrated blade that he plunged into the loose rolls of skin around Neller's throat. A shower of blood spurt-ed from the wound, staining the front of his tight suit and spraying across the grass in a crimson jet. Korden cringed and drew closer to Winstid. The fat man gurgled blood and clawed at his open neck as his killer stepped away.

People in the crowd shrieked. Entire sections drew away, on the verge of flight—and what sixty or seventy achy-jointed crones and bodlas would look like sprinting down this hill, Winstid didn't want to think about. Neller pitched forward and collapsed over the fence, his rotund form causing the posts to break and the twine to sag. At the same time, Becks scrambled to draw his shooter.

"Nuh uh, everyone stays where they are, or my boys get some much needed target practice!" Heater shouted, sliding the bloody knife back into its sheath. Dostey and the rest of the crew—three filthy Trikers and another larger than even Heater—already had their shooters up and ready to fire. A few folks ran anyway, limping on stiff, crackle-jointed legs, but the majority of the mob settled back into place, husbands and wives clutching at one another with whimpers of fear. "Boys, why don't we eliminate temptation and round up the Peacekeeps' weapons? Anybody else have some of my merchandise they need to be relieved of?"

"We're the only ones that carry in town," Winstid spoke at last, with some difficulty. His tongue felt leaden, but his spine limp. All this seemed to be happening at a detached, maddeningly slow pace, except for the sweat beading on his brow. "The rest are locked up in the Keep."

"That's good! I like to know my products are used responsibly. Speaking of which, now that I see this place, I think I was getting a little shortchanged on our trades. Might have to renegotiate my asking price."

Dostey came to take their weapons. He yanked Becks' pistol from the holster on his belt and then lifted Winstid's longshooter out of its sling. "Told ya you'd pay," he whispered, throwing an elbow into Winstid's gut hard enough to make him grunt in pain. Korden uttered a cry of surprise and grabbed his arm to steady him.

"Let's be civil, Dostey," Heater scolded, coming back across the yard. With one hand he stroked the length of his scuzzy beard like he was petting a dog. "After all, Peacekeep Crane wants to continue doing business with us. Isn't that what you said, Peacekeep?"

"Heater." Winstid cringed at how lifeless and flat his own voice sounded. "There's no need for this. What happened yesterday, we didn't plan to hurt anyone, we just—"

Heater brought a hand up, grabbed Winstid's lips, and squashed them together. His fingers smelled acrid and oily. "Let's not talk about the past. It's over, it's done, just like the old world. If we're gonna rebuild things, we have to look to the future. You *do* want that, don't you?"

Winstid nodded with his lips still held shut, cheeks hot with the indignity. Sweat trickled under his collar. Korden's terrified face was visible at the very edge of his vision, and he could see the townspeople watching over Heater's shoulder, Neller's corpse face down on the ground in front of them. For one moment, he felt like he stood on a stage, like all of this was one of the plays they put on at the Pavilion, and then realized that Heater probably saw it this way as well; the man had a captive audience, and he was pouring on the theatrics.

"Good." Heater released him. "Then we just need to square our accounts and I can be on my way. First off, let's settle our initial disagreement by going back to what caused this mess and doing it right this time."

He turned to Korden once more. "All right my man, you wanna come with me, go for a ride on a hovertrike? It's fast, it flies, you'll love it."

The kid opened his mouth and spoke for the first time since leaving the Keep. "I...I can't, I have to go..."

Heater clapped him on the back hard enough to make him stumble forward. "Naw, you don't have to go anywhere, except with us. Otherwise...well, I might have to keep hurting these good people, like I did Mr. Mayor. You wanna be responsible for that?"

Korden's eyes met Winstid's briefly. He shook his head. "No. Please don't."

"Smart kid. I think we'll get along just fine." Heater snagged the kid by the wrist and began to drag him away, back toward his men. Korden looked back at Winstid, confused and helpless.

"Wait. *Wait!*" Winstid took a step after them in sheer desperation. "Heater, you can't take him, you don't understand!"

"I understand." Heater halted long enough to look back. "I understand you have a gorgeous wife, and a lovely home. I saw them both this morning, when you gunned down my three little bloodhounds."

It took Winstid a moment to decipher the meaning of this, but when he did, his skin prickled in horror. Had the man somehow *used* those Incarnates to track down Korden? Winstid had never heard anything so revolting.

"So you decide," Heater continued. "I can take the kiddo as my payment...or *her*."

"Winstid, it's all right," Korden said quickly. "I'll go with them. As long as they leave Cheree and everyone else alone."

Heater frowned and lifted a shoulder. "Weeell, I can't promise that just yet. I'm afraid there's one other bit of restitution I'm owed. For the loss of manpower."

"What are you talking about?" Winstid asked.

"You killed one of my men. Someone has to pay for that."

Winstid pointed at Neller's body. "There's your payment."

"No, that was for rudeness. The man who killed Cloonan is the one who's in debt. Which one was it, Dostey?"

The triker leveled a finger at Becks. "This framming asshole right here."

"Then settle up with him, and let's get going."

Dostey walked over and jammed the barrel of his shooter in Becks' cheek. "On your knees, cursehead. I'm gonna enjoy seeing the inside of your skull."

"Heater, don't do this!" Winstid pleaded. "We can solve this some other way!"

"It's a lesson that has to be learned," Heater told him, still grinning. "No one uses our own weapons against us. *No one.*"

"Then shoot *me!* It's *my* fault!"

"But I so enjoy working with you." He nodded at Dostey.

"*On your knees!*" the triker roared. He brought a boot up and kicked the back of Becks' leg. The Peacekeep dropped heavily to all fours, then looked up at Winstid with jaw set.

"Say hello to Cloonan for me." Dostey aimed the shooter at the back of his head, finger on the trigger.

And then the triker went flying across the dooryard like he'd been swatted aside by a giant, invisible hand.

2

For Korden, events sped by with blinding speed, too fast for his sluggish brain to process and prompt him to react. Even if Winstid hadn't told him about these people, he would only have needed to glimpse the *mohol* of the man named Heater—a cruel shade of vermillion—to know he was dangerous. The casual murder of Hidden Glen's mayor not only confirmed this, but chilled Korden's heart in a way even the Incarnate attack at the village had not. When Heater grabbed his arm and began to drag him away, Korden went willingly, but panic squeezed his ribcage in a fist of ice.

WARNING! THIS COURSE OF ACTION IS NOT ADVISED! Stone counseled. THE FIRST FEW MINUTES OF AN ABDUCTION ARE THE OPTIMAL TIME TO RESIST!

I can't let them hurt anyone else. We'll try to escape after we're away from the Glen.

But then Becks was forced to the ground, and a gun aimed at his skull.

"You might wanna watch this," Heater told him, giving his arm another jerk. "It'll be a good reminder of why you should always obey your Uncle Heater."

Korden saw the anguish on Winstid's face as he waited for the other Peacekeep to be executed.

He couldn't let this happen. Not when he had the power to stop it.

Korden stretched out his fingers at his side and felt the artcraft flow in hard waves through him, like lightning striking steel.

The man called Dostey was lifted off his feet and pitched through the air in a series of full body somersaults, much harder than Korden intended. He flew past the Peacekeeps and landed on his back against the fence, not far from Neller Laman's corpse. The thud of impact was drowned out by the gasps of surprise from their audience.

A stunned hush fell over everyone gathered in front of the Keep. They all seemed afraid to move, afraid to breathe. Winstid looked back and forth from Dostey to the place where he'd been standing, as if expecting him to come zipping back. Heater's eyes bulged from their sockets as his man moaned and stirred on the ground. And thank the Upper for that; Korden feared he'd killed him.

Molinda broke the standstill. The old woman who'd made such a passionate speech lunged forward, wrenched the shooter from Dostey's limp hand, and began to fire it at the trikers with both hands wrapped around the butt. From her mouth came a shrill, broken war cry as she jerked the trigger.

Korden had always imagined gunshots to be massive, earth-shattering explosions, followed by a trail of fire as the bullet zipped toward its target. Instead, he got a series of anticlimactic *cracks* which seemed to do nothing at all, until the skinny triker standing just to his left spun around with a bleeding hole in his shoulder and a look of comical shock on his face.

"*Kill them!*" Heater bellowed. "*Kill them all! Burn this cursehole town to the ground!*"

3

Winstid was terrified Molinda would hit the boy with her wild shots, but he couldn't help feeling a small measure of triumph when one of them struck true, even though he was sure it did the recipient no serious harm.

Then Heater gave the order to start the slaughter, and the scene in front of the Keep erupted into chaos.

A terrified stampede began in the crowd. They screamed and surged as one, attempting to turn and flee, but succeeded only in trampling over the less spry. Brittle bodies sprawled left and right, some of them falling backward over the fence, burying Dostey in a pile of elderly limbs as he tried to stand. Winstid knew that, if the town survived this day, there would be broken hips and fractured legs to mend.

But Molinda stood her ground as her fellow Glenners panicked. The bony old crone cut a brazen figure as she used her commandeered weapon, pulling the shooter's trigger until it clicked dry on spent rounds.

The remaining trikers came out of their own stupor. The one Molinda hit leapt for cover behind the horse trough at the far corner of the yard, but the other three obeyed orders and turned their shooters on the crowd. They fired round after round from weapons that held considerably more ammo than the ones they sold to Winstid. The back row of Glenners was cut through as they fled down the hill, the injured cries of the survivors adding to the cacophony from those already on the ground. Winstid saw Molinda's thin torso chewed apart just before she collapsed.

"*Inside!*" Becks shouted, barely audible over the gunshots and fearful bleating of the mob. He was already up from the ground where he'd narrowly escaped execution and running for the door of the Keep.

Further out in the dooryard, Heater was on the move as well, dragging Korden away from the gunfire, toward the side of the Keep. He grabbed two of his men along the way, the big fellow and another greasy specimen. They broke off the attack to follow their leader. Korden looked back once more before all four of them disappeared around the corner of the building.

Winstid took a step forward to go after them.

"*Come ON!*" Becks bellowed behind him.

The man was right; the remaining two trikers were preoccupied with the crowd, but they would be out of targets soon. If Winstid tried to help the boy like this, unarmed, he would be an easy goose to butcher. As hard as it was to do, Winstid turned to retreat inside, then stopped once more.

Jakel stood just a few steps away, staring slackjawed as he took in the pandemonium.

Winstid reached to grab his shoulder. "*Jakel, you idiot, get in here!*"

Another sharp *crack* sounded.

Jakel's nose and the lower right side of his face sheared away. A red mist coated the front of Winstid's embroidered shirt. The other man dropped to the ground, clutched at his head, and rolled back and forth, shrieking in agony.

From the far end of the dooryard, Dostey brayed hysterical laughter as he shoved his way free of the tangle of moaning Glenners. He held the rifle he'd confiscated from Winstid, and raised it for another shot.

Then Becks slipped a hand into Winstid's collar from behind and yanked him toward the Keep. Winstid clambered up the stairs as bullets peppered the doorframe behind him.

4

They moved single file through the narrow corridor between the fence and the timbered side of the Keep. Halfway down, Korden's wits returned and he finally began to put up a fight, planting his heels and struggling against Heater's grip on his arm.

"Let go of me!" he demanded. More of those flat bangs sounded on the other side of the Keep as the shootfight continued, along with a wave of fresh screams.

"Kid, you're comin with us whether you like it or not," Heater growled, pulling until Korden thought his arm would come loose from its socket.

"But you promised! You promised you wouldn't hurt them!"

"Actually, I'm pretty sure I specifically said I *didn't* promise. You gotta learn to pay more attention to the fine print."

The two other trikers that Heater grabbed during their escape caught up with them just as they reached the rear corner of the building. The hulking one—Korden thought he'd heard Heater call the man 'Weryl'—panted, "What was that back there? Dostey just went flying…"

"I don't know, and I don't care." Heater pointed at the four saddled horses grazing behind the Keep. "Grab a few of those. We're taking the brat back to the trikes."

"What about the others?" the second man asked. "Shouldn't we help them?"

"For fram's sake, if those three can't handle a dusty town full of wrinkled geriatrics, they deserve whatever they get! They'll catch up after they've scorched this place off the face of the earth! *Now get the horses!*"

"I'm not going anywhere with you!" Korden raised his hand again, felt the artcraft building in his head, ready to be released at his direction.

But before he could lash out, Heater reared back with one fist and brought it in low and quick, slamming his knuckles into Korden's stomach hard enough to drive the air from his lungs.

He was used to not being able to breathe from his asmah, but this was still far worse. White hot pain radiated out from his stomach, a weight on his chest. He choked silently, panic setting in, as the color drained from the world. All sound fell to a murmur, even Stone's frantic internal advice. He would've fallen, but Heater grabbed a handful of his tunic and kept him on his feet. The man's lips moved, but Korden could hear no words.

Then the weight lifted, and he could breathe again. The details of the world rushed back in at him all at once. He sputtered and sucked at the air.

"There we go, you back with us?" Heater lifted the strap of the carry pouch over Korden's head and transferred it to his own neck, then took the knife from the sheath on his belt as well. "You know, you're really gettin on my last nerve here, kid. So if you don't get on that horse, I'm gonna knock you out cold, tie you to it, and then we'll go pay a visit to the Peacekeep's wife. You can watch everything I do to her."

"No," Korden gasped. The pain kept him from concentrating on anything else. "P-please…"

"All right then. Saddle up, and you can get started on your new life."

5

The interior of the Keep seemed dead silent after the din outside. Winstid took cover on one side of the door while Becks did the same on the other.

"Jakel's hurt, we can't leave him out there!" Winstid insisted.

"Get the other shooters! I'll watch the door!"

Winstid nodded and hurtled across the room to the heavy oak trunk behind his desk. Inside were the four other longshooters and three pistols they'd purchased from the very men who were now trying to kill them. Winstid loaded ammunition into one of the pistols, tucked it in the back of his belt, then picked up two of the longshooters and a small wooden box of shot. He went back to the door and tossed one of the rifles and the box of ammo to Becks, then eased up to look through the closest window.

All those residents who were able had now fled the hilltop where the Keep sat. Some of them still hobbled down the slope, but Winstid could see the rest gathering at the bottom, along with more Glenners who cautiously emerged from homes and stores to gaze upward at the commotion. The ground around the Keep was still littered with bodies, some still, others feebly moving. Jakel moaned piteously just a parg from the door.

No sign of Dostey, but the other two trikers finally turned to face the building. When the one behind the trough saw Winstid looking out, he started shooting again.

Glass rained down on him as he ducked. Bullets thunked into the inner walls of the Keep, splintering his desk and tearing apart one of Cheree's paintings (which he'd always loved, even if he did complain about their pointlessness). At the same moment, Becks yanked open the door and fired twice through it.

"Put the one standing in the yard down," he remarked casually as he slammed the door shut again.

"What about Heater? Can you see him?" Each frantic second seemed to jab Winstid in the side as it passed. There were no windows in the back of the building for him to check. "*Becks, where'd they take the kid?*"

"No idea. Haven't seen them since they hightailed it."

More rounds thunked into the exterior of the building.

"He's just keeping us penned up in here!" Winstid lamented.

"Not for long. Keep his attention on you."

Winstid did as asked, rising up cautiously to peer out the now shattered window once more. As Becks claimed, one triker lay face down in the dooryard. The other still cowered behind the horse trough. He popped up to take another hurried shot, not even aiming. Winstid returned it, starting a continual back-and-forth volley.

At the opposite window, Becks calmly raised the glass, braced one arm against the sill, leaned the barrel across his forearm, and took careful aim down the notched sight.

When the triker rose again, he squeezed the trigger.

An angry string of curses drifted up from the trough. Becks silenced them with another measured shot.

"*You got him!*" Winstid jumped to his feet. "Help Jakel, I'm gonna find—!"

The window in the eastern wall, next to their single jail cell, blew inward. A round glass jar came flying through the wreckage, filled with a brownish fluid and with a burning strip of cloth tied around the lid. It hit the floor in the middle of the room and shattered, spraying liquid fire. Flames coated the floor and the front wall and even splashed on Becks' leg. He beat them out before they could spread.

The rest of the inferno, however, worked too quickly to be extinguished. Hungry fire consumed the wooden floor planks. Smoke that smelled of burnt cedar filled the room. Within seconds, the heat was blistering, the air too thick to breathe. Coughing madly, eyes watering, Winstid helped Becks up, then threw open the door and lunged through, desperate to fill his lungs with fresh air.

Rough hands grabbed the front of his vest and shook him. Winstid blinked away tears and looked up to find Dostey leering down at him. Becks stumbled through the door right behind him, but Dostey laid him out on the steps with a backhand that knocked one of his teeth out.

"*What hit me?*" the triker demanded, shaking Winstid again until his head flopped bonelessly. His vest tore with a purring rip. "*How'd you do that, you worthless old fram?*"

Winstid still held the longshooter. He tried to get the barrel up between his chest and the triker's, but Dostey wrenched it out of his hands and brought his bald forehead smashing down across the bridge of Winstid's nose.

A galaxy of angry light burst across his vision. The pain tore through all other thought, a spike driven straight into the center of his forehead. Before he could recover, Dostey gave him a hard shove. The ground rushed up to meet him, a full-body wallop that jarred along the entire length of his spine. Something sharp dug into his lower back; it took him a moment to realize what it was.

Dostey stood over him. He looked down at Winstid's longshooter in his hands and then tossed it aside. "Too easy, bodla. I want this to be nice and personal." The triker slid a blade from a sheath built into the underside of his holdout cape.

Winstid raised his waist, reached beneath his body, and yanked the pistol from his belt. "I'll go with easy every time," he said, and shot the triker in the stomach. Dostey grunted and fell back a step, then peered down at the new hole in the front of his leather jumpsuit as if he didn't understand how it got there. Winstid shot him again higher in the chest and watched as he fell over.

Getting to his feet took monumental effort. The world swayed back and forth in drunken lurches, his face throbbed, his side hurt all over again, and his back felt crooked after his fall. But he forced himself to stand and then surveyed the area to get his priorities straight.

The Bloom grasses were stippled with maroon blood in lazy swaths. Dark grey smoke boiled from the Keep door. Flames blazed in the windows; as fast as it went up, the entire building would reach the point of collapse in minutes.

The injured still on the ground were all far enough away to be out of danger. Further down the hill, some of the braver residents were banding together to creep back up. Winstid ignored them all and hurried to where Becks knelt over Jakel.

"C'mon, let's get him away from the fire!"

"Too late." Becks shook his head. The left side of his face was swollen from the blow Dostey had doled out, bloody drool leaking from his mouth. "He's dead."

Winstid winced at the news. So much death in Hidden Glen today. And it was his fault, all of it, plain and simple, but there was no time for guilt. "I have to find the boy. You stay here, try to get things under control."

Becks picked up his longshooter from the ground and held it rigid across his chest. "Try to keep me away."

They eased around the flaming Keep cautiously, Winstid on one side, Becks on the other, and met in the rear, where they found only Becks' horse remaining. The large animal neighed in fear and struggled at his bridle to get away from the fire.

"God curse it!" Winstid put a hand over his eyes to block the sun and scanned the meadow, looking for any sign of the boy and his captors. The grassland was empty as far as he could see. "We have to find them."

"Which way you think?"

Without hesitation, Winstid pointed toward the high embankment to the west.

"How can you be sure?"

"They didn't ride their fancy flying machines to the Glen, which means they left them on the road somewhere. And the fastest way to get back there is through the canyon."

"Then get on the horse. Maybe that maze'll slow them enough for us to catch up."

"If it doesn't kill them outright. That skilne hasn't been trimmed in a season or two."

Winstid climbed onto the huge animal just behind the other Peacekeep. The promise he's made to Cheree burned in his mind brighter and hotter than the flames behind them as Becks urged his horse into an earth-churning gallop.

BLIGHTED

1

They'd slung Korden face down over the back of the gray mare that would've been given to him. His arms and legs dangled to either side, next to the animal's pumping appendages. The triker known as Big Weryl rode high on the saddle just behind him, so he could keep one giant hand on Korden's neck to hold him down. Sweaty horseflesh burned his nostrils and the awkward position combined with the galloping motion quickly curdled his stomach. It was all Korden could do not to vomit as Stone gave him constant suggestions for escaping his current situation, none of them with a high chance for success.

Finally, after what seemed an hour of hard riding (but which Stone insisted had only been eleven minutes), Heater called a stop.

"Where the hells are we?" Big Weryl rumbled. The pressure lifted from Korden's neck, and he could raise his head at last.

The horse stood in a tight corridor with walls made of crumbling dirt that stretched out of sight overhead; Korden figured it must be the narrow canyon leading up through the embankment that Winstid had mentioned. He could see multiple openings and offshoots from here, some of them leading into even smaller passages, forming a maze of random branches. High skilne choked one that began just a few pargs from the mare's rear flank, like the thickets growing close to Winstid's farm.

"This ain't right," the skinny triker said, sitting atop Jakel's mount and looking around uncertainly. "Did we come through here on the way in?"

Heater waited just beyond him. He swung his leg over Starry's saddle—where Korden's carry pouch now dangled from the horn—and jumped to the rocky ground with a thud. "Don't know. Not only was it dark, but I was a little busy following three Incarnates that would've cut our heads off if they'd had half a chance." Despite his agitated tone, he gave an unconcerned shrug. "Can't be too much farther though. We've been heading uphill the whole time. Let's stop to give Dostey and the others a chance to catch up. Get the kid down too and we'll all take a breather."

Weryl dismounted as well, then lifted Korden off the horse with one hand through the back of his belt and dropped him like a stack of cordwood on the ground. He scrambled away, crawling under the animal toward the closest opening in the canyon wall.

"If you like crawling so much, you might enjoy doing it all the way to our compound," Heater called after him. "Only a few hundred spans or so from here. If not, I suggest you stop right there."

Korden froze. He rolled over to find Heater walking toward him. The leader of the trikers hunkered in the dirt so that their eyes were level. His scraggly beard hung low enough to brush the ground between his legs. "Look, kid, I don't want us to get off on the wrong foot. Let me just…let me apologize for all that back there, all right? I didn't wanna do any of that. I don't like hurting people."

His face remained stone sober as he said this.

His *mohol*, on the other hand, did not.

"Yes you do, you liar."

A toothy grin spread across Heater's face, visible through the matted tangles covering his jaw. He reached forward, slipping a hand behind Korden's head as though to cup the back of his skull. Instead, he grabbed a handful of hair and pulled hard. Korden let his neck go limp and head fall back to relieve the pressure, but tears still sprang to his eyes.

"You're right. I do. But I'm a businessman first and a sadist second. And those people back there, they were customers. I don't mistreat my customers. Unless they need to be reminded who's in charge. What the Peacekeeps did to me and mine...that couldn't go unpunished."

With his head still craned back at an uncomfortable angle, Korden looked down his nose at the other man and said, "They were my friends. And you killed them."

Heater snorted and released him. "Friends are overrated. You'll learn that one day." Korden straightened and wiped the moisture from his eyelids. The triker regarded him for a long moment with dark blue eyes the color of twilight, which slipped from Korden's face down to his flaming sneakers. "Where did you come from, kid? How'd you live this long? From the sound of it, those old frams thought you were some hot curse."

Korden said nothing.

"Fine, don't talk. We'll have lots of time to loosen that jaw once we get to the compound. One way or another."

Fear burned the back of Korden's throat at this, even though he wasn't quite sure he understood the implication. "What do you want with me?"

"At first, nothing. Not a cursed thing. See, I made it a point to allow no women or children into my ranks. Hells, I won't even let my men fram a wombie that they don't kill immediately afterward. My little business venture is still finding its feet, and I damn sure didn't want anything that would draw the Incarnates and screw it all up. If my boys had brought you back yesterday when they found you, I would've sold your lovely ass as fast as possible, just to get you away from us. I only came after you today to show the good Peacekeep Crane there was nowhere he could hide from me, and nothing I couldn't take. Now though, after everything I just went through to find you...I have something better in mind."

Heater ran his tongue around the inside of his mouth, creating a roving bulge in his cheek, then glanced over his shoulder at his men, who were conversing on the far side of the horses. When he spoke again, his voice lowered to a conspiratorial volume meant only for the two of them.

"Here's the thing. My business, it's important to me, as you've probably guessed. I want it to grow, but if there ain't any more customers to buy my products, that's gonna be a little hard. And ultimately, that's what the Incarnates are gonna do. Oh sure, there's the whole 'covering-the-world-in-darkness-thing,' but what are we really talking about? The end of all commerce, am I right?" He smashed a scarred fist down into the ground between them and twisted his knuckles back and forth against the dirt, leaving minute smears of blood. "But the only way we're ever gonna change things is if we *take a stand*. Start creating little consumers to get the economy rolling again. Based on what I saw with the three pushovers that led us to yon town back there, the time to do so is now, while the Incarnates are weak. That's where you come in. You're gonna stay with Clan Triker for awhile, as our honored guest. When the Incarnates come for you—and they will—we'll kick their rotted Commie asses all the way back to the Shroud. And once people see that it's possible, they'll start doing it, too."

Heater Kay finished this monologue with a distant, wistful gleam in his eye.

Korden burst into laughter.

He tried not to, tried to contain it in his stomach, but it boiled out through his nose and forced open his mouth. Stone cringed away from the sound in his head and urged him to stop. On the other side of the canyon, Big Weryl and the other triker broke off their conversation and looked back at them.

Heater's brow lowered until his eyes were no more than paper-thin slits. "What's so funny, kiddo?"

Korden stopped his laughter just long enough to say, "I'm sorry, it's just that…"

This course of action is not advised!

"I've been saying pretty much the same thing to everyone…"

Mr. Bright, please stop this provocation!

"But coming from you, it just sounds…"

Do not say—

"Really, really stupid."

A low growl issued from deep in Heater's throat. He lunged forward with hands outstretched, fingers hooked.

This time, Korden was ready. He threw a handful of dirt into the man's face, then pistoned a foot into his groin. Heater's lunge became an awkward roll onto his side, his hands attempting to go to both eyes and crotch at the same time. Korden jumped up and ran as Stone cheered him on.

He sprinted toward another of the canyon branches, but Weryl rushed to cut him off. When he spun away, the other triker was there. The two men circled at a distance, chuckling as he looked back and forth between them.

"That's just great." Heater regained his feet and stood next to the horse, wiping at his eyes. He looked calm, but his aura radiated pain and fury in alternating bursts. "Now I gotta make good on my promise to kill the Peacekeep's wife. A man's work is never done, I suppose. But first…" He pulled Korden's own knife from his belt and tossed it to the skinny triker. "You boys have some fun with him. As long as he's alive when you get finished, that's all I care about."

The two men closed in.

Korden raised a hand, concentrated, felt his mind touch the Upper. This time, nothing interrupted the flow of artcraft. He imagined the knife plucked from the triker's hand. The man gave a surprised squawk as it happened in real life, then watched in amazement as the weapon hovered in the air in front of him, surrounded by a faint blue glow.

With a flick of his fingers, Korden sent the blade sailing past his own head, and into Big Weryl's abdomen. The huge triker doubled over and roared in pain.

Before the sound even finished, Korden sent a blast of pure artcraft at the skinny triker, just as he had back in the Glen. It felt so good to unleash that energy again, like stretching muscles that hadn't been properly exercised in days. The other man lifted off his feet and tumbled away through the air, a leaf picked up by the breeze. He flew into the offshoot choked with skilne and landed with a grunt somewhere amid the tall grass. The entire thicket sprang to life, the blades whispering and shushing against one another as they groped at the heat of his body. His scream sounded for only a split second before being choked off.

Korden spun, seeking his next target, and had his arm grabbed and yanked up between his shoulder blades hard enough to make him cry out. The conduit in his head slammed shut.

"A little hard to concentrate, ain't it?" Heater snarled in his ear. "Pain'll do that to you. I'm gonna let go, but if you so much as twitch an eyebrow in a way I don't like, I'm just gonna blow your head off and call it a day."

The barrel of a shortshooter dug into the soft meat under Korden's jaw, but his arm was released. Heater stayed behind him with the pistol jammed in his throat while he asked, "Weryl, you all right?"

"I...I don't know..." The other triker had pulled the blade from his stomach and stood clutching the wound. Blood trickled through his fingers.

"Can you ride?"

"Yeah. I-I...I think so..."

"Get mounted." As Big Weryl began the slow, painful process of climbing back on his horse, Heater leaned forward over Korden's shoulder to speak into his ear again. "So when Dostey went flying back there...that was *you*, wasn't it? You're a Crafter. Answer me, or I swear to the Upper or Aged God or Saint of Christ or whoever you worship, you'll be seein how many of your little tricks you can do with only two fingers."

Korden nodded.

"Hoooly curse." Heater sounded amazed. "You just keep finding new ways to surprise me, kiddo. I never met a Crafter before. Maybe you'll have some other uses after all."

From the east, the low drum of horse hooves drifted through the canyon.

A split second later, Winstid's voice called out. "*Heater! If you can hear me, let the boy go!*"

Joy and relief flooded Korden's heart in equal measure.

"You motherframmer," Heater hissed through clenched teeth. He gave Korden a hard shove toward the closest horse, which happened to be Jakel's. "Get on! Go! Hurry up! You cast any more of that magic and you'll be sorry!"

2

Winstid and Becks charged through the canyon, taking the twists and turns without hesitation. Both knew the branches of this earthen corridor by heart. In fact, they were moving so fast, they were almost thrown from the saddle when they came around a curve and found Starry waiting alone in front of them.

Becks reined up hard enough to send the huge palomino rearing back on its hind legs, then pulled his rifle when the animal settled again with an angry whinny. "Steady on. Could be an ambush."

"There's blood." Winstid pointed at a maroon puddle on the ground, next to a familiar knife. "If they hurt that boy—"

"Listen." Becks held up a hand. Somewhere ahead of them in the canyon, the staccato echo of hoof beats was audible. "They're close."

"So is the road." Winstid jumped from Becks' saddle, scooped up the knife, and climbed onto Starry in just a few seconds. The horse jerked his head against the bit, as if eager to get moving. Korden's satchel hung from the saddlehorn, and Winstid dropped the knife inside. "We can't let them get to those speeders. Not just for Korden's sake, but the rest of the Glen as well."

"Then let's go!" Becks spurred his animal hard, and the two of them bounded on toward the mouth of the canyon.

3

Korden rode the last leg of the journey with Heater's weapon jammed into his side, but at least he sat upright on the horse this time instead of being draped across it. The walls of the canyon got steadily lower around them, and then, all at once, they burst out onto level ground again. After riding across a short stretch of open grass, the gray ribbon of the road unspooled along the countryside ahead. Just on the other side, the sequoias pierced the sky once more. Korden's breath gave a fearful hitch at the sight of them.

Heater slowed the horse as they reached the road, directing the animal toward three strange hunks of steel sitting beside the road which Stone identified as HARLEY RIPCORD HOVERTRIKES. He leapt from the horse and dragged Korden down so roughly that he twisted his ankle and fell to one knee, tearing a hole in his dungarees. Heater barely gave him a chance to stand again before driving him forward with the barrel of the shooter.

"Move! Go! Don't even look at me!" Korden couldn't see the man's aura, but his short, quick commands sounded frightened now. As they approached the machines on the roadside, he ordered, "Sit on that one! The front seat! Weryl, you comin?"

The other triker didn't answer as he slid off his horse and slouched toward them with both arms crossed over his stomach. He wore red gloves all the way to the elbows now, and his grizzled face had gone at least three shades paler.

"Take the one in front," Heater urged him.

"W-what about…the o-other one? C-come back for it?"

"Fram that. They're not gettin their hands on one of my rides." Heater aimed his shooter at a box mounted on the front and fired three quick shots. Something inside sizzled and released a thin stream of smoke from the holes he'd put in it.

"They will pay for that," Heater muttered under his breath as he straddled the machine on the seat behind Korden. He produced a pair of tinted goggles from a bag on the vehicle's side and positioned them over his eyes, the effect like that of an Incarnate. "Oh yes. Once we get you squared away, I'm comin back here with every man I got. I'll make them scream for days. I'll—"

"*Heater, stop!*"

Korden looked over his shoulder to see Winstid and Becks fly out of the canyon's mouth. Both men held shooters. As they charged forward, Becks let go of his reigns, put the weapon to his shoulder, and fired a shot that spanged off the rear of the trike just behind Heater.

"God curse it! Get outta my way, brat!" Heater shoved Korden aside and leaned around him to punch buttons on the vehicle's control board. Korden didn't see how such a contraption could possibly fly, but a split second later a whooshing roar came from between his legs. A pale yellow glow washed across the pavement beneath them, and then the entire machine lifted a parg off the ground and hovered there. It gave a shudder as Heater gripped the steering bars and maneuvered them onto the road with Weryl at their side. The motion was smooth, but still strange enough to make Korden's stomach flutter.

Heater twisted in his seat, held up his little finger at the approaching Peacekeeps, and then shoved a lever that sent them zooming down the road.

4

"*Noooo!*" Winstid shouted, furious at his own futility. He stopped in the middle of the road and watched helplessly as the trikes accelerated away, with a bass rumble that he could feel right through his boot soles, leaving behind one machine that had smoke pouring from whatever passed for its engine. It took only a few seconds for him to lose sight of the hovering vehicles as Old Five curved left into Big Woods and got swallowed up by the redwoods.

It was all over. They had the boy, and there was nothing he could do now.

Grief burned his skin, stung his eyes. Dear Aged Lord, he'd failed yet again. First his own child, now this one, which had been delivered unto him for safekeeping. Even worse than that, he had no doubt Heater would be back, with an entire army of trikers this time, to finish what he'd started in the Glen. The whole town was already lost, whether its remaining residents knew it or not.

And Cheree. His wife, his beloved, the mother of his unborn offspring. What would he say to her? How would he ever tell her that he'd broken his solemn vow to protect the boy…?

"*Would you stop staining your shirt with tears and c'mon?*"

The cry shook Winstid out of his depression. He looked up to find that Becks had never slowed after the speeders took off, just urged his horse onto the road in their wake and charged after them.

"*What are you doing?*" Winstid demanded. "*We'll never catch them!*"

Becks, standing in the stirrups and hunched over his mount's bunching muscles, yelled over his shoulder, "*The road hairpins just ahead! If we cut through the woods, we can still head them off!"*

Winstid cursed his own stupidity. The lay of the land had forced the ancient architects of the Old Five to sweep its gray lanes back and forth to avoid steep ridges and rock formations that lay not half a span away to the north from the canyon mouth.

With a last kernel of hope burning in his chest, he urged Starry into a gallop.

5

Even in his current predicament, Korden couldn't help finding the speed of the hovertrike thrilling. His insides felt like they were pressed against his spine, and he squinted his eyes against the rush of wind. Trees flashed by, first on their left, then on both sides, as the road carried them northwest, back into the forest. Stone calculated their speed at close to 240 kilometers—forty spans—per hour, a rate that astounded Korden. If he only had one of these vehicles, he could reach the Shroud in no time.

Then he realized he would never reach the Shroud at all.

Not if Heater had his way.

The man continued to lean over him to steer, all his attention focused on piloting. Every few seconds he would jerk the handlebars one direction or the other, zipping them around debris or places where vegetation had broken through the pavement, his reflexes so quick that Korden didn't even have time to comprehend the obstacles were there. He saw now that a vehicle like this could only operate on a road; to drive it at this speed over uneven terrain—or worse, through a forest—would be suicide. Heater slowed the trike for the first time as the road took a sharp turn to the right to avoid a stony ridge. It curved even more right after, doubling back on itself to follow the grade of the land. Korden lurched as they slewed around the bend, then grabbed at the seat between his legs to keep from flying off it.

Beside them, Weryl's vehicle took the turn too wide. The rusted metal side of his trike scraped against theirs, throwing up a brief squall of sparks and narrowly missing Korden's leg.

"*Watch it!*" Heater bellowed. The words were all but lost in the awful roar of whatever powered their hovertrikes. Weryl's vehicle straightened out, but the big man sat slumped over the steering bars with his head down. As his front end began to wobble crazily across the center yellow line, Heater backed off.

And then two men on horseback came darting out from the trees on the right and directly into their path.

6

The land ascended sharply once they left the road and entered a long tract of forest. Becks' powerhouse-on-four-legs seemed to have no trouble climbing the rise, but Starry fell even farther behind. Winstid reslung his shooter and pushed him faster, steering the horse through trees and around the thicker vegetation. Between the dim woods and his own poor eyesight, he expected to be thrown from the saddle at any moment after the animal busted a leg. Starry's breath snorted out of his nostrils in exhausted chuffs by the time they crested the ridge.

Here the redwoods were too dense to see ahead, but the road must be close; Winstid could hear the trikers coming, a building growl from somewhere off to the left. He saw Becks racing on to intercept them and hurried to catch up.

"*Becks!*" he shouted. Starry hit his second wind on the level ground and closed the distance between them to just ten or fifteen pargs. "*What are we gonna do when we—?*"

Without warning, unfiltered sunlight struck him in the face as they burst from the trees. The edge of the road lay immediately in front of them. From the very corner of his eye, Winstid sensed the trikers bearing down on them like twin bullets. He yanked the reins, turning Starry's nimble form aside in the nearest lane, but Becks' thunderous momentum on the larger horse carried him right across the crete.

The seconds slowed and separated into islands of eternity, where Winstid could see every detail of the horror that happened next, even though it was all over faster than he could blink.

In one smooth motion, Becks dropped the reins and swiveled in his saddle, trying to bring his shooter up, even though it was obvious he had no time to target the machines bearing down on him. For the barest of heartbeats, it looked like the lead trike would buzz past him in the southbound lanes, but then it veered drunkenly off course and collided dead on.

Except 'collide' was far too kind a word.

The horse seemed to disintegrate as the trike punched through its hefty middle. Chunks of metal and gore exploded outward from the impact in a grisly shower. Winstid glimpsed Becks' legs torn away at the waist by the machine's sloped front end; his upper half launched high into the air before smashing into the trunk of a redwood on the opposite side of the road. The remains of the trike skidded sideways and then began tumbling over, a fountain of sparks and machine parts spewing in all directions. Its pilot flopped like a ragdoll as he was beaten against the unforgiving pavement again and again before the whole conglomeration burst into a rolling fireball.

Winstid looked away, a retch working its way up his throat, and caught sight of the second vehicle. This trike was far enough behind that it had time to brake before driving into the minefield now scattered across the road, but it was a close thing. He saw Heater jerk the steering bars to avoid a burning chunk of wires and metal covered in horse intestine.

The sudden turn caused the vehicle to lean so far over that Korden slipped from his seat and plunged toward the ground.

7

Stone warned him that the angle was too steep even before Korden began to fall. He clawed at the air, grasping for something, *anything*, to save him.

His fingers hooked into the greasy tangles of Heater's beard.

The man howled in pain as the trike straightened and righted again. Korden hung from the side now, with one foot caught on the seat and the rest of him supported only by the extraordinarily long hair sprouting from the triker's chin. The surface of the road flowed past just cupits from his own face. He clung desperately to the makeshift rope as the vehicle swerved around more wreckage.

"*Leggo of me, you whoreson!*" Heater took one hand off the steering bar to pry at Korden's clutching fingers. He felt his grip loosen.

And then Winstid was there, racing up alongside them atop Starry.

"*Give me your hand!*" he shouted.

Korden let go of Heater's beard with one hand and reached for the Peacekeep.

8

The trike continued to decelerate sharply as Heater divided his attention between the accident debris and the sixteen-year-old boy now dangling from his whiskers. Winstid spurred Starry back to a gallop. They leapt over the hollowed-out carcass of Becks' horse and fell into step beside the vehicle, easily matching its speed now.

Korden heard his shout and threw out a hand to reach for him. Winstid leaned down from the saddle, grabbed for him, missed, and went to try again.

He was so intent on rescuing the boy that he never saw the shooter Heater produced.

But he felt the bullet when it burrowed into the middle of his chest.

9

Korden heard the shot.

Saw Winstid fall off the far side of his saddle.

Something inside him—some fragile, vulnerable, and still very optimistic part; the last vestige of his sheltered youth—shattered into a million disillusioned pieces.

Above him, the leader of Clan Triker bellowed mad laughter.

Black rage replaced the blood in Korden's veins, every bit as potent as that which set upon him when his father died.

The hand that had been reaching for Winstid filled with fire. Not a big flame, little more than a palmful, but as dense and blue as sapphire, one whose heat could've melted this flying hunk of metal to slag.

He found the strength to pull himself up by Heater's beard and then jammed his fist—and the fireball—into the man's open mouth.

Heater's scream this time was high and full of agony. The fire consumed the lower half of his face in a flash of blue, boiling his skin, turning his facial hair into a raging inferno around his jaw. He released the trike's handlebars to beat at the flames.

Korden let go before the fire could reach him, not caring anymore if he fell to his death. He hit the pavement hard and rolled, heard strange cracks and snaps, felt pain shooting throughout his entire body. When he came to rest in the road, he forced his head to turn so he could watch the aftermath.

Heater's hovertrike cruised on for fifty or so more pargs with the controls unmanned, its rider far more concerned with extinguishing himself. The man looked like a lit candle as he wailed and thrashed. Then the vehicle either hit debris or had its steering knocked askew by Heater's flailing, because it made an abrupt left turn and shot into the forest with a fair amount of speed. The triker just about had the flames extinguished when Korden lost sight of him among the trees, but a moment later a rumbling explosion shook the ground.

"Good riddance," Korden whispered.

10

Minor bruising to temporal lobe, possible concussion to frontal, contusions to vertebrae T4 through

T9, ONE SPRAIN TO RIGHT WRIST LIGAMENTS, THREE BROKEN PHALANGES IN SAME HAND, SEVERE ABRASION TO LEFT HIP AND BUTTOCK, SEVERE EPIDERMIC TEAR TO BACK OF LEFT LEG—

"Enough," Korden muttered. The words meant nothing to him. All he cared about was that his legs still worked, which they seemed to.

BUT SIR—!

"No, Stone. Switch off until I call for you."

The computer knew better than to needle him this time. In the new silence that followed, Korden limped back down the road. Utter destruction stretched from one side of the pavement to the other as far as he could see, smoldering metal and glistening chunks of flesh no longer identifiable as equine or human.

Starry stood over his master, with the carry pouch hanging forlornly from his saddle. Korden patted the horse's flank as he sat down heavily next to Winstid, thinking yet again of Redfen Bright's last minutes.

The Peacekeep lay on his back, with a red stain on the breast of his shirt that seemed to spread even as Korden watched. His chest rose and fell, but a thin wheezing sound came from the man's mouth with each breath.

His eyes jittered as they met Korden's. One lid drooped. "Hurt?" he asked, expelling a fine mist of blood along with the question.

Korden shook his head slowly. "No. I'm all right."

"H...Heater?"

"He's dead."

A smile touched Winstid's bloody lips. "Good."

"I'll get help," Korden told him. "I'll go back to the Glen and bring someone..."

Winstid shook his head, his eyes round and fearful. He grasped Korden's arm with strength he didn't look capable of, and gasped, "N-no. Stay away. You p-promise me, boy. Don't go back there. Not ever."

Korden nodded agreement as tears pricked the backs of his eyes.

Of course the man didn't want him to go back to Hidden Glen. He'd caused enough damage there, just as he had his own home, and every place he'd come to along the way.

His father should have changed their last name to Blight rather than Bright, because that's exactly what he was. Cursed by the Upper. Luckless to all who had the misfortune to lay eyes on him. He deserved nothing and belonged nowhere.

Not anymore.

Winstid seemed to be aware of the affect of his words. He eased his grip on Korden's arm, but didn't let go. "T-take Starry," he said, nodding at the horse. "Ride south for a hundred s-spans or so...then head due east. S-stay off the r-roads...in case any more of the trikers are looking for you. Watch for signs to Ida. I've n-never been there, but...supposedly they try to k-keep civil. If there really is a Prophet... maybe they can p-point you in the right direction to find him."

"But...what about you?"

Now the Peacekeep did let go of him. He folded his hands over that spreading stain on his shirt and closed his eyes. "You're g-going to leave me right here."

"No!" Korden exclaimed, horrified. "I can't do that! I won't!"

One of Winstid's eyes cracked back open. The other one tried and then fluttered closed again. "I've done all I can for you, boy. My c-conscience is clean…for the first time in years. It wasn't much, but maybe it's enough that the good Aged Lord…will let m-me see my child again. Now go on. I'd l-like to die in peace."

Those tears pushed to free themselves from Korden's eyes once more, but he blinked them away. If the world wanted any more tears from him, it would have to fight for each one. When he finally got to his feet, Winstid Crane's chest gave no more than a shallow, labored rise every few seconds.

Korden limped to Starry. He tried to put a foot in the stirrup and cried out as something in his back lit up with pain. The horse nuzzled against his neck and then knelt until his belly touched the ground. Korden scooted his weary, aching body up the animal's back until he was positioned on the saddle.

As the horse clopped up the pavement, back in the direction they'd come, he looked back to find that the Peacekeep had stopped breathing. His lips formed a pleasant grin.

And then Korden Bright faced forward and rode hard toward the future.

Like this novel?

YOUR REVIEWS HELP!

In the modern world, customer reviews are essential for any product. The artists who create the work you enjoy need your help growing their audience. Please visit Goodreads or the website of the company that sold you this novel to leave a review, or even just a star rating. Posting about the book on social media is also appreciated.

Russell C. Connor has been writing horror since the age of five, and is the author of two short story collections, five eNovellas, and fourteen novels. His books have won two Independent Publisher Awards and a Readers' Favorite Award. He has been a member of the DFW Writers' Workshop since 2006, and served as president for two years. He lives in Fort Worth, Texas with his rabid dog, demented film collection, mistress of the dark, and demonspawn daughter.

His next novel—*The Halls of Moambati*, Volume IV of *The Dark Filament Ephemeris*—will be available in the fall of 2021.

Heater Kay—whose given name was actually Haddin—
was born one of a set of twins.

He never met his father. The man was just one of a string
who paid his mother for sex in a far southern settlement that
no longer existed, then smartly walked away before finding
out that his seed had taken root. His mother, for some sen-
timental, womanly reason, felt some kinship with the lives
inside her, and refused to rid herself of them. She was run
out of the settlement and spent the next five years of her life
attempting to keep her two sons out of the clutches of the
Incarnates before expiring from a gruesome case of carnal
scourge that rotted her from the inside out.

Haddin and Happum Kay were taken by their mother's
last client—himself already showing the first black lesions of
the scourge—and sold to an old man who owned a travelling
oddity show. He put the boys on display for those who wanted to see children without the danger of having any themselves. His circuit kept them on the move and well ahead of
the Incarnates, but his cruelty had been, perhaps, far worse
than the quick death those demons would've offered. His

sexual torment of the boys resulted in Happum's expiration at the age of seven. Haddin endured all the way to free age, at which time he dismembered the old man to such a degree that even his toes were no longer connected to the rest of him, then joined the roughest, meanest clan of marauders he could find.

Right up until Happum's death, the two boys were identical. Looking in a mirror, they could scarcely even tell themselves apart. For the rest of his life, when things got particularly bad, Haddin would pretend his twin brother still lived, a perfect double that resembled him exactly.

That was why, as Heater lay burned, bleeding and broken on the forest floor near the flaming remains of his hovertrike, he wasn't all that surprised to see himself come walking through the trees and squat down beside him.

"Oh brother," the other him bemoaned. Heater's beard was nothing but a few charred bristles growing amid the blackened skin of his lower face, but this new arrival still possessed a luxuriant scrub of hair that reached down past his genitals. "What have you gotten yourself into this time?"

"You're...not...Happum." Each word—no more than guttural grunts that he could barely understand himself—shredded his broiled throat.

"No. No, we're not," the duplicate admitted. "We're someone far, far better. Someone that can make all your fondest desires come true, if you agree to help us out." The other Heater leaned closer to the one on the ground and purred, "So tell me: what do you want more than anything in the entire world?"

Heater didn't even have to consider that question.

"Kill...boy."